The Frangitelli Mirror

G.R. Thomas

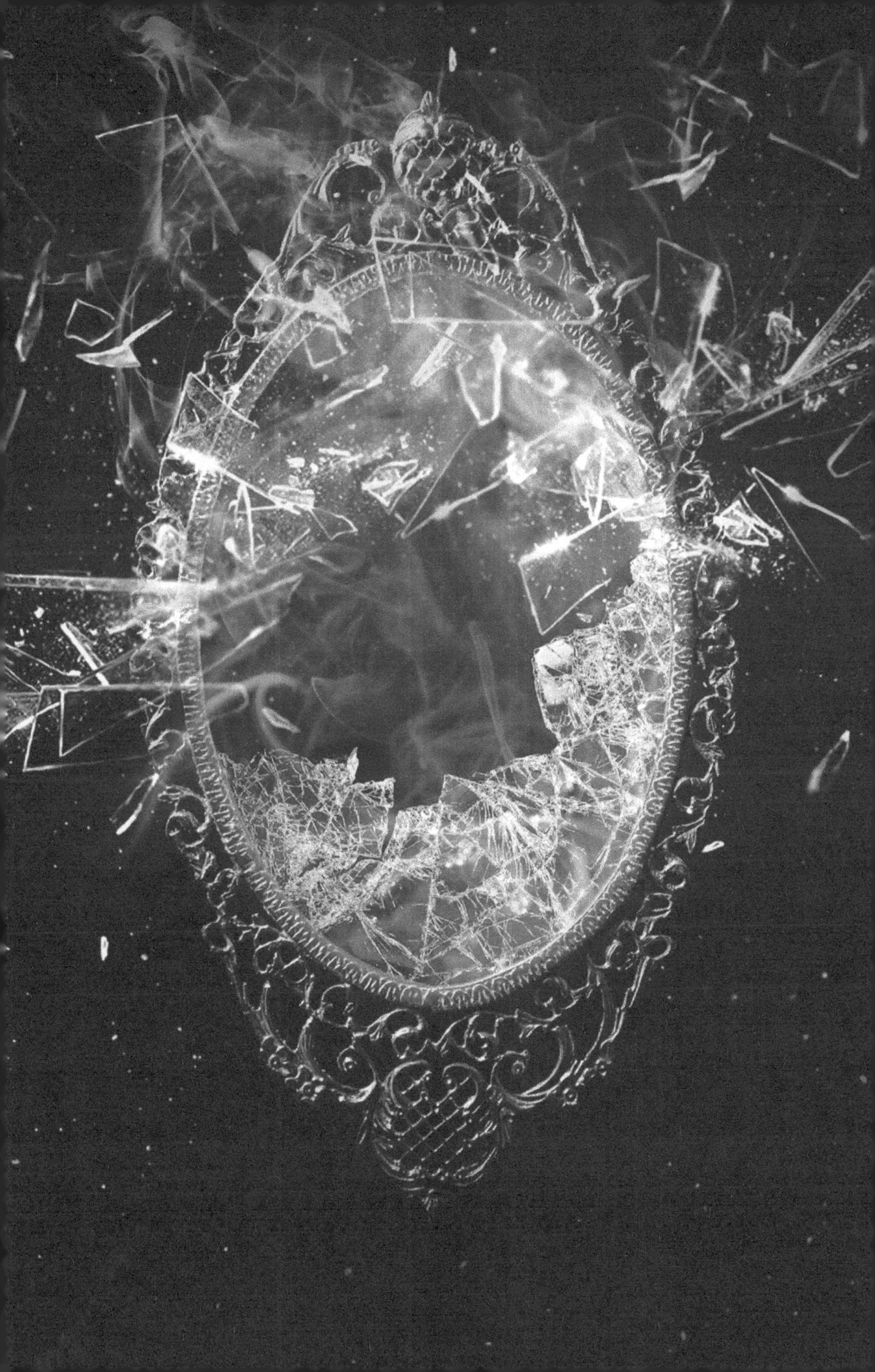

Content Warning

The Frangitelli Mirror contains horror themes, violence, death of a child, death of an infant, blood and gore, and paranormal violence. Please read according to your comfort level.

To my husband;
my best friend, my biggest fan, your support,
love and belief drive every word I write.

You may not have appeared in my books so far,
but you are, and always will be my hero.

Actatos Adibaga Sabaoth Adonay-
Spell to summon Bruxas and null all its power.

Actatos Adra Arata Alal de Bruxa-
Spell to drive away a demon.

Alria Garia Ananus (to reverse, say Contrarum in beginning)-
Spell to stop someone speaking.

Amatiano veru cedata-
Spell to stop someone moving.

Agla Aglala-
Spell to stop haemorrhage: thumbprint their own blood on their forehead.

Actatos Alrax de Braxa-
Spell to summon a demon to show itself in a non-threatening way.

Buona Jacumora-
Spell written in your own blood, worn on your body to protect you from enemy.

Anul liberatum-
Spell to deflect the power of a demon.

Nascondodmerato-
Spell to hide something.

Through nature we walk, in whispers we talk.

—Masciara Unknown.

CHAPTER 1

Darkness haunted Rose Carbonelli. It brought fear and sleepless nights, staring wide-eyed at the bleak grip of night upon every corner of her room, listening to the door knob twist, the window pane rattle. Rose fought sleep, sometimes until the roosters crowed, before she allowed her eyes to give in. The velvety spread of a star-pricked night sky, so favoured by lovers, set Rose into a state of terror.

She craved daylight, the warm hug of the sun that kept the shadows of the night at bay. Daylight had, until recently, been a place of safety. But something had changed the day the crow with the gold-flecked eyes arrived.

It first appeared on a hot December evening when it was more than shadows keeping sleep at bay. Rose sat on the back porch, mosquitoes buzzing in her ear, tasting the blood of her bare feet. She itched her ankles, red spots raised and punishing with their irritation.

The sun set late; its summer glow smeared the horizon in apricot and red. The crow made its presence known when it landed amongst the purple blossoms of a Crepe Myrtle tree that grew by the back porch. Its inky wings shone in the waning daylight; the gold of its eyes glistened like gems. It cried out, settled snuggly on the branch, and stared down at Rose; she stared back. It had not let her be from that day to this.

The crow paced by her window day and night, sometimes it tapped the glass with its long beak, sometimes it just stared.

But really, it all began when Rose did something careless; something desperate. She had stolen. Each night since, as she lay awake, she chastised her younger self, who in 1915 had sought help where she shouldn't. When she found the book, took the book, and read the strange words on its front page aloud;

Ticanim Invocatum.

Rose had been seeking an answer; wondered if perhaps she was praying to a new God, one that would actually listen. Instead, she had invited in darkness when she had been seeking light.

She had not spoken aloud any of the other words she read. She understood nothing of them other than that she had dipped her toes into something stinking of rot.

The ensuing years had taken a toll. Rose was a shell of herself, but she suffered her lot resolutely. It was the only way to survive the darkness, the only control she had. Each night Rose scoured the book, tried to reverse what she had done, to understand exactly what it was she had done, if, in fact, it had ever been in her control at all.

She sought to return calm to the storm of her mind, but something was changing; not just by the rise of the moon did terror stalk her. Now daylight had her in the grip of fear, and it all coincided with the crow she had named Devil.

It had not always been this way, but when Europe went to Hell, something within Rose altered as well, as it did with everyone and everywhere. Yet, with Rose, it was more than just war. It was 1917, and she was nearly 18. For two years, Devil and the shadows had made themselves known, and life had thrown all its ugliness in her face.

Rose sat upon the edge of her bed, rubbing her eyes, her back to the door, attention upon the corner to the right of the window. The small book slipped to the floor; its curled pages fell open.

She slid to the floor, closed it, and ran her fingers across the cracked leather. She pressed the golden crescent, and across the outline of the crow that adorned the ancient cover. She licked her lips, looked up to the window; dawn, not Devil, looked in upon her.

The morning light struck across the floor and onto the book as though Mother Nature herself was in on its secret. Rose drew a wearied breath and studied the book for the thousandth time.

It was old, how old she couldn't guess. There were no publication pages within, no evidence of the author. Its pages were yellowed, and it smelled of dust and dry rot, of the thousand fingers that must have thumbed through its vellum. It was written in many different hands, with notes throughout the margins. Rose opened the first page and bit her lip as she scanned those words.

She flipped through, a page at a time, past languages she could not understand. There were sketches of things best left in nightmares, as well as herbs and vials of tinctures lost to time. She had wondered if it was merely a book of medicine, of old wives' tales, but this book didn't feel like others. It had a weight to it that didn't match its size, a feel to its pages that made one not want to close it. Day after day, despite her resentment of it, the book called her to pick it up and sink into its words.

Rose recalled the day she had seen the book fall from the cart of an old woman who began appearing in town each Friday, selling her wares, dried herbs and fruits, knitted bits and bobs. Rose had been fascinated by her in the beginning. Something about the stoop of her stature, the way the lines on her face crisscrossed, her pewter hair in need of a brush. Mama had warned her away, as had the priest on Sundays. Rose, however, followed the woman who carried a black-eyed crow upon her shoulder.

One day she had set up her cart at the bottom end of the high street in town, catching the passers-by as they entered. Most gave her a wide birth, suspicious of her accent, the strangeness of her clothes, and the odd things she sold.

Rose was with her mother on a reasonably pleasant autumn day. At a time before things had become too hard, when food and money were still reliable. Mama had been caught by Miss Ray, the local gossip, undoubtedly relinquishing nothing but shallow details of their lives that would be fed instantly to the grapevine.

Distracted, her mother had not noticed fifteen-year-old Rose wander across the road, eyes wide, watching the old woman complain as she packed up. A constable tapped his truncheon impatiently in his hand.

"No permit, no trade." He spoke loud enough for the gossip mongers to feed upon.

In her haste, as she slapped her horse upon the rump, the old woman hadn't noticed the tarp of her cart was loose, didn't see the small book tumble to the ground.

Sunlight glinted upon something on its cover. Rose watched the old woman disappear over the rise of the road, the constable wander away, and the book left in the dust.

With her mother still humouring Miss Ray, Rose made her way over, looked down, and squinted as the sun glanced across something golden on the cover. Her fingers twitched.

Pick it up.

Rose looked over her shoulder guiltily, but no one was there.

She checked her surroundings again. It was hustle and bustle. No one noticed the daughter of a seamstress, so she picked it up and ran her hands over the golden crescent embedded into thick leather, a crow, open-winged underneath. She flipped the cover open. The spine cracked, the pages within thin and water-stained, inked words illuminated in a practised hand seemed to leap from the page. Despite her youth, Rose instantly recognised this to be very old and unusual, something that the church would very much frown upon. She drew her fingers across the pages and flicked through the delicate paper. A strange feeling coiled within her, stoking the idea that she should keep it, that she should have it all to herself.

"Rose? What are you doing?" Her mother had asked. Rose had startled, not noticing her in the haze of excitement. Rose's fingers curled around the pages; her hands slipped behind her back. She felt strange, her thoughts somewhat separate from her body, and it was this strange sensation that made her slip the book into her pocket.

It was a week to the day that Rose knew she had made a mistake. The whispers had begun on the first night, movement out of the corner of her eye on the second. On the third night, she saw her brother Matteo staring at her through the open door of her room, wet, bloated… dead. She did not sleep that night.

The fourth day she threw the book in the hearth. It flew back out, landing at her feet, hot to the touch but not a mark upon it. The fifth night, Rose tossed it down the well out the front of Mr Wilson's house in the middle of the night. By the time she had returned to her bedroom, there it lay, upon her bed, glistening beads of water upon its leather, otherwise intact. On the sixth night, Rose lay a rosary across the book. The chain snapped, and all the beads rolled away, some remained stuck in the grooves of the floorboards.

On the seventh night, Rose listened to the voices, watched the movements in the corner, and knew she was being haunted.

On the eighth day, Rose went in search of the old woman. She asked everyone, but no one knew who she was or where she had come from. On the way home, halfway down Banksia Lane, the cart was parked, the horse grazing, a crow sitting upon its rump.

"Hello? Hello? I need to return something you lost." Rose's heart beat furiously, whipped along by relief that this nightmare would soon be over.

Rose rounded the cart, saw no one, rounded it again, and there the old woman was, stoking a fire that was not there a moment ago. Smoke curled from a robust flame, something delicious bubbled in an iron pot above it.

"Something *I* lost, you say?" The woman had an accent like Papa.

"Yes, it fell from your cart last week."

"Did it now?" She stirred a little faster, then sipped noisily from her ladle.

"Yes..."

"And you only saw fit to return it now?" The woman reached into her pocket and sprinkled something in the pot.

Taken aback, Rose pushed her glasses up her nose and sought the right words, but they would not arise.

"I...I..."

"You looked upon what was not yours to do so, or... perhaps it was? Who am I to say such things?" The old woman shrugged and stirred her pot with more enthusiasm, uncorked a jar, drizzled the contents in. The pot bubbled faster; a rich meaty smell hit the air.

"What's done is done, young lady." The old woman dipped her ladle again, sipped and smiled to herself.

Rose pulled the book from her pocket and offered it to the woman; her heart kicked a little faster.

"I'm sorry. I should have given it back immediately. Please accept my apology." Her hand shook, the leather slippery between her fingers.

"You are bound, I cannot take it. It has shown you a course. That is all an old woman can say."

Rose's body shivered with cold despite a warmth in the air. Her teeth clenched, she sucked in her bottom lip, held her breath and set the book upon a log by the woman's side, careful not to get too close.

Rose backed away and felt something slap her leg. She shuddered as her hand fell upon the book which was back in her pocket. Her lips quivered, that same, *not quite there*, feeling engulfed her.

"That which has been seen cannot be unseen, my dear. That which has to be learned must be learned." The woman tasted her brew again, this time chewing and nodding to herself. She sprinkled more powder from her pocket into it and stirred, softly mumbling to herself.

The wind whispered through the trees, and tugged at her fire. A black feather flickered in the woman's hair. Rose's fingers dug through her dress until she felt the bite of them on her thighs.

"I don't understand, and I don't want to have it." Her eyes were hot, the old woman blurred, she held the book out again. "Please, take it?"

"You have opened the door, Dear. Now you must enter."

Rose shook her head, and backed away.

"Follow the sign of the crow." The old woman nudged her own crow gently, it squawked, looked at Rose and settled snuggly into the crook of the woman's neck.

Tears blurred Rose's vision again, fear drove its way deep into her belly, making her queasy. Rose blinked until her eyes cleared, wiped her glasses clean on her shawl, and gasped. She spun around.

The woman was gone, just the lingering smell of her potion upon the air.

CHAPTER 2

Tap, tap, tap.

The gold-eyed crow visited the day after the woman disappeared in plain sight. The same time as the shadows, and the sounds began their campaign of terror… the same time that Matteo began to appear every single day.

It sat outside her window, feathers wind-tugged, its eye cocked so as to see Rose.

Rose held the book sandwiched between her hands; her middle finger wedged into a well-worn page.

"Go away." she snapped. The crow fluttered from the ledge, and settled upon the arched wire of the front fence. There it stayed, cawing melodically with the magpies and kookaburras.

"That's not what I meant, but better." Rose flicked through the book, ran her fingers across the page, a flicker of something indefinable warmed the cold that normally gripped her.

Grubby marks blackened the edges, the writing penned on its face a little blurred in places, undoubtedly from many fingers scanning across the strange words.

"What is it you say?" she browsed through some more pages, nothing resonated with her, but something tingled in her belly when the book was open. Something strange washed through her; it was gone as if never there once the book was closed.

She held it to her chest and sighed, wondered if she would ever understand what the old woman had meant. She couldn't seem to be rid of the book, had even grown strangely fond of it. Perhaps it was because it was something she had all to herself, something the war in Europe had not robbed from her?

Rose dangled her legs over the edge of the bed and watched the morning light probe the shadows. It made little progress into the corners, leaving them heavy, dark and watching. Her toes curled as they hit the cold of the floor, one stocking snagged upon the wood.

"Damn it!" The fabric ripped; her big toe revealed. She pulled the thin wool back over her toe, lifted the loose board next to her bed and slipped the book into the small hiding space.

"Perhaps another day I will understand what you are."

Rose slipped her boots on and a threadbare coat over her nightdress, then clicked her door shut, relieved to leave the room behind. The house was quiet apart from the tick of the clock in the sitting room and a gentle murmur across the hall.

Her mother was yet to rise, still finishing her morning rosary as Rose slipped past. Rose grimaced; she couldn't remember the last time she'd uttered the same words. If Mama only knew what had happened to her rosary beads, Rose would surely be pulled kicking and screaming to confession. Rose backtracked, and pressed her ear to her mother's door.

"Oh, gracious Lord, please look kindly upon us. I beg you to watch over dear Rose, guide her back to your light."

Rose scoffed quietly. *Light?* She searched for it, ran to it, but light didn't seem to show its hand, not with the eagerness that darkness did. Rose moved on, eyes upon every other corner, wary at each turn, searching for movement. She stoked the kitchen hearth on the way through, set the kettle atop its grate. Even the sooty blackness behind the flame seemed to reach under her skin. She turned away, wiped the sleep from her eyes, and headed for the safety of daylight.

Yet still, darkness followed Rose, it stuck to her like mud to a sole. As much as she pushed at what she saw, what she felt within the shade of a tree, the corners of her room, it clung to her very soul. It felt impossible to escape the coaxing, the fingers of shadow that licked along the walls, curled under her bed and sat there awaiting her attention. She refused to listen to the voice of the old woman, still, so crisp her memory, but she could not shut her eyes at night lest the shadows finally reach their claws out and touch her.

Rose pulled her coat tight and shuddered as the door slammed behind her. Winter… the seed of death, the bearer of the deepest shadow, hit her like a frigid wall. Its icy breath pushed at her, blew her down the back steps. As with every day, a morose repetition of the last, Rose urged herself into the day's chores, bleary-eyed, and yawning. She lazily made her way down the yard, only half aware as she urged wakefulness on.

Dawn's apricot glow faded into a cold, grey smudge, the air blustered around her ankles and smelled of rain. It was only when the building squall quelled for a moment that Rose noticed the silence.

"Oh no!" Hands slapped to her mouth, her pace stuttered, eyes wide, disbelief a curtain of numbness.

The chicken coop door was open, the latch left unlocked the night before. Her task. One she did every morning and evening. Let the chickens out at dawn, lock them up at dusk. Her bottom lip quivered; her insides ran cold as she remembered she had fallen asleep late yesterday afternoon. The hand of darkness had wrought its power over her.

Rose fell to the ground, cold and unforgiving, it yielded to her the fruits of her exhaustion.

Blood pooled in the life lines of her hands. Eyes squeezed tight, she willed this to be yet another nightmare. The wish was slapped away, truth a slick wetness coating her skin.

The cold stung Rose's eyes as she peered at her blurred palms. They burned around the edges, fear tugged for tears. They set forth, cutting hot ribbons down her freezing cheeks as she unwound her fingers, pulled her glasses from her nose and wiped the fog from them. She slid them back on, the frames as cold as ice.

Rose winced at the strings of red that whipped away from her skin, yielding to the gusts of a brewing storm; they were there, then they were not. Her own life felt as fleeting. She was here now, but for how long until the shadows won?

The crow circled.

Her hand found the back of her neck, she rubbed at the familiar rise of fine hairs. Rose's eyes snagged upon the willow tree Papa had planted when she was born. Then a sapling, now its shade owned most of the yard. Its naked branches swayed, raked the ground like skeletal fingers. The crow settled in its branches, using its wings to balance. There it gloated over Rose, silent, watching. She squeezed her eyes tight, willed it away, saw the book in her mind, knew in her bones it was all connected but didn't know how or why.

She looked away from the tree, refused to acknowledge the other thing that lurked in plain sight, in the light of day. But she heard its whispers.

Ba...no...ba...no

Fingers curled back in; she couldn't help herself and peered back at the gnarled trunk. The shape faded away; its voice quieted. Her nostrils flared, the decay and desperation of it assaulting. Rose pressed behind her glasses, pushing at the vision that seemed to paint itself upon the inside of her lids. It was gone. She looked around, it was definitely gone, yet now her face smelled of blood.

Rose leaned down, picked up a carcass; the hen's head flopped, blood dark and dry, sticking its feathers into clumps.

Rose held it to her chest.

"I'm sorry little one." She stroked it tenderly, then gasped and held it away from her body, her mouth a little drier than before. She lay the carcass back down, rubbed her eyes, mouth agape. Did its eye blink? An image of jaws flashed through her mind. Rose yelped, rubbed her eyes again. The hen's beak opened and closed; its lower lid slid across a dull, dilated eye. Rose thought she had made a mistake, that it was alive. She quickly checked the hen over, parted the feathers to find the wound she would tend, to nurse it back to health. A groan rumbled in her chest as Rose slumped; the ground shot its cold through her. The hen's innards were gone, the feathers hid the gutting.

"How..." she scooted away, the hen once more a ruined, dead thing. The willow branches creaked. Rose snapped her head up.

The crow set off high above her house, blending into the stormy sky.

Rose swallowed hard, scrambled back to her feet, and gripped the bridge of her nose between thumb and forefinger.

"You're exhausted, that's it… you're in shock."

She took a deep breath and gave attention to the greyness of her once vibrant home. Corrugated sheets spotted with rust patched the roof where last winter the tiles had been ripped away in a sudden squall. The morning's gusts lapped at the metal, lifted it up and down, a rhythmic tap, tap upon the gutters. The entire back of the house leaned to the left. She sighed at the slackness of its shell, the sheer lack of will to stand for much longer.

She sometimes felt the same. Haunted, weak; wracked with a loss of control, no matter what her desire; her purpose. Rose knew that in the end her destiny was caught between the pointless feuds of men and the whim of a cruel Mother Nature... and something else altogether unspeakable. The book flashed into her mind again. The shadows were her irrefutable proof, the voices could not be unheard, the visions could not be unseen.

A life of love and a little comfort were small goals. Still, as the hands of time ticked mercilessly forward, with each rise and fall of a new day, with every moment she slept with an empty belly, Rose felt any semblance of such folly evaporate. Each night she lay, quilt bunched in her fists, eyes upon the right-hand corner of her room, book well hidden under the floorboards. All night Rose ignored the beckoning to listen, stuck her fingers in her ears when Matteo called her to play. Life would not be the same, not in this house, not whilst her mother carried on as if all would be well. Not while the corners held her attention, and the dead commanded her to notice them.

CHAPTER 3

A bitter world clawed for Rose's attention, sucked in its' breath, and whipped hard against her frame. Each gust snatched soft, russet feathers from her grasp. Rose snatched back at the wind, screamed at it, tried to claim them back, but the wind was too clever, too quick, and her fingers too sticky with blood.

Nail beds tinged blue with cold, Rose's skin flaked around the cuticles, worn and calloused. Lean, pale bones strained through meatless flesh. Old lady hands, tired hands, hands that longed for silken gloves, shiny rings and another warm hand to hold. She could not envisage a wedding ring sliding across such ugly claws. Her chin quivered, she averted her eyes from the willow tree, squeezed the sting from them and cast such thoughts aside.

Rose moved her hands down, gripped her legs instead as the smell of death upon her fingers brought acid to her throat. She retched and shook with more than cold.

"Why are you doing this?" she whispered, but no more did the willow hold the shadow.

"Rose? Rose? Where are you? Hurry up and come inside. You'll catch your death."

Rose stilled, hot guilt warmed her momentarily as Mama called from the house, her breath thin, almost lost in the gusts. Rose pulled back to the reality of the moment, bunched an edge of her apron and blew her nose. She became aware once more of her limbs, pulled herself up, eyes upon a wooden shed. Capped with a metal roof that curled at its edges, the coop leaned into the back fence, both holding each other aloft.

Thick bushland beyond was the only colour in a bleak day. A smudge of green and brown beyond the boundary, interspersed with skeletal trees that died each winter, born anew each spring. Rose couldn't see her spring, imagined she'd never feel its warmth again. Body pressed against the weather, hair whipping her face, she moved towards the coop. The open maw of darkness behind its door set a clawing cold down her spine.

Pulsing gusts pushed Rose onwards. One unwilling step at a time, arms wrapped about her body, she held her breath, not wanting to inhale death. The door of the coop banged with the rhythmic rise and fall of the wind, chomping at the world each time it opened, the darkness within too close, too unknown.

Please don't be in there. She peered back to the willow. It was as any normal tree should be.

Rose rested a hand on the door frame, the blood stuck her skin to the wood. She leaned in. Her knees stung when she fell at the coop's doorway. A small cry escaped around her hand that pressed hard against her mouth. Bloodied carnage; headless chickens filled the belly of the coop.

"You didn't even eat them!" Rose sobbed. "You beast!" Unrestrained tears burned her cheeks, the warmth sickeningly comforting against the stabbing cold. Her hands bared down into the ground, nail stubs bit into her palms, and she pounded the ground until her fists pulsed.

"No, no, no!" Mud splashed across her face, and speckled the lenses of her glasses, but she didn't care. Rose's fingers ran across a pattern in the mud. They sank into fox prints that fanned out the doorway, a frenzied lacework of devils stalking the night. Defeat burned under her skin, an itch of that prodded, teased and coaxed at emotions that clouded her thoughts. She slumped against the coop; shawl caught in its wire. Frustration had her yank at the wool, its delicate loops snapped. Rose's head felt suddenly too heavy and fell into her hands. She indulged the sobs, released the tension that squeezed her chest like a vice.

"Why?" Her fingers hooked through the new hole in her shawl, grey fibres shredded away, captured in the glue of blood that clotted the creases of her fingers. The shawl was already threadbare, this new hole unspooling before her eyes, like the world both there and afar. Rose stared, bleary-eyed, past browned flower beds to the smoke pouring from the laundry room.

Despite the loss of everything, hunger pains, and cold nights when the single hearth log burned out, Rose had never wanted for cleanliness. Her mother boiled their sparse linens and dresses every other day, wear aside, she was clean each morning, presentable to the world, as wretched as it was.

For a moment, just a fraction of time, Rose smiled, lifted her arm to her face, smelled the sharp starch of her sleeve. It mattered for that brief moment until the edge of her vision caught sight of another carcass at the outhouse door.

The serenity of calm peeled away, like a protective outer skin leaving her raw and angry. Rose pulled herself up and connected her boot with the coop. The metal roof rattled; the wooden frame shook. She yelped, grabbed her boot; blackness filtered her vision as pain sung in her toes. She hopped around, teeth gritted, shawl slipping from her shoulders. The wind caught hold and whisked it away into the arms of the willow. Rose screamed in frustration.

Temper causes nought but anguish, Mama would say, but the rush of sudden emotion came so easily these past years. The taste of hastily spoken words, burning with ill feeling, held an addictive comfort, a strange sense of power. Words more suited to the docks threaded through Rose's mind. She silently mouthed them, then screamed them into the wind until her throat hurt. Puffing, sweating; that release of profanity eased a portion of the fire that had taken possession of her insides. Rose set her pounding foot down, the wind obliged again, gusting more heartily, and she screamed some more. The way these vulgar utterances rumbled from her chest and rolled over her tongue felt so very good.

When the flush of emotion settled and her breath was caught, she spotted her shawl snagged and flapping wildly high in the willow. She hitched her dress with a mind to climb for it, however, her mother's more intemperate voice carried downwind again.

"Rosa? Hurry up out of this weather this instant!" Shawl forgotten Rose grimaced; she hated when her mother used her Italian name, she only did it when she was impatient. It was the cause of so much bullying at school, the sound of it when Mama accented it grated on her ears. Rose actually liked the name, just not the sour stares of her classmates.

Rose reached down to her pounding toe. Old leather boot peeled away, stocking in hand, she winced at an emerging blue swelling ringed with red.

"Damn it." She dabbed at the toe gingerly, a sharp breath sucked between gritted teeth as she forced the stocking and boot back on.

"Bloody bastard!" Rose yelped as her foot set back down, the ground tended to the pain with a now welcome, numbing cold. She set off, hobbling on the outside edge of said foot, scouting around the coop, hoping to find at least one chicken left alive.

"Chook, chook, chook?" Little hope lit her voice, "Come on, chook, chook, chook?" Around the far side, a flash of caramel caught her eye. A hopeful race of her heart instantly quelled at the sight of more bloodied feathers wedged in splintered wood at the base of the fence. Her shoulders slumped; her movement halted. Rose stood still and just stared. The wind whipped her apron up, it thwacked and snapped, the weather tugged it almost gleefully as her vision glazed at the nothingness they had left.

Rose curled her fingers in, her palms stung; hurt bristled inside and out. She snatched the edge of the apron from the wind and wiped her face and glasses again with the least muddied corner, making her way closer to the fence. There was a hole in the palings, another flurry of fox prints around it. A tuft of orange fur tangled in the grey wood.

"You evil creature." Rose plucked one of the feathers from the fence. Soft white down at the base, a rich ochre towards the tip. This one had a brown spot.

"Dear little Queenie." She held it against her chest, her other hand pressed against the growl in her stomach. It was as though her body understood the gravity of the situation.

The mid-August weather sliced through her dress, wicked through her stockings, and a creeping cold settled beneath her skin. She shivered until her teeth chattered. Her eyes crusted with dried despair and watered anew. But tears weren't going to put food on the table, weren't going to bring prosperity back to her home. They certainly wouldn't make people not do stupid things that broke your heart.

She sniffed, opened her fingers, and let the feather flutter away. Mama called again; her words almost entirely lost in a deep rumble of thunder.

Rose sleeked her dress down to her ankles, wiped her hands on her apron and cleared her throat. Hands on hips, she counted the remnants of the flock and gathered up the corpses. She tried to forget their names, cast away pleasant memories of hand-raising fluffy chicks in the kitchen by the warmth of the hearth. She couldn't look at them now, tried to ignore the stiffness of their legs, the glazed, unblinking eyes. Her little pets were now cold and hard in her hands.

Rose ran. Thoughts of life before 1914 flashed through her mind. Was it all just a fairy tale? A false memory? Had life not always been so miserable? The corpses swung like pendulums as her pace hastened, still hampered somewhat by the pain in her foot; feathered bodies banged against her legs.

Once upon the back steps, Rose stopped to gather her breath, to calm herself lest Mama think her weak. She lay the carcasses atop the kindling box at the back door with a gentleness they could no longer appreciate. She patted them, knowing they could not feel the love, but something made her do it anyway.

Reaching for the door, Rose's body shuddered when something banged. The suddenness of the sound pounded in her head, rocked her on her feet. The coop door, it was just the coop door at the mercy of the storm. Relief washed through her as she watched the door flap open and shut. A spittle of icy rain began, slicing through the greyness of the sky. Despite the fact she didn't want to go back to the puddles of blood and decay, she dashed back to the coop, secured the door, putting a stop to the rhythmic banging. It was too much like gunshots. Gunshots reminded her of war, and war was a dirty word. It had changed the world; it betrayed all that she knew; it slit her heart in two.

As she turned to dash back, by pure chance, Rose spotted three chalky eggs nestled in a clutch of weeds at the base of the willow. She'd forgotten that the hens liked to lay in strange places, leaving her a treasure hunt every other day. The sight alleviated the tightness in her chest, mouth already watering at the thought of soft scrambled eggs.

Rain hardening, Rose quickly scooped them up, held them like precious jewels before wrapping them gently in her apron. She took a step and stopped; her boot dwarfed by larger footprints pointing towards the house. One step at a time, she followed them, numb, not numb, every part of her tingling, dread curled in her gut. Thunder rumbled more deeply. She hitched up her dress and splashed past the prints. Lightning forked beyond her house as she jumped the steps onto the back porch, coming to a stop near her father's gardening boots. There they sat, old and cracked, cobwebs stitched across the top, soles caked in fresh mud. Thunder cracked above the house. Rose jolted once more.

CHAPTER 4

The kitchen smelled of charcoal and not much else.

"God walks quietly, Rose," Edith said as Rose pulled her boots off and threw them by the door. Rose rolled her eyes, quickly averting to innocence when Mama peered over her shoulder.

"I felt those eyes, Bella. You ought to say an extra prayer before bed tonight." A gentle smile softened new lines around Mama's mouth; eyes sunken, ebony hair more silver-streaked each day. Edith's chin trembled as she noticed the blood streaks upon Rose's arms. She blinked, straightened from digging in the hearth, wiped charred hands along her apron. Edith cleared her throat and reached for the eggs.

"Well, the foxes have certainly eaten most heartily, and so too shall we eat a good breakfast. Where are the hens?" Edith's voice wavered.

"On the kindling box." Rose slipped her glasses into her pocket, wiped her eyes on the damp of her sleeve and jutted her head towards the back porch. Relieved that there was no shadow upon it, she was instantly annoyed at her Mama's lack of outrage.

"I'll stew them later." Edith stepped out to retrieve the birds; frigid air pushed inside, making Rose shiver more deeply. Edith treated the birds with the same gentleness as Rose had. Laying them by the sink, she draped a dish towel over them like a shroud.

Rose slumped at the small table by the larder, wiping the feel of dead things from her hands more forcefully against her apron. Cold hard limbs, clawed toes curled over in rigour felt way too fresh. Rose stared at the lumps under the dish towel.

"I won't eat them." She knew it to be a lie as the claw of hunger was more painful than before. "I'll not…"

"You'll be thankful to have anything in your stomach, Rose." Edith sloshed her hands in some wash water, scrubbing them more briskly than necessary as though she, too, needed to scrub death away. "Your Nonna and Nonno ate whatever they could scavenge as children, don't you remember the stories your father told you?" She wiped her forehead and sighed, "Oh, the poverty they endured. You may think us unfortunate, but I am forever grateful to have been born here, Bella. Despite everything, there is hope in this country." Edith placed a bowl upon the bench, cracked the eggs with one hand whilst whisking with the other. Rose squeezed her lips tight, lest she said anything more, despite the fact she wanted to say so much, to scream, to yell about anything, about everything.

Instead, Rose fidgeted, ran a thumbnail along a crack in the table top. A thread of grime curled away, staining underneath the nail. She pressed a little harder, not caring about the pale scar left behind in the wood. The sound of Mama mixing, the whisk scraping at an increasing intensity, set Rose's teeth to clench. The edge of her nail snapped away. A thin line of blood coursed the curve of the nail bed.

All the while, Edith broke the cold draught of silence with a soft hum. A familiar tune, one that spun upon the long-gone gramophone years ago. Rose shook her head, watching Mama's body sway to her song. She couldn't fathom how Mama could relax like this, how she seemed to always find a spark of pleasure in the most mundane moments. A scream brewed in Rose's chest. She wanted to hate the world; she, in fact, did hate the world and everyone who had hurt her. She didn't understand her mother; she barely understood her sinfully, hateful self.

As though the world cared for just a moment, the storm quieted. The rain ceased its thrashing against the roof, and the wind released its hold of the windows and doors. A wedge of pale sunlight streamed in; a mild winter warmth sliced across Rose. Her body relaxed, muscles unwound, the thrashing pulse in her temple eased. The warm light reflected off the two remaining spoons they had left; its glimmer glanced across a silver frame that sat alone upon the mantle over the hearth. It held Rose's attention, bringing selfish thoughts of her plight to an abrupt halt.

Her father's portrait, the only photograph they owned, the singular item of unnecessary décor that remained. His proud expression in hues of cream and brown stirred a myriad of emotions within her. When he had volunteered for the war, Rose had been distraught. When he hadn't come home, she was heartbroken. Now, every night she was wrought, watching the corner of her room, twisted with fear and anger.

Rose made her way towards her father's likeness and held the frame carefully. The cold silver was a satisfying weight in her hand. Mama's humming ceased.

Rose slipped her glasses back upon her nose, bringing Papa's image into a more satisfying sharpness. Chest tight once more, she felt the weight of Mama's attention. Rose sniffed away her feelings… private emotions she once shared so freely but now were locked away as securely as any safe. She found a clean corner of her sleeve, swept it in gentle circles across the frame until it shone haphazardly, tarnish long set in. It would have to do. Papa had the same dark hair as her mother, as Rose herself had. Rose and Papa wore a golden skin, a tone both admired and reviled, depending on which locals one came upon. The photograph, however, couldn't capture the amber of his eyes, a deep rich sunset that she too inherited, unlike the brown of her mother's.

"It was those eyes that caught my attention. Oh, the way the sun caught them." Edith's shoulder brushed Rose's.

"I'd never seen your father before; he was new to town after years working the docks abandoned by those who ran to the gold fields. He was still a young man exploring the world." Edith's eyes were closed, a smile lifted hollow cheeks.

"And then he saved your life," Rose finished the story.

"Yes, Bella, it's still a wonder. How I heard him tell me to look up from so far away… well, it was God's work." She smiled wider.

Edith had recounted, numerous times, the day she was near-squashed by a ton of flour being hoisted up into the bakery loft. She promised she hadn't heard those closest to her yell at her to jump out of the way. Edith insisted she had heard a voice in her mind tell her to look up. She saw the pully lurch and dashed to the side just as the flour fell. She had fallen, dusting herself free of flour and dirt, when her attention was caught upon a stranger, knapsack on his shoulder, walking towards her. Rose's father. Edith, despite being put to bed for a week for her ramblings, just in case she'd hit her head, to this very day, insisted she heard his voice call to her. When he had leaned down to offer her a hand up, the amber of his eyes stole her heart.

Rose saw wistfulness hold Mama a moment, and wondered if she would ever feel that way? Eric's face flashed through her mind; she felt the gentle pressure of a dozen stolen kisses on Sundays at the back of St Paul's. Heat warmed her cheeks but was immediately doused with the anger she now coveted towards him. Anger felt safer, it hurt, for sure, but not the way love did.

Rose's eyes cleared, Edith's complexion had returned to the sallowness of hunger and exhaustion. Rose sat her father's picture back upon an embroidered doily, the first one she had made with all its missed stitches and patch-ups. She was sure Papa had been proud of the effort. *Edith* and *Giacomo* were a little crooked, sewn in a faded red, a heart on each side of their names.

"I'm sorry for being ill-tempered," Rose whispered.

The whisk resumed for a moment before Edith looked over her shoulder, a gentle smile softened the worry in her eyes.

"Cut up yesterday's bread, Bella." Edith nodded towards the breadboard, "But mind you wash those hands first."

"Yes, Mama." Rose filled the sink with an inch of brackish water and rubbed a little lye soap into her skin. She winced as it seared into the needlepoint bites that dotted her fingertips, the torn nail an especially refreshing sting.

Rose sliced slowly through the stale loaf, wondering how many more times the blade would do so. The flour urn had one day's bake left, two at best.

"What are we to do without our chickens?"

"God will provide my sweet," Edith answered. Rose cringed inside and threw the knife down. She slapped the bread onto a plate.

"God will provide, of course, *He* will," Rose mumbled to herself in a mocking tone as she watched Edith smear a thin line of beef fat into a hot pan. Rose had all but forgotten the taste of butter.

Edith pushed the scrambled eggs gently across the pan, her movements smooth, as delicate as always. Her dress was worn, hems tattered from too many repairs, her beautiful, sweet mother looked more a pauper than ever, yet she held herself with a poised countenance, a dignified woman Rose secretly aspired to. Rose sucked in her bottom lip to halt her tongue as reality smacked her in the face. The dilapidated state of Mama was all the evidence she needed. God wasn't providing for them at all. Rose's grumbling belly was easy evidence of that, her mother's state of dress, a professional seamstress, absolute proof. It seemed in 1914 that God went abroad and forgot about humanity.

CHAPTER 5

The homely sound of bubbling water filling a teapot tempered Rose's sour thoughts, however, an irrational jealousy struck when Edith slid a knitted warmer over the teapot. It seemed even that silver dome of metal had more comfort than they did. Rose's wilful temper clawed to the surface.

"I think God is too busy for the likes of us. If he cared at all, he would never have let Papa go to war." Rose dragged a chair from under the table, its legs squeaked as she flopped down, most unladylike.

"Your father enlisted voluntarily, as have many good men, Rose. God had nothing to do with it." Edith scooped a modest golden mound of egg onto one plate, the largest serving onto Rose's. Edith's face pinched; the only time any hint of anger coloured her complexion was talk of her father's enlistment.

"I don't feel like saying grace," Rose mumbled, not really knowing why she wanted to aggravate her mother so. It didn't bring anyone back, not in the way she wished.

Edith drew in a breath, mouth open to speak but then closed her eyes, clasped her hands and quietly prayed alone.

Rose's fork screeched as she pushed eggs around the cracks on her plate. Despite the urgent clench of her stomach, she couldn't eat them just yet. She wanted to savour their richness, breathe in the aroma for as long as hunger allowed.

"Have you heard anything from the bakery?" Edith asked, watching the movement of Rose's fork.

"They have no work either." Rose sighed; her fingers tightened around the cutlery. "I've been thinking… I'm old enough now." Rose swallowed, "I could apply at the munitions factory. Nellie Bailey went there last month. Her brother told me she's making enough money to pay the rent."

Edith rubbed her lips together and took a sip of tea.

"That's very nice, Rose, but that is too far away. I can't have you moving to the other side of the city."

"Why? Money is money. Why should it matter where I work. The girls are lodged together; it is perfectly safe and proper. I don't know why you fuss so much, Mama!" Rose clipped her words the way she knew it needled Mama, apologies already forgotten. She had thought many times of moving away for work, away from the corners, out of the reach of the shadows.

"We will take in more sewing," Edith said, annoyance oozing from her like a vapour. "We have discussed this one too many times. You know my thoughts about you leaving home. Who knows what could happen?"

Rose's attention fell back to the hearth, the dying embers of it exaggerated the darkness under the flue. What mother feared and what Rose feared were two very different things. She couldn't tell mother why she wanted to leave, what she saw, about the book, Devil, the crow, that she was trying to find a way to right it all. The fire crackled. Rose looked to the back door to see small, wet footprints leading all the way to the hearth.

Matteo smiled at her, blue and bloated, his eye lashes wet and stuck together in the corners. Her brother appeared to her every single day, so far only in the kitchen, always by the fire, sitting, warming his cold grey hands.

"Sewing won't pay enough, you know that," Rose's voice wobbled as she forced her eyes back upon her mother, trying to forget the day her brother was dragged from the river, trying to forget that she was supposed to be watching him.

"We may have to sell some things, just until your father returns and we have a stable income once more." Edith took a tiny mouthful of food, chewed slowly, sipping more tea in between each morsel to stretch the meagre meal out. The fire sizzled and popped.

Matteo watched them with wide eyes, licked his lips as he always did, as though hunger remained in death. Initially, Rose had left a corner of bread, a cup of water, anything to keep him happy, to keep him away. Of course, they were never touched, and her mother had begun scolding her for leaving a mess for the rats.

Largely, Matteo just sat there, trying to warm what would be forever cold.

Rose slammed her fork down. Matteo jumped; her mother flinched.

"What do we have left to sell?" Anger slid across Rose's tongue all too easily. "This war is killing more than the soldiers. It's turning everything upside down. It's destroying everything!" She fanned her arm around the kitchen, pointing at Matteo, who was blowing into his cupped hands.

"Just look at us? Look, Mama!" She pointed around the room.

Peeling wallpaper, an empty larder, a dusty sideboard that once brimmed with floral porcelain. Rose wanted to scream *and look at all the dead things,* but she couldn't, she wouldn't. She knew that would be too much for her mother, yet the sight of their home set a flame under her anger. The bareness of their life, the lack of anything of comfort, the lost warmth of family sitting by the fire at night reading. It bellowed that rage into a small inferno.

Rose had lost the gentle ease she once possessed, an ability to see so easily the light in the dark, to feel joy at the smallest of things. Now she was an echo of her former self, haunted, the negative of the girl who once dreamed of her future as a beautiful adventure.

Edith's movements had stilled, the hope in her eyes dulled. Rose bit her lip, stilled the vinegar of her thoughts.

Perhaps it was the hunger? Perhaps the emotions, the visitations, maybe it was that she was living each day in plain terror? Maybe the book had nothing to do with anything. Rose snatched up her fork, fingers curled tight and shoved a mound of eggs into her mouth.

Edith's plate clinked as she placed her cutlery down, dabbed her mouth with a napkin. She slid her chair out silently, her movements considered as she disappeared into the sitting room. She returned with a glint of silver in her palm.

"No! Not Papa's pocket watch. Please, Mama? It's the most precious thing he owned… uh … owns. Besides, it was Nonno's." Rose stood in protest, her chair crashed to the floor, the dishes rattled as her fist hit the table. Edith barely flinched, her eyes a little harder, holding Rose's with a sharpness that made Rose's chin tremble.

"No, you *won't* sell it!" Rose's chest tightened; she pushed her glasses back up her nose, but her vision clouded with anger.

"I'll… I'll shovel shit at the blacksmith's if I have to!" The pulse in her head rushed until she couldn't hear anything but the panic within. Her head spun. Rose leaned onto her hands to steady herself. Heat clawed under her skin. Everything tingled.

"You will watch your mouth, Rosa." Edith's brows arched, her eyes steely, but her voice remained annoyingly calm, it lacked the heat that Rose cultivated so very easily.

Edith flicked the watch open and closed a couple of times. Candlelight deepened the dark crescents ever-present beneath her eyes. She pressed the watch over her heart. The sight of its perfect shine between her fingers a memory of nights when Papa would tuck Rose into bed, flick the watch open and say, *"There now, my angel, the hour for sleep has come."* He would shut it, but not before letting Rose hold it in her tiny hands, wide-eyed. Rose liked to raise it up to catch the candlelight, just so, until it glittered like a star. Fingers curled over the table top; she recalled the heavy silver in her palm, could feel the filigree pattern engraved into its casing.

Rose watched her mother's fingers trace that same pattern, as though she had the same recollection. Edith sighed, her eyes softer, smiling at a secret memory before the emotion drained away and the lines around her mouth deepened. Edith's arms dropped, but she held tight to the watch.

"You simply can't sell it, Mama, please?" Rose's head hurt; a creeping feeling clawed the base of her skull. The hairs upon her neck awoke anew.

"Please, Mama…" her voice faded.

Edith cleared her throat, eyes flitting between the watch and Rose.

"Rose, Bella, your papa has been gone two years come this September. His presence, his income, his love… we are left wanting." Edith's voice hitched; her breath shaky. She took a sip of tea, set the cup down with a trembling hand. The thumb of her left hand rolled her wedding band around, its silver tarnished like the photo frame, like her, like their entire lives.

"They said the war would be over quickly, that our men would be fine. Well…" Edith held the pocket watch to her heart again. The dying hearth crackled softly behind her, its flame dulling to embers. Matteo was no longer there. Cold now clutched at Rose's ankles, her toes curled in.

"Clearly, things have not gone as expected. Apart from those first few letters when he arrived in France, we've had no word of him since he left. We need to be realistic; pragmatic, Rose. We have to survive for him, be ready when he returns." Edith blinked rapidly and cleared her throat once more, but those deep brown eyes betrayed her. Tears were diamonds upon her lashes; the angles of her face hardened by shadow and a flash of emotion.

"Rosa, do you suppose your papa wishes to return home to an old watch and our bodies decaying along with our Matteo in the grounds of St Pauls?" The stark reality of her words stung as keenly as a slap in the face. They forced Rose to sit back down. The room felt small, the air heavy, and it drew those diamonds down Edith's cheeks.

Rose flicked a crust of bread around her plate, picked it up and chewed it slowly. It served to suppress another rush of regrettable words and tempered the biting hunger within. It tasted sour, matched perfectly with her temper. Edith sat back down, leaned back in her chair, poured another cup of tea for herself, and they finished the meagre meal in silence.

CHAPTER 6

Dishes clunked in the sink as Edith washed whilst Rose swept the floor. The rhythmic swish, swish drew Rose's mind away awhile, to sunsets by the river, picnics after church on Sundays, cordial spilled down pressed dresses. The image of Eric Wright, her absolute best childhood friend offering her a handkerchief to clean it up brought a warm flush to her skin. Prior to fifteen, she would have grabbed it, shoved it in his face, run away and giggled as he chased after her. Now though, things were different, and not in the way she had envisioned, not the way her heart had hoped for. Her nails dug into the broomstick, she swept harder and faster, yet his face stayed planted in her mind.

"Here." Edith pulled the broom from Rose's grip and slid the watch back into her hands.

"We'll have no floor left if you keep that up." She gently folded Rose's fingers over the watch. Her hands warmed as they sandwiched between her mother's.

"I will finish tidying up. Put on your Sunday dress and head up to the haberdashery. I hear Mrs Wright is taking goods in lieu of money for a while. Such a good Christian soul she is."

Edith looked to the ceiling, nodding a quiet prayer of thanks.

"That watch should buy us enough thread and candles for a good while." Edith looked to the flour urn; Rose caught the fleeting guilt wash pale across Mama's face. Edith turned away and began sweeping the floor, hiding her emotions as best she could, as she always did.

"We may be able to purchase some more chickens sooner rather than later and, perhaps, purchase the watch back if Mrs Wright hasn't sold it before our fortune turns about." The sweeping slowed, then became almost as frantic as Rose's efforts.

"I'll ask Mr Wilson next door if he might spare us some eggs in exchange for housework in the meantime. He's very lonely since Mrs Wilson passed. I'll drop by later today to ask." Edith herded a small tuft of dust into a corner and leaned the broom against the wall, ran her hands down her sides and took a deep breath before turning around, a warm smile plastered across her face. Matteo appeared behind her; he slid his hand into Mama's.

"It is a little colder than usual today." Edith pulled away, and rubbed her hands together to warm them.

Rose's fingers curled tight around the watch, she pressed it against her chest, watched Matteo's shoulders slump, his smile wane as he faded away. Her heart thumped hard; her nostrils flared. The moist pungency of death infused Rose's senses once more, Edith none the wiser of what mingled amongst them.

"Hurry now. All will be well, Rose. I'm quite positive a letter will arrive before you know it with word of your papa." She waved Rose away.

"Get along now before this storm turns any worse." Edith peered out the window, its edges caked white, only the middle clear enough to see through. Mama didn't see the face that stared back.... an unknown corpse hung with patches of leathered skin and tufts of black hair. Rose's skin crawled; she looked away and it was gone when her eyes flicked back up. Something within her pushed her to take notice of these things, to give them her attention, despite the gut-churning fear of it all.

The wind had picked up again, sucking in dark, greenish clouds. Droplets slid down the window panes, tinkered like piano keys upon the roof. The sun had all but given up, the far end of the backyard deep in shadow. Edith pulled the kitchen window firmly shut, latched it and lit a miserable candle stub; the amber flickering made little difference to the recesses that rapidly filled with darkness.

Rose left her mother to the cleaning up. Edith began humming to herself, a prayer as usual. Rose dragged her feet, stopped inside the hallway, and peered back around the corner. The shadow rose behind Edith; Matteo also was back, a wad of Edith's skirt in his hand; he watched the shadow as well, dull eyes wide as though in death, he too was scared.

The shadow looked at Rose, eyes dull and rolling, mouth gawping.

Ba… no… ba… no

Its head bent towards Edith, something foul eked from it, the stink unmistakably death. Rose slapped a hand on her mouth, gagged upon the stench of sloughing, rotten flesh. The shadow did not move, arms lank by his side, Edith none the wiser that she was being watched.

Rose slipped away, ran on tiptoes to her room. Pressed her back against her closed door, eye narrowed towards the loose floorboard, gasping to fill her lungs.

"Please stop, please?" Sweat beaded on her temple despite the sharp cold of the air. She pressed the edge of her fist to her lips to quiet the roar of her breaths. When she calmed, Rose looked about her room… checking. Dimness claimed most of it, that right corner always the deepest, always drawing her attention, yet it was empty for the moment.

"He's with Mama," she whispered. "They're both with her. Calm down, get dressed, and get out."

She made her way to the wardrobe, head swivelling to ensure she was, in fact, alone.

Rose gripped the handle. It was cold; the dangling tear drop of metal filled her palm in a satisfying way; she held onto it, a thread to what was real and normal.

"Come on, Rose, pull yourself together." She tugged the door open and yelped.

Matteo sat in the base, beneath the only other dress she owned. Rose slammed the door. It stuttered against its frame, coming to rest ajar, a sliver of darkness struck between inside and out. That thin shadowed seam gripped her attention.

"Go away, Matteo." Rose stumbled back, and pressed herself hard against the wall. The wardrobe door creaked open a little wider. Grey fingers wrapped around the wood; a tuft of matted brown hair poked out. He whispered to her, a gurgling of words she couldn't understand.

The noise in Rose's head was deafening. She couldn't drown out the whispers, the cries … the outright screaming.

"I can't do this anymore." Her voice was thin and wispy… defeated.

Matteo's fingers slid away; the wardrobe door closed with a soft click.

Rose dove for the floor, gouged the loose board out and retrieved the book. She flipped hastily through the pages to the one scribbled in a rushed hand, the only words in English. She had until now been too frightened to say the words out loud. She was desperate though, and thought no worse could come of her for trying something… anything.

She held the book up and faced the wardrobe.

"With a full heart of peace and grace
I call on you to leave this place."

CHAPTER 7

Devil tapped its beak upon the window. Its claws made a *tip, tip* sound as it paced left to right. It appeared after Rose had uttered the words, was it a prayer, a curse… she didn't truly know. She watched that bird, saw the intelligence in its eyes, and felt a strange tug in her belly, a connection she couldn't explain. The book fell from her hands, her head dipped, and she sobbed.

Rose felt a draught behind her, and saw her Sunday dress somehow laid out neatly on her bed.

Her muscles tightened, and she grit her teeth. She kicked the book. It slid across the room, coming to a stop beneath her bed.

"Useless," she snapped, then a sudden panic surged through her. She ran to the book, grabbed it, dropped it back into its hiding place, and stamped the floorboard down. Rose stared at the dress, splayed her hands across her cheeks, calmed herself… tried to think things through.

If Matteo was trying to help her, were the others also? She reached for the dress, eyes on the wardrobe, on the corner. No, no, they couldn't be. Wouldn't they leave her with a feeling of comfort rather than snakes writhing in her guts?

Mama's footsteps tapped along the hall. Rose snatched the dress up quickly, retreated to her dresser and held it against herself. She kept an eye on the corner in the reflection as she appraised her own miserable reflection.

Another few months and the dress would have no more seams to let out, no more hem to call upon. Despite hunger, her bosom had still grown, the only part of her, in fact. She stared a little harder behind herself; the corner was empty.

Rose let out a long breath, now focused on the face she knew, a face that housed a body she didn't understand. The plumpness of youth had given way to more refined angles in her cheeks, her eyes shaded by thick lashes, even her glasses beheld a more mature countenance. She once hated them, but now… not so much.

Thunder rumbled; she could feel its power underfoot. The patter of rain still a light trill, but the day quickly dimmed. Devil was now atop the letterbox, shaking the rain from its feathers. It glistened glossy black, the only darkness that seemed to behold any beauty, despite the disquiet of its presence.

The laneway that led to town was already hunkered in shadow. A small, muddy tide rushed down the left side of it. The avenue of trees lurched, succumbing to the growing storm's will. Branches snapped and bent like fingers, begging her in.

Her room shrunk as the storm claimed the light, the air a thick blanket, hard to breathe in.

The floor creaked behind her, she turned around, but nothing was there. The dress slipped from her grasp, she kneeled to pick it up, eyes wide upon the corner to the right. Rotting flesh wafted her way again. She opened her mouth to recount the strange words but stopped. It wasn't working; she didn't at all know what power, if any, they held. Everything had begun because she had opened a door she had no right to when she took that book, and Rose had no clue what she was doing.

"Why don't you just tell me what you want?" The window rattled, and she bunched the dress in her fists, the door seemed so very far away. Rose reached for her neck again, the skin cold and bumpy.

"Please leave me alone… pl…" Her voice hitched this time. The corner was full, a deeper, thicker umber. The whispering was indecipherable.

"You don't belong here…" Her eyes stung. "Not anymore. I'm sorry for what I've done… if that's why you're here, it was an accident. I shouldn't have taken the book." Rose pushed herself up, took a step back, tripped on the loose tread of her old boots and collided with the wall. The mirror banged behind her. She spun and steadied it lest it fall and break like everything else. Once still upon the wall, she released the mirror, and spun back. The corner felt empty again. The room smelled of dust and nothing more.

She stared a long while at the corner, just as she did each night. The cycle was repetitive, day after day, worsening as the money ran out and food became scarcer. She was in this very moment trying to convince herself that it *was* the hunger… or perhaps that she was altogether going a little mad, but Rose knew all too well that she had opened the veil between the living and the dead.

"I need to leave this place," Rose whispered, hands balled against her chest, not knowing how that could ever be possible in any manner other than within a wooden box pointed towards St Paul's. She fumbled on her dresser, pulled the latest letter seeking work from the pile of apologies. Rose uncapped a pen, rolled it between her palms to warm the ink. She signed her name below an application for the munitions factory.

Footsteps closed in towards her room. Rose dropped the pen, folded the paper and slipped it into her last envelope, unsure what money she might use to post it. She quickly slid it behind the mirror before stepping into her dress. She started brushing her hair more aggressively than required, wincing as it caught in knots, one eye upon the reflection of the corner, the other upon the wardrobe. The footsteps halted outside her door. She sat upon the stool beneath the mirror. There was a knock.

"Rose, may I come in?"

"Of course, Mama."

Edith entered; her hands clasped something to her chest. She eyed Rose's room, that same pale dismay drained Edith's complexion of a once beautiful glow. Rose's eyes flickered between Mama and the mirror; the edge of the letter was only just visible. She checked the corner again, nothing; there was nothing. Edith made her way over, the heels of her shoes clicked as the floorboards groaned, the loose one rattled.

She motioned for Rose to face the mirror.

"You're nigh on eighteen now, a young woman." Edith took the brush from Rose. She stroked the length of Rose's hair; each slide a step back in time to simpler days, more innocent moments. It brought forth memories of years gone by when Mama would brush her hair one hundred times each night. Rose studied her mother's reflection; the gentleness of her face stirred an undeniable love each time the brush ran the length of hair. What would she do if the shadows made themselves visible to Mama? Rose shuddered at the thought. Perhaps she needed to draw them out, away from Mama? She wondered if that was her lot in life? Had she, by interfering with the book, set a destiny so very dreadful?

"It's time you wear a more mature style, I think." Edith's voice jarred Rose, who was lost in macabre worries. She swept Rose's hair up into a chignon, pulling a few pins from her pocket to hold it in place. Edith then flashed her palm in the mirror's reflection. Rose gasped.

"You still have it?"

"Of course! This is one thing I was holding onto for you, for your wedding day."

Edith pressed the ivory hair clasp over the chignon, threaded its pin through the middle.

Rose couldn't help but smile at the weight of it, the sleek reflection of herself. She looked immediately more mature, her cheekbones higher, her lips fuller. One nice thing, something pretty and light in a world of death and darkness.

"This world is turning in unexpected ways, my love. Nonna would not have wanted this to be wasted." Edith leaned down and kissed Rose's cheek.

Rose stood up and kissed her mother. Matteo peeked through the doorway, milky eyes under arched brows; he stared at Rose, shrugged his shoulders and misted into nothingness.

Her bedroom door slammed, the mirror shuddered, and the envelope sailed out, landing at Edith's feet. Rose's mouth dropped, the shadow followed Matteo, its lingering umber sliding across the floor, disappearing underneath the door. Rose's hands splayed before her nails dug hard into her palms.

"What's this?" Edith picked up the letter, saw the address in Rose's neat cursive.

Edith's face pinched. "This will make fine kindling." Her nostrils flared subtly.

"Mama let me explain."

Edith shoved the paper in her apron.

"Off with you to town."

CHAPTER 8

The high street was awash when Rose turned the corner from Banksia Lane. She had run through the depths of its shadows, past its claws, chased by something unseen, deafened by the voices that invaded her mind. Rose held onto the milepost that marked the edge of town, bent over where the lane spat her out, heaving for breath. The air was so cold it hurt as it hit her lungs, she coughed, and her eyes watered.

There was no comfort in drawing her coat tighter; the weather cut through as easily as a scythe. Rose's boots sucked in and out of thick, stinking mud, each breath fogging thickly, her glasses more a nuisance than anything. She slipped them into a pocket and hurried onwards past a man slumped on the ground, leaning against a tree, smoking a pipe. He turned his eyeless head towards her as she passed, held his pipe up in greeting, and set it back into his fleshless mouth. She heard the click of it against his teeth; she ran.

Gutters flowed, rich with debris, an odour to it so ripe that she shielded her nose with her coat lapel; her breath, stale with tea and eggs, didn't help matters. Neither did the horse trotting past with a gunshot wound in its head. An open-top cart rumbled by, its passengers unaware of the man with a noose around his neck who stumbled along behind. His head twisted to one side; his neck elongated where the bones no longer connected to the spine. He didn't notice Rose, to her relief, as he tried to right the angle of his head.

Rose slipped, righted herself, finding a page of yesterday's Melbourne Herald stuck to her sole. She peeled it away, and read the bleeding ink of the headline.

French Repel Enemy. Attack Fails at Verdun.

Her breath caught, her chest a vice. Was Papa lying in a field in France? His letters had stopped so very long ago, they had been from France, and that was when the shadows became inhabited.

The newspaper was soft, its fibres sloughed away as she tried to read the small typeset, just in case there could be a mention, a clue. But the words bled too quickly until they were no more than blackened streams coursing down the soggy page. Rose balled up the paper until it wadded, her hand squeezed it tight until water oozed through her fingers. She imagined it was the war mongers' necks in her grasp, her knuckles whitened a moment longer. Rose threw the paper into the flowing gutter, teeth clenched, anger tempered the shiver that had a hold over her body. None of this would be so if the war had not started... or if she had left that book alone.

The wind whipped her faster along the street, her mind playing awful games. She couldn't stop the visions of her father's body in a ditch far away, slowly being covered over by other bodies, until he was squashed down, forgotten under a pile of death. Dead, discarded, forgotten. Is that what the shadows were about, clawing back, trying to not be forgotten?

She skirted a woman covered in pox, garish mouth wide, eyes bulbous bloody orbs, a dead child to her slack breast.

Rose quickened her pace, shook her head.

"Just don't look at them!" Her head shook sharply, Rose scolded herself, "If you don't pay them attention... they'll disappear." But they didn't, they were always there. Rose's jaw clamped, her teeth squeaked, her feet moved faster. The weight of her father's watch in her pocket, the news headline, the hunger that relentlessly gnawed at her... and now *they* pursued her in the daylight. She felt a breath away from fainting; her legs burned. She turned a corner, leaned into the squalling wind, and sucked in the cold of it. Rose ignored her peripheries, didn't allow her eyes to linger on a man with a slit throat stagger past, she fought it all the way up the rise of the main street of town.

Pretty dresses and debut balls flooded her thoughts instead, but at the corners of her vision, *they* fought for her attention. The shadows pushed in relentlessly, so she ran faster. With her dress hitched up, her legs pumped as hard as they could, desperately hoping the visions would not seek to chase her as a predator would prey.

"Rose? Is that you, Dear?"

Rose slowed, bit her tongue, intended to keep running; she was so close to her destination.

"Rose Carbonelli?"

Rose sighed, rolled her eyes, pulled her glasses from her pocket, wiped them and placed them upon her face, slipping them neatly over the small rise in the middle of her nose. She summoned a smile and turned.

"Miss Ray." Rose inclined her head and ignored the gold-eyed crow that circled above Miss Ray.

"I haven't seen hide nor hair of your mother and yourself in weeks. Is everything alright, Dear?" Miss Ray's watery eyes judged Rose from head to foot.

"You look peaky, Dear, lost that Mediterranean look about you." Her fingers laced over the rise of a paunch belly of plenty. Rose grimaced inside. Mama had taught her about the unkind ignorance of some people, Miss Ray being the Queen of them all.

"Well, there's not been much sun, has there? I'm quite sure I'll darken up soon enough." Rose smiled her fakest. Miss Ray grimaced, arched her thin brows, but then she too returned to the falsity that was a plastered-on appearance of compassion.

"Where is your dear mother?" Miss Ray's mouth puckered as she leaned to the left, and eyed the new style of Rose's hair.

"Hmm, rather gaudy for the day, don't you think?" Miss Ray pinched Rose's arm.

Rose stepped back. "Please don't do that!"

"You're as thin as a whip." Miss Ray tutted. "Told Edith a year back she should have sent you off. A woman like that trying to raise a young lady on her own…"

"Woman like what?" Rose glared at Miss Ray but was distracted when lightning flashed a distance away. The old woman and her cart were down the bottom end of the street. Thunder clapped, lightning flashed again, making Rose jump; the old woman had disappeared. Miss Ray seemed to read her nervousness as something else.

"Mother keeps us both very well. She is very stoic," Rose said, not wanting the old busybody to know too much, but in truth, she would have loved to slap her face.

"I imagine she would be, marrying a foreigner and all." Miss Ray's smile pinched in smug judgement. "It's not unexpected that you have struggles, poor dears," Miss Ray said. She shook her head and tsked her most condescending false empathy.

Rose bit her lip to halt more of those words from the docks. Instead, she envisioned Miss Ray's buttons popping open, the indulgence of her life falling out in public.

"We do as others do, Miss Ray, work hard and wait for the return of Papa."

"Not much work, Dear." Miss Ray could barely suppress a smile. "Well, I suppose it's the way for many these days," her eyes swept over Rose's hair once more. "What means of income are you seeking, Dear, out on your own, all dolled up like that? I'd be mighty careful young lady, what traps are lying in wait." She shook her head and clucked her tongue again. "I expect you'll be quite the prey; men do like something a little avant-garde now and then. Mind yourself now, Dear," Miss Ray said.

"Miss Ray? I… I'm here on errands for Mama!" Rose's mouth was agape, embarrassment clawed up her neck. She knew, of course, Miss Ray would read this as guilt.

She glared at Miss Ray, imagined that crow plucking her tongue out, forever quieted of her nastiness. The crow swooped by, circled higher, coasting on each gust as though it knew Rose's thoughts, as though it just might do as she wished. Rose's heart beat a little harder.

"I'm looking for shop work, as a matter of fact." Rose nudged her head towards the opposite side of the road in the direction of the newsagency. "I've skills enough to sell a paper or a sweet."

"There's no good work about; you well know that, girl!" Miss Ray nodded; eyes too shiny with delight. Her judgement of Rose too easy, too enjoyable.

Rose imagined those judgemental beady orbs plucked out one at a time... slowly.

"Well, whatever I do, it will surely pay better than petty gossiping!" Rose hitched her dress and turned away, her feet pointed at the newsagency, her ears too keenly hearing the shocked gasp of Miss Ray. A smile spread across her face.

"Good Christians lean upon the Lord, Dear, not the flesh!" Miss Ray yelled loud enough for all to hear.

Rose's legs moved faster for the insult and to prevent herself screaming one of those ugly words.

"I'll pray for you and your dear mother." The rest of her insults were lost in another rumble of thunder.

As Rose's feet thumped onto the boardwalk, she heard a scream, then shouting. She turned back to see Miss Ray slapping at the crow with her bag, a thin stripe of blood on her cheek. Laughter bubbled in Rose's throat, but it was cut sharply down by an ensuing terror.

Devil? Can you hear me? The crow arced up and away, landing upon a street lamp. It cawed and cocked its eye to Rose. Miss Ray's screams carried away on the next gust of wind as she was ushered to the opposite side of the road by a passer-by.

Rose returned its stare, open-mouthed. Devil shook its feathers, cawed at her, one amber-flecked eye focused upon Rose, the only colour in a colourless day. It turned from Rose, strutting along the arm of the lamp, its attention now across the road.

The steady, drizzling rain seeped beneath her coat, but Rose didn't notice it, a strange feeling burned away the chill of its bite. Hair heavy, she felt the clasp coming loose. She took it out, slipped it into her pocket, the protestations of Miss Ray catching her attention again. Rose smiled as Miss Ray slapped away the good Samaritan, Devil cawed again as though enjoying the fruits of its attack.

"You can stick your prayers…" Rose whispered as thunder vibrated the ground. Rose kept the rest of the thought to herself. Miss Ray gawped open-mouthed as Devil swooped for her again. She yelped hoarsely, pulled her coat tight and bustled away towards the butcher shop, straight through a shadow. Its darkness rose up behind her, Devil alongside it. Fleshless fingers flicked Miss Ray's hat, a gust of wind caught hold and ripped it from her head. For the second time this morning, Rose felt the urge to laugh.

She left Miss Ray chasing her hat and moved along the boardwalk to the newsagent.

Devil arced overhead and fluttered to a stop upon the horse tie-up.

"I don't need your help," Rose snapped. Devil cawed, head down low, feathers bristled along its neck, and sidled left and right. Teeth clenched anew, Rose wasn't sure she actually meant that, she wasn't at all sure she didn't secretly covet whatever this strange crow was trying to communicate. She sighed, averted her attention and hoisted up the heaviness of her dress, hem blackened. Entering the newsagency, a sudden burst of hope lit within her when she realised only living people were inside.

Her boots were heavy and squelched upon the floor; she grimaced, stepped back, double wiped them on the door mat whilst smoothing wet strands of hair behind her ears. She pinched colour into her cheeks so as to not look quite so undernourished.

The familiar wood-panelled walls embellished with warm glowing gas lamps tempered the anger flowing hot in her veins. It smelled of paper and ink. A wall of maps and brochures lined the rear of the serving counter. Mr Andrews had his back to her, a pen behind his ear and a leather apron snug about him while stocking a shelf of fountain pens. The emptiness of the shelves had increased as the years went by and the war raged on.

Rose cleared her throat.

"A moment…"

He stepped down from a step stool and wiped his hands down his apron.

"Ah, Rose, hello, how's your mum?" Mr Andrews asked, scratching a shiny bald patch on the crown of his head. A finely curled, perfectly white moustache tweaked above his smile. He ushered himself behind the service desk.

"She is well, thank you."

"How can I help you today?"

Rose wrung her hands, and hesitated. She could already see the answer in his face, but her stomach growled, and Miss Ray's high-pitched trill still rang in her head.

"I know I was in recently, but I thought I'd ask again if you might need help in the shop? Anything at all. Serving, cleaning, I could even sell papers on the street with young Thomas." Rose bit her bottom lip, held her breath and reached for the tiniest spark of hope.

Mr Andrews rubbed a finger across his moustache, smoothing one end into a perfect upward curl. He stepped around the counter, wiped his hands upon his apron again when there was clearly no need to.

"I'm sorry, Rose." He pressed his lips tight, pensive and sighed. "There's just no work; you know I would help out if I could." He shook his head. She could see him awkwardly appraising the state of her.

"Have you tried the bakery? People need bread; there's always a line out the door."

"Yesterday," she answered, shoulders slumping.

"I'm sorry, things are not easy for anyone these past few years."

"No, they aren't." Rose noticed the heavy blue crescents under his eyes.

"Heard anything on your father?"

Rose shook her head. "Not for a while now."

Mr Andrews averted his attention, wiping at his clearly polished service desk.

"I'm sorry to hear that… most sorry."

"Thank you." Rose couldn't stand the sympathy that shadowed his face. She had to get out. As she turned for the door, Mr Andrews called out.

"Rose, here. It's not much." He was folding the top of a paper bag down and set it in her hands.

Rose opened the bag; confusion creased her brow before a smile cut through her misery.

"Folks seem to prefer fountain pens these days, I've a few spares I can't seem to sell. Perhaps you could use them to apply for other employment?" He nodded enthusiastically as Rose pulled out a soft feather quill. The bag was weighted down with a new bottle of ink. Rose ran the feather across her cheek, enjoying the soft newness of it.

"Thank you, Mr Andrews, that is very kind." She tucked the small parcel into her deepest pocket and nodded politely.

"Goodbye." She left quickly, the vibration of the door rocked the boardwalk as the wind caught it and slammed it shut behind her. Her father's watch tapped against her leg, where it snuggled in her pocket, her new quill light as... well, a feather, in her other. She stopped, leaned into a lamp post, and watched the hustle of life pass by for a moment. Devil was in the same place; it cawed, and cocked its head to watch her once more. She looked away, observing the street, not at all sure what she felt towards it after it attacked Miss Ray.

Two constables, cloaked in leather from the rain, strode along the boardwalk to her right. A cart horse reared up as it was being led into the farrier for a new shoe, a man lay in the gutter across the road, clawing at his open belly, trying to shove his guts back inside. The sight transfixed Rose; he didn't look at her, didn't notice anyone else, he was simply trying to put himself back together, and Rose was his only witness.

Disgust coated the back of her throat; she pressed a hand to her mouth, and swallowed the urge to retch. She hitched her dress again and ran across the road towards the haberdashery, only to hear someone yell.

"Watch out!" Rose glanced up just in time to lunge out of the way of a large carriage. She swayed on the spot; the sleek black shine of the carriage sparkled with raindrops. It was polished; she could see her outline sway in its shine as it passed her by. Curtains drawn; a golden crest was carved into its side; an ornate letter R surrounded by flowers.

The carriage held her attention as it pulled up just short of the haberdashery.

The disembowelled man continued his work, not at all concerned with the fact that Rose was nearly run down. Devil fluttered overhead and settled upon the carriage roof, cawing more heartily at her than before.

Follow the crow to seal the door," the old woman had said to Rose when she had tried to return the damned book. Rose frowned and watched the crow pace upon the carriage roof, its claws tapping sharply upon the wood. Rose inched closer to the carriage, attention upon the crest.

She peered up at the concealed windows. The carriage lurched as someone got out on the other side. She rounded the front, past the horses, the driver nodded as she walked by.

"Careful crossing the road Miss; lucky they're experienced stock. Younger ones might not have seen you so safe!" He jutted his chin at the four horses tacked to the carriage. Their black necks arched with an aristocratic air.

"I'm very sorry; I was distracted."

"Well, best you be paying attention next time." The driver tipped his hat and sat back, flicked a newspaper open, awaiting the return of his passenger.

Rose admired the horses a moment. She really quite loved them, had always wished for one herself. They shone with well-polished finery upon their harnesses, and looked every bit as though they'd not deign to graze near Mr Wilson's old gipsy cob. One ear bitten off by a wild dog as a foal, old Ned was famous near and far as the most trustworthy of steeds, but would never do for such transportation.

Rose felt suddenly sick at the sight of such wealth at the very same moment as wondering what such comfort must feel like. Arms crossed, fingers circling her sleeves, she imagined soft velvet and satin, warm leather boots, and hand-spun lace. She wondered what they would have for supper and if their hearth was brimming with wood each night?

She also wondered about Devil. Why was it here? Why now? Was this the time to pay it attention… to follow it? A new chill slipped under her skin and tightened around her heart. Rose drew a calming breath, "Stop being ridiculous," she whispered to herself.

She resisted the temptation to look back at the carriage and Devil, drew herself up with the poise Mama had taught her, and stepped onto the boardwalk, heading towards her destination. A few moments later arriving at the haberdashery, Rose peered in the windows, its warm, amber glow a beacon. The cold that gripped her eased a little.

Rose took the first step up to the door and hesitated. Her fingers curled in, the cold seeped right back in. Eric was pressing a sign inside the front window, their eyes met. Rose looked down, her heart thumping too heavily. When she looked up, he was gone. She sighed with relief, leaned in, and read the note.

Devil cawed loudly. Rose looked over her shoulder. Devil dipped its head, and cocked an eye at Rose. They held each other's gaze a moment.

Rose wet her lips, hugged her body, turned back and read the advertisement again.

"Live in?" She rubbed her gloved fingers across her chin. "Live in..." she whispered, an idea forming in her mind. She looked back to the crow; Devil watched her in patient silence.

The gutted man wandered past along the edge of the boardwalk, hands pressed against his stomach, congealed fluid slipped slowly between his fingers. He was heading in the direction of St Paul's. "Live in…" Rose whispered as his image evaporated on a gust of wind.

The wind whipped more furiously along the boardwalk, an unnatural howl in its song. A strangely herbed rot flavoured her next breath. She saw the shadow slide across the corner of the boardwalk. Were her days and nights to be tormented forever more? The need to escape was strong, to never see her bedroom, those corners again… Rose wished to not set eyes upon fleshless limbs and eyeless sockets for the rest of her days.

She looked at the advertisement again, her heart rushed a little faster, but for a very different reason. She was here anyway; Mama had wanted her to visit. She could ask about the position at the same time. This was a way out, a place to hide, to save Mama, maybe to find a way out of the nightmare she found herself in. As if to encourage her, Devil swooped around her. She slapped at it, the crow cawed and flew away.

Rose recovered herself and smoothed the skirts of what was once a baby blue dress. Mouth pinched; she slapped away the mud that weighed at her hem. The fabric was rich with stains and, after this morning's journey to town, looked worse than ever. She sighed, clucked her tongue and reached for the door.

The shop's electric light shone invitingly. Windows frosted around the edges brimmed with an array of luxurious fabrics, household goods and curious knick-knacks. Her hand shivered in a sudden hesitation upon the handle and slipped away, eyes stuck on the advertisement.

A lady's maid? How ridiculous! What did she know of this? She had no references, no idea what such a position would entail. Her shoulders slumped; she turned to leave but noticed Miss Ray waddling back down the street, her cheek still plum red from the crow attack.

Rose watched the old biddy, hat back on, post parcels in hand, nodding with false care at the odd passer-by. The old woman followed behind Miss Ray; she looked over to Rose. Another crow landed upon her shoulder, she nodded, expressionless to Rose, and as a cart rumbled by, both the old woman and her crow were gone, as if never there.

The smell of rot intensified, drew her attention from Miss Ray, from the disappearing old woman and her crow, back to the corner of the boardwalk. The shadow melded within the grim greyness of the day. It moved, slipped along the ground, past the carriage and dissipated into the wind.

Rose bit into her fingers, the cold of them shocked her teeth. She hesitated, then moved to the edge of the boardwalk, and actually searched for the shadow. Where had it gone? Had Mother Nature gobbled it up, freed her from its attention? Could Mother Nature do that with the others? She moved a few feet further along. The air smelled of dirt and water, of horse manure and burning wood. Relief washed over her, her hands fell to her sides, reprieve for a moment. She wondered if it had merely gone back home, fled to the corner of her room...waiting.

CHAPTER 9

Rain slammed down, separating Rose from the darkness that surely awaited her at home. A white curtain barricaded her between town and home and the Rutherford carriage. The metal awning overhead creaked; its wooded struts groaned under a roaring deluge. The noise at least drowned out intrusive thoughts of helplessness and anger; of people with more than they required; of resenting her mother's calm acceptance of their situation... and of what lay within the shadows, of the things that haunted her.

Devil reappeared, shook the rain from its feathers as its claws clicked along the boardwalk. It bobbed its head, scuttled forwards, as though urging Rose towards the haberdashery.

"Are you watching me?" Rose felt ridiculous talking to the bird. It cocked its head at her as though it was listening, as though it understood her words. It dipped its head low and cawed a deeper tone. Rose took a step back towards the shopfront. She shivered deeply. It felt like an omen was falling upon her, pushing her in a particular direction. She licked her lips, cold and cracked. Why did she think so much? Why couldn't she just sew and pray like Mama?

Rose's fingers laced through her shawl, one she borrowed from Mama, her own still flapped in the branches of the willow. The bite of the weather stirred a cough, made her nose burn and run. She slicked it dry with the back of her hand, and peered through the white haze towards home. The road ran a river, people dashed for cover. The wind renewed its hungry gust for her comfort; even the things that were dead were nowhere to be seen. Mother Nature had made the choice for her that morning… and the crow still hopped around her hem urging her choice in one direction.

Hovering once more in front of the haberdashery entrance, eyes upon that note, Rose pressed the door.

A brass bell chimed much too happily as she entered, but an instant relief hit her. She inhaled. Wood polish and potpourri, sweet and heady. The temperate air was a welcome hug, her skin's numbness melted into pins and needles. Her cheeks warmed, hands and toes once more felt their coverings.

"Minute…just attending another customer," called Mrs Wright from somewhere out back.

Rose rubbed her arms, sealing heat into herself. She watched for movement at the back of the store, when she realised she was alone, she quickly peeled the note from the window and tucked it into her pocket atop Papa's watch. When the heavy curtain scraped open at the back storeroom, Rose spun, and pushed the paper further down in her pocket. She set her hands behind her back, innocence upon her face. No one else would see the advertisement; she needed this job.

Mrs Wright bustled from the storeroom to the front counter. The curtain settled closed, apart from one edge. Eric, Mrs Wright's remaining son, peered out. He watched Rose, eyes on her hand that slipped guiltily back into her coat pocket. He wore his hair longer these days, not in the short style that was so popular. As if knowing her thoughts, he pulled the copper locks further across the left side of his face, hiding what was there. She didn't care about that; it was the scar on Rose's heart that caused her to coldly avert her eyes. The curtain slipped back, and he was gone.

"Rose, dear, what on earth are you doing out in such weather? You'll catch your death, come, come." Mrs Wright waved Rose over, stuck her head back through the curtain, speaking to someone.

"Yes, yes, I think that suits splendidly." She then made her way back to Rose, pulling a blanket from the back of a chair behind the service desk. Lily of the Valley mingled with the polish and potpourri as Mrs

Wright wrapped the blanket tight around Rose's shoulders, strands of her voluminous pompadour tickling Rose's face. The heavy wool was a welcome warmth, and her body seemed to melt into the comfort.

Mrs Wright rubbed Rose's shoulders vigorously until her powdered cheeks jiggled.

"My word, you're frozen to the bone." She guided Rose towards a golden damask chair and gently sat her down next to a bolt of royal blue silk. Rose shifted her attention from such beauty, trying not to remember the nice things they once had.

"Sit yourself here a moment, my love." Mrs Wright crossed her arms and studied her. Soft brown eyes swept head to foot.

"Hmmm, well now, don't you look like the cat who caught the pigeon?" Mrs Wright's fingers drummed upon her arms; arched brows framed a kindly face.

"Is everything alright, Dear?"

"I'm fine," Rose said, not at all wishing to talk any more than she had to lest her thievery be found out.

"Is that so?" Mrs Wright took a handkerchief from her pocket and dabbed at Rose's face. It came away spotted with mud.

"That flush upon your face says otherwise." She shook her head. "Well, well, whatever it is, let's have you warmed up first."

She called towards the rear curtain. "Eric… Kettle!" Mrs Wright turned back to Rose; her expression more sombre.

"'Tis hard to find comfort in these times, Rose." She opened a pouch on a silver chatelaine that sat snug around her hips, pulled a sweet from within and passed it over. Rose took the black and white humbug more eagerly than intended. The sugary peppermint brought her tongue to life; she sucked so hard her mouth hurt. Mrs Wright smiled.

"We can however find some solace, humble as it may be." She patted her chatelaine and disappeared beyond the curtain, again chatting to someone.

Alone in the shop, Rose's hand burned to look at the advertisement again, at the possibility of being anywhere but there, of leaving her home, this dreaded town, and never seeing that corner in her room again. The sweet rolled across her tongue, and clinked against her teeth. She bit it in two at the sight of the shadow behind a mannequin on the far right. The sweet crushed between her teeth; its richness could not erase the smell of death that had followed her.

There was a tapping sound. Devil bounced upon the boardwalk outside, tapping its beak against the window. She turned back to the shadow; it was closer, lingering behind a table laden with thick and thin fabric bolts.

Rose stood, backed away until her hip hit the counter, her fingers mindlessly pulling at a thread along the edge of the blanket that gave no further warmth.

Mrs Wright reappeared with a steaming tea cup and a broad smile.

"Sit, Dear, come now." She waved her hand back to the chair, oblivious to what lurked. Rose obliged, her movements unwilling and jerky. Mrs Wright took it as evidence of Rose's chill.

"I was just feeling like a pot of tea. Here now, drink up. Let it warm and fortify you. I put an extra spoon of sugar in." She winked, a hand out for Rose to sit down.

"Come, come, don't let it get cold."

Rose slid sideways into the chair, eyes flitting to the shadow, then back to the rear curtain. A tall man appeared from within, Eric handed him a parcel. Elegantly dressed in grey tweed, he shook Eric's hand, turned towards the front door, and his gaze settled upon Rose. Devil tapped more fervently upon the glass.

Mrs Wright huffed, "Blasted thing." She opened the door, stepped out, waved her hands. "Off with you… get away!"

The bell tinkered as the door shut.

Mrs Wright shook the cold from herself. "Pests! They make such a mess!"

Rose's attention was for once not upon a crow or a shadow, but upon the bronze-skinned man who looked intently upon her with deepest amber-hued eyes. She pressed the hot edge of the cup to her lips; it chinked against her teeth as her hand shook. She couldn't avert her stare from him. The lights cast a shadow across the sharp angles of his face, accenting the tone of his skin that seemed to glisten in the ambient light. Tea aromas wafted beneath her nose, but that herby rot had her eyes searching the shop for death and then back again to the stranger who was now talking to Eric at the counter, his lack of attention leaving Rose strangely hollow.

"It's not polite to stare, Rose," Mrs Wright whispered.

"I'm... I'm not..."

Rose focused upon her drink, blew the steam across the surface of the cup, and let it coil back to warm her lips. She swallowed the milky sweetness.

"Another spoon of sugar to sweeten the fibs?" Mrs Wright winked, shrugged her shoulders and smiled wider. Rose felt her cheeks burn.

"Oh, don't fuss, Dear. Mr Borgia does draw a lady's attention!" She, too, blushed a little. Rose squirmed in her seat and sipped more eagerly at her tea.

"I'm surprised you've not seen him before; he has lived here a while now... goodness... must be ten years, I believe. A quiet sort though, he does tend to keep to himself. Looks after the Rutherford estate. I suppose when I think about it, I'm not surprised you've never seen him, he only pops into town every once in a while. Most of the estate requirements are sent monthly by messenger." She leaned in close, placing a hand on the side of her mouth to contain her whispering.

"No one's seen the lady of the house since... well, since the tragedy. I often wonder if the poor dear is still alive... but then Mr Borgia is often seeking new staff, so..." Her eyes rolled, and she nodded more to herself.

"Mary Rutherford must still be kicking on. Enough of my gossip," she laughed, and stood up. "I'm starting to sound like that old barb, Frances Ray, heaven forbid!" She threw her hands up and wandered out back briefly. Rose's attention fell straight to the back of Mr Borgia, her hand in her pocket, making sure the advertisement was still there. It wasn't how handsome he was that held Rose's attention; it was how much he reminded her of Papa.

Mrs Wright returned in a flurry, a small plate in her hand.

"Only for special customers. Let's put some curves onto those bones. This preserve will surely do it." She smiled warmly and held a thick cut of bread under Rose's nose.

"I made this last summer, picked the berries myself along the river." Rose pictured her mother's bony frame but couldn't control herself, mouth-watering. She took the bread, spread thick with jam, and pushed it into her mouth so quickly she coughed. It wasn't fresh, the crust hard, but the sweet tang of blackberry was bliss. Rose groaned; Mrs Wright waved another handkerchief in her face.

"Lord, don't choke, Dear, slow down."

Rose swallowed the deliciousness and wiped the stickiness from her lips.

"Thank you." The ache in her stomach waned.

"It's the most delicious jam, Mrs Wright."

Mrs Wright huffed contentedly.

"Well, don't tell your Ma." Mrs Wright waved a finger.

"She is the reigning marmalade champion of the Northern Regional Ladies Auxiliary." She chuckled, collected the empty tea cup and set it aside.

"Now, to the matters that bring you here on such a dreadful day?" Peaked brows framed a glint of concern.

"You ought to be home by the fire with your Ma." Mrs Wright pulled another chair a little closer and sat, her own teacup in her lap, forefinger tapping the rim of it.

Rose hesitated, attention still hooked on Mr Borgia, who was now chatting to Eric by the door, pointing to the window and shaking his head. He passed Eric another note, Eric stuck it in the window. Rose cursed inside. Her pulse thundered in her temples; she took a deep breath, and slid her hand back into her pocket. The watch within cold against her now warm palm, the advertisement wrapped around it.

Rose looked at Mrs Wright. With her soft brown eyes, smooth plump cheeks, Mrs Wright was a woman of indeterminate age. Rose pushed her glasses a little higher up her nose.

"Mama and I were hoping you might have some extra sewing work for us. But…" Nervousness tightened Rose's chest, made her tongue thick and awkward, her attention upon the doorbell that tinkered as Mr Borgia left. Her heart sank a little, and she wasn't sure why. His silhouette stalled in the white haze outside, something fell upon him… a bird. Rose squinted. A different crow sat upon his shoulder. He disappeared into the carriage. Something twinged in her chest.

"Rose, dear, are you okay?" Mrs Wright asked, clicking her fingers at her.

Rose shuddered, "Sorry, yes, um… we've run out of thread and candles." She pressed her lips together; her words ran too quickly, her attention now upon the gleam of the pendant that hung from Mrs Wright's neck. *Why does she still have nice things?* Rose glanced over her shoulder, Eric was actively ignoring her, and the carriage had not moved. Her mind raced, thoughts everywhere… she felt like she was shattering. She repositioned her glasses but couldn't quite find a place of comfort for them.

"We've no money left and can only get a small basket of canned goods once a week from St Vincent de Paul," Rose's voice fell to a whisper. Mrs Wright reached for that pendant, and twirled its teardrop shape between thumb and finger, eyes averted to the roof in thought. A soft *hmmm,* was her only response. Rose waited a moment, toes tapping, biting the inside of her cheek, a dozen comments upon her tongue swallowed away. The weight of the silence unbearable, Rose spoke quickly before her words dried up again.

"We could do repairs in return for candles and thread." Rose's eyes sparkled with a sudden gush of hope; she leaned forwards, her words hastened.

"And then take in a wage once we've paid them off. You know we work quickly; it will be just a few days, that's all," she nodded as though that would encourage Mrs Wright. Rose balled her fingers and crossed them, bounced her legs up and down, all the while feeling the shame of begging tremble through her voice. She saw a flush of discomfort colour Mrs Wright's complexion.

Mrs Wright dropped the pendant, bit her bottom lip and sighed.

"Oh Rose…" her voice trailed off. Rose's eyes lowered to her lap, disappointment pressed upon her, forced her hand to slide her father's watch out, leaving the note tucked within. The lights struck the watch just the right way, so it sparkled like a diamond between the slits of her fingers. Her stomach tightened as she offered it to Mrs Wright.

"I can exchange this for what we need," Rose's voice hitched.

"Will you take this… for now at least, as collateral? The foxes took all our chickens last night; we've not an egg to eat, only a day's worth of flour left. All of Papa's savings are gone." Her eyes stung; she couldn't take them off that damned pendant.

The fabric of Mrs Wright's dress whispered as she shifted, seemingly unable to find comfort in her seat. There was a long pause as Mrs Wright stared at the watch, brows pinched; she placed her tea cup upon a table nearby and clutched her hands upon her lap. The shop was pin-drop silent, even the storm seemed to hold its breath in anticipation. Mrs Wright's mouth opened then closed, she sucked her teeth. She cleared her throat behind her hand.

"Dear, dear Rose." She leaned in, placed a hand over Rose's, keeping the watch firmly in Rose's possession. Mrs Wright's skin was warm and soft; there was meat on her bones.

"I have indeed been bartering a little here and there, but a pocket watch won't pay my bills. Unfortunately, it's not a coveted item at market at present. People are wanting food and fuel, medicine and such. I've young Eric bringing in a few shillings helping at the docks, but it's barely enough to cover the electric light costs." Her eyes swept up towards the warm glow of her coveted Baker light fittings. Her throat bobbed, and she sighed, colour still staining her cheeks.

"I know it may seem I am wanting of little, but appearances can be most deceiving, my dear. Now, if it was eggs or even a chook that you could offer, I could help. I've no time to find a dealer to try to sell such a treasure." Her eyes flitted back to Rose's fist before she stood up, seeming to need a moment of distance. She ran a finger across a rich emerald fabric next to the blue silk, a line left behind on the fabric in a fine layer of dust. Only then did Rose notice how very full the shop was; only then did she notice the undertone of mustiness.

"I'm not sure I know anyone taking on anything but the absolute necessities," Mrs Wright sighed heavily, sat back down and fiddled with her pendant again.

Shame dulled anger into embers within Rose, but the hope in her pocket kept a taught smile on her face.

"I understand." But Rose didn't really understand at all. Nothing made sense; nothing was fair. She opened her palm, the watch fell back into her pocket, fingers curled into a ball, the ghost of the watch still present against her skin. She hadn't wanted to sell it, but when a refusal came, her stomach clenched harder than ever. Panic rushed in her head. What would she tell Mama when she came home empty-handed? Perhaps they might peel the paper from the walls and lick the glue for supper?

An ache arced across her skull; she heard bells, and footsteps, she looked to the shadow behind the mannequin once more. There he stood, a putrefying hollow carcass, eyes sunken and withered in their sockets. He whispered as he always did.

Bam…no, Bam…no

Rose reached for the scrap of paper, clung for escape, for hope, for freedom from the shadows, from whatever was pleading in his dead eyes. What if that hope in her pocket was a last chance that was not hers to have? Her vision clouded, and she leaned forward, head in hands, shoulders slumped. She drew for breath; each intake burned and was harder than the last. Each gasp was flavoured with the taste of ghosts.

"Dear, dear!" Mrs Wright pressed a warm hand to Rose's forehead, tilted her chin, and looked into the flush of Rose's cheeks.

"Eric, dear, fetch me a finger of sherry!" Mrs Wright's voice wavered with panic.

Rose's heart hammered harder; she was falling. Darkness pressed against her, the cold of it forced its way in. She couldn't breathe, her fingers grasped the edge of her seat, but her vision was gone, and she felt herself sliding away. Mrs Wright's soft voice was the only anchor left; she reached for it as she felt her head ease onto something soft.

"There, there, Dear, calm yourself now, breathe now, nice and slow."

Light pierced through; Rose felt the cool of a cloth pressed against her forehead. She could see once more, eyes wide with panic; she arched her back, straining to see the mannequin and the secret it hid. It was more than just *him* now. They were all there, leaching like snakes from the corners, oozing down the walls. Shadows that sucked the breath from her lungs again and didn't allow her to turn away. Rose didn't want to see him again, she closed her eyes, slapped a hand across her mouth so as not to smell the rot. She didn't want to see the whited-out eyes, the mouth gaping with words she didn't want to hear.

Rose was falling again, unable to see what was behind her, her body light as a feather, the comforting aroma of tea and fabric, of dust and potpourri, faded away, replaced by a stomach-churning stench. Her fingers were numb, and then her toes, her body weightless.

A high-pitched ringing, a gentle bell, overtook the quiet of her fall. It summoned that part of her not yet gone… sound. The tinkering was louder; she felt the floor move beneath her, heard the click of footsteps, and felt the pressure of hands upon her. Within the blackness of the abyss, Rose squeezed her eyes tighter, refused to see *him*, reached towards warmth, grasped for help, and breathed in a new smell. *Not rot, not death… familiarity.*

Rose's body moved, jostled upwards, then down, she was floating, and then her body stilled. She leaned towards the new scent; the panic of her breathing drew it in. She groaned, and tried to speak, but her attempt at words halted when something cool spilt into her mouth. It burned sweet down her throat, made her cough, her eyes fluttered. Light blinded her momentarily before feeling returned to her body, and her eyes fully opened.

Rose lay upon the floor of Mrs Wright's haberdashery, Eric behind his mother, face pale, the stem of a sherry bottle pressed against his chest. Their eyes held a moment, he brushed his hair forward to cover the left side of his face, and he averted his eyes. Rose looked away too. Mrs Wright hovered above her, damp cloth wadded in her hands, her face flushed with relief as Rose roused.

Rose's head rested upon something; she slid her head back, following that familiar spice and warmth that drew her from the chasm she had nearly succumbed to. She realised quickly that it wasn't a pillow upon which her head lay, but the lap of a stranger. Her eyes rolled upwards and met his.

CHAPTER 10

"Forgive me, Miss Rose, you fainted." Mr Borgia helped Rose from the floor. His voice was silken and deep; rich with a familiar accent. It reminded her of Papa, and her chest clutched.

Rosa, vieni qua, Bella. She could almost hear Papa calling her to help in the garden when she was little.

Rose immediately liked the smooth roll of the letter *R* when Mr Borgia spoke her name.

A heady mix of smoke and spice wafted from him. He smelled like bitter coffee and grappa… like Papa. As soon as her feet felt flat on the floor and her back lost its sway, Rose quickly slipped her hand from his; the warmth of him lingered upon her skin, and she missed her father more than ever in that moment.

She felt colour flood her cheeks; she didn't want to appear weak. She wasn't like every other girl, she was strong, independent, and she was as stubborn as her mother. Rose struggled to decide whether she was embarrassed, angry or grateful, so she decided on all of them at once, and her heart thundered. Her attention quickly shifted back to Eric. His attention was heavy upon Mr Borgia; he poured another finger length of sherry into a tiny glass and swallowed it, then poured another, offering it to her.

"Rose?" Her finger grazed his, a nip of golden brandy spilled to the floor. She rested the small glass to her lips and sipped, letting the heat bring her fully back. Mr Borgia and Mrs Wright guided her back to the chair. Rose sat and downed the rest of the fiery drink.

"Thank you, Eric," her voice cracked. He took the glass from her, both careful not to let skin touch again. Too much attention was pressed upon her. Despite herself, her eyes slid back to Eric again. In a fraction of a second, a flash of their childhood ran through her mind.

Pulling their milk bottles from the river to drink at lunchtime, making stick and leaf boats and watching them sail away upon the current. That first secret kiss that changed everything and then… the day he left… the day that destroyed everything. They rarely spoke since, the days of easy company and conversation seemed nothing more than a wishful memory.

"Thank you, Eric." Mrs Wright dismissed him. Worry feathered Eric's jaw, his attention remained heavily upon Mr Borgia. A dark hue underpinned a tiredness in his eyes, and deepened the flush of the scars not hidden. Eric looked back to Rose, an echo of a smile somewhere just beyond that worry. He turned away, Rose watched him limp towards the back, shrapnel a permanent resident in his right knee. He was alive but so very damaged, as Rose felt her heart was.

"May I be of any further assistance, Mrs Wright?"

Rose snapped her attention back to Mr Borgia.

"You have been most helpful, Mr Borgia; thank you kindly. I believe I can take things from here on." Mrs Wright gestured towards the men's section, "I do apologise about your order; I will see to the rest of your parcels momentarily."

"Thank you," Mr Borgia bowed, sliced a hand through glossy black hair before setting a fedora upon his head. His skin was darker than Papa's; it glistened with the kiss of a more southern Mediterranean sun. His gaze fell back upon Rose. She didn't know where to look. Her hands twisted in front of her belly. She studied her overworked fingers, and admired the colour of her own skin, just like Papa's, a skin she once hated. Rose swallowed, feeling the heaviness of Mr Borgia's presence; she looked back up to find him still watching her.

His eyes narrowed, head tilted, he stared beyond her shoulder. Rose twisted around; the shadows were deep; they were not vacant. A nervous sweat sprung upon her palms.

"I hope you are feeling better, Miss Rose?" He asked.

Rose's attention averted to the floor.

"I am quite well."

She shifted in her seat, not missing the curtain flutter shut as Eric unsuccessfully hid his spying. The air felt uncomfortable again; it was thick and rotten. She stood, ready to leave, but found herself watching the measured movements of Mr Borgia as he wandered away amongst mannequins of tweed… into the shadows. She felt his attention on her still, despite the fact he seemed thoroughly occupied with the price tag of a suit.

Rose's mouth was closed with a tap of her finger.

"Now, now, Rose. Stop your gawking," Mrs Wright whispered. Embarrassment heated Rose's entire body, it crawled up her neck, and for the umpteenth time in a matter of moments, Rose felt her cheeks bloom.

"Sorry, I just…"

"He does look quite like your father, Rose." She nodded; lips pressed firm. "Perfectly understandable to catch your eye so, but no reason to stare." Mrs Wright shook her head, "Quite the likeness, but I believe he may be from a different region of Italy." She guided Rose towards the counter.

"Are you feeling yourself again?"

Rose nodded, the desire to turn back to Mr Borgia almost too strong.

"Good. My heart isn't what it used to be. I'll not appreciate another turn like that, my dear… now, let me see here…" Her voice trailed off. She opened a large ledger with a red spine. It slapped loudly onto the glass top; the sound shuddered through Rose. Mrs Wright licked a finger and flicked through the pages, seeing Rose peek again at Mr Borgia, who had come to wait patiently upon the chair she had just fallen from.

"He wasn't supposed to stay, so I hear. But all these years on… well here he is. Quite the mystery, really," Mrs Wright whispered; her eyes widened with intrigue. "Unlike your father, he wasn't sponsored by an employer to immigrate. I'm not even quite sure what his trade is, but he always seems flush with money the way he spends it here. Besides being the Rutherford Estate's caretaker since old Johnathon passed on, he keeps to himself really. Oh, will you listen to me gossip!" She chuckled to herself.

Rose had been barely listening, she couldn't resist the urge to stare over her shoulder, pretending to readjust her hair. A bang startled her again, and her attention swung across to the storeroom. The curtain fluttered again.

"Sorry, Mum."

The curtain peeled back a fraction. Eric's eyes bore into Mr Borgia.

"You best not be breaking anything out there, my boy," Mrs Wright tutted and shook her head. She took a deep breath and returned her attention to the ledger. The curtain fell away again, the quiet in the storeroom intense. Rose knew without a doubt Eric was eavesdropping.

"You two on speaking terms yet?" Mrs Wright's right brow arched.

Rose couldn't draw a word across her lips.

"Seems a shame. You're both as stubborn as an ox. A battle of iron wills can spoil such a friendship, or whatever you two pretend to call it." She flicked through the ledger some more, mouth pursed, pausing long enough to realise Rose wasn't going to add anything further to the matter. Mrs Wright sighed, disappointment flattened the hope in her eyes, but she let the matter drop. Rose's body uncoiled, glad Mrs Wright hadn't pushed her on the subject of how she felt about Eric now or in the past.

"Now, let's see how I might be able to help you in some way." Mrs Wright tapped Rose's shoulder, catching her once again peeking at Mr Borgia checking the time on a golden pocket watch. Mrs Wright tapped the ledger with a finger, bringing Rose's attention to its perfectly orderly script of goods and costs.

"I may just be able to solve your immediate problem." She bent down and poked around underneath; boxes shuffled about unseen. Rose stepped to the left, a mirror behind the counter sitting just the right way so as to…

Mr Borgia was looking straight at Rose. With a deep, furrowed expression, his amber eyes seemed to glow from within. Rose startled when Mrs Wright slapped a box on the countertop.

"Decorum, Rose," she tutted under her breath.

Rose shifted again so that she couldn't see Mr Borgia. He had caught her staring, by the state of her dress; she surmised he had probably realised her destitute situation, felt sorry for her, or revolted… or both. Shame washed over her; she slipped her hand into her pocket, and crushed the advertisement.

"Sorry," Rose whispered. Mrs Wright shook her head as she tipped a small box onto the glass countertop.

"Well, now, I can't sell these." She slid a half dozen cracked beeswax candles into a paper bag along with a half skein of cotton.

"I've a decent amount of work coming in next week. I'll call on you and your dear mother then, shall I?"

Rose nodded gratefully and did really feel thankful despite the resentment she so readily stoked.

"Here you go. I've just a few small repairs, for now, hems and such." Mrs Wright passed her a neatly wrapped bundle that represented food on the table and not much else.

"We will take anything, thank you." Rose scooped up the bag of broken candles and parcel of repairs into her chest.

Mrs Wright skirted the counter, and slipped an arm around Rose.

"Tell your mother I'll pop in later this week. I've a lovely fruit cake marinating. It will be sure to put some colour on her cheeks. I'm sure I've a spare egg or two as well." Mrs Wright squeezed her shoulders.

Humiliation sizzled under Rose's skin; it fought gratitude and quickly evolved into anger again. Her head felt tight, the lights too bright. Rose turned to leave, quickly muttering her thanks.

Mrs Wright grabbed her elbow.

"This blasted war is making skin and bones, widows and orphans of us all; you're not alone, Rose, don't ever think that." Mrs Wright dipped a hand into her apron, passing over two thimbles.

"Your fingers are red-raw, Dear. Please, use these and sew only in daylight, not all night by the hearth."

Rose slipped the thimbles into her pocket, where they chinked against the watch and hair clip.

"You're too kind."

"There, there, now." Mrs Wright gave Rose a gentler squeeze about the shoulders. She smelled of dust and sweat now, the truth of her situation as bare as her own.

"Can you have those repairs back tomorrow evening?"

Rose nodded, "Yes, without fail." She slid the blanket from her shoulders, her fingers already stinging at the thought of the fine needlework ahead. Mrs Wright put a hand up in protest.

"You've more need of that than me." She pushed the blanket into the bundle of goods in Rose's arms.

"But I…" Rose tried to decline.

"I'll hear none of that now. These times don't tolerate pride. You take it and be grateful young lady." The warmth of her smile softened her stern words.

"Thank you." Rose wrapped the blanket back over her shoulders, immediately feeling richer under the thick, green warmth. She pulled it protectively over the package now tucked under her left arm, her attention caught on Eric peering out from the storeroom again. His hair now swept back, revealing the truth of what divided them. It was never about the scars, but what caused them that haunted Rose, and it had closed off her heart to him.

Eric didn't smile when their eyes met. He tugged his hair back over his face, and his attention returned to Mr Borgia.

"I'll see you tomorrow then?" Mrs Wright retrieved some parcels wrapped in paper and deposited Rose at the door. She wandered away towards the hat stand, where Mr Borgia bowed politely. Rose hesitated, hand on the door, her ears strained to listen in.

"It's been quite a while since you've been in, Mr Borgia, I'm glad to see you looking so well. And thank you so much for your help with dear Rose." Her head shook, and she shrugged. She leaned into Mr Borgia; her voice fell to a whisper. His head nodded, then shook; he snatched a quick glance Rose's way, his expression solemn. He reached into a pocket, and passed Mrs Wright a slip of paper.

Rose pulled the door ajar but stood there a moment longer, lingering, holding onto the sound of his voice, wondering upon the judgment she assumed he would make upon her situation. Now she was the eavesdropper. Gossip and scandal were all people had to hold onto these days; little else enlivened the depressing state of a country at war. She turned away; the floor creaked behind her.

"May I?" Mr Borgia's hand slid over hers, his fingers warm. He twisted the handle.

"That is quite the handful." His breath brushed Rose's ear; it smelled richly of coffee, so very much like Papa. Her heart ached. He was taller than her father, young enough to show no particular age. Yet, there was something deeply wizened about him, as though he had lived a dozen lives already, something altogether unsettling.

"It's... I'm fine..." Rose stammered.

"Are you sure I cannot help you?" He pulled the door open.

"Thank you. I can manage from here, Sir," Rose said. She braced and stepped quickly out onto the walkway and hurried.

"May I ask you..."

Rose walked determinedly towards home. His voice carried strong on the wind as he called after her. She stepped from the boardwalk back into the mud, the rain-scented wind gusted against her, slowing her down. She leaned into it, invited it in, relished the howl that drowned out Mr Borgia and the whispers calling to her. She averted her attention from the shadows, and did not acknowledge the dead that accompanied the living.

The rain had settled into a lighter sprinkle as she approached Banksia Lane. There was even a glimmer of sun pushing through the clouds that clung to the hills beyond town; she could almost taste the warmth of it. It seemed a beacon, drawing people from indoors, and the main street seemed a sudden hive of activity.

Laden carts rattled along the road; the horses struggled to churn the wheels through the stinking sludge. White foam dripped from their muzzles, their heads bobbed forward in effort, and their exhausted snorts underpinned the rhythmic song of the wind.

The local paper boy, Thomas Whitaker, shouted loud for business across the road outside the publican house. Rose thought he had called her name, but when she stopped to see what he wanted, Thomas was in the midst of a sale with someone, and she found the call of her name to be coming from somewhere else.

"Miss Rose?" Rose felt the vibration underfoot before she saw the grand carriage pull up behind her. She gritted her teeth; the package under her arm crinkled, the contents squashed against the pounding in her chest.

She hesitated, considered running to get home and be done with this horrid day. But annoying curiosity piqued her interest. She wanted to hear his voice again, drink in the richness of its tone, the memory of Papa that it drew, raw and painful… irresistible. And, of course, Rose wanted to know why on earth he had followed her.

She turned; the wind now buffeted her back. Mr Borgia stepped from the carriage.

"I am sorry to bother…" Mr Borgia was cut off as a passing carriage sloshed through a puddle; freezing mud splattered them both head to foot.

Mr Borgia winced, removed his fedora, flicked the mud from it, smoothed his dark hair and set it firmly back on. He slipped a handkerchief from inside his jacket and offered it to Rose.

Rose shook her head and dabbed her face with the edge of the blanket, her dress wetter than before. She shivered anew.

"Miss Rose, please?" He stepped closer with the handkerchief, and guided her away from the edge of the road as another carriage rumbled by. Rose hugged her parcels closer; she shook her head again, unsure why she felt so conflicted by this man.

"I insist," he said, warmth in his smile.

Propriety said no, but politeness said yes.

"Thank you." Rose took the edge of the cotton square and dabbed at her face. The fine cotton was perfectly starched; it smelled crisp and fresh. It smelled of him...of Papa. Her guts twinged; her eyes burned.

"Weather is terrible, is it not?" Mr Borgia said, a small chuckle rounding out his words. "I do not often see this kind of cold where I come from."

"Where are you from, Sir?" her voice wavered. She knew exactly where he was from, but wanted to hear his voice, close her eyes and imagine it was Papa.

His smile deepened; his teeth were white with a single gold tooth on the left. *That would buy a good bag of flour or ten.* Rose scrunched the handkerchief in her fist.

"Sardinia, I'm sure you've heard of it?" He tilted his head, his eyes sparkled brighter at the mention of his home.

Rose nodded. "My papa was born near there." Italy was as far away as the moon and the sun from her small world. She often wondered if she might ever see the country Papa had fled to make a better life. The thought made her grimace; *better life?* She studied Mr Borgia's clothing, the healthy glow of his face. *Better for some.*

She shivered as the wind gusted her body, cut right through to her skin, the rumble of thunder upon it. She glanced longingly towards Banksia Lane.

"Did you need something, Sir?" Rose wished to be home, not for the shadows but to extricate herself from the situation that created a disquieting anger and longing all at once.

The circling crow cawed, settling on a water trough by a horse tie-up. Its eyes were inky, not flecked with gold. It was not Devil. Who was this crow, she wondered? It jostled in the wind, its shiny feathers fluttering wildly, and its claws slipped as it tried to find purchase on the thin edge.

The old woman's words about awaiting the crow rang in Rose's thoughts. As though the crow could hear unspoken words, it launched into the air, circled above Mr Borgia, sharply cementing the point.

"Miss Rose? Are you alright?" Mr Borgia's lips quivered with cold as well, despite the thick finery he was layered in. His tweed coat was clearly expensive but no match for August weather.

"Sorry, I'm just a little tired," she said. Rose shook the handkerchief out and offered it back, but he shook his hand.

"Keep it, please." He reached into a pocket of his coat.

Her fingers curled tight around the cotton; she waved it more insistently at him.

"No, thank you." Anger clipped her voice a little more sharply than she had intended.

"Then take it home, wash it and bring it back to me tomorrow," he said.

A closed-mouth smile quelled the cold's grip on Mr Borgia's lips. Rose frowned and inched her hand closer to him.

"I don't know what you mean." She waved the cotton for him to take, impatiently needing to press away the prickling in her neck. The deep decay of death passed through her; she felt the weight of the shadow nearby. *Why was it following her? Why now had it shown itself during the day and so far from home? What had she done?* She peered over her shoulder towards home; Banksia Lane seemed so very far away.

"I must get home," she said.

Mr Borgia's kind expression waned. The amber of his eyes lost their sparkle as they turned up towards Banksia Lane. There was a moment of strained silence between them.

"I apologise for unsettling you, but I just wanted to ask..." An envelope fluttered in his hand, but Rose's legs were already moving.

She bent into the weather and ran towards Banksia Lane, the crow following, cawing loudly overhead.

"An interview... I want to offer you an interview," Mr Borgia called, his voice nearly lost in the wind.

Pungent rot pushed into her lungs, she ground her heels into the path, her body came to a sudden stop. Rose slid in the mud, gasping for breath; she leaned into her legs to steady herself. Her boots sucked out of the ground; she plucked hair from her eyes as the wind taunted with a new storm, a fine spray of rain teasing what was to come.

She shielded her eyes from the sickly green glare of the sky to see Mr Borgia running towards her, his eyes gleaming gems, eyes like Papa's, eyes like hers.

He came to a stop, leaned onto his legs as well, gasping, fedora in hand, hair a wild mess. A bemused smile barely covered his exhaustion.

"Will you..." He puffed, the crow sat above them upon a branch that swayed and creaked. "... Meet me tomorrow..." He coughed into his sleeve. A second crow arrived, side-stepped up to the first and leaned its head into it. It was Devil.

"... For an interview."

Something twinged in Rose's gut.

Mr Borgia called her attention back from two pairs of glassy eyes that stared down at her. He held out the creamy envelope; it wavered in the shake of his hand. Rain dripped onto it and slid like grey tears down the fine paper.

He finally straightened, smoothed his hair and put his hat back on.

"We may be of help to each other. I will be in the rear of the haberdashery a 10:00 am tomorrow."

The ground was softening, colder, the mud sucking her in place as though it wanted her to stop, to listen. Rose took the corner of the envelope; it was soggy. She jostled the package under her arm so as to use both hands to carefully slip out an appointment card.

"You want to interview me?"

"I believe you have one of the advertisements in your pocket. You *are* interested?" His brows quirked; amusement tugged the fullness of his lips as he caught her out with her deception.

"I... I..." Rose's hand slid guiltily into her pocket. She licked her lips, tasted salt, her skin flushed hot; words of denial faded in her throat. One of the crows cawed, and one took flight; the wobble of the branch caused the second to flutter onto a lower branch, closer, its head tilted towards Rose as though listening in.

"I am looking for work, but..." This was all unexpected, too quick for her usual overthinking to wrap around.

"Good, very good. I am in urgent need of staff." He rebuttoned his coat and looked far less ruffled than moments before.

The wind deepened its moaning, the trees lurched, leaves swirled around their feet... and the shadow drew up behind him. Rose stumbled back; breath punched from her lungs... but she just stared. She didn't say a word, didn't intervene as it rose dark and blurry, its ramblings upon the howl of the wind. It hovered behind Mr Borgia, Rose dared not breathe lest it might strike.

Mr Borgia cocked an ear as though he heard something, peered over his shoulder and back again. His complexion was a shade darker than before, the sunset of his eyes deeper. Thunder rumbled. He seemed to take her behaviour as a reaction to the storm.

"Hurry home. I'll see you tomorrow." He tapped his hat and left, this time at a casual walk, seemingly unaffected by the weather or the shadow he walked right through. Rose watched him get smaller, saw the shadow follow him a while before it misted away, swallowed by the darkening sky.

Rose slid the envelope into her pocket and ran until her boots left the main street and skidded into the slush of Banksia Lane. With the blanket pulled half over her head, she rushed towards home, fled death and rot, ran towards hope.

CHAPTER 11

Rose lied to Edith the next morning. It came so easily to bend the truth.

"Mrs Wright said she would have some extra work to pick up this morning. I'll be back soon."

"Don't be too long. We've a lot to get through."

"Of course, Mama."

Rose left with a spring in her step and guilt on her shoulders. The sun shone warmly for the first time in weeks. It left no room for shadows, dried the puddles and erased the boot prints. The air was still and smelled of wattle and eucalypt. Rose felt lighter... unwatched.

The main street was bustling; she was just one of many today and found herself outside the haberdashery in quick time. When there was no sign of the Rutherford carriage, she panicked, retrieved her father's watch she'd kept with her and checked the time. 9:45am. She wasn't late.

The brass bells announced Rose's arrival; she shook off her coat and lay it across her arm. A customer was being served by Eric, who was quick to register Rose. He nodded curtly at her, no love in his expression. *Good*, she thought and looked away with as much feigned disinterest as she could muster.

Rose searched the shop and found Mrs Wright.

She caught sight of Rose, and the warmth of yesterday drained from her. She excused herself from a customer.

"Rose, I'm rather surprised to see you here this morning." Her lips pressed firmly; her skin was less powdered today. She looked older like she hadn't slept well.

"I'm here to interview with Mr Borgia." For some reason, her voice was thin... she stuttered her words, affected by the dour expression of Mrs Wright. "The position… lady's maid… at the Rutherford Estate."

"Hmmm."

Rose felt colour crawl up her neck. She stammered again, "I know I've no experience, but..."

"Work is work in these times." Mrs Wright pretended to busy herself re-rolling a length of red fabric.

"I expect your mother doesn't approve."

Rose didn't respond. Mrs Wright clucked her tongue.

"She doesn't know? Well, now, you've a conundrum to solve there, haven't you, my dear?"

"Please don't tell her? She thinks we can manage, but we can't. This could literally save our lives." Rose hid her hands, balled tight with anger. Why was it so dammed hard to be a woman? Why couldn't she just do what was needed to be done, like any man could?

Mrs Wright set the fabric aside, her attention flitted between Rose and the curtain at the back of the shop.

"Please, Mrs Wright?"

"Very well. I suppose it's really none of my business. But…" She wagged a finger at Rose.

"If she comes calling after you, I'll not lie." Mrs Wright frowned and gestured to the rear of the shop. They passed through the curtain into the storeroom, a tight space packed high with goods on either side. The floor was uneven; it groaned underfoot. Mrs Wright pressed another door that led into a dimly lit hall, and this short walk led to their living space. It immediately struck Rose that it smelled of food, of tea and toast, roast meat and fat. Her stomach growled.

"In the parlour, Rose." Mrs Wright opened a leadlight door to reveal Mr Borgia seated, a small teacup steaming in front of him.

"Don't make any rash decisions, Rose. Think of your mother," Mrs Wright whispered.

"Ah, Miss Carbonelli. I was worried you might not make it." Mr Borgia stood up and gestured towards a chair. Rose forced a smile, unsettled by Mrs Wright's odd behaviour. He rounded the table and pulled the chair out. The light of a walled gas lamp caught his gold tooth as he smiled at her.

Rose sat. The chair was hard, exacerbating her instant nervous wriggling. She glanced around the parlour, trying to push away the tremble in her limbs, the nauseating roll of her stomach. He set himself down, then shuffled through a leather case. It was quiet, so very quiet she wondered if Mr Borgia could hear the wild thump of her heart. A crow flittered past a small sun-drenched window. Rose curled her fingers, digging them hard into her palms.

"Will you be needing anything else?" Mrs Wright lingered, one hand upon the door. Her fingers tapped silently upon the wood.

"Thank you, we won't be long." He nodded for her to leave. Her attention snagged on Rose before she nodded to herself; that frown weighed upon her. She shut the door with a gentle click. Rose did not hear receding footsteps; instead, she saw the shape of Mrs Wright in the warped patterns of the leadlight.

It only added to her nerves. Rose shifted in her chair, unlaced her fingers, cupped her hands in her lap, knitted them again until her knuckles were white. She checked the corners of the room. They were thin, empty; she could breathe, yet Devil paced the window ledge, golden eyes upon her.

Mr Borgia shuffled some papers in his case, pulled up a thick bundle clipped together and set it in front of himself.

He sipped from the cup; this one hand gloved while the other was not. Rose could almost taste the richness of the coffee that lingered in the air. She followed the cup to his mouth. "You like coffee?"

His lips lingered at the rim of the cup.

"Papa used to drink it, he would let me sip it, but Mama says it's too strong for my stomach."

His brows arched. "My mother said I was born with a taste for espresso, fed it to me mixed with sugar and a raw egg."

"Zabaglione?" Rose asked.

"Indeed." He sipped again.

"Mama made that for Papa for breakfast, it was his favourite thing."
She smiled softly. Familiarity seemed to settle the air. Her fingers relaxed;
her seat now more comfortable.

"Cook brews a decent coffee after I taught her the correct method.
If you're successful today, perhaps she might make one for you." He
sipped again.

Rose watched the way his throat bobbed as he drained the cup, the
way he licked his lips and set it gently back down. He moved precisely,
deliberately, with a calm she never had. He cleared his throat, her
attention again upon that single gloved hand. *Odd.*

"I understand through my inquiries you've not worked in private
service before?"

Rose's blood drained; she felt like she was sinking. She'd lost the
position before she had even spoken. She just knew it. Her hands balled
again.

If he'd inquired about her, he'd surely know how little they had, how
they'd fallen on hard times, and that she'd left school at fifteen to help
Mama.

"No, I haven't, Sir," her voice hitched as she caught movement to
her right. Two silhouettes hovered outside the door. It was enough to
drum up an annoyance that numbed her nervousness and sparked a
determination within her. Rose straightened her back, squared her
shoulders, and forced a more confident presence on Mr Borgia.

His nostrils flared ever so slightly as he flicked through some papers,
yet her annoyance grew as she heard the floor creak outside. *Busy bodies.*

Mr Borgia looked up, mistook her frown for something else, and
poured her some water.

"Please, don't be nervous."

"I've not had a formal interview before." She smiled and took the
glass, sipping merely to be polite. It was hard to draw her eyes from Eric
and his mother's snooping.

"Well, let's get it done quickly then." Mr Borgia smiled but not
enough to flash that tooth.

He slid a stack of papers in front of Rose. The first page was printed
with the Rutherford crest, words typed in black ink beneath. *Privacy
agreement.*

She frowned.

"Miss Carbonelli, I have been the caretaker of the Rutherford Estate for many years." He uncapped a pen and set it down.

"I was appointed by Mr Rutherford, that upon his death, I should install myself as its head and attend to the care of his wife, Mary, as well as the upkeep of the estate. Rutherford House is unique in that the only family that resides there is Mrs Rutherford, a few select staff and myself. The work is targeted to her care and welfare; it is quite different to working anywhere else." He poured more coffee from a silver pot and sipped, his eyes never leaving Rose.

"It is in your favour that you have not worked in service. Your expectations and experience will not colour your ability to fit into a somewhat unusual position." He paused again; relief flooded Rose.

I have a chance.

She remained silent; her thumbs rolled over each other.

"Mrs Rutherford remains in mourning for her husband. Her needs are peculiar to her particular situation. I am looking for someone I can trust, someone with discretion, who will care for and provide companionship to her."

His thick brows arched, he leaned on the table, his hands clasped under his chin. The gas lamps flickered.

Rose opened her mouth. The light in the room felt heavier, the edges of her vision a little dimmer.

"Of course," he pointed to the papers in front of her. "You cannot begin without signing those. A privacy agreement to ensure your urge to speak of family matters outside the house is clipped. Any breach of trust will be instant dismissal with no references or severance wages."

"Will be?" Rose asked, heart thudding harder. The lamp flickered again.

"Yes. Terms of your employment commence the moment you sign; the end of the week should suit to begin?" Those brows quirked again.

"You're offering me the job?"

"Only if you sign that document."

Her head spun.

"But I've…"

"I'm quite sure you know how to wash clothes, tidy a bed and make conversation. Mrs Rutherford's needs are unique but few and quite simple."

He picked up the pen and offered it to her.

"The wage will change your life. As we do not retain a butler and have few staff, I am at liberty to offer a butler's wage." He smiled and nodded at the papers encouragingly.

Rose, open-mouthed, reached for the pen; it was heavy, made of wood with gold detail. Borgia, with a crow next to his name was inscribed along the side.

The side of her hand grazed along the paper; her name appeared atop a line before she realised what she was doing. Sun struck across the room, sliced over the desk, illuminating her name on the document.

The paperwork slid away, back into his hands; he looked at the signature, then across to Rose.

"Very good. I would like you to commence on Friday of this week. Can you organise your affairs by then?"

Rose leaned back in her chair. "Of course... I ..."

"Excellent. You do not need anything other than essential personal effects. Everything else you require will be provided for you." He pushed his chair out and placed all the papers into his bag. Rose also stood, fingers gripping the back of the chair. *A butler's wage!*

"How will I... I don't know an address." Her lips felt dry, she licked them. Something akin to fear-laden excitement lashed her heart. It thundered in her ears, louder when she saw a silhouette still lingering outside the door.

"Miss Carbonelli?"

"I'm sorry, what did you say?"

"I will have our driver pick you up by the river at pier 3, 10am on Friday. There will be transport waiting at your house at half past nine to get you to the river."

Rose nodded; things were happening so quickly.

"Thank you." Her head thundered, she secretly pinched herself... yes, she was indeed awake.

Mr Borgia reached for the door, hand hesitating on the knob allowing a moment of pause as footsteps retreated outside. He made a subtle sound in his throat, annoyance perhaps. He pulled a wad of money from inside his jacket.

"Goodbye, Miss Carbonelli. I look forward to welcoming you to Rutherford House." The door clicked behind him; his muffled voice acknowledged someone outside.

Rose was still white-knuckled upon the chair when Eric entered, tucking money into his trouser pocket. A moment of tense silence ensued. She still felt the weight of the pen in her hand along with the burden of their eavesdropping.

"What was that all about?" Eric asked.

Rose gripped the chair harder. "An interview for a position at Rutherford House, as if you didn't know. You're not that good at snooping." She pushed away from the chair, indignant.

"I wasn't."

"Eric, don't treat me like a child, I could see you outside the door." Rose drummed her fingers along crossed arms.

Eric's shoulders slumped; he sighed and raked a hand through his hair, careful to keep his left cheek covered.

"I just worry about you, Rose. There's something about that man." He shook his head.

Rose laughed, "Are you serious? You're worried about me? You? Of all people, *you* are worried about *my* welfare?" She threw her hands in the air and pulled her coat on.

Rose brushed past him, "*You* worried about *me*!" She laughed. She glanced down at his right leg, at the hint of silvery scarring along his jawline.

"Clearly, whatever bothers you about *that man* doesn't stop you from taking money from him." Rose eyed his pocket.

Eric's face reddened; his freckles faded beneath the anger. He dropped his hand to his pocket and clutched the cash inside.

"You don't know what you're talking about."

"Neither do you. He is merely offering me a wage. What *you* did was inexcusable." Rose slipped through the door and down the hall.

"It was different then, and you know it." The floor moaned underfoot as Eric followed her back into the shop, his voice an angry whisper.

Rose rounded on him.

"Different? Of course, it's different. You running off on a fool's errand with a death wish is in no way the same as me trying to find employment to put food on the table! You..." She breathed hard and stared unblinking at him, "You volunteered to put yourself in a war zone a million miles away. Did you care about how *I* felt about that?" Rose let the anger flow. "You *chose* to leave me," she poked a finger accusingly at him, felt dizzy, and ran from the shop before she made a fool of herself and fainted again.

"Rose?" Mrs Wright called after her as the bell jingled, and she slammed the door behind her. Rose stood outside the shop; anger trickled like lava through her skin. "How dare he?" She muttered. The doorbell chimed again.

"Rose, please?"

Eric was half out the door. "I had my reasons. Please try to understand?"

"And I have my reasons, Eric. Unless you wish to bury Mama and me by the end of winter, mind your own business and understand that." They stared hard at each other, neither relenting until Miss Ray appeared, slowing her bustling pace so as to eavesdrop on a morsel of gossip. A faint red line lingered on her cheek from the crow attack the day prior.

"Young Eric." She nodded. He slammed the door shut and stood inside the front window glaring at Rose.

Rose ignored Miss Ray's complaints about his rude behaviour as Eric's lachrymose eyes bore down at her through the window. He snatched the Rutherford House advertisement from the glass and slowly screwed it up, exactly as he had done with whatever it was they shared it the past.

CHAPTER 12

It had been three days since the interview with Mr Borgia. Three days of constant sewing, of stinging fingertips, of stale bread fried in near-rancid beef fat. Three days of no shadows in the corner of her room, three days of recalling the way Mr Borgia's voice sunk beneath her skin.

Three days of recounting her argument with Eric. Part of her remained indignant, another part sorry for leaving him on such bad terms. The same had happened when he left for Europe. Back then, she'd let her fear turn to anger, and now, she'd done it again.

Rose sat in the drawing room, Mama's seat empty, a pile of darned socks neatly stacked upon it. The thump of an axe cleaving wood told Rose where Mama was. That had been her father's job. Every Saturday morning, Papa would sing out back whilst he cut enough wood for the week and stacked it neatly on the back porch. Some, in convenient shards of kindling for the kitchen, some, more robust logs to keep the house warm all night. She smoothed out the paper in her hands and read the writing for the hundredth time.

Lady's maid for immediate employment

She'd meant to throw it in the fire, not think of it again until Friday, but there it was, crinkling in her trembling hands. She had succumbed to self-doubt about being somewhere new and unfamiliar. She worried on Mr Borgia, there was a strangeness about him, but this position was a way out, a way to live, an escape from the dead and whatever ill that book had brought upon her. Rose was not going to give in to circumstance, not like Mama had done.

Mama, how was she going to tell her?

The wood chopping had stopped. She could hear Mama running water in the kitchen, then striking a match for the hearth. It drew her attention to the small fire in the sitting room. Today it was lit for the first time in months, Mama only allowed it because they had work coming in. Rose's fingers were a testament to how much they'd sewn to earn the extra warmth.

The house had not held such gentle comfort in a long time, yet Rose still shivered. Since Papa had left, even in the height of summer, there was an undercurrent chill that clung to the walls. The lack of him had taken more than just money. There was no joy. It was like the day he left the world sucked the life from their home.

Rose folded the paper away, picked up her sewing again. She may as well get as much done as she could, she had precious little to pack, and she needed Mama to think everything was normal, not that she was preparing to leave.

Her needle dove into guipure lace trimming, pulled up gently then plunged down again until the fine collar was restored. She held it up, rubbed her thumb across the delicate fabric, and wondered if she might afford such a nice thing in the future. She put her thumb in her mouth and sucked the rawness of it. The thimbles Mrs Wright had gifted her were helpful to a point, but hours of fine needlework still wrought havoc upon her fingertips.

Rose rested back, rubbed her temples with her thumb and forefinger. She breathed slowly, recalling the smell of coffee and how it reminded her of Papa. None had brewed at home for such a long time.

A small clock ticked away on the side table upon which she kept her sewing supplies. The large hand was a minute from striking 9:25 in the morning. She felt the urgency of time advancing. The truth would soon reveal itself to Mama, Rose wondered what words, truth, or lies would spill from her until then.

Rose yawned and felt the stretch of it click her jaw. She was so very tired. She'd been awake a day, maybe two. Her nights were still long watching the corner in her room, and she couldn't wait to leave it and the book behind.

The weather was at least bright. A winter sun cleaved through a thin film of cloud and struck a pale line across the floor. A small wedge of blue sky was just visible above the tree line. She leaned forwards; someone was riding down Banksia Lane. She squinted, but couldn't yet make out who it was.

She set back to sewing, but the light faded, the room darkened, and her candle struggled to do its job. The air became heavy with the wetness of dead things. Rose dropped the sewing, her spool of thread slipped from her lap and rolled away to the middle of the room, coming to a stop in a puddle, a boot print rimmed with mud.

Rose slowly stood, one hand on the arm of the chair; every inch of her skin tingled, her mouth dry; she held her breath as though it would make her invisible. Her thimble fell from her thumb, the tap of it on the floor so very loud.

The corner nearest the window deepened its umber hue. The fingers of it stretched across the floor, over the dark rectangle where a rug once lay. The whispers felt wet in her ear. Rose wanted to move, but her legs were frozen. She stared between the darkness and the rider that neared her house.

Screams rang in Rose's head; they were not hers. She squeezed her eyes shut; chin pressed upon her chest.

"Please stop. I don't know why you're doing this." Something banged against the window.

Tap, tap, tap.

She peeled open one eye. Devil ruffled its feathers and tapped its beak upon the glass. Rose pressed her palms against her eyes and pleaded, "Stop, stop!"

She eased backwards; the crow tapped more earnestly. Rose caught her foot on a chair leg and fell back. She squealed, but something caught her, pushed her back to her feet. A pressure stilled upon her shoulders, her breaths hastened, her head swam. She twisted around. Mama wasn't there. No one was there. Her arms stiffened by her sides as something squeezed her, ran down the length of her arms, cupped her hands, cold fingers probed at hers. She had no control, couldn't pull away, could not curl her fingers from the invisible touch. The room began to swirl.

Tap, tap, tap. The crow squawked.

Rose felt as though she was falling; her blood drained to her feet. The sound of a heavy knock on the front door snapped her back from the nightmare, the grasp on her hands evaporated. Breath pushed into her chest, and feeling returned to her skin. The room smelled of embers and dust. The crow took flight, the window empty.

Her legs moved; she fell back into the chair. Hand on her chest, her sewing crumpled upon the floor. Her mother called out.

"Rose? See to the door."

The knocking was more urgent. Eye on the puddle that still held her spool of thread, Rose reversed from the room and rushed to the door, checking behind herself constantly.

Leaning against the front door, she ran her hands down to the cool of the handle. Trembling words spilt from her.

"Who is it?"

"It's me, Rosie."

"Eric? What are you doing here?" She pressed her ear to the wood, her heart raced for a different reason. His voice was so beautiful, but what he did was unforgivable.

"Freezing my arse off, actually."

Rose smiled despite herself. That sounded like Eric of the past when life was simpler and feelings didn't get in the way so easily.

"Are you going to open the door?"

Rose turned the key, the door creaked. Light poured in; Eric smiled, peaked cap in his hands, his horse munching weeds by the front gate.

"What are you doing here?"

"Is it so unusual for me to drop in?"

"No… actually yes, recently anyway." Rose wondered why she didn't just invite him in, why she needed to be so difficult, why forgiveness eluded her.

"Things haven't quite been the same recently." Eric's eyes lowered; his cap circled as he worked the grey fabric through his fingers. The wind tugged at his hair, and he pulled it down over his left cheek, but Rose knew what was there, and she didn't at all care. It wasn't what angered her, it wasn't what made her heart harden.

Her knuckles whitened on the door frame as memories flooded her. Tear-stained pillows, a hollowness so deep she thought it might suck her into oblivion. The memory of the day she threw the engagement ring into the river took her breath away.

Rose's nails dug into the door; she felt the weathered edges. Whilst Eric's eyes were averted to his cap, she took a moment to really notice him for the first time in a long time. His clothes were too big, or his body too small, she didn't know which. His cheekbones were more prominent where once his face was round and always held a smile. Even the smattering of freckles across his nose seemed faded. The scars he thought he hid were inside as much as outside. Scars scored his heart, just like Rose. He was a shadow of who he once was to her, and he had lost a father too. Guilt slithered within her; she had treated him so poorly; they were both a mere phantom of their former selves if she was to be perfectly honest.

"No, things have not been at all like they used to be." The door creaked again as she opened it further.

"Do you want to come in? I can't really offer you anything, but I'm sure Mama would love to see you."

He folded his cap, wedged it into a back pocket, and then pulled open the bag that was slung across his shoulder.

"No," his voice was a little cooler, he shifted on his feet. "Mum wanted me to deliver this."

Rose's eyes widened as she took the parcel. It was light, but an armful, wrapped in paper with Wright's Haberdashery printed ornately upon it.

She slipped two fingers between the seam of paper, saw black fabric, and pulled a small card from within.

"Rutherford House." She rubbed her neck, swallowed as her mouth dried.

Eric nodded at the parcel. "Burn it."

"What?" she pressed the parcel to her chest.

"You opened it before me?" Anger curled in her gut.

He shook his head.

"Then why on earth would you tell me to burn it? How would you know what was in it?"

Eric ran a hand through his hair, pulled the strands hard over the scars.

"I saw mum sew it. She makes all his staff uniforms, done so for years. Trust me, there's plenty of work in it. That's how often they leave." He swallowed hard and leaned closer to drive the point home. He stared at the parcel as though he could combust it on sight.

"I don't want you to take the position… please, Rosie." He reached for her; Rose stepped back.

She set the parcel down inside the front door, then crossed her arms. Annoyance flashed across her face; all semblance of compassion dissolved.

"And we are still at the same crossroads. You wish for me to *not* do something?" She snapped.

"I just want you to be safe, that's all." He eased away; his arms dropped to his side.

"My safety is important to you? How nice."

"Please, Rosie, just listen to me. That house, there's…" He bunched his fingers, pressed a fist against the door frame. "I don't know, I don't trust him."

"My name is Rose. I'm not a child anymore." She pulled the door against her so as to avoid their argument carrying to Mama.

"Damn it, Rose! Don't be like this." Eric pulled his cap from his pocket and bunched it in his hands. The wind whipped up and blew his hair back. Long silvered scars threaded along his jaw, crossed his cheek and ended in a knot of thick skin where an ear should be.

His mouth was pressed tight, she could feel his desire to cover up, to hide, but in this moment, she could feel the same passionate anger that she coveted oozing from him.

His eyes watered, so deep, so intense, it felt as if they could scoop her up, carry her away. She wanted to reach for him, to heal their hearts, to run her fingers over those scars, tell him none of it mattered, but she hadn't forgiven him, didn't know if she could. She bunched her fingers tight, just in case the part that still loved him betrayed the anger she fanned so fervently.

"I seem to recall a similar conversation I had with you about not going somewhere dangerous," she said, cool and sharp.

"That was different," Eric's voice softened.

"Oh really? Begging you not to volunteer for war was different? Begging you not to throw yourself on a minefield was different? Begging you to stay so we could make a life together was different?" Her voice fell to a hurried, angry whisper. "Unless this is a call to arms sending me to the front, I am pretty damned sure you caring for my welfare is the height of hypocrisy."

He punched the door frame and sighed with frustration.

"You don't understand, Rose."

"I understand you want what you want, but I can't have what I want."

He shook his head, pointing behind him.

"I've heard disturbing things about Mary Rutherford too, that house, it's…" Eric's face was grim. "She's not right, Rose. There's something wrong with that place."

"So now I need to fear a widow? Fear washing, cleaning and helping an old woman with her daily life? You're being ridiculous. In all your snooping, have you not seen the wage? Sixty pounds a year, Eric!" She pointed sharply. "You want me to forego sixty pounds a year? Are you serious?" Rose threw her hands up in frustration.

"There are other positions…" He pushed back from the door. "Don't you think it odd to offer such a large wage?"

"Where are these jobs? Tell me of one? You want me ferried off to the other side of the state to the munitions factory? Far away from Mama, away from you? Do you hate me that much?" Her breaths came too fast, blood rushed in her temples.

Eric's face flushed. "That's not fair, Rosie... Rose, you know that. I could never hate you." His voice trailed off, he licked his lips, eyes glassy. "Don't say that." He pulled his hair back down over the scars and slipped his cap back on.

"Well, what is fair, Eric? Tell me, what is fair? Me begging you not to head to war straight after my father, after your own father? Do you think it was fair to leave me? Your mum? To have me cry myself to sleep for months, wondering if you were lying on the ground with a bayonet in you? Tell me?"

"Calm down… please." He held out his hands pleadingly. "You're right."

"I'll calm down when we no longer have to worry where our next meal comes from, when you care about what I need, just for once."

"You know I care about you. I…" He looked down, shook his head, his hands balled tight. "I'll give you everything if you give me the chance." He looked back up to Rose; their eyes held a moment. "I just don't want you to go to Rutherford House, please, Rose."

Rose stepped back and shut the door in his face, leaned against it, and tears flowed.

The door shuddered behind her. Eric knocked earnestly.

"Please, Rose, please don't go. You heard the stories about that place when we were kids." His voice was muffled.

Rose laughed and pushed away from the door.

"Stories, Eric, that's all they are. Go home." She turned from the door, tried to ignore the new shoe-shaped puddles beside her, held her sleeve to her mouth to drown the rot in the air. She headed back to the sitting room and listened to Eric's uneven footsteps recede, the distinct pattern of his limp, before the sound of his horse trotting away allowed her to breathe.

She sat in the sewing chair, parcel on her lap, sweat beaded at her temples, her attention hooked upon the shadow in the corner.

"You can go away too." She ripped the paper, ran her hand over the black cotton dress, felt the starched, perfectly white apron, eyes upon the corner still.

It was thick, darker than the other corner, its reach deeper into the room. A curl of mist tested the boundary of the darkness, crossed the barrier, and slithered across the floorboards. The uniform bunched in her fists.

The white ether snaked around her ankles; she kicked it away; it coiled back upon itself and returned to the corner, disappearing into the depths of it. Death fanned its stench, smoke and bone, blood and gore; they brought bile to her throat.

"I am not afraid of you," she whispered, knowing the words a fundamental lie. She smoothed the dress out across her lap, admired the stiff white cuffs and rounded white collar.

It somehow made her feel important like she had a place in this world other than rotting away in this house, terrified of everything in the corners of her vision.

She watched the corner, the shadow caught between a strike of sunlight and herself. Rose had no knowledge of what it was to be a lady's maid. No real insight into the secretive Rutherford family. What she did know was hunger, cold and dread. Sleepless nights, looking over her shoulder, feeling the constant need to flee. Could this be her opportunity to stop seeing ghosts?

CHAPTER 13

"Please, Rose, you don't need to leave home. We will manage. What would your father say?" Edith's eyes were wide and watery as she rolled up a shawl for Rose's luggage. Rose carefully inserted her new uniform into the bag, ignoring her mother.

"I don't have shoes." Rose frowned and looked begrudgingly at the worn, cracked leather on her feet. She sighed.

"Rose, Rose, please listen; that place is..."

"Mama! You sound just like Eric." The floor creaked underfoot; she dared not look back at that corner, even with her mother in the room. She stared at the loose floorboard and contemplated bringing the book but decided the shadows, the creaks and the book stayed here. Rose turned around to Mama, the blanched eyes in the right corner cemented her resolve.

Rose took a step, but Mama grasped her elbow.

"What has Eric had to say about this?"

Rose tried to ignore the white terror coating Mama's face.

"Too damned much!" Rose snapped. "This is my business and no one else's."

Edith rounded on Rose, lifted her chin so their eyes met.

"You've a mind to listen to me, young lady. This is very much the business of those who love you. Where there is a rumour, there is *always* a grain of truth." Edith's bottom lip quivered. She pulled her rosary beads from her pocket, held them to her heart.

"You're as bad as Miss Ray, Mama." Rose rolled her eyes.

"Rosa! You will not speak to me like this."

Rose turned on Edith.

"And you will not let us starve like this!"

Silence. Cold, sharp, cutting silence. They stared at one another; Edith's knuckles whitened around the rosary. Shame and anger flamed the rim of her eyes.

Rose felt her blood drain; guilt ran hot in its place.

"Mama…" She reached out a hand to Edith, then let it fall back to her side. Rose softened her voice; her heart hammered with shame.

"These past years have been so hard. I'm worried for you, you're not well, Mama. I can get us out of this, keep a roof over our heads, make Papa proud."

Edith took a deep breath, swallowed her emotions and spoke in her steady and measured way.

"Your father would be proud of you… is proud of you. *I* am proud of you. But Rose, everyone in town…"

Frustration took over again. Rose slammed her bag onto the bed.

"You're going to risk our welfare on gossip? Mama! Please, I can help us. I can make sure Papa has something, someone to return to." The lie about Papa stung deeper each time she gave it life.

Rose felt pulled to that loose floorboard, closed her attention to the whispers stoked up by the lie. It all stayed here. It stayed here until she could find a way to stop it, or make enough money to buy their way out, to escape the shadows.

Rose peered through the front window. Her ride had not yet arrived; she wished it to hurry before their argument worsened. She didn't want to fight with her mother, didn't want to part with a sour face.

"Mama," Rose took a deep breath. "I'm moving an hour away. I'll be safe in the comfort of a rich family; my wage will soon fill our larder with food and the pen with chickens."

"But I don't know these people, Rose." Edith kissed her beads, pressed them into Rose's hands.

"How can I protect you?"

Rose sighed. "I don't need protecting, Mama."

Something flashed over Edith's face. Her hand clenched over Rose's, pressing the beads almost painfully into her palm. Edith spoke in an angry whisper.

"You, young lady, know nothing of the world. You do not know these people, that man, that woman. You don't at all know their intentions."

Rose unwound their hands, pressed the beads back into Edith's possession.

"Did you know the people who took Papa to war? Did you fight him when he told us he was signing up? Did you argue with him on the very real possibility of violent death? You didn't stop him from leaving, did you?"

Edith flinched as though she'd been slapped. She took a step back, hand over her heart.

Rose quieted, too; she knew that she'd gone too far. Her rebellious lips quivered. She glared at the corner, dared it to step out of line. *It's all your fault*. Rose retrieved her bag, pulled a threadbare shawl back out. She wrapped it angrily around her shoulders and secured it with the ivory hair clasp, which did not seem to want to stay in her hair.

Her fingers shook as she patted her left pocket and felt the shape of Papa's pocket watch. She took a deep breath and spoke softly.

"I'm not going to war Mama; I'm going to wash clothes, tidy a room, earn a wage. Unlike Papa, you can count on me; I'll be back for a visit once a month."

Edith was pale. Rose felt sick to her stomach. Her anger released something, but seeing her mother look so defeated was a knife in her heart. She put a hand on Edith's shoulder, couldn't stand the tear slipping down her mother's face. Mama would be alone, with no family to turn to. Only the old man next door and Mrs Wright to keep an eye on her. It wasn't as though Mama had no actual family of her own, but those ignorant and cruel people disinherited her when she married Papa. They had refused to attend the wedding, claimed Mama was hysterical to be marrying a foreigner. Mama married for love, she loved so hard and so deeply she endured twenty years of pain in the knowledge that her family were only a town away, living in comfort, living in ignorance.

Rose's heart hardened towards them; she resolved herself to raise Mama up, to see her saved, elevated, respected. Rose would repair Mama's heart, save her body and soul. But for a short time, Mama would have to endure her time alone, a short time, so that Rose could work hard, pave a brighter full-bellied future. She would see out the war, and brace for what was to come when her mother learned the truth of Papa. Until then, Mama needed something to cling to.

Rose took Edith's hands in hers and kissed the bony ridges of them.

"Everything is going to be alright, Mama. You've raised me well; you've taught me so much. Now it's time I return that love to you. I can do this." She hugged her mother, kissed her sunken cheek. Edith's fingers dug into Rose's ribs; she clung as though she may never do so ever again.

Rose unpeeled herself, tucked sweaty strands of her mother's hair back over her ears.

"I'm not leaving forever. Won't Papa be so proud to see this house as it should be when he returns?" Rose's voice hitched with yet another lie. The floor creaked whilst neither moved, and she felt the weight of the shadow's presence. She held her bag protectively against her chest, her fingers fumbled with the buckle that closed it.

"Yes, he would," Edith said, kissing her rosary. She twisted her apron in her hands, the rosary still threaded through her fingers clicking. She touched the back of one hand to her eyes, drying the tears. Edith's pallor didn't warm. She reached for Rose again and ran the back of her fingers down her cheek.

"Rose... dear..."

Rose couldn't think of anything more to say and was relieved to hear carriage wheels grind to a halt outside.

"It's just another house, Mama." Rose reached for her dressing table. "Look," She grabbed her new quill and inkwell. I'll find some fine paper to write to you every other day to tell you how beautiful it is, all the magnificent stuffed wild duck they must eat." She squeezed them down into the side of her bag.

"All will be well, Mama."

There was a knock at the door.

Edith didn't move, so Rose made her way to the hall and opened the door to a well-dressed but scrawny, silver-haired man; her ride to the Yarra River, where she would cross for another connection. Excitement tingled under her skin.

"Rutherford House Miss?"

"Yes, thank you."

He gave Rose a strange sideways glance, screwed up his face so as the wrinkles on his cheeks met those around his eyes.

"By yourself, Miss?" He took her bag, peering over her shoulder to Edith, who was worrying her nails against the door frame, rosary pressed to her lips again. Rose leaned into Edith, hugged her tight, and breathed in the smell of her one more time. Perfume had long ago been sacrificed, but she still loved that smell of charcoal and flour. Rose kissed Edith's cheek again and whispered.

"I'll be fine. You wait until I send my first wage. All your worries will be forgotten."

Edith gripped Rose harder; she said nothing as Rose slid away. Edith's hand reached back for the door; it seemed to be the only thing holding her up.

The driver hovered, rubbed a scrawny finger under his nose, his attention on Edith.

"Uh, it's an awful long way from home for a young lady," he said. Rose glared reprovingly at him, grabbed Edith's hand as her body seemed to waver.

"I'll be ready in a moment, Sir. You can wait by the cart, thank you." Rose's voice was knife sharp.

"All good then, Miss." He shrugged and took up a position just outside the front fence. Rose turned back to her mother.

"Pay no attention to him, Mama; it will be such an adventure." She hugged her hard again, held on a little longer before letting Edith go with an extra kiss.

Rose waved. "I'll write to you once I've settled in. I promise." She walked ahead of the driver, a spring in her step, a pull in her gut as she moved away from her home.

"Sure you're alright travelling alone, Miss?"

"Am I to be concerned with your ability to drive this thing? Can you not keep a single person safe?" Rose frowned, annoyed at his nosiness.

He rubbed his nose more aggressively and sniffed. "Of course, Miss, it's just that…"

"You, by chance, related to Miss Ray?" Rose rounded the offside of the cart, running her hand down the warm neck of the horse in harness.

"Pretty boy." He bobbed his grey head as though it was perfectly obvious he was beautiful. Rose smiled. To be so assured of oneself, if a horse could, why couldn't she?

She cupped her hand, and his soft muzzle dipped into it; he nudged her palm, looking for a treat.

"One day, I'll have a bushel of apples for you."

The driver was still scratching his head in thought, still considering her jest about Miss Sticky-Nose Ray. Confused, he dropped her bag into the back of the cart and offered a hand to help Rose up.

"Don't know who this Miss Ray is… er … Miss."

"My mistake, Rose smiled to herself, feeling mean for teasing him as he tipped his hat very gentlemanly and pulled himself up onto a simple wooden bench next to her. Rose looked up to a clear azure sky; distant ominous clouds threatened the hint of Spring. She peered over her shoulder at the grey face of Mama. She lifted a hand, and smiled as wide as she could, which at that moment was nigh impossible as she saw the face of her father in the window of her bedroom looking straight at her.

CHAPTER 14

Athready young man, devoid of conversation, dug hard into the current that drew them across the Yarra River. The Rutherford House carriage waited upon a hilly incline on the other side. The punt lurched. Rose gasped, grabbed the side; brown water splashed in, the cold of it seeped in immediately. The sun dipped behind those encroaching clouds; the air dipped to a sharper cold that drummed the wind to drive the waves higher.

"Is this normal?" Rose's stomach turned at the same time, but not because of the movement of the vessel. The air sharpened its cold; she peeked over her shoulder, wanting to believe it was the fetid smell of gutted fish that ripened her next breath… but she knew it wasn't. It couldn't be? He couldn't be following her? Her jaw clenched; she held her breath and searched the shadows lining the shoreline. Bustling activity left no room for things to hide, no corners for the dead to slither into. Life was rich, loud and busy. Papa wasn't there, neither was Matteo. Rose let her hands fall, quietly chided herself for being dramatic and utterly ridiculous.

She held tighter as the river current roared beneath. The power of its pull strained the arms of the punter. He bent his knees and grunted as he balanced the small wooden float, guiding it slowly across. Sweat stained the back of his shirt and beaded down his neck.

The approaching side was heavily bearded; eucalypts on one side, a barnacle-clad jetty and a smattering of buildings, all pertaining to shipping on the other. The shore was crammed with boats and fishermen and people selling wares straight from the boats.

The young man rowed harder; his arms shook as he guided them up to the lean of the jetty.

"Bluey, hurry up!" He threw a rope into the hands of a young freckly-faced boy who ran from the shore.

"Alright there, Jimmy?" He caught the rope, wobbling under its weight before wrapping it around a thick metal moulding. His cheeks blossomed with the cold and effort.

"Ta, Bluey, get on over the other side now." Rose's punter, who she now knew as Jimmy, nodded to another punt floating in on the other side of the dock. Bluey saluted Jimmy and ran to grab the rope of the other vessel.

The punt lurched as Jimmy climbed out, her bag slung over his back.

He reached down for Rose's hand and nodded politely. "Miss?"

She took the slippery wooden steps carefully until she found her footing. Jimmy walked her to the edge of the river, where a muddied path married up to the dock.

"Take care at Rutherford House, Miss." He tapped the front of his peaked cap, nodded and ran for the carriage with her luggage, leaving Rose frustrated at yet another warning about her destination.

"Miss Carbonelli?" A tall man in black and white livery of a bygone era called out. His accent was British, his face as old as time.

"Yes." She picked up her skirt, stepping this way and that, avoiding puddles until she hit a dry patch just outside the carriage.

"Morning, Miss. You may call me Charlie." He bowed as much as his arthritic body allowed.

"Good morning, Charlie. Please call me Rose."

He smiled; his entire face crisscrossed, and pale blue eyes appraised her. He wore fine, wired spectacles, not unlike her own; they lent a knowledgeable air to him.

His attention was soft and kind, yet a weariness sunk his eyes. Charlie flipped down a step and offered a gloved hand. "My bag?" Rose asked.

"Safely loaded, Miss Rose." He smiled again; this time, it seemed a little forced.

"Thank you." Rose hesitated to take his leather-gloved hand. She'd wondered only days earlier what kind of luxury lay within this very carriage. Apprehension gripped her momentarily, but the whisper of excitement pushed her forward; she took his hand and stepped inside.

The door clicked shut. She sunk into the seat and drank in the pomp that entombed her. The intense smell of flax hit her; the dark wood of the carriage recently polished to a high shine. The inside was richly accented with red and gold trimmings. The carriage pitched and groaned as Charlie climbed aboard. Rose rested deeper into the rich velveteen seat. Despite the cold, she pulled a glove off, ran her fingers across the fabric, it was smooth, luxurious. Gold-trimmed drapes shaded fogged windows allowing just enough light in but not enough that anyone outside could see who was inside. She relaxed back and smiled.

The carriage lurched forwards after the crack of the whip. Rose sighed and pressed her hands deeper into the seat. She felt a warmth curl about her feet and found there was even a hot wrapped brick to tend her comfort.

She shook her head, part in wonder, part in disgust. So much poverty, yet some had such indulgence. Rose settled back into the seat, knowing the ride would be some time. She let her mind wander as the outskirts of her town bled away.

Would she be a capable lady's maid? Would she even know where to begin? Was it more than dressing and undressing the lady of the house? Where would she sleep? What would they feed her? *Oh, food, there would be food, lots of food.* Her mouth watered, imagining the fine silver it must be set upon, silver she assumed she might have to polish.

She pushed the curtains aside, the river skirted the road, the riverman staring in the direction of the carriage departure. The undertone of concern about her destination in their weathered faces stirred a voice that told her this was a mistake, told her to go home as quickly as she could. She bit her lip, fingernails digging into the window ledge, condensation drizzled from the pane to her hands. She opened her mouth once, twice to call *stop* to the driver, but the words faded in her throat. That pull towards Mr Borgia was still present, a strange need to follow him, to know him.

Then there was Eric, the image of Matteo's bloated corpse giggling by the hearth, all the shadows that haunted her, the dead that pushed hard to seek purchase in her thoughts. She squeezed her eyes closed. Whatever the concerns of Rutherford House were, surely, they could not be worse than what tortured her day and night?

She watched out the window a moment longer, all that was familiar faded away into the distance.

"It's going to be an adventure," she whispered, the grimness within quashed with a forced smile.

The journey was uncomfortable. Rose became more claustrophobic by the minute. She loosened the top button of her blouse, slipped her shawl off and fanned her face with her gloves. The stink of the polish gave her a headache. The carriage jostled around potholes after they turned off the road that ran along the river, that didn't help either. She tried to keep her mind busy.

Rose drummed up all she knew of Rutherford House. The family were made wealthy last century upon the toils of the poorest of workers in local goldfields. For that, they were not popular or respected. Papa immigrated among thousands and for a time, he worked those same fields and often spoke of the poor conditions. Perhaps that was the source of everyone's concern? *Through jealousy and judgement, were rumours birthed?*

The carriage heaved to one side; the sudden movement jolted her from her thoughts. Charlie called down; his voice muted.

"Sorry, Miss, potholes from all the rain."

Rose clung to the window ledge until the carriage settled into a smoother motion. She studied the changing landscape. The road was rimmed with vast farmland. Orderly rows of some kind of lush green crop awaited the warmth of Spring to blossom.

The carriage jolted again. Rose grabbed the handle of the door for support. They slowed, coming to a stop.

Rose pushed the curtain all the way aside. A tall iron picket fence separated them from the here and there. Her heart beat a little faster, fingers clawed a little deeper into the ledge. *This must be it,* she thought with girlish excitement.

Regally arched wrought gates set into an equally tall brownstone entry. Rose sucked in a breath and held it for a moment. This was all that separated her from poverty and hope. The letter R swept dramatically across the middle of each gate. She let out her breath as she felt the weight of the coach shift when Charlie alighted. Rose pulled her coat tight, slipped her gloves and shawl back on, and shifted to the edge of the seat.

Charlie hopped across a number of puddles on his way to the gates, pulling an oiled coat over his head as rain pitter-pattered the roof again. The gates moaned as though they'd not been opened in a long time.

The carriage moved up the drive quickly, and Rose had her first glimpse of the famous Rutherford House. She leaned forwards, slid the window open, not caring about the rain and drank in a shock of cold, refreshing air.

A thick fog clung to the ground. It swirled lazily as the horses cut through, curling up in gentle sweeps of white before settling back within itself. The air smelled clean, of fresh earth and grass. It was still and silent but for the gentle song of light rain. Rose smiled, not missing the odours of town, the brash sounds and hustle.

Rutherford House emerged as the driver took a large sweep to the left, a monolith floating upon silvery, blanketed grounds. Large bird-like topiaries erupted from the mist, brown and skeletal, touched by winter, awaiting Spring's paintbrush.

Rose's nails dug harder, nearly piercing the thinness of her gloves.

Agapanthus lined the drive. Long silken green leaves glistened in the rain, a few with tall white flowers, the rest hibernated.

They rounded a large fountain, three white hippocampi galloped from its centre, green and black algae discoloured their undersides. Water arched from their muzzles, landing below in foamy plumes.

A Victorian mansion loomed ahead. Italianate arches curtained a balcony trimmed with laced iron. Creams and browns added a sense of warmth to the wintery landscape. Lush greenery hugged its perimeter, and a foggy glasshouse clung to the left of it. As the carriage slowed towards the entrance, Rose looked for the bustle of neatly dressed staff, but the house dripped with abandonment. She had imagined a swathe of staff lined up awaiting to greet her; she shook her head. *How ridiculous. Who do you think you are… King George?*

The carriage stilled in front of a grand double-doored entrance under a columned portico. At a distance, everything looked perfect. Up close, the worry of time was evident. Cracks ran the length of the portico supports, and mildew drizzled down the window ledges, lending the effect that the house had wept.

A thick wadding of leafless ivy netted the right side of the façade; it clawed possessively all the way to the roof. Its bony web almost entirely covered the front of the house, perhaps holding it all together, perhaps hiding what was within. Rose buttoned the top of her coat; the heated brick no longer kept the cold at bay.

Rose's attention trailed the ivy. It curled around the windows, a ragged nest except for a neatly clipped area beneath a second-story window. She thought she saw a curtain shift, a person, a shadow behind the glass. Rose adjusted her glasses, squinted, but the curtains fell back into place, sealing the day from whoever was within.

CHAPTER 15

Charlie helped Rose from the carriage and set her bag on the steps near the front doors.

"Take care, Miss Rose. You'll see me here 'n there." He pointed to the front entrance. "You'll be needing to ring the bell now." His old eyes settled upon her a moment too long, making Rose shift in discomfort, pick up her bag and hug it protectively.

"Thank you, Charlie." She made it halfway up the sandstone steps, felt his gaze upon her still. She turned back to ask him what it was that he so very much needed to say, but he was already back in the seat, snapped the reigns upon the horses' rumps and pulled away. She waited until the sound of the wheels died away, took a few grounding breaths, shivering, unsure, her attention wandering across every detail of the façade.

A crow cawed; it sat upon the portico above the entry doors, stepping sideways, back and forth, tilting its head this way and that as though studying her. *It can't be Devil, can it?* Rose sighed, acknowledged her utterly ridiculous thoughts, but kept her bag pressed against her body like armour.

She gasped as the crow swooped down; the breath of its wings fanned her cheeks. She scrambled to the top step and watched the bird fly off, rounding the water fountain before disappearing over the roof of Rutherford House.

Rose shook her head, hand to her chest. "Stupid bird." Something fluttered past her again; she swatted at another crow cutting a path through the fog, revealing a vast lawn in need of a scythe.

A half dozen more crows circled, cawing, their button-black eyes watching. They were loud, their conversation earnest. Rose jumped when the front doors sucked open, drawing her attention from the murder of crows serenading her arrival.

A middle-aged woman bustled out mid-argument with someone inside.

"I'll not have it! I'm done with this place. No, Sir, you will have to make do on your own henceforth. Martha can bake bread and scramble an egg well enough!" She hastily shoved her arms into a heavy coat, her fingers fumbling with the buttons. She pushed a burgundy felt hat on more aggressively than one should.

"And good luck trying to find anyone who'll put up with the likes of her... and *you*, for that matter!" The woman glared up at one of the dark window panes.

"Don't touch this, don't look at that... it's an asylum she needs, Sir, that's for sure. Good, proper medical care." Her jowls wobbled as she jabbed a finger sharply towards the doorway, face florid. Rose side-stepped, sucked in her cold, cracked lips, and tried to look invisible.

The woman performed a sign of the cross, then shuddered to a stop at the unexpected sight of Rose. One hand clutched at her bosom with fright.

"Jesus, Mary and Joseph himself! You half scared a poor old woman to death!" Her lips firmed as she looked Rose up and down, settling on Rose's bag. She hugged a small leather bag under her arm and stepped in closer.

"I hope you're a worldly, patient girl because there isn't anything but the devil himself in this house. I'll bet you won't last a week here!" She turned back around and snapped at whoever was in the house.

"The carriage Mr Borgia, call it around! I shall meet it by the gates." With that, the woman strode off towards the front gates at an angry pace, splitting the fog, pulling her hat harder down as she went.

The front door closed again. Unsure of what was occurring, Rose stood there, mouth slightly open. She rubbed the back of her neck, eyes wider, heart more earnest. The excitement of the day seemed to shrivel a little.

Horse hooves drew nearer as the carriage returned a few minutes later and headed towards the angry woman who sat on the edge of the fountain. She threw her bag into the carriage, alighted and slammed the door so hard it echoed across the gardens.

The carriage disappeared around the drive. Rose bit her knuckles, completely confused, alone on the steps. She looked upon the front gardens, the wearied and naked wintery trees seemed suddenly bleaker. Hope seemed to drip away from the façade that only moments ago was fresh and bright, made her feet feel light upon the ground.

Someone cleared their throat and drew her attention back to the doorway.

"Good morning, Miss Carbonelli." Mr Borgia stood as composed as a statue. She hadn't heard the doors open. Prim and neat, perfectly presented in stately black and white, he was tucking a pocket watch back into his waistcoat.

"You have arrived on time. This is a very good start." He smiled; that gold tooth caught some light and glimmered richly.

"Please, come in." He reached for her bag and opened the heavy door wider, his other hand swept towards it. She clutched her bag closer; he inclined his head acceptingly. Rose hesitated.

"Apologies for that outburst by the now-former cook."

Rose alighted the last step, legs a little more unwilling than earlier.

"Is she okay?" Rose asked softly, unnerved.

"Yes." The song of his voice seemed immediately harsher but the mystery of him lingered, and Rose still felt an instinctual urge to follow him.

Mr Borgia entered the house; Rose placed a foot on the threshold and smelled polish and candles. Mr Borgia waited a few feet inside the entry hall, hands clasped behind his back.

"Please." He swept his hand once more, and Rose stepped in, struck by an unexpected stillness, a thick and heavy quiet. A clock struck on the hour, the vibration of it a shock; she shuddered. She took another few steps feeling the resonance of the clock's voice on the parquet floor.

"We have a lot to get through to settle you in. This way, please." Mr Borgia nodded and marched on at a brisker pace.

Rose followed him quietly; her boots sank into a rich red Persian carpet runner after a few paces. She moved slowly, immediately drunk on the ornateness, unable to ignore a life she could only dream of.

High ceilings and walls richly hung with art. Candelabras burned brightly underneath gas lamps all the way along the hallway. The air was heady, rich with incense. The roof misted with smoke that erupted from a number of silver thuribles, just like the ones at church.

The quiet was so very unusual; even the tick of the grandfather clock held a reticence. Despite what Mr Borgia had said in her interview, Rose had still expected a bustle of staff. Footmen, doormen, valets, maids and butlers; that's what she knew from her reading. She hadn't at all believed there would be anything else. But it was just her, Mr Borgia and the tick of the clock.

"I'll take you to meet Martha first; she has worked in service here for many years. She may be in a disagreeable mood now that Cook has left. It adds pressure to her busy schedule." He wriggled his fingers, urging Rose on faster.

"Come, come, you will need refreshment, I imagine?"

Rose nodded, "Thank you, that would be nice." She swallowed, only then noticing the parch of her throat.

"Follow me." He walked on, stopping a moment to collect mail from a silver platter outside the open doors of a grand dining room.

"Mail goes out each morning at midday. If you have any correspondence, please leave it here. Please adhere to the privacy agreement, keep your communication to matters other than your business here." He arched his brows in silent question.

"Of course," Rose answered.

Mr Borgia flicked through his mail a moment, so Rose occupied herself by sneaking a peek into the closest room.

A grand dining room was fully laid with pink dinnerware and curling silver candelabras, ready for a dinner party at any moment. Rose stepped into the doorway, noticed then that a thick crust of dust dulled the mahogany of the table and blunted the shine of the porcelain. Oval paintings of strangers with cold expressions hung neatly from brass chains across picture rails on either side of an ornately carved mantel, its hearth boarded up. Unusual objects and oddities dotted the walls and filled every space. It looked not unlike things in glass cabinets at a museum.

"This way, please, Miss Carbonelli." Mr Borgia touched her shoulder, and the zap jerked her back to the hall.

"Please call me Rose." She rubbed her shoulder.

"Indeed, Rose, it shall be."

Rose withdrew her attention from the dining room, eyes hooked a moment longer upon a carving with a wide maw, white stone eyes, a tuft of what looked like real hair upon its chin. She grimaced; her fingers dug into her bag a little tighter. She quickened her pace to catch Mr Borgia, noting a musty undertone; despite the thickness of the incense, the air had the taste of desertion.

A lump rose in her throat, and she rubbed her neck again. This place had corners; would it have shadows too? She tried so very hard to not be captured by them, looked down, concentrated on the back of Mr Borgia's gleaming black shoes, and kept in time with his rhythmic pace.

A set of double doors to her left caught her attention, though. She couldn't help but stop and admire a stately library with ceiling-high shelves. Thousands of books lined them, each shelf perfectly set out by colour and size. Her heart skipped at the sight. Rose loved to read, but they had long ago sold off everything to pay their bills. She wondered if a copy of Jane Eyre might be somewhere in there. The only book she had now was *the* book, the book that had altered everything, the book she needed to be rid of. Her hand groped at the side of her bag, because in that moment, with that thought, she felt the weight of it in her bag despite not packing it. The hairs on her neck stood; she would have to work hard to busy her mind, to forget the anguish of the past few years, to leave the power of the book behind. Yet, her hand cupped the bottom of the bag, and there it was, a small rectangular shape. She swallowed hard, sweat coated her palm as her fingers re-traced the familiar corners of the book. She peered over her shoulder, Mr Borgia still moving ahead, thankfully unaware of the otherworldly occurrence happening right under his nose. Rose took a deep breath, let her hand fall away, and stepped into the library, and wondered if she might squirrel it away in there, hidden from her and the world?

Mr Borgia appeared in front of her quite suddenly and reached for the doors. Rose startled; the leather of her bag squeaked under her hands.

"The library is out of bounds. It is for my private business."

"Oh, I'm so sorry."

"If you need a book for Mrs Rutherford, or yourself, you only need to ask, and I will oblige." His eyes narrowed at her, as though he was trying to understand something unspoken. "Are you quite alright, Rose? You look a little flushed." The song in his voice dampened like a summer day turned into a storm.

She rubbed her neck but couldn't seem to suppress a new prickle under her skin.

"I… I am perfectly well, Sir. A little nervous perhaps." Her voice didn't carry any conviction and he frowned again.

"Well, there is little time for nerves, there is much to be done. Mrs Rutherford's comfort must always come before your own from this moment onwards." His frown deepened, "All the more reason to settle you in quickly after some refreshment."

Rose forced away any recounting of Eric or Mama's concerns that rushed into her thoughts. The strangeness she felt was the fault of the damned book, it was all the book's fault. She edged away from the doors, the library was sealed away with a creak and a click, but not before she caught sight of a document-laden desk within.

"It's so very quiet. Is Mrs Rutherford not home?" Rose inquired, trying to ease the sudden tension.

Mr Borgia slipped his keys inside his jacket and sniffed sharply. He smelled so richly of smoke and coffee… and something else.

"Mrs Rutherford is always home. She does not leave the grounds, not ever." His smile seemed forced.

"As I have already explained, she has quite particular needs. Quietude and routine are the most important."

"Oh." Rose immediately felt foolish.

"You will understand quickly how Rutherford House functions. I am confident you will do very well here."

Mr Borgia moved on, closing every other room they passed through the long entrance hall. He jiggled each door knob for good measure to ensure they were properly sealed.

"You will have access to all that you require, no more, no less. You will be comfortable and want for nothing." He turned back and looked down at her.

"And I feel you will be the first lady's maid in quite some time to be successful in helping Mrs Rutherford in the very special care she requires. I am most confident you will make a very positive change to this house." The knit of his mouth released into a more genuine smile. He turned away, his heels clicked, and he kept moving along the hall.

Rose's thoughts were chaotic. How could he seem so confident in her ability to successfully discharge such employment, yet shut her out as though he couldn't trust her? It didn't sit right, but she tried to reassure herself that it was perfectly reasonable until he did, in fact, see her to be a trustworthy employee.

They arrived at a grand staircase at the far end of the hall. Colourful rays of winter light struck red-carpeted steps through a rectangular stained window above. Rose could just make out the movement of clouds through it; they sailed past quickly as though chased by the breath of a new storm.

The colours and light seemed the only sense of brightness in the house to this point. The dark panelled walls, closed doors, and silence had not at all felt welcoming.

Mr Borgia turned to the right, away from the stairs, arm out in invitation.

"Refreshment will be down in the kitchen first." He went on ahead through an open doorway.

Rose forced a smile and followed him down the servants' stairs. She squinted in the dim light; a single gas lamp cast a sickly pale hue that barely lit the way ahead. Empty shadows pressed in on her, she felt herself shrug inwards as though their touch was poison. She forced herself to take every step, nearly reaching out to grasp onto Mr Borgia. When her feet hit the basement floor, relief punched from her lungs, loud enough that he turned around.

"Are you quite alright?"

"Yes," Rose nodded rapidly, avoiding eye contact. She hugged her coat tighter. "It's just very cold down here." The chill of the air was, in fact, breathtaking. It touched every inch of her lungs, her words misted, curled in upon themselves and faded into nothing.

"Comfort was not considered for servants of the past." He waved her on. "Mr Rutherford was more generous than his father. He placed heating at great expense in the servant quarters, but they've long been out of service. The thoroughfares are as they always were, dark, old and cold, so mind your step." He turned a corner and entered another corridor. Even in the poor light, the walls told the tale of their age and weariness. Peeling pale paint, stained skirting boards and the odd tile underfoot missing. There was a thickness to the air, a cold tactile touch to it, and a silence so deep it rang in her ears.

"This way." He hurried her along as she had slowed, about to peer into one of the open doors. Rose startled when Mr Borgia touched her elbow and guided her away from the dark eye of the room she hovered outside.

"These accommodations are abandoned, only rats for guests now."

They moved past a dozen more rooms, each door ajar, a slit of darkness so deep that Rose felt like she could fall in and disappear forever.

"Martha? Are you in?" Mr Borgia called as they neared a lighted doorway and a comforting smell. Flour and spice, the warm hug of heat chased away Rose's morbid curiosity for the silent voices of the shadows that dwelled in that corridor.

They entered a huge kitchen split with a long wooden baking table. Herbs hung from the ceiling; two skinned chickens lay split down the middle upon the bench. A large pot boiled upon an ornate cast iron wood stove, all golden and black, with a healthy box of kindling by its feet. The air was laden with the perfume of vegetables, flavour, and the richness of meat. Her mouth watered.

Mr Borgia stuck his head through a doorway to their left.

"Ah, there you are. She has arrived."

Rose heard someone fussing before Mr Borgia stepped back and pulled the door fully open.

"About time then." Martha wandered over to Rose, an aged limp in her gait, the smell of hard work about her. She was short, her face lined with life, not unlike Charlie, yet her eyes were a sharp brown that lacked warmth. Severely parted snow-white hair hugged her bony skull and wound into a neat bun set at her nape. She wore a pale blue dress, collared high on the throat, its skirt rimmed solid, sensible brown leather boots. She was a service woman of another era and one that was judging Rose's youth and lack of experience in a single glance.

"Hmm." Martha dumped dirt-clad potatoes from a basket onto the workbench. One rolled out onto the floor, Rose picked it up and placed it on the bench.

Martha's rheumatic stare held Rose hostage. Rose couldn't find words to introduce herself. Martha clucked her tongue, then re-tied a frilled apron with a yellowed hem.

"Not much of you, is there?" Martha peered at Mr Borgia and back to Rose again, leaned forward, and pinched Rose's arm.

"Don't know where you found this one; she's sicklier than the last." Martha's fists sunk into her own healthy hips.

"I only cook simple fare, Mr Borgia. She won't be getting the pomp and ceremony Mrs Denham slaved over." Martha waved her tea towel at Mr Borgia. Rose was confused as to why a servant spoke in such a way to him.

"You'll rue the day you let Mrs Denham go. A few bob extra, and she'd have stayed on. She spoiled you both, and you know it."

"Martha, enough." His eyes flashed at Rose, amusement or annoyance; she didn't know him well enough to tell.

"See to Rose settling in."

Martha pursed her lips, tongue in cheek. She curtsied awkwardly.

"Of course, your Highness," Martha muttered. Rose had to bite her tongue, or she may have laughed out loud, but when Martha wandered to the stove and stirred the bubbling pot, Rose forgot all other senses. She breathed in the aroma; her stomach growled.

"Rose... Miss Carbonelli?" Mr Borgia broke through her hungry visions of a bowl brimming with whatever was in that pot.

"Yes, Sir," Rose said. "Pardon me, Sir."

Mr Borgia's fingers wriggled by his sides as though he was anxious to be on his way.

"You will need to assist Martha where she sees fit; as she so eloquently pointed out, we are quite short-staffed."

"Short-staffed? By the blazes… we've no staff!" Martha stirred a little faster, lifted the spoon and sipped. "Hmmm…" She sprinkled something from a clay dish into the brew.

The amber of Mr Borgia's eyes shone a little brighter. He shook his head, this time chuckling to himself.

"Be kind now, Martha. Don't teach her your bad habits."

Martha waved a tea towel at him again.

"I've enough to get on with; she'll do as she's told or be off back home like the rest of them." She nodded towards the door as if commanding him to leave.

Mr Borgia smiled wryly and reached for Rose's belongings.

"I'll leave these upstairs for you."

Rose bit her bottom lip, uncoiled her fingers and gave him her bag, hoping he wouldn't open it and see how very little she had, how destitute she was; she hoped he wouldn't find the damned book and kick her out for being a heathen. He left; the sound of his steps echoed for a long while from the hallway.

"Well, girl, grab an apron," Martha said, nothing at all welcoming in her tone. Rose pulled one from a hook Martha pointed to on the wall by the dark eye of the hall. She hung up her coat and slipped on the apron. It was stained, with silver fish holes in its hems, one tie shorter than the other, but it was firm with starch and smelled clean.

"You may call me Martha, no need for formality in this place. Class left here long ago." She plucked up a sharp knife and pointed it at a stool.

"Sit yourself there."

Rose did as she was told, sitting at the bench as Martha slid a bone-handled knife across to her.

"Start peeling, then," Martha said as she set a kettle to boil and busied herself at the stove again. The smells hooked Rose; she supposed as alcohol did a drunk. It made her stomach flip; her mind go to jelly. Plain meals or not, a meal was a meal, and right then, Rose would peel a thousand potatoes, scrub a hundred stinking night pots just to feel food slide into her belly.

Rose settled into the task, peeling skins away quickly, her hands adept from years of helping Mama. The gentle bubbling of the pot on the stove remained a pleasant distraction, chased away the uncomfortable silence Martha stoked, and kept the shadows in the hallway still.

Rose studied the kitchen as the peels curled onto the bench. A long horizontal slit of a window ran the length of a peeling roofline above the sink area. It was at ground height outside, weeds pressed against the glass. It drew in just enough natural light to keep the kitchen functional under the dim hue lent by gas lamp sconces and a dozen pillar candles. They imbued nothing more than an eye-watering orange glow. It perhaps explained the redness, the overworked tiredness that rimmed Martha's eyes.

Rose absorbed every inch of the kitchen, stopping at the thin slit of blackness that sliced down the edge of the larder door. Her knife halted with half a potato peel curved over her hand. She concentrated, searched for signs, sniffed the air for the smell of death, but there were no writhing shadows, no odours other than the starch of the potatoes and a rich, salty brew bubbling heartily. She checked the corners once, twice. All was clear; nothing lurked in their depths. She sank a little more comfortably onto the stool and smiled, a weight carried for so long, lifted.

"Finally," she whispered to the potato as she dug the knife back into it.

"Who you talking to?" Martha set a tray down, a simple white teapot set with two cups and sandwiches.

"Corned beef and mustard. Had this set aside for my tea, but seems you need it more than me," Martha said. Rose squeezed the potato, placed the knife down, and pressed her hand against it lest she snatch the sandwiches too quickly.

"I can't eat your food. I mean, what was meant for you." She swallowed the saliva pooling in her mouth. She wanted so very much to plunge into it, to gorge every mouthful.

Martha slid a plate in front of her, three generous points of laden bread and poured some tea.

"Eat. I've enough for myself whilst you're skin and bones." The coldness of her voice was jarring but not enough to stop Rose from reaching for the plate, forcing herself to bite in a ladylike fashion when she really wanted to put the whole sandwich in all at once.

"You make your tea as you see fit." Martha pushed milk and a small bowl of sugar towards Rose. She watched Rose eat, watched her pour extra tea and set the pot back down. Was it in judgement? Rose didn't care in this moment of bliss. She felt she might drool if she spoke, so she poured a generous dollop of milk, delighted at the way it swirled through the redness of the tea. She stirred through a heaped spoon of sugar and washed the sandwiched down, her throat burning pleasantly, her stomach full all too quickly.

"Hurry now, you've work to do." Martha eyed Rose's plate. Rose picked up the last sandwich, closed her eyes as she bit down, and felt them roll in her head. Another sigh of relief. No shadows, a wage and food… delicious, juicy food.

Rose drained her tea and saw Martha still watching her, grey brows pinched together, plucking at her lips.

"What is it?" Rose wiped her mouth, thinking she must have smeared food on her face in her eagerness.

Martha topped up her own tea and sipped, her eyes peering over the rim of the cup. "You remind me of someone."

"Who?" Rose's chewing slowed.

"Someone from long ago and far away from here." Martha's eyes swept the kitchen and returned to Rose, glazed in a secret memory.

"Was it family?"

Rose felt she had intruded too far as Martha's eyes narrowed; she cleaned away the sandwich dishes, piling them by the sink.

"I'm sorry. I shouldn't have been nosey."

"No need to apologise." Martha's movements stilled, her back to Rose; she leaned forwards, supporting herself on the edge of the sink, as though she might collapse.

"You just look like a girl I was in service with back home, back when I was but a lass." It was only then that Rose took note of the hint of an accent Martha retained. It echoed with Irish, but she couldn't be sure.

"A young maid in a house far stranger than this… in the end."

"Stranger?" The word stuck in Rose's throat. What did Martha mean … *stranger than this place*? She poured the dregs of the tea into her cup, took a mouthful of the now bitter brew, and sucked tea leaves from between her teeth.

"I once worked for a very wealthy family, had more money than anyone would require in a dozen lifetimes. I was a scullery maid then, a busy thankless position it was." Martha wiped her hands on a cloth, moved to the stove and ladled through the pot, stirring as she spoke.

"Young girl was taken in by my cousin, Edwina; she was the cook of Norlane Hall. That's the house." She nodded at the memory, sipped liquid from the pot, and added another pinch of something from that nearby bowl. She peered over her shoulder at Rose.

"You've that same gaunt look about you, too thin, weak. You'll want out of that quick smart if you're to stay on here."

Martha looked back to the pot, stirred some more, tasted again, opened the oven and added an extra log into the fire.

"Terrible end…" Martha's head shook slowly.

Rose leaned her elbows into the table and knocked her teacup over, fumbling to catch it just in time before it dropped onto the floor.

"What happened?"

Martha shook her head quickly. "Terrible business."

Martha checked a clock above the stove and hung the ladle overhead upon a hook laden with utensils.

"Best you finish up; his Highness will be back to get you shortly."

"What happened, Martha?" Rose followed Martha to the sink to set her own cup down. She looked down at the woman who busied herself, placing a wedge of yellow soap in the soap wand. She agitated a bowl of steaming water until it brimmed with suds.

"Best not to speak of the dead." Martha signed a cross over her heart. She looked up at Rose, eyes a little more glazed than before. She wiped her nose on her apron, moved to the big bench and began butchering the chicken into small portions.

"Soup tonight; it'll fortify you both." She caught the look on Rose's face.

"Forget what I said. Norlane Hall was a long time ago and far away." She waved away her words, the matter closed. Martha hacked into a breast bone, the crunch sickening; the sight reminded Rose of the fox's handiwork. She grimaced; the reality was that foxes only did what people did, killed and ate to survive. So too, they killed for sport, leaving carcasses behind just as people murdered and left bodies for others to stumble upon. She suddenly felt less anger towards them; they were just trying to survive like she was. The foxes were doing what nature instructed... who was she to judge them? Would the loss of her chickens upset her as deeply if she had a full belly every night?

Rose was pulled from her thoughts as Martha hacked the last leg from a bird.

"You'll be treated fairly here as long as you do your job now, you hear?"

Rose nodded, picked up another potato and started peeling again.

"I'll need a few more." Martha pointed with the knife; bloodied juices dripped from the blade. "That was the last from the garden. Head down that hall, last door on the left, vegetables are kept in there. It's dark and cold, just the way they like it. Take a candle, so you're not tripping over yourself."

Rose picked up the empty basket and wandered down the hall she had arrived through, past the servants' quarters. The candle spilled light into the darkness, took the ominous weight from it. Curiosity and opportunity had her push some doors open. She held the candle aloft; it drenched the small rooms, each furnished with a bed, washstand and robe. All had an old mattress tipped on its side. They smelled musty, old, long unused. Rose found the potatoes in a small room next to a broom closet, rushed back up the hall and dumped them on the bench.

"Martha, the servants' rooms are... well, where do you sleep?"

"No one lives on site other than myself, Mrs Rutherford, and now you." Mr Borgia's smooth timbre interjected and made Rose drop a potato. It rolled along the floor, coming to a stop by his feet.

"It's time you meet Mrs Rutherford, Rose."

CHAPTER 16

The servants' stairs creaked beneath their feet this time, or had she just not noticed it before? Rose counted them in her mind. Twenty up to the ground floor. They paused at the base of the formal staircase; Mr Borgia patted his coat until he felt what he was looking for and pulled a set of keys from a pocket.

He moved, then halted on the first step, a loud thud upon the coloured window panes. His head snapped up to the glass, fingers drummed silently on the balustrade. A bird repeatedly fluttered against the window. Mr Borgia didn't move for what felt like a long while; Rose heard only the steady woosh of his slow breaths. The bird tapped and banged at the glass until it departed in a sudden raucous fluttering. Mr Borgia glanced back at Rose.

"Don't worry about them; it's near Spring; they get more excited at this time of year." His cheek feathered, and he walked on.

Rose placed her hand on the balustrade in the same place his had just been. It was ember-hot; she jerked away before placing it back down above the heat, ascending behind him, her fingers grazing over numerous gouges and scratches in the otherwise well-polished wood.

The walls along the way were studded with more oddities she could not identify. Paintings, carvings, and trinkets filled with gemstones hanging from small hooks. Interspersed among these was an array of dead things, stuffed heads of various creatures with snouts and horns.

Rose hated the way it felt like they were staring at her, so she trained her eyes on the back of Mr Borgia again, rather than their dead, glassy attention.

Thirty steps passed before she alighted upon the second storey. The landing faced a bank of arched windows that gazed upon the frosted front gardens. Heavy red brocade curtains draped the floor, guarding the privacy within. The house sucked thick beams of winter light through the lace in between.

The air was stale and flooded with dust motes. Rose ran her fingers through a cold slice of window light and watched the motes curl from her touch. Mahogany wainscot walls absorbed the light within a few steps, the way ahead dusky. Flame-shaped sconces lent a dull night-like glow to the oncoming hall. Rose blinked, readjusted her glasses, but the ambience strained her eyes; she pulled her glasses from her face, polished them with a sleeve and set them back on. It was still dull.

Mr Borgia wandered ahead, halting in front of a large gilt mirror.

Their reflections caught Rose off guard. Haloed by the window light, Rose saw how very small and bedraggled she looked, whilst Mr Borgia was so richly clothed, refined with a well-fed glow to his skin. Rose clamped her jaw; anger swirled fresh in her veins, hotter with each pump of her heart. *How could some have so much when many have so little?* The urge to say as much was quashed as Mr Borgia reached for the mirror, and to her astonishment, he clasped a handle on the mirror's frame. The mirror was a door.

"How curious," Rose said.

He paused, let go of the handle and turned back to her, clearing his throat as he did so, shaking out the keys.

He looked past her, eyes glazed momentarily as though thinking upon something. He adjusted his tie. In the brief moment of quiet, she thought she could hear singing somewhere.

"Curious? I suppose it is, but function is more to the point in this case." He flicked through the heavy set of keys of brass and silver that chinked as he sought one with a large round bow, an intricate and strange curved symbol cast within it. He slid it into the lock and turned right until there was a click. When he withdrew the key, she noticed the pattern in the bow was also engraved along the mirror's frame. It looked like a ribbon tied into a neat bow laying on its side.

Rose's heart fluttered as it occurred to her that Mrs Rutherford was locked in. She stumbled back, eyes wide. Was she to be locked away as well? She couldn't swallow all of a sudden, her arms stiffened; she looked back to the staircase; it seemed so very far away.

There was a sudden high-pitched scream, a blood-curdling, under-your-skin wail. Rose reversed until her back hit the balustrade of the staircase, mouth agape, hands balled by her sides. Mr Borgia looked at her, calm, not at all shocked, as the guttural cry peaked and slowly faded.

"You will get used to that," he said.

Rose stared at the door, a million questions in her mind. Her legs trembled; she wanted to run away and burst through the door all at once. Would she be allowed out? Would she find Mrs Rutherford prostrate upon the floor, injured or dead? Rose's eyes flicked from the door to Mr Borgia, back to the stairs and then settled again on the deep burnt orange of his all too calm attention. Her fingers curled in, pulled up to her chest as if to hold her heart steady.

Mr Borgia tucked the keys back into his pocket, a softness came upon his expression.

"The door is locked for the safety and well-being of Mrs Rutherford," he explained.

Rose swallowed; a lump of fear wedged in her throat.

"Mrs Rutherford tends to get lost on the estate if she ventures out on her own. She can be forgetful. She must be chaperoned at all times if outside this wing. *You* will not be locked up, Rose, but Mrs Rutherford requires such care. The entire point of your position is to allow Mrs Rutherford more freedom, companionship and assistance that ensures her welfare. Your presence will enable her to visit the grounds, take the air, and see something other than the walls within." He pointed over his shoulder with a thumb.

Rose nodded; no sense of his assurance alleviated the tightness in her chest. She awaited the explanation of the screaming, but his face shaded as though the sun set too suddenly.

"This is a coveted position, Miss Carbonelli. Its peculiarities are well compensated for."

Was this a challenge to leave before she had begun? Moisture finally returned, and she swallowed. She thought of her mother, of her backbones pressing through the thinness of her clothes. Rose rolled her shoulders back and looked into his eyes. "I am most appreciative for it, Sir, and I intend to discharge my duties to the highest standard."

He held her gaze and spoke as if she had not.

"This door remains locked at all times. Even when you are inside, you will ensure it is locked." He retrieved the keys, swivelled the key ring, unhooked a long silver key and handed it to Rose.

"Do not lose this, do you understand?"

Rose nodded; Eric's protests were suddenly louder in her head. She slipped the cold key into a pocket.

"What you see, what you hear, the work you perform, none of it will leave these hallways. Privacy is paramount, as I have already made quite clear. Any breach will be instant dismissal as discussed, and I will ensure you find no work within a hundred miles of Melbourne." His accent sharpened; the sunset of his eyes deepened. She couldn't hold his stare any longer; it made her shift and look at her feet.

Rose wondered if this was why staff changed so often, being locked away, unable to keep their lips sealed? She had no trouble with secrets; she had just fled from her biggest one, but being locked in? That was not at all what she expected.

"I understand," the words shuddered out.

"Do as you are asked, nothing more, nothing less. Take no liberties, and your time here will be quite simple, not too difficult."

Rose nodded.

"You attend Mrs Rutherford's private and personal needs but answer only to me in regards to her continual welfare, or any other concerns you may have during your stay."

He paused, waiting.

"Of course, Sir." Rose curtsied quickly, assuming that was what one would do and moved away from the balustrade, her balance restored.

He scoffed, "I am the caretaker; you need not curtsy. Now, I will introduce you to Mrs Rutherford, let you settle in, then I will have Martha show you around the rest of the estate." He pulled an envelope from his pocket.

"Yes, Sir," Rose whispered, wanting to ask so much more. As if knowing her thoughts, he spoke further.

"Breakfast is brought up promptly at 8am. You are not expected to rise at dawn as is traditional of a service role. We function during daylight hours only; it is what keeps Mrs Rutherford in comfort. She is not fond of the dark. You will notice her rooms are kept alight throughout the day and the night."

Finally, something Rose could relate to.

"You may come and go about your duties as needed, take your breaks when Mrs Rutherford takes her rest. The routine changes according to her needs. Each day will be different from the last. There will be times you may have no duties to attend; you may occupy yourself as you see fit in those hours."

The walls seemed to recede, and she felt she could breathe again.

He turned from her and clicked the handle of the mirror door to the right. Warm, bright light struck the side of him, he urged the heavy door a little further, and Rose was hit with a strong Rosemary perfume; it hit her like a slap and made her eyes water. It was much stronger than downstairs. Mr Borgia stepped aside, he swept his arm towards the door, inviting her in.

Rose entered a hallway, Mr Borgia behind her, the door snapped shut. She was locked in.

Rose found herself in a most unusual place. Another wood-panelled room, but it was small, like an anteroom. It was brightly lit with an electric chandelier. Hundreds of glass drops shimmered overhead; their facets caught the light in such a way that they beheld different tones of warmth depending on how the light struck through the glass. Mr Borgia hesitated at a second set of tall doors, both beset with mirrors, that same sideways bow symbol carved into each corner of the doors.

"You will address Mrs Rutherford as such unless she asks otherwise. Secondly, you will stay upstairs at all times at night. Electric light is connected upstairs only, the gas is turned off downstairs at night, and candles are doused for risk of fire. You are not to roam the house at night, especially downstairs. It is very dark; it is not safe. Mr Rutherford was an avid collector; as you may have already noticed, there are many things to trip on. A number of staff have been forced to resign due to injury when roaming around downstairs after dark, including your predecessor."

Rose nodded, mentally taking notes.

"Third, your duties are simple. You will clean this wing, Mrs Rutherford's clothing, linens..." He waved his hand, "You understand?"

"Yes, Sir."

"You will dress and undress her in the evenings if she requires your assistance and draw her bath when necessary. Her meals are always taken here." He pointed to a sideboard across from Rose. "Martha generally sets and collects meals from here, sometimes she will bring them directly in." Rose noted an intricate lace runner atop the sideboard. A silver jug with glasses sat to the side, a vase thick with lavender and baby's breath to the left. Rose stepped forward and reached for the handle of a dumbwaiter set into the wall above.

"Meals come up in this?"

Mr Borgia lurched forwards, his hand dragged hers away.

"We don't use that anymore." His hair flew out of place, a slight sheen sprung upon his forehead. He let Rose go, smoothing his hands back over his head.

"Rats… that's how the rats get in. Never open it. They terrify Mrs Rutherford."

Rose rubbed her hand. He hadn't hurt her; it was just the ferocity of his reaction that shocked her. She nodded.

"I understand." But she didn't really; her eyes roamed the dumbwaiter. It was only then she noticed the base of it was nailed shut.

"Occasionally, a picnic basket is left when the weather is agreeable. On those days, you are to take Mrs Rutherford to the orchard so she can take the air with her midday meal. Martha will show you where to go later today."

Rose perked up at the idea of a picnic in an orchard.

"You may take breakfast and lunch downstairs if you wish, but your evening meal will be in your room, which is in this wing, so you are close by for Mrs Rutherford. Nights are often when she will need you most. She can become… confused."

Rose nodded again, eyeing an envelope he pulled from his jacket.

"I have written everything down for you, should you need reminding of your obligations." He passed it to her, she held it as though it were delicate, breakable.

"Mrs Rutherford may refer to you as Josephine at times; please do not be alarmed, and do not correct her. It is one of her more peculiar maladies."

He noted the confusion that fell across Rose.

"Josephine was her lady's maid when she first married, she helped her adjust to life at Rutherford House. They had a very close relationship. Mrs Rutherford sometimes regresses to the past. If you correct her, she becomes distressed; she may scream, as you have just heard."

Rose nodded slowly, promising herself she would not induce such a sound from Mrs Rutherford. This was becoming more unusual by the moment.

Mr Borgia pointed at the doors.

"Also, do not let the cats out… ever. They are a comfort to her. I do hope you like cats?"

Rose nodded; a flicker of her earlier excitement tingled her skin.

"Oh yes, I do very much like cats." The promise of pets wrested tension from her.

"Very good." He rubbed a finger under his nose and cleared his throat.

"Lastly, under no circumstances inquire about the doll Mrs Rutherford carries. It may appear unusual, but you must not speak of it, touch it, nothing unless she asks you to, but she will not. Mrs Rutherford cares for it as though it were most certainly real. Her behaviour may seem strange, but she is of no harm to anyone. This is never to be discussed, not with your friends, your mother, not even with your priest." His brows gathered, watching her more intently.

Rose slipped the envelope into her pocket and reached for that familiar tingle on the back of her neck. A strange heaviness fell upon her shoulders once more. That same something in the back of her mind said run, but her sensible side, her already grumbling stomach, and bony frame slapped ridiculous worries away. She subtly sniffed the air but could smell nothing but the pungent incense and flowers. She looked for shadows but could see none. *Stop it.* She scolded herself.

"Yes, Mr Borgia. I understand."

Mr Borgia made a '*humph*' sound in his throat and stared at her a moment longer.

"Refer to my notes if you need reminding; they contain all I have told you, and if there is anything, anything at all in this house that should cause you concern, I want you to feel comfortable to tell me." His smile seemed forced again; his fingers drummed upon his legs before he turned and reached for the second set of doors. The handle squeaked slightly; he slowly pulled the double doors open, paused, and peered over his shoulder.

"Are there any questions before we enter?"

Rose had a million but held her tongue.

"You may find the interior unusual; it is, again, peculiar to Mrs Rutherford's needs. Some find the décor unsettling." The doors fully opened, and Rose winced.

A blinding light struck her. Red, gold and black blurred into an uncomfortable smudge until her eyes adjusted. A floor-to-ceiling window at the end of a hall invited in a rich light that glanced off the walls. Wall sconces burnt bright; a hundred flickers of light refracted along every inch of wall space. Countless mirrors hung in various shapes, sizes and styles. Candles burned on side tables in both elaborate and simple holders.

The glare of the mirrored hall was astounding. Mr Borgia proceeded, unaffected. Rose followed, struggling to adjust to the hundreds of replications of them both. Never had she seen or imagined anything like it. So many mirrors, so many versions of herself shielding her eyes. She hugged herself, concentrated on the back of Mr Borgia, and tried to avoid the bizarre spectacle. It wasn't unlike a hall of mirrors at a carnival, the ones designed to delight, confuse and scare.

"You will clean these mirrors weekly and as needed. They must stay spotless. Do not, under any circumstances, move or cover them. Lights burn day and night; as I mentioned, the darkness greatly unsettles Mrs Rutherford. Even in your sleeping quarters, do not interfere with the light and mirrors. Darkness must never fall across these walls."

CHAPTER 17

Rose's feet fell hesitantly upon the rich red carpet as they proceeded along the hall of mirrors. Mr Borgia walked to the end of the hall, opening a door on his right.

"This was a nursery some years ago. It is where you will sleep. You will find it spacious and comfortable, most unlike regular servants' accommodations."

Rose followed him into the room. The shine of a large floor-standing mirror immediately struck her. Nestled behind a metal bedhead, its silvery eye twinned a second, slightly smaller mirror hanging upon the wall just beyond the foot of the bed. The effect was such that one would not be able to escape their own reflection when trying to sleep. *So strange.*

A third mirror, silver-framed, hung above a wash stand directly across from a window. With the bed set underneath the window, there was no angle upon which a sleeping occupant would not be under a mirror's watch. Her fingers dug into her arms.

"I must have these mirrors in here too?"

"Yes." He checked the window, it seemed stuck. "This must remain closed at all times too. The rats especially like to sneak in open windows at night. Only the balcony off the day room may be opened between dawn and dusk."

"Why?"

"Because they are the rules, and they maintain the comfort of Mrs Rutherford." His voice had an edge to it. Rose decided to leave her questions about the mirrors for now.

"May I?" Mr Borgia pointed at her coat and hung it on a stand behind the door. "You will find all the necessities for comfort that you require already set up in here, or otherwise ask Martha for anything more personal."

Rose watched his movements in the mirrors.

"I understand this is all quite unusual, but in a few days, it will become as normal as any other occupation. You may dowse your lamp to sleep as long as the mirrors stay as they are and the moonlight allowed in."

Two oil lamps added their small flickers of light to an already bright electric light dangling from a ceiling rose. One on a bedside table, the other in the far left corner. They imbued the room with a warmth the mirrors did not. Every aspect of the room was under watchful silvery eyes. Light caught every nook and sunk into every space. There were no shadows. It was both comforting and jarring; Rose was not at all sure how she felt about it.

The room smelled lived in, as though not long vacated. Her nails dug harder into her arms; she released them, ran her fingers along the bed, the linen as luxurious as she'd ever seen. Gold and red brocade, with red silk neck pillows. It looked more like Versailles than regional Melbourne. She leaned across a crocheted blanket folded neatly upon the bed end and looked out of the sealed window. Sweeping blue-hued hills on the horizon separated this place from the rest of the world. A large lake with a small island lay to the right of the rear of the estate. Some kind of building was on the island; what it was, she could not tell, even with her glasses on. Just below the window was a stable yard. The carriage she arrived in was parked behind, hay bales lined up an alley between the house and the outbuilding. Charlie was hobbling along, horse in hand, leading it into the stables.

Rose turned from the window when a door creaked open. Mr Borgia was at the wardrobe, he pointed inside to where her new uniform hung, and brand-new shoes shone underneath.

"Mrs Wright informed me of your shoe size, and I took the liberty to purchase them for you." He eyed Rose's barely-there boots. Seeing the wide shock in Rose's eyes, he added,

"They do not require repayment."

"Thank you," she said, embarrassed by the charity. *I'll pay him back with my first wage.*

Mr Borgia made a satisfied sound in his throat and made his way back to the door.

"If you will?" He extended his arm, inviting her out. A cat slithered in and twisted through his legs, wandered across to Rose, rubbed against her legs then jumped onto the bed. It circled a few times, settled down into a tight wad of grey fur and purred whilst kneading the linen. Rose reached for it, it pushed its head against her hand and mewed, inviting more pats.

"That is Heathcliff. He favours this room for its morning sun."

Rose smiled. "I think we shall definitely be friends."

"Rose?" Mr Borgia's brows arched; he stepped out of the doorway. She pulled away from Heathcliff and followed Mr Borgia back into the stark glare of the hall. Rose winced; the sight pained her eyes. She bit her lip as she walked behind him a few paces, then blurted out the burning question before she could stop herself.

"Why are there so many mirrors?"

Mr Borgia stopped. His body stiffened as it had upon the staircase; he didn't turn to face her but answered her question in a clipped tone.

"Because they please Mrs Rutherford… they comfort her in her time of darkness." He turned right towards a set of double doors with large brass handles on the opposite side of the hall. Rose followed quickly; cheeks hot; she had already overstepped.

He pushed open the doors. "Mrs Rutherford's bed chamber."

Her hand flung to her mouth lest her surprise made a noise and irritated Mr Borgia further. She found herself in a large suite, brilliant with winter sunlight gleaming and bouncing across walls hung with crimson tapestries, and countless more mirrors tacked those tapestries to the walls. There wasn't a shadow to be seen. Every corner was exposed by reflections of light, and despite the displeasing sight of herself a thousand times repeated, the lack of shadow settled the tingling in her skin. It calmed the need to clench her teeth and look over her shoulder. Despite being overpopulated with furnishings, the room was otherwise unoccupied.

"Mrs Rutherford rises at 8:00am and retires by 6 pm. You will have your evenings largely to yourself." He pointed to the left, "That door leads to the bathroom for her personal needs." He skirted a round table beset with a tall ornament of deepest black. Rose grimaced at its carvings. Skeletal arms with bony fingers rose up a thick woody stem that looked like a tree branch. The fingers clawed up to hold a receptacle with a lid that hung open. She caught Mr Borgia watching her as she looked at it.

"What is this?"

"Family heirloom. Mr Rutherford acquired it many years ago in Sardinia."

Rose let her attention slip from the ornament towards a grand mahogany bed. At its foot, dominating the room, drinking in every reflection, controlling all of the light, was an immense oval mirror. Taller than Mr Borgia, it sat regally upon clawed, silver feet. The frame was intricate, smooth leafy swirls, large verdigris flowers and again, that symbol on the key, a bow, laced amongst the design.

The mirror's watery eye was heavily marked with time, its edges misty, the reflections dulled by what age claimed of it. But it demanded Rose's attention; it claimed the room even though age seemed to have diminished it.

"This seems very old."

"The Frangitelli Mirror. It is indeed very old." Mr Borgia offered no more detail about the mirror.

Rose felt hooked by it, called to its gaze until she was pulled dreamily from its attention by the click of a door.

"Mrs Rutherford, your new lady is here."

A tall silhouette glided into the room through a set of double doors off the bedchamber. A thin woman dressed entirely in black from head to foot. Her reflection coiled around the room, a faceless visage, a concealed identity. She was veiled in black lace as well, even her hands gloved. No skin, no clue as to what she looked like; it caused Rose to pause.

Mrs Rutherford turned to Mr Borgia but did not seem to notice Rose. A ginger cat tottered by her side, threaded under her floor-length skirt. Mrs Rutherford cocked her head to the side.

"Shh, Arthur is sleeping." She pressed a finger to her veiled lips and pointed to a netted crib set by a Queen Anne dressing table. She made her way to the crib, lifted the netting with a slender finger, and peered in, her other hand pressed over her heart. "Shh, dear Arthur, all is well, my love."

There was no baby crying. Rose shifted, eyes sliding between Mrs Rutherford and Mr Borgia. He appeared completely unaffected.

"Apologies for our disturbance, Mrs Rutherford," Mr Borgia whispered. He side-glanced Rose, put his fingers to his lips, and urged Rose closer to make her presence known. She curtsied; Mrs Rutherford did not acknowledge her.

"May I introduce you to Miss Rose Carbonelli, your new lady's maid. She is young but most eager to attend you to the highest of standards."

Mrs Rutherford didn't respond; her attention was solely on the crib.

"Go on." Mr Borgia looked to Rose and nodded towards Mrs Rutherford, "I'll leave you to get acquainted." He smiled in an encouraging way. "She will address you as soon as she has attended Arthur."

Rose watched the woman cooing at the crib. Mrs Rutherford reached in, picked up a silver rattle and shook it. "Shh, there, there. Settle my sweet petal."

There was still no crying.

Rose jolted when Mr Borgia leaned into her and whispered.

"Read over your daily chores and instructions tonight. Today is for finding your way around. Settle in, meet Martha again in the kitchen at 3 pm, and she shall show you the rest of the estate before dusk. I will check on you before dinner."

He left, the void of his presence broke that strange invisible connection she felt towards him and it left Rose caught in an unsettling divide between this lady in black and her doll.

CHAPTER 18

Mrs Rutherford remained by the crib for some time, soothing a babe that was not crying, a child that was not there. Rose crossed her hands over her belly; she felt exposed, standing in a strange room behind a strange woman who seemed content to ignore her. She rolled her hands over, pushed her glasses up her nose, opened her mouth to speak a couple of times, then let the words fade. Instead, Rose took a moment to study the woman; all the while, she was trying to block out the intrusive mirrors, the grey reflections of herself, the glaring flickers of electric and candlelight.

Mrs Rutherford seemed to repeat the same thing over and over as though stuck in a thought, a moment in time.

"There, there, little one, Mother is here." Her dulcet voice held a smooth melodic song to it, not unlike Mr Borgia, but without the accent.

Mrs Rutherford rocked the crib; the movement shifted her veil, a slit of milky skin exposed. She realigned it; her attention remained upon the crib. Rose could just make out a slender face through the lace of the veil, but nothing more. What she looked like and how old Mrs Rutherford was would remain a mystery for the time being. The black taffeta of her dress sighed as the fabric shimmied with her gentle movements.

"Alright, my love, you win this time; we can't wake the entire household." Mrs Rutherford reached into the crib and retrieved the baby… the doll. Although warned, it was still a shock to Rose to see her lay the doll so gently into her arms, hold it with the care one would of a newborn.

She rocked, bounced her body gently, humming an unknown tune.

Mrs Rutherford lay the doll on the bed, refolded the swaddling, and tucked it in tighter. She drew it up, and held the doll in the crook of her arm.

"Ahh, that was the problem. You were cold. Poor dear." She hummed some more, and her body swayed in rhythm.

Rose wondered, other than sweeping a floor and boiling some clothes, how on earth she could possibly be of help to this woman.

"In your room, you will find suitable attire. When you are appropriately dressed, we shall speak of what I require of you." Mrs Rutherford's words shocked Rose from her own thoughts. Her instructions were measured and soft, with a childlike tone that added another blanket of strangeness.

"Yes, Mrs Rutherford." Rose curtsied quickly.

"You may call me Mary."

"Of course… Mary." Rose hesitated. Mary looked in the direction of the doors as though to hurry Rose along. Rose headed for the hallway without delay, only to nearly trip over another cat that dashed between her ankles, rubbing and purring at her with great enthusiasm.

"Oh! I'm so sorry. Aren't you lovely?" Rose said softly. She snuck a look over her shoulder. Mary was thoroughly absorbed with the doll, so Rose knelt and patted the black and white feline whose face had an endearing black spot above each eye.

"Pretty darling." She stood; the cat followed her with its tail flicking and a couple of meows for good measure. Rose eased by the table with the black ornament, its grotesqueness hooked her and made her want to touch it despite how horrifying it was. In a room of such beautiful things, she did not understand why such a ghastly object seemed to have the centre of attention. The great mirror caused her to pause as well; she felt absorbed by it once more, lost in its smoky edges, seen by something within.

She pulled herself from it, somewhat unwilling to turn her back on it as she entered the hall.

Rose sighed as she shut the door of her new room and leaned against it. She did not like the mirrors; they were intrusive and made her feel watched. She had felt observed by uninvited and unseen things for far too long and wanted no more of it. She pulled her coat from the hook and hung it across the face of the mirror at the foot of her bed, immediately knowing she'd already broken a rule, but this was a new life, a fresh start. She wasn't about to continue hiding and living in fear.

The black and white cat had followed her in and jumped upon her bed, joining Heathcliff who rumbled in sleep. Rose smiled. A silver disc hung from its collar.

"Cathie," she said softly. "Well, someone is a Wuthering Heights devotee." She smiled as she stroked Cathie. The cat stretched luxuriously and purred before curling against Heathcliff. She wondered if it was Mary who liked the story; perhaps this would be a way to connect with her mistress?

The room felt warmer with the slumbering cats, homely and comforting. Her shoulders relaxed; hope set a gentle ember within her. A small hearth crackled quietly. She placed a new log upon it, poking at it to draw a larger flame. Rose closed her eyes, absorbed a warmth not felt in such a long time. The heat drenched her skin and left it tingling with comfort.

She retrieved her uniform, rubbed her hands appreciatively over the newness of it. Crisply ironed, it smelled so very good.

She slipped off her ragged dress and stood by the fire a moment more in her undergarments, letting heat imbue as much comfort as possible. She draped her old dress across the mirror at the head of the bed, relieved to lose a second reflection, to feel a solitude that held no malice.

Her uniform slipped on into a perfect fit, satisfyingly smooth against her skin. So long had it been that she had owned anything new, it may as well have been a royal robe, for it felt that special. She ran her arms the length of the sleeves, buttoned the stiff white cuffs, and folded the crisp collar neatly.

The shoes were snug, the buttons shiny. Her feet were secure in the hug of them.

Rose tied the frilled apron, slipped a simple bonnet over her hair and admired her reflection in the mirror above the wash basin; she had left that one alone. She smiled, liked what she saw. Pride warmed her in a way no hearth could.

"You'd be proud of me, Mama." She spun about and practised a curtsy.

"Yes, Mrs Rutherford." She bowed deeply, "Of course, Mrs Rutherford." She pretended to hold a tray, "At your service Mrs Rutherford." Rose giggled and noticed both cats looking at her with wide green eyes.

"What do you two think?"

Heathcliff yawned and put his head back down; Cathie curled over and began cleaning her backside.

"Well then, if that's what you think of me, Cathie." Rose giggled again; the feeling of joy foreign but so very needed.

Rose wanted to open the window to let the crisp winter breeze in. She breathed deeply, closed her eyes and imagined the freshness instead.

"No more shadows, no more fear."

She took one more satisfied look in the washbasin mirror, tucked in a stray hair, and headed to the door, hope in her heart.

CHAPTER 19

Mary was nowhere to be seen. Rose wandered every inch of the bedchamber. She ran her fingers across one of the wall tapestries. They were thick, old and rich with a mouldy odour. She found a seam between them, peeled it from the wall, bare, cold plaster lay behind. She let the fabric fall back.

The blood red of them made the room feel like she was traversing a body turned inside out. Long streams of crimson festooned the roof like a circus tent. Silks fanned out across a black pressed metal ceiling like chords of muscle, pale detail sewn in like the sinews and fat. Everything was so overly ornate, rich and shiny, not to Rose's taste at all. She would have chosen light colours. Pink and apricot, the colours of Spring, the season of life. And then there was that ghastly ornament on the table; she averted her attention from that.

Her new shoes clipped onto floorboards as she stepped from the carpet. They fell almost in time with the tick of a number of clocks that counted the hour in and out of unison. Five. *Why would one need five clocks in a single room?*

"Mrs Rutherford?" She called softly, opening the second set of doors to a finely laid out day room. No one was there other than a hundred more reflections of herself. Every single surface was covered in mirrors.

Why?

Rose plucked at her lips and considered sitting at a gilded pianoforte tucked in the far right corner. Her fingers twitched to touch its ivory keys, but she would see herself snooping, the mirrors a constant conscience, so she closed the doors again.

She made her way to the dressing table, noted the perfectly placed brush set. She picked up a comb, a few hairs tangled in its teeth, a hint of grey on them. She ran her fingers along its brass edge then picked up the brush, admiring the fine needlepoint flowers adorning its spine. She placed it down and called out.

"Mrs Ruth… er… Mary, it's Rose. Are you here?"

"I've lost her already." Rose chewed her fingernails, wondering what she was to do. She walked towards the crib, leaned over the wrought iron sides. She reached out, yanked her hand away, and then pushed the netting to the side.

Empty but for that silver rattle Mary had picked up earlier. She ran her fingers along the crib, dropped her hand and wandered towards the bed. The linen was unmade, so she busied herself with tidying that, being careful to pull everything into creaseless perfection. Hands-on hips, Rose looked around for another task, but was distracted by a faint scraping noise. She cocked her ear up and followed the rhythmic sound. Was it the vermin Mr Borgia spoke of? She grimaced at the thought of mice and rats scuttling unseen.

The scraping became louder the closer she came to a tall rectangular mirror on the far side of Mary's bed. Rose hesitantly put her ear near its wooden frame. That rhythmic *sh, sh,* sound seemed to echo within the wall. She pulled away, frowned. It certainly didn't sound like rats; it was too regular, not sharp-clawed scurrying at all. Curious, she leaned closer and jumped when Cathie wrapped around her legs again. Rose accidentally fell against the mirror. It clicked and popped open — another door.

Cathie dashed in through the slit. Rose chewed at her fingers again, she looked around, unsure of what to do. The ticking of the clocks was accompanied by the flick of her thumbnail against her teeth. Rose leaned a little closer, pulled the door a little wider, held her breath and listened.

Humming, more scraping. She pulled the edge of the mirror with the tip of a finger and winced at its groan. She stepped aside, peering in, her mouth fell open, and she quietly gasped. A secret passage.

The glare from the bedroom conveniently shone within the dark entrance, revealing a steep set of circular metal stairs.

Rose paused, blew out a breath.

Hand upon the frame, she leaned in, let her eyes adjust. She sniffed the musty air, examined the stairs and the shadows behind them. All was still, the shadows vacant.

A cool breeze within tugged errant hairs around her cap as though a window was open somewhere.

"If the cat feels safe…" Rose decided she should follow too. She trusted animals; they sensed things. A cat surely would never run towards a ghoul? She glanced back quickly, expecting to see Mary's disapproval at her poking about when she'd not been there an hour, but, again, only a myriad of her own reflections stared worriedly back at her.

Rose shrugged, drew a centring breath, and slipped behind the mirror. She grasped the stair rail for support, and gently placed one of her new shoes on the first rung. Nothing happened, so she stepped gingerly to the next step. Her shoes tapped softly against the metal. The scraping sound stopped. Rose braced one hand against the wall of the narrow passage, sucked in her bottom lip, ear cocked, listening. The scraping began again. Cathie's meow echoed down. Rose took another step.

"Come Girl, don't dally in the shadows."

Rose nearly fell backwards, grappled for the balustrade just in time, righted herself and hurried up the last few steps and around a corner.

She found herself in a small windowless room lit by a half dozen gleaming brass lamps. Incense burned intensely, the air thick and white. It was strong with rosemary, lavender and a hint of something else. Mary sat at a table, a white apron across her lap. In her gloved hands, she brushed gently against something round. Hanging overhead was a ghastly array of eyeless faces and limbs with no bodies, all pegged along a line of rope.

Rose curtsied quickly after realising she was staring, "Sorry, Ma'am."

"It is my hobby, Girl. What do you think?"

Rose took in the porcelain dolls, whole and in pieces. They filled the space so well that she felt very much crowded. Some were complete, delicately painted and finely dressed, but most were in parts. By Mary's chair was a perambulator with a porcelain doll wrapped snuggly like a newborn babe inside. Her baby. *The* baby.

"Does Cathie have your tongue?" She looked up at Rose, the black veil pinned high upon her head, a thinner white lace one underneath. The outline of her face was more visible; the dark rounds of her eyes and the shadow of her lips were all Rose could make out.

"Do not stare, Dear; it is unbecoming."

"Sorry, Ma'am," Rose curtsied again and turned to leave.

"It's Mary. I've not dismissed you." Her voice lacked anger or pleasure. The tone and volume, calm and measured. Rose turned back around; the space felt even smaller, a dozen empty eye sockets stared down at her.

"Sorry, Mrs... um, sorry Mary." She cupped her hands in front of her starched apron. Its stiffness seemed to help her stay upright when she felt like she might sway.

Mary continued her work, smoothing a bare porcelain head with a square of sanding paper. White dust powdered the hem of her gown. Rose took a step forward; the air held a gentle talcum smell as she admired the craft more closely.

"I'm sorry for disturbing you."

"Apologies are for the perpetrators of ill will and offence. It offers no recompense to the offended. Wouldn't you agree?"

Rose stuttered. "Umm."

"Have you done something that held ill will or offence?"

"No, of course not, Mrs... Mary."

"Well then, you need not say sorry, Dear." Mary stretched an arm out and pointed to a shelf behind the doll in the perambulator. Rose could not help but wonder on the heavy coverings she wore. Did she dress so in the height of Summer?

"This cherub is ready for a personality; please, will you pass the brushes in that vase?" Mary asked.

Rose picked up the vase Mary indicated; an old preserve jar stuffed with paint brushes of various sizes. She placed it upon the bench Mary sat by.

"You may leave. I will be down in a while to feed the babe. You should have your chores done by then." She reached to her hip, tugged at a simple chatelaine, not unlike Mrs Wright's, and flipped open a fob watch.

"It is a quarter past twelve; we will take lunch at one and then a turnabout the garden. Arthur does so love the fresh air." Mary plucked a long thin-tipped brush from the vase; she placed it next to a collection of paint vials.

"You will come to love Arthur so; he is a delight." Rose heard the smile in Mary's voice, gulped at the pretence she was going to have to muster towards the doll-child.

Rose curtsied, "Yes, Mary, I most surely will take to him like my own brother."

"You have a brother?"

"Yes… well … I did."

Mary's movements stilled.

"You have lost someone?"

Rose nodded.

"As have we all, Dear, but we get on with life as we must."

Rose turned, one foot upon the first step, when Mary called her back.

"What is your name?"

"Rose," she curtsied again.

"Rose, yes, that's right. Mr Borgia did tell me." Mary set her sculpture upon the bench, pulled a jar from a draw to her left and turned her back on Rose.

"Mr Rutherford's mother was named Rose. He loved her so." She unscrewed the jar, dipped a cloth into it, rubbed a liquid across the porcelain face. Rose went to leave again, but Mary continued to speak.

"Are you good at your work?"

"Yes, Ma'am, I will be most dedicated to your service."

"Mary, please, Ma'am makes me sound so very old." Mary set the face to the side. She turned back to Rose and pulled a thick length of silvered, ebony hair from under her veil.

"Of course, Mary."

"Are you adept with a hairbrush, Dear?" Thick wisps of wiry grey slid across the black lace of Mary's gloves.

"I can do the basics well enough," Rose answered in truth, having learned to set her mother's hair a few years prior when Mama had burnt her hands on a pot that fell from the hearth.

"Basics? That won't do at all. It is Friday. Fridays are the day I wash and set my hair. I will be attending a gala at the Royal Women's League tonight. I expect nothing less than the most perfect of mason curls."

Rose rolled her hands over.

"You do know how to set mason curls, Dear… ahem… Rose?"

Rose shook her head ever so slightly and looked down at her feet, confused. Mr Borgia had said Mary never left the estate.

Mary's chair scraped on the floorboards; she leaned to her left and cooed at the doll.

"Settle now, dear Arthur. I'm quite sure she will at least be able to sit with you then?" Mary lifted the doll and cradled it in her arms.

"Is he not the most divine little thing?"

"Yes, he… he is quite adorable." Rose cringed inside, feeling foolish, embarrassed, and utterly confused.

A crow sang its coarse song somewhere outside. Mary seemed to freeze, stare off into space. Her veil shifted almost enough to glimpse underneath, but she suddenly unpinned the outer black lace and let it flutter down. Mary bustled past Rose, doll in her arms. The energy of the room was immediately heavy; the lamps flickered, threatened to go out. Rose rushed after Mary down the stairs.

As Rose pressed the mirrored door closed, a book was thrust into her hands, Mary seemingly out of the strange reverie that had taken hold of her.

"Page twenty-five. The instructions are clear on how to set mason curls. You do know how to read, don't you?"

Taken aback, Rose nodded quickly before she could respond in a way that was anything other than respectful. She had a penchant for that, as her Mama knew all too well.

"I read very well, Mary."

"I'm glad to hear that an educated girl has made it into my employ. Johnathon will be most impressed." Mary laid the snuggly wrapped doll into the cradle.

"Have you met him yet?" Her veil swayed as she maintained her attention on Rose's confused expression.

"Met who?"

"Mr Rutherford? Did he greet you?"

Still confused, Rose opened her mouth but didn't know how to respond. She was told Mr Rutherford was dead. She wanted so badly to press the crawling feeling on her neck but clawed her fingers hard into the book instead.

Mary waved her hand, "Of course, he is away on business. Remiss of me to confuse you so." Mary tucked another blanket over the doll.

"Sleep now, my love." She kissed her finger tips and pressed them onto the doll's forehead. Mary lingered over the bassinet a moment before making her way to the bathroom on the opposite side of the bed. Whilst Mary was in there running taps, Rose peered into the cradle, a morbid curiosity overtaking her sense of propriety and the warnings of Mr Borgia.

A wrap of intricate white crochet swaddled the doll. Its eyes closed against rosy porcelain cheeks that possessed a shockingly realistic hue. A small silver crucifix dangled from the frame of the crib. Rose touched it, smooth and cold, she wondered how it may at all help, then let it drop away. She was drawn back to the doll, to the cupid bow of its lips, to the odd odour it perfumed. She leaned in a little closer but before she realised it, she was reaching in; her fingers barely grazed the cold of its cheek when everything went black.

Rose was falling, spinning out of control. Her scream was silent. She hit something soft. She was enclosed on all sides, walled in, but above, something shiny caught her eye. She wanted to reach for it, but her arms were bound. She tried to sit up, but her head was too heavy, and her body unable to follow directions. The warmth that cocooned her dropped to an icy bite. She focused on the shiny object. It swayed, shimmered in a faint light that was snuffed out. Darkness pressed in. Rose heard a scratching noise, felt whatever she lay on shift. A groan, a gurgle, an altogether horrifying cry edged closer. All she could do was look up and watch the curl of bony fingers over the edge of whatever she lay in. She concentrated harder, felt a scream build in her chest. The fingers slid in, followed by tufts of wiry grey hair. Her heart beat so fast, too fast. A forehead shiny and bone-white, eyeless black sockets peered coldly at her. Rose screamed until her chest burned. Sound erupted from her mouth, but her cries were not words or even her own voice. They were the screams of a newborn. The ghoulish head dipped over the edge of Rose's confines; a tooth-filled mouth opened. Rose screamed louder, felt her breaths sucked into the maw now hovering over her helpless body.

Rose was back in the bedroom, heart thundering, head swimming, a spring of sweat across her brow. She pulled her hand from the crib, and one of the doll's eyes rolled open. Rose jumped away when Mary's footsteps clicked along the floor. Rose spun around, hands balled under her chin, her skin tingling. Mary stood stock still.

Rose was about to be let go; she knew it. She had broken the rules twice already. She could still feel the vision sucking the life from her, wondered if she should, in fact, just pack up and run. Mary cleared her throat, and Rose prepared for the consequences.

"Do your chores, read the chapter, and you may set my hair after luncheon."

Mary brushed past Rose like a breath of wind, swiftly picked up the doll and retreated back to her workroom, humming contentedly as she climbed the stairs.

It was clear in Rose's mind that she would lose this employment before the day's end. So far, she had overstepped the rules all too easily, and realised the folly of thinking she could be at all capable. Try as she might, she could not understand how to fashion mason curls. She had read the chapter a dozen times, set out everything she found in the bathroom in an orderly manner before Mary appeared, lace flowing ethereally. But her mind was reeling from the vision. She struggled to concentrate, tried to put it down to an overactive imagination, the expectation that everywhere she went, darkness would follow. But there had been no shadows, no lingering things. She was overtired, overexcited, and told herself it was just that.

Mary sat on the chair Rose had set up in the bathroom.

"When you are ready, Dear."

Apart from Mama, Rose had never washed another person's hair before. The idea was altogether too intimate, and Rose felt her heart quicken as Mary prepared herself. Mary pinned her veil in a manner that allowed most of her hair to be seen, but her face remained hidden. Shoulder-length ebony hair, with less grey than Rose had imagined, draped into the washbasin. Mary leaned back, made herself comfortable, sighed. Rose lay a linen towel around her shoulders.

"Is that alright?" she asked.

"Most comfortable. Commence." Mary nodded sharply.

Rose had boiled water over the hearth and filled the basin in a dozen lumbering trips. She had set out all the bottles of sweet-smelling soaps she had found in the bathroom cabinet.

"What lotion do you prefer?" Rose held a few bottles up, Mary pointed to a small brown one with a smudged, illegible label.

"The Rosemary oil, please. It keeps the bad humours at bay. That is why it mists the rooms and hallways."

"Is that why you burn so much essence, to keep the bad humours away?"

Mary nodded. "Yes, Dear." She leaned further back against the basin. "Bad humours are one with the fabric of Rutherford House, it's best to go on the offensive, Dear."

Rose paused; a lid part unscrewed. "You mean the rats?"

"Of course, Dear, yes, the rats. Commenced now." Mary waved a hand at Rose.

Well, Mr Borgia had mentioned rats a number of times. Perhaps they did not like the herbs that so richly perfumed the house. Rose frowned, set the bottle down and filled a porcelain jug with water.

She tipped water over Mary's hair, her fingers awkward, tangling amongst the strands. She poured a little Rosemary lotion onto her hands, circled it through the hair. Rose began slowly, her movements light and unsure.

"One must *feel* the cleaning, Dear."

Rose rubbed a little harder, adding more of the rich lotion. She swirled it around until Mary wore a snowy bubble crown. Mary raised a hand.

"Rinse now and quickly, my darling cries, I must attend him."

Rose's fingers stilled, tangled in Mary's hair. There was no baby crying, but she wasn't about to contradict her. She didn't want to think of the doll.

"Of course, Mary." Rose quickly poured more water to wash the suds away.

"A spritz of that." Mary pointed to a small bottle by the basin. Rose squeezed the atomizer, smelled the richness of rosemary again. She towel-dried Mary's hair expediently and dotted some more oil through it, rubbing it in quickly, leaving it glistening. The rosemary aroma was clean and fresh but also reminded Rose of Mama's lamb pie, her belly grumbled.

"Thank you, Rose." Mary settled her veil back down over her hair, a towel still draped about her shoulders. She left with a hurried step.

Door ajar, Rose wiped her hands and watched Mary reach into the crib.

"Arthur darling, Mother is here." She rocked the doll, brought it up to her face. She set a kiss upon the doll's head through the lace. Mary sat upon an upholstered chair; it creaked underneath her. She fiddled with the front of her dress, undid a button, then another. Rose nearly fell back when she saw what Mary did next. The front of her dress flapped down; she lowered her undergarment and exposed a breast. Mary placed the doll to a withered nipple. Rose nearly dropped the basin of water she was about to empty.

She set the basin down, stood at the bathroom door, fingers curled into the doorframe, mouth agape and stared. Shame flamed Rose's cheeks, but a mix of horror and curiosity shoved all her decency to the side. Mary interrupted Rose's voyeurism when she called out.

"Josephine? Where are you?"

Rose pressed her lips thin; her nails dug a little harder into the wood.

"Josephine?" Mary sounded more urgent; her voice different... breathier than before. Rose split a nail against the frame.

"My hair seems to be wet. Were we caught in the rain again? I'm cold, Josephine. Bring me a warm blanket, will you?"

Rose looked around the room, as though this could be some kind of jest, but no one was there to laugh at her expense. It was just her and a visibly distressed Mary. Rose drew a deep breath, wiped her hands dry, picked up a clean towel, and hung it by the hearth for a few minutes whilst Mary continued what she was doing with the doll.

"Please hurry, Josephine. Why can I not recall how I became so wet?"

"Um… I just washed your hair." Rose struggled to pull forth a response.

"You did? My word, I must say, the effects of childbearing really do take their toll!" Mary laughed lightly, "I fear what I may be like once Arthur is toddling. Will I have lost all sensibility?" She laughed again.

Rose felt the towel to be warm enough and made her way back to Mary, faltering with every step, her eye caught briefly on the Frangitelli Mirror at the end of the bed.

"Mary?" Rose held the towel up for her to see.

"Thank you, Josephine. Dry me off; a simple chignon will do. I've no plans today."

The air felt like molasses; Rose pushed through it, wondering if she may be dreaming. She pinched herself; her skin stung. She was surely awake. Whilst Mary pulled the doll from her breast and tucked her sagged skin back into her clothes, Rose rationalised that these oddities were a million times preferable to the shadows. She could cope with the unusual, the strange, just not the dark and the wicked.

As Mary tucked the doll into the crib, Rose pulled out the dressing chair, picked up a brush. Mary sat down, rested her hands in her lap, and stared straight into the dresser mirror. Of course, Rose couldn't tell, because of the veil, if she was looking at Rose or just herself.

"Just a chignon?" Rose asked. "Not mason curls?"

"What on earth would I want those for Josephine? We aren't going anywhere special… or are we?"

"No… we… er… are home for the day." Rose answered.

"Well then, on with it, dear Josephine."

Rose brushed Mary's hair until it was tangle free; the warmth of the towel on her shoulders had already dried the ends. She folded the hair into a bun, and as she was pressing in a pin the clock struck one, the deep boom of it made Rose jump. She dropped the pins left in her hands, picked them quickly up, ascertained they were not required and replaced them into a wooden container on the dresser.

Mary prodded at her hair. It thankfully stayed in place, but Mary's fingers stiffened as they felt every crooked rise and fall of Rose's handiwork.

Rose glared at her own hands as though they were a mortal enemy. Her belly swirled; bile lapped in her throat. The ache of hunger was still too present, the touch of cold gripping her in the night still thick on her skin. The shadows in her room clawed through her mind reaching towards her, searching for her location. Rose opened her mouth, about to spill an apology for her inexperience, beg for a second chance, scream for mercy, and not be sent back home to where the dead things were...

"Lovely as always, Josephine." The way her head tilted, Mary seemed to be looking at Rose through the lace of her reflection, an image repeated too many times in the mirrors behind them, beside them... everywhere.

"Let me see it." Mary passed a hand mirror to Rose.

Rose held it in such a way that Mary's hair reflected into the oval of the dressing table mirror.

"Look how it shines; Rosemary oil really does the trick. I learned that from my Great Grandmother, you know... she had hair like silk and nary a grey hair, even on the day she died." Mary picked up a small metal jewellery box and flipped the lid open. It squeaked as though unopened for some time. A string of pearls threaded through her fingers, the luminescence of them accentuated by the blackness of her gloves.

"These will do nicely." She passed them to Rose, who had never felt such luxury. The small creamy pearls slid across her palm. They were cold and smooth, her fingers hooked around them, the clasp glimmered with a diamond setting. Rose's jaw clenched; she imagined the rent this could pay, the mouths it could feed.

"Don't dally; set them on now, will you?"

Rose eased the pearls around Mary's neck, careful not to disturb the veils.

"Mother said pearls were for mourning, that they were the tears of angels, but Johnathon, he says they make me shine like the angel I am." *But he was dead,* Rose recalled, her skin prickled. *What was wrong with this woman?*

"Quickly now, I don't want to miss the carriage to town! Go pick me an evening gown, choose whatever you think is fit for a grand occasion. I am to sup with the mayor," Mary waved Rose away.

"But …" Rose stopped herself; Mary had returned to thoughts of leaving. Rose clasped her hands and hesitated, but as she really had no understanding of the routine, she decided to go with the fluctuations of Mary's demeanour. Mr Borgia had made it clear not to contradict her, so, in order to ensure she stayed employed more than a day, Rose made her way to the armoire, trying desperately to ignore the myriad of reflections of herself, to avoid the sucking attention of that great mirror at the end of the bed.

She turned a small silver key to open the door. Confusion fell over Rose as she shuffled through the garments within.

Every dress, shawl, and stocking were exactly the same as what Mary was currently wearing. A dozen black gowns with accompanying lace veils hung neatly pressed, smelling of whatever eked from the bulbous pomander that hung next to them. Accessories were neatly folded on shelving to the left, not a splash of colour to be seen.

"Um. Mary... er… are you happy with black?"

"Of course, it does compliment my figure. Choose what you prefer, though, Josephine; any colour shall do today. Johnathon adores me in anything." Mary pushed out of her chair, checked on the doll in the crib, opened the doors to the day room and disappeared within it.

Rose sighed and pulled a dress out, "Well, that's a nice shade of… black." She closed the armoire, followed Mary into the day room. It was a large room, airier, the balcony doors open, a welcome breeze lifted the strange thickness of the air in the house.

She eyed the pianoforte again, only now noticing its lid was plastered with a mirror too.

So very odd.

There were a number of settees and armchairs. A tapestry stand sat to one side by the windows, she assumed to capture the best natural light. Rose wandered by it; dress draped over her arm. Half complete, the tapestry was a teddy bear cushioned upon a bed of flowers, the name Arthur stitched along the bottom with a birthdate.

April 4th, 1905

12 years ago? Was that how long Mary had been mourning a lost child? Had she been in this state of mind all that time?

Rose felt tears prick the back of her eyes. She knew loss, understood the gnawing pain of death. Matteo and Papa's images flickered through her mind. Rose wondered if she might end up like Mary, alone and living in a world split between the present and the past.

A coldness suddenly demanded her attention; the caw of crows turned her to the balcony. Mary's silhouette cut sharply against an overcast sky, and her clothes billowed in the wind.

Rose followed; the smell of rain thick upon a misty air now devoid of that momentary sunshine. Fog probed along the ground, fingers of it climbed the brickwork, slithered across the tiled balcony and towards the doorway, as though seeking entry. It curled around her new shoes. The cawing made Rose hesitate; she stopped at the doorway, poked only her head out, the curtains snapped against her face. A crow sat upon the balustrade. It shuffled left and right, peering up at Mary. Its glassy eyes held an intelligence, a knowing… and a hint of amber. It made Rose think of the old woman and the book.

Surely that's not Devil?

Mary seemed unaffected by the fog, the crow… by anything. The crow tapped its claws along the balustrade, edging within reach of Mary.

Rose swallowed hard; her words seemed so difficult to get out.

"Mary, your dress is ready."

Mary turned around, the wind tugged hungrily at her veil, but she held it in place.

"Dress? What dress?"

Rose frowned. "You asked me to get you a dress to wear, to go into town, to meet the mayor?"

Mary seemed to go rigid, her head tilted towards Rose as though she were staring at her in confusion. Rose shifted the dress, laying it from one arm to another.

"The mayor? What on earth are you on about, Dear?" A gentle laugh trickled from her. She waved her hand. The crow took flight, circled around and back again, landing closer to Mary.

"You *are* the new girl; it is understandable that you will take a little while to become accustomed to the routine. What is your name again, Dear? I am so forgetful, what with being a new mother."

"It's Rose, Ma'am."

"Ah, yes, Rose, a favourite flower of mine. I adore white ones. Johnathon's' mother was named Rose… such a pretty name." She raised her head, Rose thought she heard Mary sniff. "Rain is on the way. I think I will take a rest and read whilst Arthur is settled."

"You don't want to go into town now?"

"Town? Goodness, the air there doesn't at all agree with me. Bad for the complexion, all that smoke and dirt." Mary rested her hands upon the balustrade, her shoulders lifted as though she was drinking in a large breath. She reached for the crow, and it leaned into her hand. She stroked it; it made a sound akin to a purr. Mary stood in serene stillness; frost glistened upon her veil, it sparkled upon her shoulders. She didn't seem to shiver as Rose did.

"Are you sure you do not wish to change?" Rose asked.

"Tend your duties. What a fuss you make. But I do desire some tea, Dear."

Rose retreated from the balcony, glad for the hug of warmth within, away from the crow but surrounded again by the mirrors. She stared a while at the crib, promised herself she wouldn't dare touch the doll again.

There was something very odd about this place, something very wrong with Mary. This was a house with secrets, everyone was right about that, but what family didn't have secrets… Rose surely had one of the worst?

She pushed aside the lace curtains, watched from inside, and wondered what exactly Mary was thinking as she gazed over the winter-laced gardens. Did she have more moments in reality or in the past? Rose sighed to herself.

"You don't have to understand her; just do the job, get the money," Rose mumbled, turning away, glad for the empty corners, relieved that Matteo was not hiding behind the furniture. Despite this house being stuffed full of wealth and strangeness, it held a satisfying emptiness of other things.

Rose thought she best clean up before sourcing tea. She hung the dress away, patted Heathcliff, who was slinking about her ankles whilst she made her way to the bathroom, where she began to tidy up. He followed her all the way, the others nowhere to be seen.

She emptied the wash water, rinsed the tub, leaned against the green porcelain basin, cloth in hand, ready to polish the mirror.

She reached for the reflection, her fingers trailing its edge where time had spiderwebbed fine cracks in the glass, small fields where only darkness lingered. Within these imperfections, Rose's attention was drawn deeper. The slightest flicker of movement, a shadow within a shadow out of the reach of the silvery grasp of the mirror's attention. She was reaching to touch it...

"Rose?" Mr Borgia's voice made her shudder, she stumbled back, knocking over the rosemary oil. "Damn!" She muttered only loud enough for herself to hear. She scooped up the bottle, set it on the vanity next to the basin, and quickly sopped up the oily puddle as Mr Borgia called for her again.

Rose wiped her hands, exited the bathroom, her attention fleetingly upon Mary, who sat once more at the dressing table, doll in her lap.

As though he instinctively knew what Mary desired, Mr Borgia held a silver tea service; he set it down on a table next to the great mirror. *How odd he, the caretaker, serves her tea?* Rose thought.

"I have come to take you to Martha. It is time for your tour of the rest of the estate." He poured a steaming cup, lay a biscuit on the saucer, placed it directly in front of Mary; not a word was exchanged. Mary reached for the cup and discreetly lifted her veil.

"Have you settled in?" He glanced between Mary and Rose.

Rose nodded, "Of course, Sir." She heard the wobble of her words and knew she didn't fool him in the slightest.

"May I ask a question?"

"Of course." He held another tray in his hand with what appeared to be breakfast dishes upon it.

Rose pointed to the Frangitelli Mirror. "Is it an heirloom as well?"

He quirked a brow. "Somewhat. It was gifted to Johnathon Rutherford some years ago."

"This may sound strange, but it has a feeling about it…" Rose's words faded as she watched Mary, in its reflection, slip a biscuit under her veil.

"Indeed, it does." Mr Borgia stared at Rose a moment too long, his attention lingered between her and the mirror. The quiet pause made her feel uneasy. Rose shuffled; her fingers clenched repeatedly.

Mr Borgia cleared his throat, and smoothed his hair. "It was crafted by a master glazier hundreds of years ago. Senore Frangitelli of the island of Murano. Some believe he had a touch of the occult about him, that his mirrors were more than just mirrors." A hint of annoyance washed over his face when Rose frowned at the story.

"Who are we to say what is true or not? I did not create the Frangitelli Mirror, but whatever it is or does, it brings solace to Mrs Rutherford."

Rose wondered how a mirror could bring one comfort when it seemed to bare her very soul when it caught her eye.

"How…" She was cut off, Mr Borgia, clearly done with the topic, turned away and headed to the hall.

Rose was still caught in her reflection. The Frangitelli Mirror seemed to drink her in, suck something from her, as though it saw right into her. Whilst Rose was intoxicated by the call of the mirror's depths, Mary quite unexpectedly screamed and jumped from her chair, her teacup rattling in its saucer.

Mary dashed to the crib, fumbled through the netting, and pulled the doll into her arms. She looked to the ceiling.

"Get out! Get Out! Leave us alone!" Mary wailed hysterically and ran back towards the Frangitelli Mirror just as Mr Borgia hooked his arm through Rose's and pulled her out of the way. There Mary stood, her reflection a pattern of wailing black lace on every wall. Her voice an incoherent warbling interspersed with a clear and frightening cry, "Stay…away!"

Rose's knees locked, her mouth a desert, every hair erect. She looked to Mr Borgia, who placed a finger to his lips and guided her quickly down the hall, and out the door.

CHAPTER 20

"What is wrong with her?" Rose pulled away from Mr Borgia, she rubbed the warmth of his touch from her arm.

"She looked terrified… she… she…" Rose knew she was babbling, but she couldn't keep quiet after what she had just witnessed.

"It is normal, nothing to be alarmed about." His voice was coarse, with no hint of concern for Rose's worries. He headed towards the alcove. "She may have seen a rat; they do scare her."

"A rat?"

He unlocked the main doors.

"Be sure to tell me if you see a rat, especially at night. They are most difficult to eradicate."

He locked the doors behind them.

"This appears to be a good time for you to take in the rest of the estate with Martha." Mr Borgia waved her on to follow and descended the stairs.

Rose stopped at the base of the stairs, one hand clutching the banister, the other against the uncomfortable flutter in her chest. Rose was hoping she wasn't about to ruin everything and be plummeted back into dodging the dead.

"That… that is not normal, Sir. How…" She shrugged, palms out. "I'm not equipped to deal with such behaviours. Should she not see a physician? Someone to soothe whatever troubles her? Believe me, Sir, I need this position, but I'm not sure I know how to alleviate such… Mary's… um… worries." Her nails dug into the banister and sunk into the grooves scratched deep into the wood.

"Rose, I can assure you, Mary is just unsettled today with you arriving." He waved his hand and made his way past her, opening the door to the servant's staircase.

"Please Rose, this way." There was no compassion in his eyes, yet no judgement either. There was no care to help Rose understand, just a cold hardness blunting his previous warmth. Rose glanced all the way down the hall towards the front door; her attention slid to the empty corners. Incense burned thickly, it misted the ceilings, with no hint of death on it. Clocks ticked; wind rattled the windows. The floors did not creak, the doors did not open of their own volition. Rose ran her fingers along the grooves over and over. Troubled woman or ghosts? Endless sleepless nights hiding the truth from Mama or this?

Rose followed the retreating echo of Mr Borgia's steps down to the kitchen.

Martha was nowhere to be seen, but the kitchen smelled richly of chicken soup, and that satiating sense cemented the answer to Rose's dilemma.

I can learn to accommodate Mary's quirks. She suffers from loss, as do I. I will find a way to attend to my duties and allow her to cope however she sees fit.

Rose, in some way, felt better. This must be the source of the rumours that had plagued the town for years. Past servants clearly had spread the unkind stories and conflagrated the Rutherford's private matters. No doubt it was robustly fanned by the effervescent tongue of Miss Ray.

"You may wait here; I will be working in the library should you need anything before the evening." Mr Borgia walked away, stopped, hand on the doorframe.

He turned back, he rubbed under his nose with a knuckle, then laced his fingers together in front of his stomach.

"Mary has moments of what the doctors call hysteria. She will scream for no particular reason, most often at night. This is why her rooms are kept locked and illuminated at all times. Mary fears the dark as you have been apprised." He stared hard enough to make Rose look away, study the dusting of flour on the floor. The silence between them extended so long that the discomfort forced her attention up to see if he was still actually there. Mr Borgia was staring over her shoulder, up to the slit of window to where a crow paced, bending its head down, eyeing them both.

"I assure you, Rose, it doesn't happen often and is something you will adjust to, or you will leave." His tone was so cold she felt its bite. He left without another word.

Rose stirred the soup while awaiting Martha. She worried on the strangeness of Mr Borgia. The crow tapped the window with its beak every so often as though it sought her attention. The lights flickered; a door slammed.

"For the love of..." Martha clutched her chest and put down a laundry basket. "As if there isn't enough to bring on an old woman's demise without you sneaking about!"

She leaned on the bench, dabbed a sheen of sweat caught in the middle-age hairs atop her lip. Martha wandered to the stove, took the ladle from Rose, stirred and sipped the soup.

"Pass me some thyme." Martha pointed to a dried bunch hanging overhead. Rose obliged. Martha pulled some leaves from the stalk and sprinkled them in and ladled a little soup into a cracked tea cup, "Here."

Rose sipped, pulled back at the heat of it, blew some steam away then let it coat her tongue. "Amazing," she said.

"Not as good as Mrs Denham's, but it'll do," Martha replied.

Rose set the cup down, wishing to fill it up a dozen times over.

"I expect his Highness wants me to show you around some more?"

Rose nodded. "Why do you call him that?"

Martha slipped off her apron, pulled a heavy woollen coat from a hook, took another and passed it to Rose.

"You don't mind it belonged to the previous lady's maid, do you?"

Rose shook her head and slipped the brown wool on, "Of course not." But she did wonder why someone would leave such a good garment behind.

"None of your business what I say to who and when." Martha looked Rose up and down, "Bold tongue on you. You do your job; that'll be all that needs speaking about." She frowned, buttoned her coat and turned away, muttering something inaudible. Rose rolled her eyes and silently mimicked Martha's words.

"My ears work perfectly fine, young lady. You'll watch your manners. Lucky his Highness can't keep staff, or that attitude would have seen your bags already packed. This way." She waved Rose towards the larder.

Rose clenched her teeth. She did not like this woman. She took a confident bet it was not Mary but Martha and *his Highness'* sour manners that caused a constant turnover of staff. She figured those people didn't know the ache of hunger or the pain of the cold. They couldn't possibly know fear. Rose wasn't afraid of a bad attitude, just of the things lurking at the end of Banksia Lane.

She followed Martha through the larder, which was a thoroughfare to a laundry.

"One of the few houses with an inside laundry; my arthritis appreciates it." Martha lifted the lid of the copper as they passed and stirred the contents. A hot blast of starchy air hit Rose. It reminded her of Mama, and she breathed a little deeper.

"You'll see to Mrs Rutherford's things and your own. You'll dust and tidy as needed upstairs. I've enough to get on with down here." The lid thumped back down. Martha pulled upon a heavy door to another set of stairs. "One person to pick up after won't see your time filled. I expect to see the place sparkling. No dilly-dallying, no daydreaming."

"Of course," Rose replied as Martha paused at the base of another set of stairs.

"Up here, this leads to the work yard and garden where you'll hang the clothes, dust the rugs and so forth." They reached a small landing lit by a square window in a pale green door, the paint of which was bubbled and peeled.

Light blinded Rose momentarily when Martha pulled on the door. She shielded her eyes until they adjusted to the dull glare of afternoon light.

"This way." Their feet crunched along a smooth pebble path. The air bit, the smell of nature upon its breath.

"This here is the vegetable garden. We grow what we can. This time of year, it isn't much more than lettuce and cauliflower. Herbs are over there. You'll help tend the garden; see to what I need from it." Martha hugged her coat tighter, pulled a scarf from her pocket, set it upon her head and knotted it under her chin.

The garden was well set out, with an orderly pattern of rectangular beds that were perfectly furrowed. The beds were well tended, but weeds crawled up the outside and snaked along the pebbles seeking the goodness of the manured soil. A rusty hairpin wire fence separated the garden from the rest of the estate. There was a sense of abandonment a mere foot from the vegetable patch. A dreary, mouldiness of time and weathering. Wearied garden tools leaned against the fence, a barrow full of rainwater filled by a leaking downpipe made a home for tadpoles and slugs. The step stones of the path lifted from the ground in awkward angles and Rose had to mind her footing.

"This way." The gate squealed when Martha opened it. Flapping wings had Rose glance up as the gate banged shut. A flash of black feathers disappeared around the corner. When they rounded that corner, Rose found Mary serene and still upon the balcony, a crow once more by her side. Mary's head turned as though she was watching them as they wandered past. The heaviness of that attention made Rose peer back a couple of times until Mary disappeared from view behind the rise of a large gum tree.

"You stay on this path, you hear? It leads to the orchard and arbour, where Mrs Rutherford takes the air. You come off it this time of year, you'll likely sink in the mud. You venture out on your own too close to dusk, it's as dark as Satan's backside, you'll not find your way back," Martha said.

Rose didn't respond. She absolutely would not do such a thing, she was, after all, running from the dark.

Martha walked on, her pace brisk for her age. The air chilled the further they went, mid-afternoon light fading, the clouds more bilious and threatening rain. The wind nipped at her dress and tugged her cap. Rose held it down as the weather began its dark song. It whistled through wattle trees, some with the first cottony yellow buds of Spring. The smell of moss and damp hung upon the air as the path eased toward a large lake, its water lapping at rusty rocks around its perimeter.

The tree line thickened the further they walked; the green expanse of orderly lawn eased into a more natural leaf litter-strewn ground. Branches creaked and groaned. The air was full of nature's voice… and something else… crows. They skipped from tree to tree, following along, cawing amongst themselves.

Rose hugged herself and increased her pace.

One flew down. It swooped at Martha.

"Argh, blasted things!" She waved it away, her scarf hooked on a claw, and was claimed by a gust and whipped along its current.

"Are you alright?" Rose ran to her and reached out, but Martha slapped her hand away.

"Stop your fussing." Martha smoothed her hair, she peered over her shoulder, eyes redder than before. She glared at the offending crow on a thin branch overhead, her scarf flapping wildly on the end of it.

"Shoo!" Martha waved, but the crow just tilted its head, eye keen upon her, or both of them.

"I've told *him* we need a groundsman. Need a rifle taken to them." She pointed at the crow, then over to the others who sat apart in nearby trees. "Never had a problem until a few years back. Mr Rutherford saw to all the vermin, but since his Highness arrived, the crows have wrought nothing but havoc." Martha crossed herself and bowed her head reverently toward the island in the middle of the lake. The familiar arch of gravestones haunted its rise. A mausoleum sat proudly in the centre. The sight made Rose's belly clench. Martha moved on.

"Hurry now, I need to show you the orchard arbour so you know where to go, then we must hurry back. The night air is coming on quickly, and I'd like to keep my eyes." She grimaced at the crows then took the path to her left.

Martha pointed ahead to an avenue of hibernating fruit trees, an arbour at the end of it, shrouded with the gnarled stems of a slumbering jacaranda.

"Up there, do you see it? That's where Mary likes to take a book and have some tea."

Rose nodded, attention still caught on the island, wondering who was buried there.

"Of course, when the apples are ripe in a few months, I'll need you to fetch some on occasion. Best you know where to go and how to be quick about it."

A spittle of rain began. Clouds raced along the sky, bruise-like hues promising more miserable weather. The wind sucked them along faster by the second, its moan loud and urgent.

Martha tapped Rose on her elbow.

"Best be on our way back. No one wants to be out here after dark."

CHAPTER 21

Rose and Martha crested the hill back towards Rutherford House. Mary was no longer on the balcony now that the rain pelted hard drops down Rose's neck. They made haste, leaving the garden gate ajar as they rushed to the back door.

Rose's boots skidded on the gravel path; she grabbed her stomach, and leaned against the house; the vine that seemed to hold it all together now held her up too.

She groaned at the sharp sting slicing through her guts.

"Not now," Rose whimpered as wetness seeped through her undergarments.

The backdoor hit the house as Martha wrenched it open, only turning when she heard Rose cry out in pain.

"What is it, Lass? Hurry up out of this weather!" She didn't move, but when Rose's tear-filled eyes looked her way, a knowing look softened the hard angles of Martha's face as Rose pressed between her legs.

"Is it your courses?"

Rose nodded, unable to speak.

Martha dashed back, put an arm around Rose and guided her back inside.

Once in the laundry, Martha sat Rose on a stool, pulled a basket from a far shelf, rummaged through it until she had a pile of pressed linen cloths. She filled a bucket with water, sat it in front of Rose and passed over one of the cloths.

"Clean yourself up." Martha's mouth softened, almost into some form of sympathetic smile. Rose took the cloth; she didn't know what was worse, the humiliation of having her drawers down in front of Martha, or each stabbing pain that bent her double.

"I had bad ones back in the day too, no one likes to talk about such things, so most of us women tend to find these things out the hard way. My Ma took me to a doctor who diagnosed me with hysteria, much like Mrs Rutherford, damned doctor wanted to lock me up. Fools are men. Wouldn't know a womanly pain from the back o' their arse!"

Rose stopped mid-twist of a cloth as she dipped it in the water. Her mouth pained, trying to repress a giggle.

Martha shook her head, and soaped up a fresh cloth for Rose. This time, a smile did lift her cheeks, her eyes held a wistful gleam. "Luckily my Ma was a sensible type, she had me sent away to cousin Edwina; that's how I found my way into service at Norlane Hall. Edwina taught me how to cope with the bad monthlies when they visited." Martha emptied the washbasin into the trough and Rose quickly removed her undergarments and balled them up so as the blood was hidden and dumped them in a soaking bucket next to the copper. She wiped fresh blood from her thighs, but it flowed on; the sight of it made her nauseous. She leaned forwards, elbows on her knees.

"I'm sorry, Martha, it comes unexpectedly and not often."

"Don't need apologies, just a solution. Edwina knew a thing or two about nasty courses. Runs in my family... perhaps yours too." Martha handed Rose fresh undergarments and an older uniform in a pale shade of grey. "I expect the shock of moving away might have brought it on." She nodded and helped Rose into the clothing. "These will do for now. You can finish dressing yourself then meet me in the kitchen. You will see to your own laundry in the morning." Martha left; Rose could hear the sound of china tinkering.

Rose slipped a wad of linens into her fresh drawers and finished buttoning up the clean dress. It was a little tight but clean and dry. Her whole body ached as she entered the kitchen. Two cups of black tea already steamed hot on the bench.

"Sit, drink."

"It's not a good start to my employment."

"Drink and stop your worrying on things out of your control. It is what it is, Lass."

Rose did as she was told. The coarseness of Martha had softened, something a little more kindred in her manner.

Perhaps she doesn't hate me after all?

"Getting old has its challenges, but I've never missed that," Martha nodded resolutely, stirred the still bubbling soup pot, then chopped something by the sink.

"Chew on these," Martha dropped an inch of ginger and a sprig of fennel into Rose's palm. "It'll help the pains." She nodded encouragingly, "You've a tough job here looking after Mrs Rutherford. Best get on top of the pains quickly, can't have you infirm now, can we?" She waved her hand impatiently at Rose, urging her to eat the herb and root. Rose's tongue burned but in a pleasant way. The ginger was fresh and especially strong, the fennel a little like a liquorice. She chewed until it wadded into a fibrous ball and swallowed with a sip of tea.

"Go back to your room. Mary will not be wanting anything now until she needs dressing for bed. I'll do it for you just this once. Rest tonight. Tomorrow, if you've got the pains, you know where to find these, and you can tend to your own personal matters," Martha pointed to a clay pot of ginger root and fresh fennel fronds in a glass vase.

"Thank you, Martha," Rose said, the pain easing a little.

"Don't thank me, Girl; this is a thankless position you've got yourself into. You must really need the wage. For your sake, keep your head down, do exactly as you're told, and you might last the week. I'll not baby you any further." Martha made an annoyed *hmpf* sound that erased the small feeling of warmth Rose held for her in that moment. She disappeared up the hall of deserted servants' quarters, returning with another pile of cloths.

"That's all I have, no one else here your age, so you'll make do with what I've given you, you understand?"

"Of course." Rose missed her mother more in that moment and felt guilt strike through her for leaving the way she did. Mama had been gentle with these matters, understanding. Martha… well, she looked to show an act of compassion but erased any kindness before it could settle in.

"Thank you, Martha." Rose took the cloths and slowly made her way upstairs.

CHAPTER 22

Rose sat bolt upright; bed covers tangled about her feet. She had no memory of falling asleep, and still felt the hand of exhaustion upon her. She leaned forwards, the pain in her belly still gripped like a fist. She grimaced, took some slow deep breaths, and pressed her hand against her stomach. She found her glasses in her lap, fallen from her face in sleep. Rose slipped them on and looked about her room.

It was dark... too dark. Everything Mr Borgia said it should not be. *These rooms must always be light. Mrs Rutherford does not like the dark.* And neither did Rose.

Lightning flashed through the window, a white sheet across the sky. Thunder crashed too close; the house creaked under its power. She peered outside. A storm raged, the outline of the gardens pulled and tugged by it. Rain blurred the window, but the silvery crescent of the moon appeared momentarily behind a bustle of rushing clouds. It shone a blue hue through her room before blackness claimed it again.

Apart from Mother Nature, all was still, all quiet, the type of quiet that unsettled Rose, the type of darkness that set in her bones and made them shudder. But... she wasn't at home; the shadows here were empty, the ghosts far away.

Yet still, the dark was not a comfort, and she wished for light like she hungered for a meal. Rose yawned, wiped the grit from her eyes, slid from the mattress, and felt her shoes click on the floor. She was still dressed. She fumbled for the hearth, followed the gentle smell of old embers. Her hands ran along the floor until they found the kindling bucket. Her fingers wrapped around a small strip of wood. She dipped it in the deep orange of the embers, took the flame about the room, lit the lamps and found the light switch. The brass toggle snapped a couple of times.

"Hmm." Nothing happened. With the electric out, Rose returned to the hearth, chose the plumpest two logs and set them on the embers in a pyramid, poking gently at them until a hungry flame took a bite. She sat by the heat, watched the flickers grow, and relished the strangeness of easy warmth and comfort with minimal effort.

With the room now warmly glowing, she unbuttoned her boots, stockings still damp from when she was in the garden with Martha. She stood and pressed the pain in her stomach; it was swollen and sore but not quite as bad as earlier. She went to the washstand, splashed cool water on her face, and utilised the linen cloths Martha had given her. She pulled on a night dress, held up a candle and looked at her reflection. Her cheeks were flushed, her eyes a little glassy, but despite her courses giving her grief, just a day at Rutherford House, with food and warmth, the gauntness of her complexion already seemed lessened.

Silvery snippets from the other mirrors caught her movements, so she pulled a towel from the wash stand and the lace coverlet from her bed and obliterated the stare of the two that looked upon her bed.

"Better." Now, there was just one reflection. A normal room, with normal things, no shadows, no ghosts, just comfort and sleep.

Rose tidied her bedclothes but something seemed tangled in them. She shook the sheet and a thud sounded on the floor. Rose gasped. By her foot lay the book. Its ancient pages lay open, words she did not understand underpinned a symbol... the same symbol on the keys to these rooms, the one adorning the frame of the Frangitelli Mirror. Rose kicked the book away, slapped her hand to her mouth, looked around as though someone or something might see. Of course, she was alone, the corners were empty, the air not fetid. *How did that get out of my bag?* She wondered. *How did it get in her bag in the first place?* She countered her own thoughts.

Rose stared at the book a while. The glow of the fire made its pages tarnish a deeper yellow, they flickered under the draught of the hearth. Rose fiddled with her glasses, chewed her nails. She dashed forward, snatched it up, opened the wardrobe and stuffed the book roughly back in her bag and slammed the door. The hearth hissed; the room glowed a little brighter for a moment. She stood a while, glaring at the wardrobe, her heart raced. Thunder startled her and Rose backed away until her legs hit the bed. She sat.

The clock by the nightstand sat at 8:17 pm, well past Mary's retirement. Rose eyed the door and the wardrobe; she rationalised that checking in on Mary was perfectly acceptable and not a childish need to escape her room and the book. She really should see if Martha had indeed seen to Mary's nightly ablutions as she had promised. She took a centring breath, her nerves settling. On her way to the door, the firelight glinted upon something. A silver tray was set on a small table behind the mirror at the foot of her bed.

Her stomach rumbled. Martha, perhaps wasn't as cold-hearted as she'd seemed. A round of sandwiches were covered with a doily, another sprig of fennel and ginger bulb sat on a saucer, all neatly laid out, along with a pitcher of water. She smiled, ate a sandwich point, enjoying the soft-boiled chicken, leaving the herbs for later, just in case. She was tempted to eat the rest when a scream shattered the silence.

"Josephine? Josephine? Where are you?" Footsteps pounded outside her door.

Rose ran from the room, her door slamming behind her. She shuddered to a stop, bedazzled by the intense glare of the mirrors in the hall. It was worse than when she arrived; someone had lit dozens more candles. Rose shielded her eyes until they adjusted to the luminescence.

"Help, help, Josephine!" She dashed to Mary's room, and pushed open the doors. Heathcliff and Cathie were arch-backed upon Mary's unmade bed. They hissed, not at Rose, their eyes trained upon the ceiling. Another set of eyes glowed green underneath the bed; it must have been the third cat.

Mary was nowhere to be seen. Rose pressed her knuckles to her mouth, heart thundering when moments ago she was calm, peaceful... almost happy.

"Mary?" Rose called; hesitation tempered her voice. Mary's bed was a mess; the covers spilled onto the floor. The cats howled; her skin prickled. Rose followed their gaze to the ceiling. The loops of drapery moved as though a breeze were present behind it, but the air felt still. Nothing was there. The cats circled each other, leapt down, and all three scattered in different directions. One through Rose's legs, out to the hall, one under the armoire, and the other, a ginger, into the bathroom.

Rose held her breath and listened for Mary, there was no sign of her, the crackle of the hearth filled a heavy silence, full and rich. However, there was another sound just under the pitch of the crackling logs. Scratching, the etching of nails or claws, the scuttling of feet.

"Rats," Rose whispered, her eyes upon the ceiling again, her face screwed in disgust. She followed the sound past the Frangitelli Mirror, averting her eyes from that dark vessel upon the table.

There was a bang above her head; Rose startled, hand on her chest.

"Mary?" She looked up, followed the skittering within the ceiling, seeking the flash of a rat tail. Past the hearth, she found herself wide-eyed, then squinting deep into the sharp angle of the cornice, one of the few tiny places the mirrors failed to penetrate, one place that held a shadow that seemed… occupied.

Something moved, a flicker of something pale. Cold coiled around Rose's ankles, despite the robust hearth a mere few feet away. She watched that corner intently, quashed intrusive thoughts and unwanted memories.

"Josephine!" Mary screamed from somewhere behind. The thing in the shadow moved; it fell to her. Rose screamed and stumbled back onto the bed. She flapped at her face, breathless, slid to the floor and began to laugh hysterically.

"Moth… it's just a moth!" Her head fell into her hands, and then she pulled herself up to find herself face to face with the silhouette of Mary.

"Rose, what are you doing on the floor?" Mary asked, calmness drenched her voice.

"I… um… I heard you calling… screaming. I came to your aid, Ma'am, but could not find you."

"You intend to aid me whilst on the floor?"

Rose still felt the bite of cold; the doors to the day room were wide open, the curtains through the balcony licked into the room, caught in the howl of the wind that rattled the house. Mary moved towards the crib.

"I do not scream, Rose, I am not at all sure what it is you think you heard. But, since you are here, I'll take water, please." She picked up the doll, kissed it and laid it back down, "May the angels bless your slumber, darling Arthur."

Rose pulled herself together, poured a glass of water from a pitcher on a bedside table. Mary slipped the glass behind her veil, a white one, matching her all-white sleep attire. She passed the empty glass back and swung herself upon the mattress.

"You may tuck me in now."

Rose did as she was told. There was no explanation as to where Mary had been, and Rose did not ask, lest she provoke another episode. Mary set her arms upon the neat fold of the bedspread as she settled into her pillow.

"Light an extra pillar, Rose, it's far too dark."

Along with the electric lights, there were dozens of candles licking darkness away, all of which were magnified by the mirrors. Rose searched, an empty candlestick in hand.

"In there," Mary pointed to a chest next to the dressing table.

Rose flipped a brass latch, eyes wide at the contents. Hundreds of candles lay in neat piles, each neatly wrapped in a sliver of brown paper with the words… *Finest Beeswax* stamped on it. Rose lit two slim candles and placed one on each side of the bed.

"Would you care for anything else, Ma'am?"

"That will be all, Dear," Mary lay in a death-like repose, hands clasped atop the covers. Rose backed away, turned to leave. Cathie reappeared and leapt onto the bed, curling instantly around Mary's feet.

"Rose?"

"Yes, Ma'am?"

"Do not call me Ma'am; it is Mary. Goodnight."

"Yes, Mary," Rose blushed for yet another faux pas, and curtsied. She closed the door behind her, entered the dayroom and leaned against the wall, breathing heavily.

"Be patient. She's traumatised," Rose whispered to herself, rubbing her temples.

She made her way to the balcony to shut the doors to the weather, she grabbed the curtains as they snapped wildly in a frigid draught. She reached through the material… to find the doors were closed. Rose tested the handles; they were locked, the key in the slot, turned to the left. The curtains fell limp, the cold dissipated. She backed away, felt the drain of her blood tug at her consciousness.

Pain surged like knives in her belly again, joined by rolling nausea. She arced over, pressed her hand into her belly, peered quickly around the warm ambiance of the room. The corners were clear, there were no shadows. Rose shook her head. "Stupid," she chastised herself and made her way out of the day room, a last unsure glance back at the stillness of the room as she pulled the doors closed.

Mary was as still as a corpse laid in state. The bed linen rose and fell, Mary's breaths the regular slow rhythm of sleep, Heathcliff curled by her side. The third cat was tucked in a ball by the hearth, she made her way to it, kneeled and stroked its back. It looked up at her, blinked sleepy eyes and mewed. A silver collar told her its name.

"Goodnight, little Romeo," Rose tickled under its chin and stood to find Cathie cleaning herself in front of the Frangitelli Mirror.

Such a strange place.

Sleep called earnestly to Rose. After years of restless nights, curled up in terror, she could finally slide into a bed and close her eyes, rest her mind, no longer afraid of the shadows. She shut Mary's door, her body aching for rest.

CHAPTER 23

Rose found her room with the electric lights blaring. She flicked the switch, they went on and off easily, unlike previously.

"Hmm." Exhaustion weighed upon her limbs; her eyes stung. There was no energy left to wonder on the strangeness of the day. She picked another sandwich from the tray, the bread was a little dry, but she ravenously ate it in a single mouthful. She washed it down with more water and made a beeline for the bed where she readjusted the garments that she had thrown over the mirrors.

"Better." She smiled once the mirrors were thoroughly covered. All be it her own image, it was unsettling to catch glimpses of her own movements, like ghosts of herself were watching.

Rose slipped into bed but immediately felt another tug of pain in her belly. She eased out of the soft warmth again, bleary-eyed, back to the platter, reaching for the relieving herbs. Her hand came up empty, she patted around and sighed.

"Silly." Rose shook her head, made her way back to the bedside table for her glasses, she polished the lenses on her sleeve.

But when she returned, glasses on, vision clear, the herbs were nowhere to be found. She looked under the table and around the general vicinity.

"Huh?" She tapped her lips, wondering if she had already consumed them? The ache was not as bad as earlier, tiredness the worse of the two sensations, so she slithered back under the sheets, pulled them up under her chin, set her glasses back upon the bedside, and, for the first time in so very long, closed her eyes at night.

Sleep was difficult. Despite a warm bed, the comforting glow of the fire and light burning the shadows away, Rose tossed about for hours. It was the noises, the flurry of feet scurrying within the walls, scratching claws dragging across the ceiling. Rats. Mr Borgia had warned her of them. The noise was incessant, but at least the storm had ceased; no more did the gale claw at the window. After laying for hours, sleep cruelly eluding her, Rose gave up, the rats just too much. She unwillingly forced her eyes open. Her lashes gluey, she rubbed them with the back of her hand whilst she reached for her glasses. She patted the bedside table twice, but her glasses were not where she had left them.

Pushing herself up, she rubbed her eyes again, tried to clear the blur and squinted. The table was empty but for a simple white doily. Frowning, Rose was sure she had set her glasses directly onto that doily. She patted about the bed, on the floor near her slippers, and then down the small space between the window and the bed.

She bit her thumbnail, gasping when the sheer lace that dressed the window moved. She reached out, flicked it aside, thinking a rat was scurrying along the windowsill. Nothing was there but the pearlescent glow of the moon at its zenith. She sighed with relief but felt the familiar rise of goose flesh on the back of her neck. Her head snapped to each corner of the room. Nothing, there was nothingness in them.

"Stop it," Rose pinched the bridge of her nose and shook her head. She sat a moment, attention upon the frost that haloed the window pane. She eased onto her knees and squinted at the velvety darkness outside. The gardens below were nothing but blurred shapes bathed in the gentle blue light of midnight. She felt awake now, annoyingly alert but not wanting to leave the delicious warmth of the bed. But she slipped from the covers, padded about the room until she found her glasses on the washstand. She put them on, and peered around the now crisp room, eyes set upon the bedside table. She was positive she had left them there.

She shrugged. It had been a big day, so much to absorb, it wasn't surprising she may have misplaced them in the rigours of exhaustion.

Rose cracked her door, tip-toed to Mary's room and peered in, her reflection caught in the Frangitelli Mirror again. All was quiet in this strange room of glass and light. She shut the door and wandered to the window at the end of the hall. The roofline of the long stable row drew her eye outside. Beyond murky darkness was a world without light where shadows thrived. She shivered, glad to be where she was, relieved to be rid of what had haunted her beyond the gates of Rutherford House.

Rose pushed the drapes further aside and followed the line of the driveway from the stables all the way to the silvery glisten of the lake. The island upon it was a dark blob, the mausoleum and graves hidden within the night's embrace.

Movement in the corner of her eye had her sweep her eyes back. A light bobbed in and out of the gardens, crossed the drive and cut across the expansive lawns. She leaned in, forehead against the chill of the glass, her breath misted against the pane.

A lantern swung left and right, the person holding it blended with the shadows leaching across the lawns. Then the light disappeared as whoever possessed it passed beyond a clutch of trees. Clouds banked in front of the moon, its light momentarily cut off, leaving the estate indistinguishable from the starless slick of the sky.

Hands now splayed upon the glass, Rose ignored a renewed scurrying in the walls, eyes wide, searching the thickness of the night. The golden light flashed here and there, like a firefly probing the dark. The clouds parted, leaving a thin strike of moonlight across the gardens.

The silhouette emerged from the bony clutches of dormant trees close to the house. The lantern bobbed more erratically as whoever held it moved swiftly. They came to a stop, something silvery flashed, making Rose wince; she lost sight of whomever it was.

The moon reappeared in its fullness as the clouds drifted away. It dampened the shadows, revealing the crisp outline of the gardens once more. Rose searched for the light, she saw nothing but skeletal treescapes and bushy blotches. As she let the drapes drawback across the window, she glanced down to find the glimmer of the lantern directly below, the shadowed figure looking directly up at her.

CHAPTER 24

Rose collapsed, sank to the floor, gasping. The rats increased their fervour, marching through the ceiling. The electric lights flickered, the candelabras in the breezeless hall flared.

She pulled herself up just enough that only the top of her head breached the sill. All was shadow and gloom again, the moon lower in the sky. The lantern, the person… nowhere to be seen.

Rose pushed away from the window and eased Mary's door open once more. Mary slumbered, her breaths slow and even, all three cats now purring upon her bed. The hearth was low, the room a little cool. She tiptoed in, rushed past the attention of the Frangitelli Mirror, and ever so quietly set another log upon the grate. The embers hissed, their flame claimed the wood, its orange deepened and Rose backed quietly away. Cathie raised her head, one eye open a slit, and mewed gently, then lay back down.

Rose rounded the table that sat in front of the great mirror, made it past, hand upon the door when something made her stop. She looked back. The garish bony ornament was gone. The intricate lace doily on which it sat bare. She paused a moment, thinking that perhaps Mary had decided it indeed was too horrific to look upon in an otherwise beautiful room. She wouldn't miss it and let it sift from her mind.

Rose checked the main door; it was locked, she pressed her ear to it, all was quiet beyond. She turned to shut the second set of doors leading to the hall, but something hooked her attention on the sideboard below the dumbwaiter.

A slice of ginger and withered fennel frond was set directly in front of the sealed service elevator. Rose frowned, wondered if, in her bleary-eyed state had she moved them or had Martha sent up extra? She shook her head, picked them up, slipped a sliver of ginger onto her tongue and made her way back to her room, enjoying the heat that oozed down her throat.

Rose found the lanterns out in her room again. She lit them once more, still needing their comfort despite the lights that blared overhead. She took a small bite of the fennel, not particularly enjoying its flavour, but the pains were so much better than earlier, so she chewed, grateful for the ease.

She removed her glasses, folded the arms, and most assuredly set them on the bedside, this time next to the remaining herbs. She slipped back into bed, groaning with relief. Covers tight, she checked the corners of the room habitually, and felt comfort in their emptiness. With the stranger outside still on her mind, she stared out the window and let the smooth flow of clouds lull her into sleep.

Rose woke with the call of the rooster. A smudge of red-hued dawn told her rain was likely again, but even with the prospect of dreary weather, she felt a lightness long forgotten. She yawned, reached for her glasses, and felt the herbs but nothing else.

She pushed herself up and rubbed her eyes. The rooster crowed with a more enthusiastic gusto as she patted over the bedside table.

"Where on earth…?" She rubbed her eyes again, slipped to the floor, and caught the blurred smudge of her face in the mirror at the end of the bed. She grimaced and tugged the makeshift coverings back over the glass where they had slipped away.

"Hmm." She frowned. Seeing a hundred visions of herself was like being haunted by her own shadow, a ghost of herself, and she'd had quite enough of movement in the corner of her eye. The relief Rose felt in less than a day was immense, and she planned to maintain that ease. Whilst

Mary's rooms were a nightmare of reflections, her own room would not be.

Satisfied, she narrowed her eyes and searched again for her glasses, shivering as the hearth was nothing but ash.

For no other reason than its where they'd turned up yesterday, Rose made her way to the washbasin, and there they were. She frowned again, bit her lip as she slipped them on, instantly seeing everything sharper.

"Strange." She put it down to her courses; when they did arrive, she was never quite herself, she often felt as though her mind was filled with a fog. Perhaps she'd got up during the night again and forgotten? Pouring water into her basin, she splashed her face; the cold of it brought a rosy flush to her cheeks. She cleaned her teeth and freshened up her body with a dusting of talc before dressing. Her belly remained bloated but not as uncomfortable as the previous day. She twisted off a small wedge of ginger and chewed on it whilst she buttoned up the old dress Martha had given her.

Rose did pay attention to her reflection in the washbasin mirror. Where once she'd dreamed of grander plans than service work as a child, she felt a warmth run under her skin. It felt like pride. She nodded at herself. Yes, she was proud to have found a way to help herself, support her mother and put the hauntings in the past. While some felt service work to be a low pursuit, Rose felt taller, braver, and stronger.

The rooster crowd more heartily, the sky outside now haloed with the rising sun. Rose was smoothing down her uniform outside Mary's door, Mr Borgia's instructions fresh in her mind.

Wake Mrs Rutherford at 8 am.

She searched for a clock, catching her own face too many times glaring back from the walls. A small cuckoo clock between her room and the hall window announced it was 7:15 am. She leaned closer to it, wondering if it may be broken as the little blue cuckoo bird dangled in front of the glass dome of the clock face, its paint scratched, the arm that once pushed it in and out stretched out of shape. The clock still ticked; the second hand moved smoothly around its repetitive life cycle. The sun was low on the horizon, and a morning frost still hugged the gardens, so she assumed it to be correct.

Tapping her lips, she wondered if it was too early to enter. Slipping Mr Borgia's instructions from her pocket, she read the rest of the notes whilst she considered this.

Set her breakfast out; it will be left by the service elevator for you.

Tend the tidying of her room whilst she takes breakfast, then you may take your own with Martha.

Mid-morning, if the weather is not inclement, offer to take Mrs Rutherford for a turnabout the orchards. Otherwise, she likes to read a book.

Lunch is served strictly at 1 pm. You may take yours with Martha after Mrs Rutherford has finished.

In the afternoons, Mrs Rutherford will spend time in her art room. Leave her to this and tend her laundering.

Dinner is served at 5 pm. You may take yours in your room as Martha will have left for the evening. The ground floor will be off-limits at this time.

If you have any concerns, I can be found in the library or in the evenings in Mr Rutherford's rooms across from Mrs Rutherford's.

Rose folded the notes and slipped them back into her pocket. She gently pushed Mary's door open and poked her head through the crack. All was quiet other than the many clocks ticking wildly out of unison. The closest read 7:18 am. Mary slumbered; the covers pulled tight. The cats all now balls of fluff in front of the dying hearth.

Rose entered and felt like an intruder in someone's sacred and private space. She stopped at the table in front of the Frangitelli Mirror. The ghastly ornament had returned. Had she imagined that it had been missing? She shook her head, pushed it from her mind, not wishing to look upon the terrible thing.

She tiptoed past the bed. The crib was close by, Mary's hand dangled over the edge of the bed as though she'd been rocking it before falling to sleep. Rose dared not look into it, let alone touch the doll as she had yesterday.

The chill of the night still curled around her heels and she worried that Mary might feel it more keenly than she did. Wanting Mary to be comfortable when she awoke, Rose stepped past the cats and set about tending a morning fire. Setting the logs upon the ash, she pulled a sliver of kindling from the stack, lit it on a pillar candle that sat upon the mantle, and set the flame to the wood. It took a moment to catch, and when it did, she leaned in and blew gently on the flame until it bit comfortably into the wood.

Rose took a brush and pan, swept ash from the floor and tipped it into a copper pail to the left of the now crackling hearth. The pan caught the pail and made a loud, reverberating sound. Rose winced, hunched her shoulders and held her breath as Mary groaned. She rolled over in bed towards Rose, the white sleeping veil slipped from her face.

Rose dropped the brush and pan; this thud startled Mary awake. She sat bolt upright. Their eyes met; Rose's mouth bone dry. Mary's corpse-like complexion held no hint of emotion. Hollowed cheeks sagged beneath prominent bones. Pale lips pressed into a thin line, her chin may or may not have quivered. Mary blinked a few times… from the one eye that was present. She lifted a hand, set it across the deep red grooves that gouged the left side of her face, the side with an eye socket grown over with thick, shiny scarring. Without a word, Mary pulled the veil back into place and lay back down.

The rooster crowed, its sound now mocking, laughing at Rose's foolishness, her ineptitude at being quiet, discreet. Rose had no breath, her fingers splayed, eyes on the door, wondering if she should leave, say something, or stand there like a fool?

It must have been some time that she had been frozen, for she heard the doors open and the tinkle of porcelain on a tray. Her uniform was hot on her back, where she had stood too close to the growing fire. Mary remained still, but there was a distinctly faster rise and fall of the bedclothes. Mary was most definitely awake, the strained silence too much to bear. Rose moved away, sweat ran down her neck. The clocks all struck the half hour in teeth-grinding disunity.

"Blasted things," Martha grumbled as she pushed through the still-open doors and set breakfast on the table. She startled when she saw Rose.

"You trying to frighten me to death again? That's three times now!" Martha hissed through her teeth and took a cloth from the pocket of her apron and fanned herself.

"You're too early; she's not yet awake."

"But…"

"No arguments, you wake her at 8 am promptly, not a moment before or after."

Martha set about sorting the breakfast. "Thought I'd bring it directly in to help you just this morning. Tomorrow it'll be by out there on the sideboard as usual. Pay attention now to see how she likes things."

"Won't her breakfast be cold?"

"The Misses takes a cold porridge, and this pot keeps her tea warm enough. She likes her napkin folded just so and placed with the cutlery to the right. Sees it better that way."

Rose felt she understood why Mary might need help with her vision, having witnessed her unexpected appearance only moments ago.

The clocks seemed to tick louder as Martha set everything out with precision. A doily-covered porridge bowl sat perfectly in the middle of a linen placemat. A rose-painted tea cup with a gilded rim to its right, the handle facing precisely to the east. A small milk jug in the same design as the teacup to its immediate right. Three lumps of sugar were placed upon the saucer, with a delicately small stirring spoon.

"There now. All in easy reach, just as she likes it."

When Rose remained silent, Martha looked her up and down, hands on hips. "You look peaky; what is it? Need more ginger, fennel? I've a touch of laudanum, but I fear that'd put you out for a week, and that wouldn't do at all." Martha arched her brows, awaiting her answer.

Rose shook her head

"It's not my courses," Rose whispered, a little embarrassed. She didn't know this woman and had only ever spoken of such private things with her mother.

Mary moved in the bed; the mahogany creaking underneath her. Rose's hands rolled together, and she peered back over her shoulder; Mary seemed to be asleep again, her breaths slow and deep.

"Out with it then," Martha whispered; her fine nose held a sharpness that seemed to slice her face in two.

Rose moved close to Martha, unwillingly paying heed to her reflections. To the right, the left, in front, her own self stared back, pale, worried, eyes too wide. Martha seemed completely unaffected. She sighed and rolled her eyes.

"I've no time for your histrionics. I've got work to do, as do you." Martha's words were tight, impatient. She picked up the tray and headed out the door. Rose followed quickly.

"The mirrors?" Rose blurted in a louder whisper.

Martha halted but didn't turn around.

"I saw her… just now. Her… um… Mrs Rutherford's…" Rose felt a sweat spring above her lip. She was embarrassed to ask such questions, it was unseemly, and Martha's demeanour seemed to leach any semblance of kindness with every mumble Rose made.

"What I'm trying to say is…" Rose licked her lips; they were so very dry. She pushed her glasses back up her nose, over the small bump in the middle.

"Why would Mary want so many mirrors when she…" Rose twisted her hands until her fingers reddened. "When she… she covers her face all the time anyway?"

Rose couldn't bring herself to mention the actual scarring, the eye socket that seemed to glare at her with its emptiness. She didn't dare ask how it had happened.

Martha's shoulders rose and fell as she took an impatient breath. She did not turn.

"Be careful of what you ask in this house. You may well find you do not like what you hear." Martha walked out and shut the doors behind her, leaving Rose alone, speechless and afraid.

CHAPTER 25

"Josephine? Where are you?"

Mary's panicked timbre reverberated up the hallway where Rose polished one of the numerous mirrors, awaiting the clocks to strike the hour.

She found Mary in half undress; her linen undergarments stained brown. It was still ten minutes short of 8 am. She hadn't heard Mary rouse. Heathcliff threaded through Rose's legs; Cathie lapped at the floor under the breakfast table. Romeo still slumbered by the fire.

"Oh, there you are!" Mary threw her hands in the air. "Arthur cried quite suddenly. I spilt my tea everywhere." Mary pointed to the armoire, "Be a dear; choose me something pretty and some fresh unmentionables."

Rose suppressed a smile, curtsied and opened the armoire, gathering stiffly starched 'unmentionables' and a fresh dress.

"Will black do today?" Rose asked.

Mary stopped by the cradle, checking the doll within the crib.

"I suppose it will have to do if that's all that's come up from the laundry." She then clapped her hands, 'Let's take a turn about the orchards. It does settle Arthur so, and I could use some air. Black at least will not show the muck about the hem."

Rose curtsied and set about undressing and dressing Mary. Once the buttons were tended on her shoes, she handed Mary a fresh black lace veil.

"That should keep the sun from your skin."

Mary halted, head turned to Rose slowly, in such a movement that the hairs on Rose's arms lifted. It was a thing to behold to never see someone's face, to not know their expression, to have only their voice and movement to read their intent.

Mary stared uncomfortably long, ran the veil through her gloved fingers, her breaths audible, rapid. She bunched the veil and then seemed to shudder as though coming out of a trance.

"Of course, so thoughtful of you. One must tend one's complexion." Mary set the outer veil upon her head, picked up the doll, and wrapped it tightly.

"After you," Mary indicated towards the hallway.

"Now? What about your breakfast?"

"No time like the present. Johnathon may be home soon. I like to be available to him, and he does so miss Arthur when he's away on business. This morning I dine on life and love."

"Of course," Rose nodded, and followed Mary's brisk pace out and down the hall. She unlocked the main doors to the staircase, let Mary out and locked up behind them. Mary walked on ahead. She moved with a liquid silence; her body seemed to float, her black dress trailing behind.

At the base of the stairs, Rose heard voices up the hall. Mary waited at the front doors, repositioning the folds of her veil, cooing all the while at the doll she held.

As Rose approached the library, she heard someone speaking, one of them all too familiar. She quieted her breaths and lightened her step. The doors were open a crack, and she caught a flash of red hair, a peaked cap stuffed in a back pocket. Eric was shaking Mr Borgia's hand.

Her pulse rushed in her head. The echo of love for Eric that still pressed from the depths of her mind was squashed with the heat of anger. She leaned her ear closer, her nails bit into her palms.

"You can start today?" Mr Borgia asked.

"Yes, Sir." Eric's voice was light with excitement. He pulled his cap from his pocket and circled it through his fingers as he habitually did.

"Very good. It will be nice for Mrs Rutherford to see the gardens tended once more. I'll see that Charlie sets you up in the old stable house. Martha?" Mr Borgia waved his hand at the door, calling for Martha, eyes squinted at the sliver of hallway through the crack of the door. Rose nearly fell backwards; she twisted from view; absolutely sure he'd seen her.

"Martha will see to your meals and laundry. You will meet her soon enough, don't let her sharp tongue worry you. She's like that with everyone."

"Thank you, Sir. I appreciate this opportunity. You don't know what it means, Sir."

"I do indeed, Mr Wright. I do indeed."

Footsteps had Rose scuttle to the front doors, her shaking hands fumbling with the lock.

Mary remained oblivious to the goings on, humming a lullaby. Rose felt the weight of someone's attention upon her back.

She swallowed, twisted the door handle, and ushered Mary out. She was set to close the door and get on with her duty, but the rush in her head and the clench in her belly made her look up.

Eric was staring at her as the door of the library clicked shut.

Eyes locked for a moment, Eric nodded at Rose, he opened his mouth to speak as he pulled his cap on…

Rose slammed the door shut.

Distraction pulled Rose from her task, Eric's surprised expression when their eyes connected imprinted in her thoughts. It was Rose who followed Mary along the path around the back of the house. Martha appeared, leaning over the fence of the veggie patch, carrying a basket of freshly picked vegetables. She waved at Rose.

"It's still wet out, Girl. Mind Mrs Rutherford doesn't slip."

Rose nodded, eager to keep moving, not wanting the flush of her anger to be noted.

She followed a quick-paced Mary through a flock of happily roaming chickens.

The sun shone a wintery heat, melting the tension that gripped her body. As they turned down the path towards the lake, Rose's thoughts settled into two tracks.

Because of their last meeting, she quite irrationally settled upon the former and allowed anger to fan like a wildfire. It was always the easier emotion. It ran its course with little effort, required nothing of her… but that was a lie. Rose felt it drain her, draw all her energy stoking its hunger, yet, she pounded her steps behind Mary, her teeth clamped, choice words collecting in her memory banks for when Eric had the misfortune to next cross her path.

A pleasantly blue sky streaked with clouds brought a Spring-like feel to the gardens. It settled the emotion that clawed up her throat. Rose almost smiled at the splash of emerging buds upon a circular rose garden. Mary left the path, crossing into an untended patch of grass splashed with white patches of early jonquils. Bees circled busily above these buffets.

"Mary, aren't we going to the Orchards?"

"Yes, Dear, I just wish to visit Josephine first."

Rose frowned, confused, but was already used to these quick changes in Mary's perceptions. She followed on. Why Mary would find Josephine in the gardens, Rose couldn't imagine. She supposed it was just another one of her idiosyncrasies.

Mary crossed onto another gravel path, her pace quicker, yet she still maintained that illusion of gliding. This new path skirted the opposite side of the lake. Large gumtrees arched across the path, immediately dropping the temperature and dappling the light. Rose hugged herself, wishing now she'd brought a shawl.

Mary bent, plucked a jonquil growing at the base of the rocks that fenced the lake in. She continued on towards a bridge. As they neared, the wind picked up, its melody brushed through the trees, joined rather harshly by the call of a crow that fluttered overhead. Rose felt the beat of its wings, a surge of air as it swooped down, sure that it grazed her cheek; a soft featheriness made something twang in her chest. An image of the book flashed in her mind.

Her hand flew to her skin, her cheek warm, smooth, unaffected. The crow cawed once more and settled upon the metal balustrade of the approaching bridge. It cocked its head at their approach, ruffled its feathers and shook; its amber-flecked eye followed Rose, not Mary. Rose looked away as their heels clacked over greyed wooden slats, her heart aflutter for a different reason. Some wobbled underfoot, Rose grasped the cold of the balustrade, old paint splintered into her skin, and she pulled away. She felt uneasy, her head light as murky lake water lapped hungrily below, churned by the wind that now sang a more forceful note.

She shivered, stepped gratefully onto the solid ground of the island and followed Mary around a wiry hedging that was in dire need of a trim. Devil zoomed past, cawed and disappeared over the hedge.

"Nearly there," Mary said lightly, as though the darkening sky, the chill in the air and Devil bore no effect upon her. Rose thought of the warm hearth that awaited her when they returned, of closed windows that crows could not breach and hurried around the corner of the hedge…

Rose stopped, a shudder ran through her, and her blood ran cold.

CHAPTER 26

Mary knelt and laid the jonquil in front of a weathered gravestone. It lilted deeply to the left.

"Forgive me. It has been too long," Mary picked at bushy grass claiming the lower half of the gravestone.

"Arthur has been so very fussy; he keeps me up all night. I've been so tired, but that really is no excuse, my dearest Josephine," Mary's voice withered into a whisper; she stilled her weeding, hugged the doll closer.

Rose stared open-mouthed. Mary bowed her head; her words so soft Rose could no longer hear them. All the while, she rocked the doll, tending it so very carefully. Her reality seemed a blur of what was and what wasn't.

Rose stood well away, not wanting to encroach on a private moment. Her attention swept across a number of graves with Rutherford etched into the stones. Some stood tall and proud, and others lurched as though the ground was slowly swallowing them. Behind them all was a mausoleum on the far end of the small island.

Josephine's grave was set apart; its stone held a gloss to it that suggested it wasn't as old as the others. Curiosity got the better of her manners, and Rose edged close enough to read the words upon it.

Flynne, Josephine
Faithful
Servant of the Rutherford Family

Rose read the epitaph again. Josephine was dead… and buried on the estate. Her fingers dug into her palms; she didn't feel the sting on her skin. The air chilled to ice.

High turnover over staff… is this what happens to their staff? They die?

Rose stared between the grave and Mary. *Did she do this to Josephine?* Rose stepped back, all manner of images flashing through her mind.

Mary hummed to herself, still pulling weeds, oblivious to the dread that now pressed upon Rose. The wind gusted, Devil returned upon it; it circled, sailing on an updraft. Rose watched the crow, it eyed her from above, swooped towards Josephine's grave, as though to emphasis it.

Go away! Rose thought, stumbling a little further back, away from Mary, away from more death, away from questions she wasn't sure she wanted answered. Devil cawed coarsely, flapped its wings twice and arced over the mausoleum. It disappeared for a moment, then rounded the old structure from the offside, its feet grazing another little grave, then onwards past Rose once more. She gasped, ducked, flicked at the bird, grabbing her glasses just as they were about to fall from her face.

"Go away!" she hissed. Rose wanted to yell, but didn't wish to startle Mary, or somehow aggravate the bird further. It finally settled upon the small grave with a tiny metal fence. This almost innocuous, simple little grave seemed to interest Devil, and, for some reason, Rose felt compelled to know more about it.

Mary remained deeply occupied tending to Josephine. Rose didn't want to hear any more of her mutterings about the doll to the dead, so she wandered amongst the other graves, pretending to pay no heed to the crow. Habit forced her to search for shadows behind this stone, beyond that one, under a great eucalypt that overcast half of the island. She looked for the dead to ensure they were exactly where they should be… below, not above the ground.

Her skin did not prickle, her blood did not run cold. Tension dripped away. There were no shadows, no odours, no movement, nothing coaxing her towards darkness. It was just a collection, mementoes to loved ones long passed… and a dead maid, but Rose quickly rationalised she could have succumbed to anything. Yet that crow and the tiny grave it guarded had some kind of pull that she felt unable to ignore any further.

Devil shuffled more excitedly across the small grave as Rose approached. It cawed, head low, tapped its beak on the face of the gravestone. *You do want me to look at it, don't you?* The thought made Rose feel utterly ridiculous and she halted. The crow stretched its wings, shook its shiny feathers, it tapped its beak more enthusiastically on the grave as though it heard Rose's thoughts.

The wind whipped a little harder, blew the clouds from the eye of the sun. A stream of pale light struck the crow and glanced from its eyes. Amber eyes, knowing eyes, eyes like Mr Borgia, eyes like Rose and her father.

Rose pushed her glasses up her nose, they slipped straight back down a nervous sheen on her skin. She felt a little breathless, and pressed her hand to her heart. It hammered against her palm. For a brief moment, the corners of her room didn't seem quite so sinister. The crow bobbed up and down with more gusto, its claws tapping like typewriter keys. It seemed excited, as though it was trying to tell her something.

Ridiculous.

Yet, intrigue urged Rose to move towards the little Marble cross within the fenced plot. The cross leaned heavily to one side, just like Josephine's grave. The crow flapped its wings and paced more excitedly. Rose moved with apprehension, unsure what exactly was driving her; fear, excitement, outright idiocy?

The wind drew in more clouds, the sun once more hidden.

Rose licked her lips, but her tongue was dry. She checked over her shoulder; Mary still tended to Josephine, a thick wad of weeds in her hand. Rose kneeled before the small grave, one hand rested upon the cold steel of the picket fence encircling it. The earth was concave in front of the cross, somewhere underneath a coffin claimed by the ground. She reached forward, an irrational quake in her hand. Rose pushed aside the grass that climbed like ivy around the little cross.

A simple inscription, the carving lacked the finesse of the gothic devotions on the other stones. Rose pressed a hand to her heart as she read the words that lacked the affection of Josephine's grave.

Rutherford

The sun breached the clouds again, highlighting smatterings of scratches in the stone cross. Rose reached for them, letting her fingertips sink into their depth. *What in the world…*

Her vision greyed around the edges, something curled in her gut; she yanked her hand away, her fingertips powdered with marble dust. As she wondered what wild animal clawed at grave stones, Devil called its coarse song, took flight, and swooped low enough that she felt the breeze tug her cap. Rose ducked, toppled forward across the little fence, and fell into the grave. A wave of terror washed through her, a momentary vision of a bone-white face hovering over her, just like when she had secretly touched the doll. Rose rolled away from the cross and over the fence, her dress catching and tearing at the hem. The moment her skin lost contact, the vision faded, and her sight sharpened.

Hand on chest, she sucked for a breath and fell onto her backside, awaiting the thrash of her heart to settle. She gathered up her skirt, found the hole, it was small, nothing a short length of thread wouldn't fix. Rose looked up; humiliation already set in with her predicament. Mary was no was no longer at Josephine's grave. Rose scrambled up, flicked her dress back down, she turned around… to find Mary standing right behind her, silent and all too still. Rose yelped.

"Mary!" Rose curtsied.

"I am fatigued. Arthur needs feeding. I wish to leave," Mary said flatly.

Rose curtsied again, "Of course." Rose followed Mary back towards the bridge, one swift look back at the tiny grave of the real Arthur Rutherford.

CHAPTER 27

After Rose finally ate a late, cold and stodgy porridge, the afternoon passed with silence between Mary and herself. Mary 'fed' the doll, then retired to her art studio. Rose tended the laundry, stirring clothes through the starchy water of the copper. Her belly pained her again, but she had too much to do, so she tried her best to push through the slices of heat that endeavoured to double her over.

Rose remained unsettled by the visit to the family plot. She stirred the linens faster and faster, her mind frequently returned to the vision, wondering why Arthur had a single date upon his gravestone. She couldn't help her mind wander into dark thoughts as to what had happened to Josephine. The distractions meant she dawdled with the laundry, realising she had yet to drain and roll the clothing as the clock struck midday. She dumped the clothing into a rinse tub, rolled the excess water off as quick as her arms would wind, and hung everything on a wooden drying rack instead of the clothesline. It was sure to rain again, and she didn't want to have to re-wash everything.

By the time she finished, Rose took a moment to rest in an alcove under the stairs on the ground floor. After resting a while, she stood to leave, but her attention was hooked by voices drifting from the library. Despite herself, she was drawn to eavesdrop. She edged along the hallway, passed by stuffed heads of this and that, skirted around hall tables packed with ornaments she didn't recognise. They caught her attention with images and writings of far-off places she could not comprehend.

The air remained thick with incense; it threatened to draw forth a sneeze. She pressed her hand against her nose, felt a tickle, and wished it away.

Mr Borgia's voice travelled well enough that she could hear the anger in it. His accent deepened, he spoke a mix of English and Italian. Rose replaced a wooden ornament beset with shells back onto a side table that her movement toppled, and pressed her back to the wall. She edged a little further until his words were clear.

"I understand that, but I am bound. I cannot leave her here; I owe it to her. You understand this. We are few this far from home, but this one… I know this is the one. She can help me save Antonietta."

Rose frowned. *Antonietta?* Mr Borgia was a caretaker, why was he speaking of saving someone who didn't even live here?

He then spoke even faster in Italian. His tone desperate. Rose didn't understand much, not until English began to pepper his distress again.

"I know she sees them; I know it. Her familiar … *e un corvo*. It has told me what she sees. She can bring this damned thing to an end."

Rose held her breath, her glasses fogged. She polished them on her apron, then edged a little closer.

"She has yet to declare herself. It won't be long. *Io sono sicuro*… she has the sight; I can smell it on her. I want nothing more than to return home *Cara Mia*. Please be patient, just a little while longer. You understand I must right what has been wronged?"

There was more arguing in Italian, his words softer, his voice hitched with emotion. Rose searched her memories, trying to recall the little Italian Papa used to speak. Corvo… her eyes flashed wide. *Crow*. Rose's fingers curled into the wall; her shoes whispered across the floor, a little closer to the library doors.

"I have insurance should there be any resistance. Please, believe me, Angelica, I want to come home, we will be a family once more, I promise."

Something banged.

Rose jumped, fists tight, eyes closed, imagining Mr Borgia rushing out to find her frozen form just waiting to be dismissed on the spot.

He did not. Mr Borgia mumbled rapidly under his breath; these words were definitely vulgar ones she'd heard Papa utter more than once. His footsteps paced heavily; the floor creaked under him.

"Dio!" Mr Borgia snapped. "Antonietta, why have you done this?" There was another bang.

Rose was shaking but moved just enough to her right that she could see through the crack of the door. *Bang, bang, bang.* Mr Borgia slammed the receiver of the telephone against the edge of the desk, his normally serenely poised face red, his hair astray. Documents slid from the desk, a small brown book amongst them. A book with a crow upon its cover.

Rose stared at it; her eyes grew wider by the second. The cover, the golden crescent moon, and the crow blazoned across it. How did he have her book?

A hot sweat ran down the small of her back, her thoughts a chaotic blur. Rose wanted to move, wanted to run to the door, open it and flee… but to what? Back to the ghosts and the shadows? Back to skin and bones? Back to a paltry life where she had no control over anything?

Her thoughts quickly ran over Mr Borgia's conversation as she slid back from the door.

Bound? What did that mean?

She rubbed her head, forced her breathing to relax, and tried to make sense of things. She fanned the heat from her face, anger was not her friend, even though it tasted so very good. She overheard half a conversation; she couldn't possibly know what it was all about. Her understanding of Italian was poor; she probably completely misunderstood the words. But that book and the desperation in Mr Borgia's voice chilled her, it fanned something under her skin until her mind was cluttered.

Rose slipped her glasses back on, pushing them until they hugged her nose tight. She listened to his rhythmic pacing a little longer, imagined barging in and confronting him, to demand why he had her book, to ask who this Antonietta person was.

As she imagined such folly, she startled as the front door banged open.

In the glare of an overcast sky stood Eric.

CHAPTER 28

"Rosie?"

"What are you doing here?" Rose snapped and launched away from her position of eavesdropping.

"Glad to see you too." Eric half-smiled.

The conversation in the library dulled from her attention. Rose crossed her arms, walked a little closer to Eric, whom she now saw was holding an armful of cut wood.

"Anywhere else a man can get employment, but you choose here! I don't even get a day?"

The joy at seeing her drained from his face. Eric's cheek twitched; the scar of his ear reddened.

"Think what you want, Rosie. Mr Borgia came by yesterday. Said he was desperate…"

Rose laughed, "So, you jumped at the opportunity to get your spying off to an early start?" She crossed her arms, shifted her weight. She wished to be anywhere else in that moment.

Eric hoisted the firewood higher and shook his head.

"Yeah, I did, Rosie, Mum hasn't paid the rent in months. We received a letter to vacate the day you were interviewed."

Rose's smirk waned, she bit the inside of her cheek, focused on the floral patterns of the carpet runner.

"It's Rose, not Rosie." She turned, picked up the basket of clean laundry she'd dropped by the stairs and ran, two at a time, until she was leaning against the balustrade outside Mary's rooms.

"Damn! Damn, damn, damn it to hell!" She set the basket down again after hearing the front doors open and close. She rushed to the landing window and watched Eric head towards the stable block. Beneath his cap, she could see that he had cut his hair, his scars bare for all to see. Rose's fingers twisted around the curtains as she watched him disappear. Unlike Mary, whose disfigurement was hidden, mysterious, Eric now let his be seen. She released the curtains, and sighed. Some part of her unlocked, proud of him, scarring and all, but anger held older, more delicate emotions hostage. She shook her head; she couldn't let her heart rule. Rose looked back to the mirrored door, thought of why she was here. She felt the ivory clip Mama had gifted her, holding her bun together… holding what was left of their old life together. It was all to save her mother, to save herself, and she didn't need Eric as a distraction.

She ran to her room and threw her bag onto the bed, not to leave, but to make sense of things. She felt the vibration of its presence before she saw it… the book was still in her bag, unwanted, but still there.

"I don't understand." She plucked her lips, not touching the book, simply watching the way the light caught the golden crescent moon on its cover.

How did he take it and get it back here? Why did he take it at all?

She reached forwards, her hand grazing the edge of the bag, a mind to fling it into the hearth, but she hesitated. Rose peered into the empty corners of her room, back to the book, and she buckled the book safely back in the bag. Something itched inside her to keep it, just in case.

"What are you?" she mumbled before closing the wardrobe door upon the book that started a strangeness in her life she just could not understand.

With Mr Borgia's telephone argument and the book on her mind, Rose spent the afternoon tidying Mary's barely out-of-place rooms. Already a little less reactive to the mirrors, she polished a few more along the hallway but still avoided the black vessel whose image seemed more sinister in the eye of the Frangitelli Mirror. That mirror too, it sucked her reflection in, she couldn't walk past it without watching until her image disappeared from its eye. Something about it made her skin tingle.

Rose bunched up her cloth and dusted the table around the black vessel, eye on her reflection, her little finger twitched, tempted to reach out and touch the mirror's frame.

"Stop it," she chided herself, her hand circling harder on the same over-polished spot of teak. Rose looked beyond herself, at the reflection behind, noticing Mary in the day room, shuffling a deck of cards. Mary set out her cards for another round of Patience.

Mary faded when Rose's knuckle tapped against the base of the black vessel. She jerked back, a strange urge to reach out and touch it again itched under her skin. Rose looked down, studied the outline of herself in the gleam of the polished table, but her fingers inched back to the table centre.

Her fingertips slipped towards the doily upon which it sat. Her palm was sweaty and stuck a little as it glided across the wood. It was a momentary caress, so quick she wasn't sure she'd even made contact, but her skin stung, burned like she had grazed a flame. The sensation raced up her arm and set her heart at an uncomfortable pace.

Rose sucked the affected fingers until the feeling subsided. She retrieved her dropped cloth, eyes glued to her reflection in the Frangitelli Mirror once more, attention drawn to the space between the mirror and the roof; one of the few areas free of the silvery watchmen. In between the sweeps of red fabric was the black, pressed metal roof. She pushed her glasses up and squinted. She thought she could see scratches, jagged and every bit like claw marks.

Rose's knuckle bones squeezed tight and pearlescent against the dust cloth, "What on earth?"

"Ah ha!" Mary clapped. Rose shuddered and spun around as though caught doing something she shouldn't.

"Ma'am... uh, Mary, is everything alright?" She curtsied.

"Yes, Dear, I just finally made Patience game." Mary held up the pack of cards, complete in their service.

"I'll have a book now, Dear, before supper. See what you can find in the library."

Eyes still caught upon the ceiling, Rose headed into to the dayroom, towards a bookstand opposite the pianoforte.

"No, something from downstairs, Dear. I've read everything in here a dozen times over."

Rose checked a small gilt mantel clock over the hearth. 4:30 pm. The windows revealed a sinking daylight, the horizon already blushed with the deeper blues of encroaching dusk.

"Are you sure, Mary? Is there nothing here I can find for you?"

"Downstairs, be quick now, don't get caught in the dark." Mary slid her deck into a small box and made her way into the bedroom, back to the crib.

"Perhaps Grimm, I shall read fairy tales to Arthur."

"Of course." Rose felt for her key. It sat snug in her pocket.

The library had so far been an unwelcoming area, an off-limits part of Rutherford House. Would Mr Borgia allow her to browse for books? If he wasn't there, how would she service Mary's request? She honestly was not sure how to find him; he seemed to just appear and disappear. Rose chewed her thumbnail, twirled the key through her fingers and wondered some more on the book she had seen fall to the floor earlier…

How had he obtained her book and put it back in her bag?

Rose shook her head as she gripped the dayroom doorhandle. All these thoughts cluttered her mind with Mary's simple request for a book of fairy tales.

She dashed down the hall and into her room, pulled her bag from the wardrobe and rifled through it.

"No more snooping for you, Mr Borgia."

Rose slipped the book under her mattress.

"Now I'll really know you're a sneak if you find it there." She stared at the slight rise of her mattress, looked to the hearth again, her shoulders slumped.

"I suppose you're with me until I understand what you are." She placed her bag away, not before pulling Papa's pocket watch out and slipped it in with the key. She didn't want Papa's ghost, but she coveted something of his, something tangible; the weight of it in her pocket calmed her overactive worries. She forced herself to recall days of old, when Papa read to her, when he also regaled her imagination with fairy tales. Rose decided she would choose a book for herself, too; just the thought stirred excitement and drowned out worry.

Rose slipped back into the hall. Mary called out.

"Are you still here? Do you expect me to invent a story on my own?"

"Yes, Mary, I'll fetch a book immediately," Rose called, and set off down the hall, a dangerous excitement licked at her fears. She locked Mary in, a skip in her step, as she once again took the stairs two by two, Jane Eyre on her mind.

CHAPTER 29

All was quiet on the ground floor. Rose peered around the last turn of the staircase for Eric, the hallway was smoky with incense and nothing more. The house creaked, the clocks ticked, her fingers gripped the banister. She sighed, brushed errant hair from her face, and readjusted her cap, crossing the floor swiftly. The double door of the library came up quickly; her fingers curled around the brass handle and she hesitated. She leaned close, her ear against the cool wood of the door. Silence. She knocked tentatively; the rapping echoed the length of the hallway.

"Mr Borgia?" No answer. Rose double-checked the hallway. She was quite alone. She pressed her lips tight, remembered his warning about entering the library and reminded herself she was just doing as Mary had asked. He did, in fact, tell her to tend all Mary's needs. She grasped the handle tighter and pressed.

Locked. She frowned and rolled her eyes.

"Of course, nothing would be simple," Rose hissed and jiggled the knob a few times. She ground her teeth, but that made absolutely no difference. It was locked tight. She sighed more deeply, pushed her glasses up her nose and plucked at her lips; her shoulders slumped. She looked around, her attention caught across the hall. She wandered into the formal dining room, hoping a small bookshelf might be in there as well.

Rose ran a finger along the table, leaving a thin line in the dust. The dining room brimmed with stuffed dead things and portraits with ancient eyes that followed her. Even in a state of starvation, she wondered how an appetite could be stirred with such garish décor.

A large portrait above the hearth caught her eye, she made her way over. A young couple stared across the room. The woman was milky skinned with rose bud lips, she had warm brown eyes with a sparkle of humour within. The man was handsome, dressed in naval regalia, he wore a perfectly trimmed beard, and his hands rested protectively upon the woman's right shoulder. Rose found a plaque on the base of the painting.

Mr and Mrs Johnathon Rutherford, 1897.

"So that's who you are," Rose smiled, seeing that happiness once visited Mary in her youth.

"Looking for something?" Rose spun around to see Martha in her coat, wicker basket in the crook of her elbow.

"No… I… I was just…"

"There'll be no dawdling around here, you see now?" Martha waved her free hand.

"I'm off home early today, seeing as another storm is on its way. I've left you both some boiled eggs and sandwiches for tea. See to it you bring it up from the kitchen to Mrs Rutherford before dusk."

"Of course," Rose curtsied, not quite sure why, as Martha was of no higher station than she.

Martha's pinched face tightened further.

"You'll mind what you poke around in." She buttoned her coat to the neck, shuffled around in her basket.

Horse hooves and carriage wheels ground on the gravel outside. Martha wandered to the window and pushed the drapes aside. She drew the curtains closed, cutting out the waning afternoon light.

"You ever stop to wonder why so few servants work here?" Her left brow crooked.

Rose shook her head.

"Because too many of them poked around in business that wasn't theirs. His Highness trusts no one, be sure to mind your sticky nosing, or you'll be no better than Josephine!" Martha slapped something on the table. Rose flinched; her nails stung her palms.

Martha's shoes clicked quickly away; the front door slammed shut.

Rose's hand curled around a new bulb of ginger that Martha left on the table. Open-mouthed, searching the corners once more, Rose slipped the bulb into her pocket, Josephine's grave imprinted in her mind. She ran.

Rose's feet sunk into the landing, her hand white knuckled on the banister as she leaned forwards, urging the stitch in her side to ease. The corners were darker, the drapes fell like sinuous musculature around the windows. She licked her lips, slowly straightened, and managed to move a few paces. She stared harder at the corners, they were still empty, but it gave her no solace. For the first time a thought struck her. The shadows at home, although frightening, had never hurt her. Her hand slid into her pocket, and felt the comfort of Papa's watch. It was warm, familiar in her palm. She turned slowly; her breaths stuttered. The corners surrounding her were empty, yet they now felt somehow rich with an altogether different energy that had her press on the back of her neck. Her legs felt heavy, thighs still burning from running upstairs. She moved; Papa's watch seemed to tingle against her palm. She halted and found herself in front of Mr Borgia's room.

When she should have made her way immediately to Mary, she let the watch slip away, her hand now reaching for his doorhandle, her fist knocking on the wood, her voice a distant, trembling call.

"Mr Borgia?" She knocked with a little more force. "Mr Borgia, are you in?"

Silence.

"I… I need access to the library; Mrs Rutherford requires a…"

The door clicked; it creaked slowly open. An empty darkness sucked her in.

CHAPTER 30

Rose fell into Mr Borgia's room. She gasped as her hands hit the carpet. She quickly pushed herself up, pulled her dress down, intent to immediately leave. Dusk light struck across a plain room, neat and orderly. It smelled like a man, of musk and cigarettes. Intrigue gripped her and overtook sensibility. It smelled like Papa.

"Mr Borgia? It's Rose," she called tentatively. Silence answered. A second set of doors lay open on the far side, a deep blackness interrupted by a flicker of light.

"Mr Borgia?" Rose took a few steps, emboldened by the silence, her movements quickened and more deliberate.

She pushed her glasses more snuggly up her nose, rounded the bed past a valet that held a fedora and woollen coat. *He's somewhere on the estate if they're here.* She peered over her shoulder, she felt thoroughly alone. Her movements hastened towards a light in an adjoining room. She reached the doorframe, gripped it and eased her head around to peek inside.

Candles, not electric light, burned vigorously, lending a warm orange halo to the room. A hearth crackled softly, a desk to its right and another junk-laded bed on the far side of the hearth. The gentle glow only just plucked the reflections of dozens of mirrors beset into the walls… just like Mary's rooms. Rose rubbed her arms, the air colder than only moments ago.

She blinked rapidly, snuck a look over her shoulder and made her way towards the bed.

Dozens of books were piled onto the bed, thick, heavy looking tomes. Before she could stop herself, her fingers were sliding across a dusty leather cover, slipping underneath and gently flicked it open. Her mouth dropped open.

Hand-inked words in a perfectly sweeping script flowed across the page. Words in a language not unlike her book. But it wasn't just the words that made her mouth dry. It was a name inked in the bottom right corner below the bow symbol that was repeated around Mary's rooms.

Giacomo Carbonelli.

"Papa?" Her voice was faint, her lips tingled. Rose looked up quickly, the room felt very small all of a sudden. The floor creaked, she dropped the book, spun, and grabbed a nearby candlestick. Her mouth was like dirt.

"Mr Borgia?" Rose stepped once, twice, eyes pained. Her candle flickered, another creak behind her. She twirled; the effort dragged her flame. She felt the heat of it as she held it close, and watched the door of an armoire creak open.

Eyes flicking between the exit, the book with Papa's name and the armoire moving with no help from anyone; Rose held her breath. Her glasses fogged, the pulse in her temples pounded. Common sense urged her to retreat, something inexplicable drew her to the armoire.

A dark slit cut between its door and frame. Rose held her candlestick out, letting its light flood the interior.

"What...?" She whispered. A flash of green within. With a trembling hand, Rose flicked the door. It whined open revealing an empty space other than a neatly hanging army uniform. Recognition washed through Rose. Her hand ran down a woollen sleeve, her fingers fumbled with a rising sun image on the collar. A slouch hat lay over the hanger, pressed against the front of the uniform. Rose leaned in and sniffed. She jerked back.

"It can't be Papa's?" She placed the candlestick on the floor, hands diving into a dozen pockets until a slip of paper slid against her skin.

Unfolding a letter had never been so terrifying. Rose's heart felt like it was rising in her throat. Her eyes burned, they blurred, she blinked hard to clear them, to read Papa's writing.

Dearest Edith,

Cara, Ti amo. I write this in earnest and desperation. I have lied to you. I cannot apologise enough. I cannot express how very much I love you and dearest Rosa. I have no time to explain, other than I did not go to war. I was called to arms of a different kind. If you receive this letter, please, get Rosa out of here. Far from this city. You must trust that this is for her own safety. I have kept this life from you, protected you from what I was, what I am, but I no longer can. I have left £200.00 buried at the foot of the willow, take this and run. This is all I can say for the protection of both of you. If you are reading this, it will be because I ..."

The ink trailed away, it smudged into the page...

Corrupted with the dirty brown of old blood.

CHAPTER 31

Rose' hands shook; the key took three passes before she could slot it into the door and another three deep breaths before the lock clicked.

She stood in the anteroom, hands splayed on the door, mind replaying what she had just seen.

"Papa?"

What had he done? What had happened to him? There had been money all this time?

Papa's letter and clothes burned in her mind. The cool of the room dissipated as her skin flushed hot, her fingers tingled. Martha's warning pushed through chaotic thoughts; Rose pressed her fingers against her temples.

What had happened to Josephine? The obvious answer was that she was dead. The less obvious, how and why? Did Papa know Josephine, did he know what happened to her?

It took a few moments to arrest Josephine and Papa haunting her thoughts before Rose pushed away from the door. She gulped tepid water from the decanter by the dumbwaiter, noting the candles were out. Rose's breaths calmed, her hands steadied, and she opened the top drawer of the sideboard, found some matches and relit them. She took the key to unlock the inner doors, felt a breath upon her neck, and spun around to find the candles were out. Rose stared at the cindered wicks, reached for the matches again, and froze when the door of the dumbwaiter rattled. The matches fell from her hand; she smacked into the inner doors and fumbled with the key again. It was too slippery, her fingers seemed to knot. She heard a woosh behind her, another breath down her neck. The key slipped in, the doors opened, and as she slammed them shut, she saw the candles had reignited.

Rose dropped the key while trying to re-lock the doors and felt the wood of the panels rattle against her hands.

"Oh God!" She yelped, scrambled for the key, mind cluttered, unthinking. She found it jutted up by the skirting board, slammed it shakily into the slot, then twisted to the left. She fell back, breathless, and stared accusingly at the door, at whatever was behind the now still and innocuous entry. The book flashed through her mind, was it the fault of those ancient pages she did not understand? Was it simply a draught and her overactive thoughts? Was it the shock she'd just had about Papa?

"It's nothing, it's nothing." Rose didn't believe herself in the slightest. Teeth clenched; she had a mind to find a time to demand answers from Mr Borgia, but how would she do that without revealing her snooping? Rose plucked at her lips. Could she just leave and go home, find the money under the willow? No, no she couldn't, because the dead things were still there, and it was more than money she had sought in leaving.

After a time, when the shake of her limbs quelled, she re-pinned her askew cap and took a deep breath. She searched the mirrored hall as she wandered back towards Mary's room, no fairy tales in hand but a heart full of questions. Eyes wide, there were no shadows, no dead things, nothing... but there was *something*. Her steps slowed, she slid her hand around Papa's watch, cushioning it in her pocket as she placed more caution in each footfall. More attune to every tick of a clock, each woosh of breath rushing into her lungs, she studied everything in more detail, even checking her own reflection, making sure that it was only herself she saw.

"It's an old house. Just a draught... or Martha... or..." Rose whispered. Martha didn't like her. She keenly felt that the old woman just wanted to scare her. Perhaps this house didn't like her either? Perhaps both Martha and the house wanted her gone?

The clocks struck 5 pm as Rose passed through the day room to find Mary on the balcony. Each chime reverberated in her chest. She took a breath, shed the last of the tremor from her hands, squeezed the vision in Mr Borgia's room from her thoughts.

You need this job, for Mama. Whatever the past, there will be no future if you lose your mind.

Thunder called in the distance, a more vigorous breeze whistled through the door, caught the drapes, rattled the electric lights, and slammed the day room doors behind her. Rose laughed softly. That's all it was, just the weather weaving its way through the house. Her shoulders lost their stiffness, she sighed, relieved, and she stepped onto the balcony. The air smelled wet; a wide grey band of rain was blowing in from the east.

Mary was stock still as she seemed so prone to do. Her veil flittered in the breeze, her hands gripped the balcony, fingers dug into it as though holding on for dear life.

"Mary, forgive me, but the library is locked. I was unable to find you a novel."

Mary turned smoothly as though her feet were wheeled.

"Locked, you say? How odd?" She turned away again.

"Johnathan never locks his books away."

"Sorry, Mary, Mr Borgia has locked it, and I am not sure where he is."

It occurred to Rose then that she hadn't seen much of him throughout the day. She wondered what exactly he did to occupy his time?

Was it keeping secrets? Hiding the past of Papa?

The wind picked more aggressively at Mary's veil, a crescent of white and red flashed momentarily.

"Who on earth do you speak of, Josephine? Goodness. Is it the new butler?" Mary waved her hand at Rose. Rigidity drained from Mary's body as it did when she fell into the time of Josephine. Martha's warning about Josephine's fate grated in Rose's thoughts again.

"Come now; you know Johnathon keeps a spare set of all the keys up here." Mary moved swiftly back inside, passed the cradle, dipped her head in, checked on the doll and then clicked open the door to her art room.

"Wait there, dear Josephine."

Rose did as she was told. Lightning flashed, thunder followed, and rain tinkered on the roof. The house groaned; its bones snapped. The flames in the hearth bickered and hissed.

Mary reappeared, arm outstretched, a large ring of old keys hooked upon her fingers. She plucked out a silver key.

"There now." She passed it to Rose, "A little fairy tale, remember?"

Rose nodded, "Of course."

Mary blew a kiss to the inert, lifeless doll through her veil and retreated back up into the art room.

Rose looked at the key, checked the clocks. 5:15pm The sky was now a dusky smudge. She could just make out the disk of the moon rising beyond the cloudy horizon.

"Well, you do need to fetch supper," Rose said to herself, faltered, drawn almost against her will back to the crib.

Don't, please don't, she told her impulsive self, but Rose was reaching for it before she could stop herself, needing to know if she had been hallucinating the prior day.

Her skin grazed through the netting, fingers hesitantly padded along the swaddling, she pulled back just before skin met porcelain.

She cocked an ear to the art room and saw the flush of guilt in her reflection. All was quiet. Tick, tock, tick, tock.

She reached in the crib again.

"Why do you do these things?" Rose asked herself. She skimmed along the swaddling again, her index finger trembling over the chin of the doll. She pushed the netting further away and let light spill onto the doll face. The forever-closed eyes had lashes so real, and a blush to the cheeks. Cupid lips puckered into a little bow. It was so very lifelike. Rose let her finger drop. The cold hardness of the porcelain spoke of anything other than life. She traced the rounded line of the cheeks in the air above, the rise and fall of a stout little brow, and even smiled to herself with the mastery Mary had with her craft. Her finger twitched and touched the doll.

Cathie's sleek body, threaded through Rose's legs, pulled her from the vision. She slumped to her backside, and scuttled back until she hit Mary's bed, knees drawn up. Rose glared at the crib, offended by whatever was within it, the strange power it had.... that *she* had to see things she did not understand. "I wish this day was over," she whispered into her hands.

She shook her head, let Cathie press a purring face into hers. Rose leaned her face into her hands. Her fingers smelled of porcelain and paint, of the rosemary that Mary liberally sprinkled around the room. She grimaced, then ran her hand down Cathie's back to centre herself, stood up and glared accusingly down at the doll. She quickly flicked the netting back in place.

"Well, it's not a dead thing, at least," she murmured to Cathie, who still threaded through her feet. "Just don't touch it, Rose, for God's sake," she chastised herself. "We don't touch the doll; we just do our job." Rose searched for her cap that had slipped away. It was next to the Frangitelli Mirror. She pinned it back on in the reflection, the unsettling ornament behind her.

"I'll leave *you* well alone, too." Rose felt for her keys and the one Mary gave her. She dashed unwillingly back downstairs, her mind a flurry about what other secrets lurked within Rutherford House.

CHAPTER 32

The key didn't work. It slotted into the library door well enough but wouldn't twist. Rose felt the pressure of time running out as the day quickly dimmed. Sweat dampened her temple as she wondered if the night was to bring any new shocks. She paused, pressed a hand against the door, took a slow, deep breath and looked out the sidelights by the front entrance. Dusk earnestly sucked away light, night's touch already shadowing the gardens into a bluish smudge.

She gritted her teeth, twisted again. Nothing. She pulled the key out, ran her fingers along its length, studied the lock, then the key. The lock was shiny brass. The key a rust-spotted silver. "Damn it to hell!" Rose hissed. This must be a part of Mary's delusions, an old key from times gone by.

Rose tried every other key on the ring; the pressure of the time of day weighed more heavily by the moment. The clocks seemed to tick quicker; her movements more fumbled. Mr Borgia had clearly pointed out that after dark, downstairs was forbidden. Rose licked her lips and twisted with more gusto. Was his warning to keep her out, to stop her discovering the secrets of Rutherford House?

When the last key failed, Rose slapped her hand against the door and let her head flop against it.

"Bloody thing."

"Need help there?"

Rose grabbed her chest.

"What are you doing? Trying to scare me half to death sneaking about like that?"

"What are you doing? Breaking and entering?" Eric was standing behind her with a box of kindling. His limp seemed a little worse under the weight of such work.

"You up to no good already, Rosie?" Eric smiled easily; his eyes able to sparkle even in the dimness of the hallway.

Rose pressed her lips into an angry line.

"You've been here for five minutes and seem to know it all?" She crossed her arms, attention fleetingly on the clock that now said 5:30pm. Night rolled in like a tidal wave.

"I know a sneak when I see one," Eric chuckled and shook his head. Rose itched to slap his face, to touch it, to pull his lips close to hers. She pressed her mouth tighter, mentally slapped herself into sense and jangled the keys in his face.

"Mrs Rutherford asked me to fetch her a book, it isn't my fault the keys don't work."

Eric set the box on the floor. He wiped his hands on his pants then leaned into Rose. Her nostrils flared subtly, he smelled achingly like home, not the thick stench of the incense that wafted day and night throughout Rutherford House.

She didn't move as the warmth of his breath wafted across her cheek; she remained frozen as he reached around behind her… and pulled.

"That should do it." He held up a pin from her hair. Rose's jaw ached as she clamped her mouth shut lest she say something she knew she'd regret; be it words of admonishment or of feelings she struggled to suppress. She couldn't admit to herself that she had breathed in a little deeper when he was his closest, could still taste his lips on hers from a lifetime ago.

Eric twisted the pin, stuck it into the lock, and wriggled it until there was a subtle click.

He pushed it open. "M'lady," he bowed over zealously.

"Hmm," Rose couldn't muster a thank you.

Rose selected a small candlestick from the dining room, lit it and let its light lead both her and Eric into the library.

She quickly surveyed the room, found two more candelabras and lit them. The space drenched to life under the flickering yellow light.

Wall to wall, perfectly placed books, and a grand desk under the drape covered window. She reached for a green-shaded desk lamp; she tugged the cord, and it flashed to life.

"Interesting." Rose was sure Mr Borgia said there was no electricity on the lower floor. She blew out the candles.

"Hmm, nice for some, isn't it?" Eric muttered, tracing his fingers along a shelf of red-bound books on the far wall, then spun an ancient-looking world globe.

"Don't touch anything!" Rose hissed, yet she was drawn to touch everything too, wanted to know the secrets of this family, see what kept Mr Borgia so busy as caretaker that he was rarely to be seen. She hoped to discover why Papa's belongings were in his room and how he knew Papa.

"Two are better than one. I'll help you find what you need. What book is it then?"

Rose waved at Eric absently. "A fairy tale…" her voice waned as she poked around the desk. It was orderly; a black and gold telephone sat on the right-hand side.

"C'mon. A bit more specific. Does this book have a name?" Eric asked, pulling out various books and flicking through them.

"Brothers Grimm, and put everything back exactly as you found it," Rose replied as she trailed a finger across the cool earpiece of the telephone. It was smooth but cracked just a little where the holes for speaking were. She had never made a call, never so much as touched one before. The only telephone she had seen was in the post office. Her fingers trailed the fabric-wrapped cord. She had always wondered how a voice might travel along it to places far away.

A pen stand and ink blotter were all that sat upon the desk apart from the lamp. Her fingers slipped into a divot along the edge of the desk near the telephone. She assumed this was the damage inflicted by Mr Borgia from the argument she had listened in on earlier.

Before she realised what she was doing, Rose jiggled the handle of the top right-hand desk drawer. Of course, it was locked too.

"That's not looking for a book," Eric said.

"You mind your business. I'll mind mine."

"It was only me who got you in here; a thank you wouldn't kill you, Rose."

Her fingers remained hooked under the brass handle of the draw; she pulled once more.

Open, damn it.

Within seconds of the thought, there was a release of tension, a subtle click. The drawer relented and slid out. Rose yanked her hand away, she stared at her fingers as though they were foreign to her, mouth agape. She quickly looked up to Eric who was busy sliding books in and out.

It's your imagination, just your imagination.

She balled her hands together, backed away from the desk, just as Eric looked back up at her.

Rose crossed her arms, walked stiffly to the section of red-toned books, pulled one out. It was Shakespeare. "The Tempest suits my mood," her voice was shaky, she cleared her throat, still feeling the drawer move at just her thought.

"What are you looking for in his desk?" Eric sighed. "I'm not here to spy on you, but if you need me..." He waved the bent hair pin in front of her.

"I don't need you!" Rose regretted that the moment it came out, but she couldn't help herself. "Better fetch your logs; I'm sure there's a fire that needs starting somewhere."

Eric slammed a book back into the shelves, "Are we going to do this forever?"

Rose found a small volume of Grimm's Tales in the red section and set it upon the green leather of The Tempest. Nothing felt right, her fingers tingled.

Get out of here.

Rose's thoughts were chaotic, she yearned to retreat to her room, sip some hot tea and calm the tremble under her skin. She'd definitely poked around too much for one day. She steered for the doors, averting her eyes from the desk. Eric followed close; annoyance flared in her.

"Forever is a long time, isn't it, Eric? You were thrusting forever upon me when you signed up to the army, so I'll be whatever I want to be for as long as it suits me."

"Are you this angry with your father too?"

The nerve was raw. Papa's image, both alive and dead, flickered through her mind.

"Don't speak of Papa. It's not the same!" Papa's found uniform was now all too present in her thoughts. Nothing was as she had thought, and whatever had happened to Papa, it was not the same as her fiancée volunteering for war.

"It's exactly the same. Your dad signed up just like me," Eric's voice was a little sharper.

Rose's jaw trembled; hot tears lingered on her lashes.

"I wasn't engaged to Papa. I wasn't in love with him, planning a life with him. I…" Her vision blurred. She didn't notice that Eric's welled up too, and didn't see the stain of emotion splattering his face. Rose left the library and pulled the doors behind Eric.

She headed to the service stairs, Eric as well.

"Are you going to follow me every single second?"

"It's the kitchen that needs stocking for the morning."

"Perfectly convenient then, isn't it?" Rose bustled faster, books tight to her chest, and descended into the thick darkness.

"Perhaps it's you following me?" Eric teased, his voice held a rawness, his hurt only just suppressed.

Rose rounded on him, "I'm fetching supper for the lady of the house, and I'll thank you to not take your liberties just because we were … we were…" She turned away and rushed past the empty servant's quarters; the open doors too dark, too quiet, too empty.

The kitchen still smelled of the day's cooking. Fat and sugar with the lingering deliciousness of fresh bread. A tray was laid out on the bench, two meals upon it. As unfriendly as Martha seemed, she had also left another plate by the side, chopped ginger, fennel, and a linen bag of which Rose knew to be personal toiletries.

She scooped up the platter as Eric unloaded the wood, stacking it neatly. He filled the oven, ready for the morning. Rose watched him in the periphery of her vision as she set the books on the tray.

Eric's shirt was stained down the back, his hair slick with a hard day's work. Both sleeves rolled up, the burn scars on his arms twinned those that had taken his left ear. Rose felt her eyes prickle again, she swallowed the feeling away as he stood up, rubbing his hands together.

"That's me, then." Eric tipped his head even though he wore no cap. He headed towards the larder and stopped, "Night, Rosie, stay safe."

CHAPTER 33

Rose had settled Mary with her supper and the book before turning her bed back and lighting her lamps. She took her own supper into her room and set it down when she noticed the mirrors were uncovered, her belongings neatly folded on her bed, a note atop.

Do not cover the mirrors. It was Mr Borgia's handwriting.

"So, you have been in my room, well, well…" Rose balled her fists. She screwed up the note and pitched it onto the fire, then headed to the wardrobe. Her bag was present, the book still inside, yet her brand new quill was snapped in two.

"And Eric thinks I'm a snoop!" She threw the quill in the fire, recovered the mirrors and sealed their view once more. "I'll use *your* quill then, Mr Borgia." Her heart raced a little, remembering the drawer opening with a mere thought. She shook her head and laughed. "One day here and you're as mad as a hatter," Rose sighed, convincing herself the drawer had merely been jammed, not locked. "Tired, I'm just tired."

She sat at her small table, spoon in hand, ready to crack open her boiled egg, but hesitated; guilt churned her gut to a state of nausea. She was so mean to Eric, and had been for so very long. But she couldn't seem to help herself. Her hackles rose every time he was near. The hurt was still too raw.

Thunder rumbled. Rain battered the house. She felt the misery of the season and wished deeply for the warmth of Summer. She looked over her shoulder to the window. The pane was dry. Rose listened closer. *Pitter, patter, pitter, patter.*

"Ugh! Damned rats." Tapping the top of her egg, she flicked its lid off angrily and gasped. She swept the egg to the floor and jumped up, the chair fell from underneath her, and she tumbled to the floor.

Her glasses slipped from her face, she fumbled for them, and the floor reverberated with a deeper, closer thunder. Lightning flashed brighter, catching the lens of her glasses by the bed leg. She scrambled for them, shoved them hurriedly on, hand on chest, trying to catch her breath.

The walls rattled as the rats scurried faster. Rose crawled back to the remnants of her meal; hand pressed to her mouth. She retched, looked away, and retched again. The smell of flesh and feathers was too much. She glared accusingly at the egg, which contained a fully formed boiled chick.

She didn't want to touch it but she couldn't leave it there. She used the hearth broom to flick it onto the flames.

The fire licked at the gore, the smell of burning feathers made her retch again. Rose watched wide-eyed, hand pressed against her lips, until it blackened and dispersed with the ash. For the first time in a long time, she had lost her appetite, pouring plain black tea, and sipping it slowly to rid her mouth of the bitter taste of sickness.

She poured cold water into her basin and splashed her face. Her skin was pale with feverish cheeks, eyes still dilated, shock still tingled under her skin.

"Oh Mary…" Rose headed for the door, lest Mary had the same issue with her meal and received the same fright.

Heathcliff met Rose along the hallway, meowed and followed on into Mary's room.

Mary was still at her supper, a sandwich barely eaten, her perfectly normal egg open and glowing a golden yellow.

Rose's shoulders relaxed, she sighed.

"Mary, is your supper satisfactory?" She poured Mary's tea.

"Yes, Dear, but I fear I can eat no further," Mary nodded, hand reaching for the teacup as Rose lifted the milk jug.

Mary shook her head, "Black will do nicely, thank you."

Rose set the jug down, pushing the picked-at sandwiches a little closer.

"Will you not eat a little more, Mary?" Rose picked up the sandwich plate, offering it to Mary.

Mary shook her head again and shuddered as the floor vibrated with a peel of thunder. Mary hastily set her cup down, hands set in her lap. Rose picked up the linen napkin that had slid to the floor, she set it back across Mary's knees. She offered the sandwiches again, unable to ignore Mary's pencil-thin arms.

"For Arthur? You must keep your strength up for him."

Mary looked up at Rose; one hand slid from her lap, and she peered back to the ever-silent crib.

"He is more unsettled this afternoon. I don't at all know why," Mary said. She took a sandwich and slipped it under her veil.

"Another?"

Mary held her hand up to refuse, but Rose insisted. This poor woman did not know how to care for herself in any way other than that which meant protecting the memory of her long-dead child. A cold pain divided Rose's chest.

I don't want to end up like this.

"Please, Mary, can't you hear him fussing just now? He'll need the goodness of your milk, Ma'am. Please, for little Arthur?" Rose winced, not knowing whether encouraging the delusion was the right or wrong thing, but Mary's son seemed to be the currency that motivated her.

"Yes," Mary reached for a second and then a third point, finishing her tea in between. She stood up before the fourth could be offered. The clocks struck six.

"I am tired; dress me for bed."

Rose followed Mary to her dressing table. She made quick work of all the buttons, slipped her barely scuffed shoes off and slid a heavy cream shift over Mary's head.

"Mary, shall I brush your hair?"

"Please." Mary unpinned the outer black veil, leaving the thinner white one in place. Rose gathered up the hair and brushed it gently. One hundred strokes as Mama had always done. Mary sat quietly, patiently, moving not an inch.

"Finished. Can I get you anything else?"

"The cats, call them in, please."

Rose called them. Heathcliff and Cathie came running, pouncing onto the bed as Mary was tucked in.

"Where is Romeo?" Mary asked.

"I'll find him," Rose looked about the bedroom, then the day room. Opening the balcony; she hugged herself, it was freezing, wet and empty. She checked her room, under her bed.

"Romeo, Romeo?" In her mind, she giggled and thought, *where for art thou, Romeo*. Rose wandered down the hall and froze. Romeo was at the threshold of the doors to the stairs.

"Oh no!"

She had locked all the doors; she was sure of it. But there they were, wide open. Romeo was growling, focused on something outside towards the staircase. Rose felt the blood drain from her.

"Come boy, it's just a rat."

He hissed, arched his back, hackles raised and darted out.

"No, no!" Rose ran to the doors just in time to see the flick of his tail disappear down the night-drenched stairs. She grabbed a candlestick from the dumbwaiter and hovered at the doorway.

Rose waved her flame to the left and wondered if she should knock on Mr Borgia's doors? She shook her head, pressed her lips hard. The last visit still had a grip of her, she didn't want to stumble upon anything else unsettling. If he answered, she would also seem incapable, two nights in and a cat already escaped. "Damn it to hell!" she seethed through her teeth.

Rose took a step forward, then stopped, her toes curled. The very core of the house seemed to speak in groans and moans, cracks and thumps; its voice vibrated up through her feet under the weight of the storm. The dumbwaiter rattled frantically; she sprang away from it and into inky blackness.

CHAPTER 34

The staircase was a bottomless chasm. Rose's candle struggled to illuminate more than a stair or two. The flame shook in her hand, her eyes painfully wide, drinking in the shadows, sniffing, tasting, listening. The house quieted the further she descended, as though listening back. Her skin chilled, and her breaths rattled in her chest.

"Romeo? Come here." *Stupid cat.* "Puss, Puss… come on." She made kissing sounds to try to attract him; her calls merely rebounded in the darkness.

"Damn it!" She conjured some delicious curse words, wanted to speak them allowed, but was overcome with a hot slice of belly pain and had to bend over a moment to catch her breath.

Oh, to be a man!

Rose continued when the pain waned to a dull ache. She turned the corner and descended halfway down the final set of stairs. The air was more frigid with every step. She braved the silence within and ignored the bellow of the storm raging outside.

"Romeo…puss, puss, come on back now," she whisper-called, kissed her lips again. Her head snapped left.

He meowed long and low, the echo somewhere below. Rose hastened her steps, hit the ground floor and called again. "Romeo… come on, boy, you'll get me fired."

The echo of his growl came from down the service stairs.

"Of course, you'd go there, you stupid beast!" Rose gulped; her flame quivered very nearly out. She held it closer to her body, but her glasses had fogged so she set the candle on the ground. She slipped her glasses off to clean the lenses, the tremble of her hands caused her to fumble with them, her fingers felt all thumbs.

Romeo meowed again, hissed and growled. The sound pulled Rose's hairs and set gooseflesh upon her body. Scratching in the ceiling ensued, she felt a cold rush of air behind her.

"Ahh!" She yelped, losing hold of her glasses, hearing them hit the ground. She quickly lurched for the candle, its glow now an orange smudge that no longer clearly defined what lay ahead. The scratching continued.

"Damned cat!" Rose hissed back at it and squatted to the floor whilst she patted around in search of the glasses. She couldn't feel anything but cold hardwood and the edge of the runner that stretched the length of the hallway. The service stairs echoed again with a long hiss.

Rats… he's chasing the rats.

"How many rats can there be?" The scratching amplified, like sharpened nails on a chalkboard. A cold rush of air surged against her again, her pains increased, she pressed her belly. Tears of pain only added to the blur of her surroundings.

Rose sniffed salty snot and moved forward on hand and knee; she had to find her glasses; she needed to find the cat. She found her way into the cavity of the service stairs, pulled herself up, and took one step at a time, feeling in the darkness for the fine frames with her toes.

Where are they? She tread each stair carefully, ensuring her balance, scared to accidently step on her glasses.

The scratching was louder the further she descended, the cold more biting, the darkness so thick she imagined it might strangle her. The candle spilled its light across the final step, and there she was, faced with the long eye of the corridor cutting through the abandoned servants' quarters.

Rose couldn't swallow, could hardly see, could barely stand straight for the pains attacking the very centre of her. Her courses leaked hot down her leg.

"No, please stop?" she sobbed; the sound echoed along the hall. One blurry step at a time, she moved past each partly open door.

"Romeo… come on… kitty kitty…"

Romeo howled up ahead, where the smells of the kitchen were strongest.

"Romeo… come on, you don't need a rat, you evil beast," Rose grumbled. "I'll get some scraps if you come here this instant." *I'm talking to a cat.* She shook her head and quickened her pace, keeping one hand trailing along the wall to keep balance. The air seemed to move, have a breath of its own; it tickled her neck and tugged at her hair. She moved faster as a faint glow cut through the darkness. Hitting the doorframe of the kitchen, she was breathless but relieved. Everything remained a blur, but Martha had thankfully left an oil lantern upon the workbench, and by it sat the fuzzy orange outline of Romeo.

"You evil devil!" Something glimmered near the cat. Rose moved towards him, but he leapt from the bench and ran back up the corridor. "Romeo!" She held the flame towards the corridor seeing his fluffy backside vanish into the shadows, "You had better run straight back upstairs!"

Rose reached for the brighter light of the oil lamp but yanked her hand back. "What in the world?" Her glasses sat neatly folded next to a small dish of ginger and fennel. She set the candle down, quickly put them on, spun around, eye on every corner, every slice of shadow. Her heart pounded in her temples.

Movement caught her eye in the corridor. Rose quickly squashed the herbs into her pocket, grabbed the candle and ran. Her legs were jelly as the cat hissed up ahead; its growling hastened her pace. Whispers tickled her ears; sinister murmurings had her run faster. Behind her, doors slammed; the floor vibrated. Each slam a bomb, like the pop of gunfire and gunfire was bad, it reminded her of war, and war took her papa… but what kind of war? Papa's uniform flashed in her mind. *What's going on?*

She ran faster, reached the stairs; they were too steep to climb, her legs wanted to give in. The cat hissed again, and the scratching intensified behind her. Rose dug deep and burst from the stairwell only to be accosted by wide, dark eyes glaring back at her.

CHAPTER 35

"It took you only two days to disobey the rules. I honestly thought it would be at least a week." Mr Borgia's voice was low, his expression strangely amused.

Shrouded in darkness, he held a mirror like a shield, that garish ornament from Mary's room in the other hand. Rose had run into her own reflection, her own candlelight. The emptiness behind her, its blackness, forced her closer to him. Her candle flickered; she held it nearer for fear it would go out.

Rose was speechless, but Romeo wasn't. He rubbed against her legs and mewed innocently. She grimaced at him. *Bloody Cat.*

"*And* you let the cat out," Mr Borgia shook his head. Rose looked away from the mirror, her reflection bone-white terror.

"Find what you were looking for?" He asked, shifting the mirror towards the front doors when the rats scuttled from that direction.

"I lost my glasses."

"They fell from your face all the way downstairs?"

Rose's heart thudded uncomfortably, her belly panged, and she was all too aware she badly needed her wash basin.

"I'm sorry, I cannot remember leaving the door open, Sir. It was a confusing day with Mrs Rutherford, and... I, I feel perhaps I may be overtired. When I realised the cat was out, and Mary... I mean, Mrs Rutherford was asking for him; how could I not go looking?" Her words were breathy and rushed, anger coloured them. Mr Borgia aimed the mirror towards the staircase, his speech smooth, the light of her candle caught on that single golden tooth.

"And did you need to slam all those doors? Make such a noise? It was enough to wake the dead."

"I didn't…"

"You didn't make all that noise? Well then, Rose, who did?"

"I was just seeking the cat, Sir. There must have been a breeze, a gust, perhaps a window open. It's a fine storm out," Rose answered, no faith in her own suggestion.

"There are no opening windows down there, Rose."

In the dimness of her candlelight, she could see his brows pinch together, hollow crescents under his eyes.

"I don't know what to say, Sir," Rose curtsied. "This is a large and unusual house. May I go back upstairs now?" The trickle down her leg was pooling in her stockings, she tried to hold her legs together.

"Unusual? What makes you say that, Rose? Are you sure you really were alone? Did you see anything… anyone down there that could have caused such a racket? I would hate to have an intruder."

The candle lurched in her grip, its flame bit her as she grappled for it to still.

"No, there was no one. Just a lot of noise from the rats you spoke of, Sir." Rose curtsied awkwardly, eyes on the staircase, Romeo now fleeing the chaos he had wrought.

"I'm glad you found your glasses," Mr Borgia nodded sharply and moved towards the front door; his attention snapped to the ceiling. Rose followed his gaze. A flash of something grey, a streak overhead that disappeared into a corner above the stairs.

She gasped and backed away until she hit the wall. Mr Borgia turned back; his eyes narrowed more deeply at her.

"Did you see a rat, Rose?"

Rose held her candle aloft; her attention was fixed upon the deep recess of the corner above the stairs. Her eyes narrowed; her mouth hung open.

"Rose?"

She remained speechless; whispers filled her head once more. Her candle quivered when something white streaked along the ceiling towards the front doors; its gust tousled her hair. Mr Borgia held the mirror in that direction and pointed the ornament as well.

"I think it is best if you retire, Rose. The rats are very bad tonight, if you do see one in Mary's rooms, please be sure to call me." He moved towards the front doors, mumbling something in Italian as his shape blended into the darkness. He called back to Rose.

"With the stealth that you move around this house, perhaps, another night, we can catch a rat together." He disappeared towards whatever had left its signature upon her skin, whatever had sucked the breath from her.

Rose dashed upstairs, for the second time that day in a panic. Romeo awaited her on the top step, she clutched him by the scruff and threw herself behind the mirrored door. He howled as he fell from her grip as she slammed the main doors shut.

"You stupid cat! Get out of my sight!" Rose fumbled for the key. The lock clicked, she pressed the handle, jiggled the door, ensuring it was locked. She fell against the doors, heaving for breath, a forgiving Romeo threading innocently through her ankles.

CHAPTER 36

Mary was asleep when Rose finally found her legs to move. She heated a little water by the hearth and tended herself. Her undergarments were a mess. They would require some scrubbing in the morning and a good dose of Reckitt's blue for the stain. Her body still shook as she slipped her nightdress on, chewing the ginger and fennel as she slid between the sheets.

Rose sat a while, replaying what she saw downstairs. What *exactly* had she seen? Had she seen anything at all? She'd been running, her glasses had fogged again, and what was Mr Borgia doing, behaving so strangely in the dark?

"You're overtired… that's all." She compulsively surveyed the corners where no shadows could make purchase. All was well... or was it?

"It's just your imagination, you need money, not theatrics." Rose coached herself as she fluffed her pillow until she made just the right indentation for her head. She lay down, clean and warm, the shivering subsided, but she watched the top left cornice on the far side of the window. The warm ambience of the hearth and lamp light didn't quite reach it, leaving a dark and suspicious splotch. The window rattled slightly as rain slid down in a steady pour. Rose stared wide-eyed at the cornice, wondering if home might be better than the strangeness of this place, but she knew she couldn't slip back into that life, she didn't want to feel the death of it upon her skin.

She watched that cornice, until her eyes watered and could no longer stay open.

Rose dreamt vividly of scratching things, of slithering unseen beasts that made the walls of her room writhe. The plaster undulated in and out, the window pane ballooned inwards. Her bed jiggled, the base of it creaked, the mattress hollowed, sucking her down. A scream pierced the room, but it was not her own. The scraping was so loud. Something tugged at her hands as she sunk away. It nibbled her fingers, gnashed deep into her palms.

Rose sat bolt upright, breathless. She quickly slid back underneath her covers, back to the safety of not seeing things. She felt as though she was back at home, the eyes of dead things upon her. The scratching of her dream persisted. She pinched her thigh, she was awake.

Rose peeled back her quilt just enough that she could peek out. Her lamps flickered as a door opened and closed in Mary's chambers. The electric light overhead stuttered; the fitting swung like a pendulum. Rose held her breath, she heard no footsteps, no voices, nothing. The scampering in the walls faded, running towards something else. She quickly checked the cornice… was compelled to check it.

Was that crack there yesterday?

She narrowed her eyes and slipped her glasses on. A hairline crack snaked its way from the cornice a foot down the wall. Rose blinked and looked harder. It was a very old house, of course, it had cracks, she just hadn't noticed.

Something banged above her, the light fitting swayed more earnestly. The floor creaked; she pulled herself up, pressed her back to the bedhead. She gripped the bedding tighter and glared deeply at her reflection in the washstand mirror, as though watching herself, seeing her fear, she would keep a grasp upon reality.

Run, Run.

But what would she be running from here? She hadn't seen Papa or Matteo in days, not a dead horse or man holding his innards in. She hadn't smelled the rot of decay, none of that. She felt draughts and heard the creaks of an ageing home. Would it be that she was merely fleeing from her imagination, from the strangeness of a house she was yet to understand? Yet Papa's uniform in Mr Borgia's room couldn't be ignored, his half-penned letter a curse on her mind. But what did it mean, if anything, to the immediate survival of Mama? She then wondered on that money? *Was it still under the willow? Had Mama ever found it? Did Mr Borgia know about it? Did he kill Papa to take it? Too many questions plagued her mind.*

Rose tried to lay back down, to shut off her thoughts. She punched her pillow back into shape, tugged her quilt straight, huffed in feigned annoyance, yet she couldn't not listen to the floor that creaked for no apparent reason. She bit into the linen. Something heavy was being moved, dragged. She watched the line of light under her door flicker as someone or something passed by. She bunched the quilt tighter, heard a grunt and more scraping. Rose sat bolt upright, looked from her reflection to the door and back again, peeled the quilt away from her ear, and listened intently. Silence.

Rose bit her lip too hard; a coppery taste coated her tongue. She pushed the quilts away with great difficulty. She knew she had to; she was obligated to check on Mary. She eyed the cornice first, nothing new. Her legs swung out unwillingly. At least her pains had dulled.

The floor was ice. She sunk into her slippers and wrapped a shawl about herself. The boards creaked under her weight; at least *that* made sense. The scratching in the walls had ceased, only the song of the many clocks sliced through the silent voice of the night.

Rosemary was strong upon the air, with a hint of food gone sour. She looked at her dinner tray and recalled the vile egg she had burned. Perhaps it was that?

Rose sniffed again; the odour stronger the closer she edged to the door. Her hand hovered above the knob before she twisted and inched the door open.

She screamed, stumbled backwards and fell. The door creaked slowly open; a dark silhouette filled the doorway.

CHAPTER 37

"Did I startle you?" Mary cut a rigid figure in the glare of the hallway mirrors. She cradled the doll across her stomach. Rose tried to utter something, anything, but the words faded at the back of her throat.

"My bed is cold; I need the warmer," Mary said and moved away ethereally, as she did so well. Rose picked herself up. The rats resumed their scurrying overhead. She looked again to the cornice. There was a hole above the crack. *Had that been there before?*

Rose felt hot and clammy, quite possibly coming down with something. She looked up again. The crack seemed a little larger. *Has it always reached halfway down the wall?* She licked saltiness from her upper lip and undid the top button of her nightdress.

She kept her eye on the crack whilst moving towards the door, she sniffed the air again and shivered as a staleness held a stronger grip. She shut her door, almost thankfully, behind her and half-ran towards Mary's room.

Mary's hearth was low, which made scooping through coals less uncomfortable. Rose yawned deeply as she closed the brass warmer and slipped it between the sheets. Mary sat upon the edge of the bed, the doll now back in its crib. She cooed at it, tucked it in, then slipped her feet under the quilts.

"Did you want to let the bed warm first?" Rose asked, worried she might burn her feet.

"No. You may go." Mary lay down, her veil fell aside as her head sunk into the deep down of her pillows. Rose caught sight of the scars that trailed the length of Mary's face. She couldn't help herself but stare.

"Does it frighten you?" Mary pushed herself back up, folded the veil entirely behind her head, affording Rose full sight of her face. Mary tilted her head to the side. A single, wearied brown eye stared at Rose, thin grey brows arched, awaiting an answer. Rose reflexively curtsied, attention fixated upon three deep scars from forehead to chin, closing over the left eye. Silvery pink, old and set in. Rose's heart hammered, wondering what could have caused such an injury.

"Well?" Mary set the veil back in place and lay her head upon the pillows once more.

"You've no need to fear me, Dear. It is me that *it* wants, not you."

Rose curtsied again, wishing now that she was still dreaming. She tried not to run back to her room, but she did when she passed the Frangitelli Mirror, the strangeness of its depths too much in light of everything that had occurred that evening.

Rose banged her door shut, gasping; hands pressed against the wood, now colder than before. She threw her shawl off, gulped water, and peered at herself in her mirror, attention upon the reflection of that hole in the cornice, blacker than before.

Rose awoke again; her pillow was wet, smelling of salted nightmares. She blinked; her eyes heavy and gritty. The room was dark; her lanterns burnt out, hearth no more than a whiff of charcoal. The electric light was out too. A stripe of waning moonlight cut through the darkness, and she thanked it for this. Immediately she searched the cornice, but it was too dark, and she was thankful for this too. Anxiety still hammered in her head, she pulled the quilt to her nose, wondering if she should re-light the lantern so she could see the hole. Instead, she rolled to her right, back to the window, face to the door. Rose focused upon the stripe of light beneath it, the brilliance of light that ornamented Mary's rooms.

Her eyes glazed over after a time; her body snuggled comfortably into the dip of her mattress. The gloom of her room began to meld with the fuzz of impending sleep. Yet, the pleasant warmth of slumber was interrupted by the rats again. Their scratching too close, she could feel the vibrations of the walls. Rose ground her teeth. She was exhausted, and squeezed her eyes shut.

"Go away."

The sound stopped.

Rose opened one eye a slit, checked the cornice, it was still too dark, but nothing moved, no long-dead faces in the shadow of it, so she closed her eyes before the scraping began again. It seemed to be right behind her. She squeezed her eyes, wished for a second that she had faith, that she could pray away her worries.

Rose's eyes snapped open, ears straining as the sound started and stopped, then started again. She lifted her head, looked again towards the cornice; it was too damned dark. The scratching continued. It no longer sounded like the scurrying of tiny feet.

Her bed shook.

Rose launched out; ankles tangled in the sheets. She tumbled to the floor. The window rattled, her bed slid across the floor, stopping a foot from where she lay.

She scrambled up, fumbled for the oil lamp, but it was empty of fuel. The window rattled again; the bed linen slid slowly away as though pulled by something. She backed against the wall, frozen, winded.

"Leave me alone!" Rose hissed.

The milky white of the moon glistened through something on the window pane. Something moving across it…. etching across the glass. Letters… being written before Rose's eyes by an unseen hand.

Scrape, scrape, scrape.

Instinctively Rose sought the corners for the shadows that had haunted her for so long.

The shadows were deep, but they did not smell the same, did not *feel* the same. The gentle softness of ash and Rosemary was replaced with stagnant water, wet and rotten. She pressed her sleeve against her mouth as the offensive air thickened. A sick, sinister intrusion curled in her stomach.

Rose edged away until she found a candle, crawled towards the hearth, her stuttered gasps drowned the scratching upon the window. She dipped the candle in the embers and caught a flame upon the wick. She held it aloft; the gentle heat of its flame struck through the darkness. Was the hole larger again? The crack now ran the length of the wall to the skirting boards. Her eyes flicked to the door, then to the wardrobe. She thought to pack her bag right there and then, but the scratching continued, her attention snapped back to the window. She felt dizzy and scuttled back until she hit the washstand.

The scraping stopped; the room silent.

Rose's eyes were hooked upon the window pane.

Va Via.

Go away. Two small words she knew only because Papa used to yell them at the birds that would peck at his fruit trees. Each letter a shaky cursive, with the tail of the last trailing off to the edge of the pane.

Va Via. Rose gripped the washstand with one hand. Something slithered up the wall around the window. Long and bone-white. Rose held her breath, wished for invisibility. The candle trembled when she lifted it higher.

The thing scrambled like a spider, its head back to front, inky orb eyes upon her. It scampered backwards, grey and wrinkled, its hands and feet human, its claws and jittery movements not. It quirked its head so as to look more intently upon Rose. Raspy breaths plumed white from its mouth. White, wiry hair clung to deathly flesh. Its mouth widened, too wide to be human, too human to be anything else.

"Va Via!" The thing whispered slowly. Rose somehow found her feet, dashed to the door, and flicked madly at the switch until electricity flooded her room. She pulled all the covers from the mirrors, and light refracted around the room. The thing's reflection was caught. It screeched and covered its eyes.

"Va Via!" It screamed before digging its nails into the wall. It slithered like a lizard, slipped a bony hand into the crack, then looked back at Rose once more. "Va Via!" It screeched, then compressed itself, pushed its bony appendages through the crack, elongating most unnaturally until it had disappeared. The hole shrunk; the cracks receded until there was nothing there at all.

CHAPTER 38

Rose waited the night out in the bathroom down the hall. She'd fled, too scared to scream, too terrified to look in upon Mary, absolutely too horrified to go searching for Mr Borgia. She hoped both he and Mary were safe, but she wasn't moving an inch until dawn broke through the grip of night.

Wedged between the toilet and window, Rose was numb with cold, she blew on her fingers to no avail. Surrounded by as many candles as she could grab on her way, she sat there for hours under a spill of flickering light, shivering, watching, waiting. The vision of the thing from the ceiling was forever tattooed inside her mind. It wasn't anything like the others. It wasn't… human. It seemed somewhere in between. Too tactile to be dead, too horrifying to be alive.

Her bottom lip stung where she had been plucking at it. Her head felt stuffed with cotton wool, her eyes too heavy, but she pushed sleep away until the rooster crowed as the first orange slice of dawn struck the bathroom floor.

Rose pulled herself up, doused the candles and turned on the faucet. She splashed her face. The water was freezing but cleared her head a little. She looked deep into her eyes, bloodshot, dark crescents beneath. Pallor drained her cheeks; her mouth was dry. She poured a glass of water, gulped it down, coughed.

Her mind was set one moment, confused the next. Pack her bags, run… but to what? Poverty, homelessness, another spectre awaiting her, or face whatever had crawled up the wall of her room last night? This idea ruminated through her thoughts… perhaps she was stuck between here and there like that thing, like all the ghouls and ghosts that had been haunting her?

She rubbed her head; it ached like a hand clawed at it from within. Her reflection once more called for her attention.

Was this the 'It' Mary had referred to? Is this what chased her from the kitchens last night?

And what of Mr Borgia? Why was he downstairs in pitch darkness carrying a mirror and that strange ornament? Why did he seem intent on knowing if she had seen something in the kitchen? Is that what the rats in the roof really were? A ghoul, a ghost… or something altogether more horrifying?

Anger flushed heat back into Rose's face and she welcomed its warmth. Was she here on false pretences? Given only enough information to draw her in, to find a worker stupid enough to stay when others had fled? Eric's protestations about her taking this position flooded her thoughts… she would have to admit he was right. She punched the sink and screamed into her reflection.

Rose pulled the plug from the sink and watched the water swirl down the drain whilst considering what to do. Mr Borgia had secrets; he had snooped at her book, he had something of Papa's. The dead inhabited her home… something unspeakable slithered within the walls of Rutherford House, and now Eric lived and worked here as well. Rose bit her nails and paced, awaiting the sun to rise a little further.

Was Eric in danger?

"Damn it to hell!" She couldn't just pack and leave… she'd have to admit she was wrong and take him with her too.

A door opened and closed. The tinker of a food tray passed the bathroom door.

Rose peered out the door. Martha was just passing through to Mary's bedroom.

"Mrs? Mrs? Breakfast. I've lovely fried ham and eggs this morning. A real treat. Hot as you like." Martha's words died behind the humming of Rose's chaotic thoughts.

Rose followed on, fingers twisted together, eyes rolling about, looking for cracks, listening for whispers. They were there; they were everywhere; they must have always been there; she just hadn't noticed. But now, they were so obvious they felt like a punch in the face. She pressed her hands against her ears, but the murmurings were deeper, they were inside her head. She grimaced, tried to squeeze them out.

"Stop!" she whispered through her teeth. This quiet old house listened, the voices ceased, replaced with the sound of her feet padding along the hallway. Her pace hastened, the fact the house obeyed eroded Rose's resolve even further.

She held the door leading into Mary's room, hesitant, watching Martha set breakfast on the table under the watchful gaze of the Frangitelli Mirror. The horrid ornament was back on the table.

Martha noticed Rose lingering in the doorway, eyed her up and down whilst Mary stirred the tea she was pouring.

"It's gone half eight. Where have you been, Girl? Had to bring breakfast all the way in myself." She set the teapot down and flicked a napkin across Mary's lap.

"You look a right sight." Martha frowned, "Tidy yourself up and see to your chores. I'll finish here with the Mrs. You've a load of laundry to get through. There's hot porridge downstairs. 'Tis the only time I'll pick up after you." The favour was barbed, for sure, but Rose took the opportunity.

Rose entered her room apprehensively, sunlight flooded it, a clear morning sky filled the window. No shadows, no holes or cracks in the ceiling. Everything was neat and orderly, as though the events of last night were a dream.

Was I dreaming?

She pinched the bridge of her nose, exhaustion engulfed her with a strange numbness. Rose leaned against the bed that was positioned exactly where it should have been, the covers folded back as though she had just slipped out of them. She held her head, ran the night's events over and again, and wondered if she had imagined it all, but the scrape marks on the floorboards where the bed had slid across the room were evidence that she had not. Her eyes snapped to the window.

Va Via. Rose mouthed the words silently, hugged herself, her decision made.

She quickly slipped into her old grey dress and left her new shoes on as she felt the itch to run, and her old boots would not do. She hesitated at the doorway and stared back. Two days had turned her hopes on their head. Two days was all it took to send her back to poverty. Two days had besieged her with more questions about Papa than before. She couldn't stay here, couldn't risk whatever this was… at least the ghosts at home had never touched her, never told her she wasn't welcome. Perhaps that old life was more comfortable than she had realised? And then there was Papa's letter and the possible money under the willow.

She made haste down the hall, ignoring the mirrors, left the doors unlocked and ran downstairs.

The library door was open. Mr Borgia's chair squeaked, the sound of his footsteps followed, and the chair creaked again. She'd have to go the back way to the stable block to find Eric.

Running down the service stairs, all the servants' doors were closed. More evidence she had not imagined it all. She ignored the enticing smells of the kitchen, ran through the steaming laundry, out through the vegetable garden and around the back of the house towards the stables.

"Eric?" She called, flinging open a set of doors that were merely storage for fodder and tools.

"Eric? Where are you?" She rounded the front and drew open heavy double doors. Devil sat overhead, upon the beams of a loft. It cocked its head and launched away towards the house.

"Eric? Are you here?" Rose's voice was thready, exhausted.

She ran past the stabled horses; they paid her no heed with their noses stuffed in buckets of chaff. It smelled good in here, the hay, the horses, freshly polished harnesses. There was no incense, no smell of rot, no fear in the air, and no whispers.

She cupped her mouth, "Eric."

"Rosie?" Eric climbed down a ladder from the loft, a tool belt strung over his shoulder. She ran to him, threw herself into his arms. Eric didn't falter and pulled her in tight.

Rose cried into his chest; she breathed in his salty scent.

"Hey… Rosie, what is it?" He stroked her hair, leaned his head gently upon hers. It could have been any moment in the past when he was her everything; her past, present and future. Rose dug her fingers into his back, clawed desperately for the past, drew in the comfort that he once offered.

"You're shaking? Did Borgia do something?" He gently pulled away, held her so that he could see her face. Morning sun caught upon his scars, these scars, his scars, they gave her comfort too, felt like home. Mary's… God… they seemed to slither under her skin.

"You… you… you were right. I shouldn't have come here."

"I'll kill him. What has he done to you?" Worry shadowed his eyes. Anger bloomed on his cheeks. He pushed her hair behind her ears, the touch of his hands so very good.

Rose shook her head and sniffed, feeling vacant when his hands left her skin.

"He hasn't touched me… it's not him… well not like that, it's… you won't believe me, Eric, you just won't believe what I've seen," Rose sobbed and he drew her in again.

"What then? Is Mrs Rutherford horrible to you? Does she beat you? There's been rumours, so many of them."

She shook her head again, choked back tears.

"She's crazy… no, that's not kind, she's…" Sobs got in the way of words. "Mary's old and lost in the past. She doesn't know whether she's here or living twenty years ago. She's a confused old woman… but it's not her."

"Then what? I don't understand?"

"There's something in that house, something evil. It wants me out."

Eric's fingers stopped caressing her face; he held her still.

"What are you saying? It's a haunted house?"

Tears streaked Rose's face, "*Something* is in that house."

He hugged her again.

"Come on now, Rosie, I've seen some awful, terrible things, but I've never seen a ghost. Are you sure you're getting enough sleep? You've only been here a couple of days. It's an old house, it's sure to have some drafts and creaks in it."

Rose pushed away.

"You think I'm making this up?" She wiped her tears on her sleeve, embarrassment coated her skin.

Eric raised his hands, "No, you misunderstand, I…"

"Oh, I understand you perfectly, Eric. You think I'm crazy," her voice wobbled. She pressed her hand on her forehead and took a shaky breath.

"You've already forgotten how hard you begged me not to take this job? *Now* when I admit you were right, you act as though I'm seeing things?" Rose walked away.

"Rosie, c'mon. That's not what I…"

"I know exactly what you said. If you find me dead up there…" She pointed towards the house, "Just remember, *you* didn't believe me."

CHAPTER 39

Rose wandered the grounds a while, wondering what to do. She looked down the drive to the gates. She couldn't just walk home; it was a long way and she honestly wasn't sure of the direction to take. The morning sun warmed her back, the crisp winter air dried her tears, their salt tight on her skin. She sat on the water fountain and looked at the house as though it were an alive thing, an entity conjured by Mary Shelley. It looked evil now; every dark window pane an eye upon her. Every door a mouth to gobble her up. Her attention sat upon the second level, flitting between the windows of Mary and Mr Borgia's rooms.

"What are you up to?" She settled her thoughts upon Mr Borgia's rooms and the mystery of Papa's uniform.

Rose sat there long enough that Martha came calling, tea towel over her shoulder, hands wringing through her apron.

"Girl! What the blazes are you doing sitting out here like a sparrow? Your lady needs tending!"

"I'm thinking."

"Thinking? Well, then, Miss La de da! If we all had the luxury of skiving in the sunshine, thinking about Lord knows what, we'd be in a right state of disarray, wouldn't we?"

Rose pushed up from the fountain, noticed Eric in the distance wandering past the greenhouse towards the front doors, tool bag in hand.

Martha stepped closer, finger pointing sharply at Rose.

"You're a state, to be sure. Your hair's a nest, you've no cap, my word, why on earth do you have that rag on? Where is your good uniform? Nought been three full days, and you're throwing your job away, just like all the others. I told his Highness you were no good, but he insisted on a youngen with no experience, as if he knows a good servant over the likes of me," Martha clucked her tongue and wandered away, throwing her arms in the air. "Just like all the others gone before you!"

Josephine sprung to mind once more.

Josephine was one of the others, and she now lies rotting on this very land.

Rose pictured the island in the centre of the lake. What had happened to Josephine, and why was a servant buried amongst the Rutherford family?

Rose hugged a new chill from herself and set her attention upon the double windows that were Mr Borgia's office. Sunshine glinted off the glass; she couldn't see if he was still in there. He had seen her book, and her life hadn't been the same since it fell into her possession. She had to find out why he had taken it, if he somehow knew what it was, and why she saw the things she saw. She had to know about Papa.

She took a deep breath, summoned her courage, and gathered her bag. Rose made her way back to the house, choice words on her mind, a false bravado shielding a deep fear coiled in her belly.

The front doors were ajar, the headiness of the incense eked outside. She entered and found the library doors open as well. She didn't knock.

The library was empty.

Rose dropped her bag, made her way to the desk, sifted through a pile of papers. Bills for this and that demanding payment, but nothing of interest. She pulled the drawers… they were locked. Her mouth wet, her lips tingled.

"Open," she whispered with little conviction and a world of doubt. She curled one finger under the top-drawer handle and pulled. It moved. Rose held her breath, listened for footsteps. All was quiet. She swallowed hard, turned her hand over, examining it for some strange sign, an indication of what this power was. Her skin looked normal, her fingers lean and bony as always. She glanced to the door once more before she slid the drawer out. It was neatly supplied with two fountain pens, an empty note pad and a silver cigarette case. Her heart thundered in her head as she reached for the second drawer.

"Open." *Click.*

This one was filled with open letters addressed to Mr Borgia. She slipped one out.

It was in Italian. She clenched her jaw, furious at herself for not being more attentive learning Italian when she was younger. Papa had never forced it, so she knew only the phrases he had used around the home. She slipped that letter back and opened another.

July 5th 1915

Ciao Amico,

All is arranged. The military paperwork has been sent and received. You may now proceed with the plan. Make contact when Bruxas has been contained. We understand this is a difficult extraction for you. We will forward the appropriate release papers so our brother can return to his family.

Letters about Papa? Rose frowned, unsettled by the lack of names on the letter. She pulled another with the same handwriting on the envelope.

September 1st 1915

I am most aggrieved to hear the terrible news. The conflict in Europe is at least to our advantage in concealing the issue for as long as possible. We do not need to immediately act upon placating the family as yet. Find the body if you can, but I fear this will not be possible until we contain Bruxas. Brother, you know what you must do. This Bruxas must be disposed of in the manner of others, in spite of this most dreadful situation you find yourself in. She would have wanted this; of that you can be comforted.

"Miss Carbonelli?"

The letter flung from Rose's hands, sailed through the air, landing at Mr Borgia's feet. He picked it up and glanced at the page. His cheek twitched.

"Find what you're looking for?"

Tears pricked her eyes; she clenched her fists. Her lips trembled.

"What is going on here?"

He walked towards the desk. Rose snatched the envelope opener, pointed it at him.

"Stay right there!"

He put his hands up, "Very well."

"You took something of mine."

"I can assure you; I have not taken anything that belongs to you, Rose." He tucked the letter in his pocket.

"My book. I saw it here the other day when you were arguing on that thing." Rose pointed to the telephone, "You took it and put it back… why?"

He opened his mouth, but Rose demanded more.

"And you can also tell me what you are hiding here? I saw what's in your room. Papa's uniform, why is it here? And… and why were you creeping around last night? What's going on in this house?" Rose stabbed her weapon in the air.

He stared at her; his cheek twitched again. She thought he was trying to quell a smile. She slapped the desk in frustration.

"I don't care, Sir, if this means I'm let go. I *want* to leave. You can pay me the wages due and send Eric on his way too. He's only here to spy on me anyway. We will find work elsewhere. Whatever is going on here is not worth the wage."

Mr Borgia pulled keys from his pocket and unlocked the top drawer of a filing cabinet.

"You mean this book?" He slid it across the desk, "Pick it up."

Rose hesitated, eyes flitting numerous times between him and the book. She could hear Eric whistling, his heavy boots pounding up the stairs.

Rose flicked the book closer; it was heavy. Too heavy. She flipped it over, opened its cover. The writing inside was different, very different. Not Latin or Greek, and there were no scribblings in the margins like hers. She wiped the pool of sweat from her lip, ran her fingers over the cover. It had the same crow emblem, but it was *not* her book.

"That is my grimoire, Rose," Mr Borgia said. "You have your own, and I assure you, I have no need to look at yours."

Rose's mouth opened a fraction. Words stuck in her throat.

"Yours is in your bag. It followed you here, didn't it? Slipped itself from under that loose floorboard?" His brows arched.

Rose's blood ran cold.

"How… how could you know that?" She backed away, still pointing the opener at him. Her skin felt too tight. Dizziness clawed at her, Rose shook her head, and tried to keep focus.

"Gianna told me."

"Who's that, your spy?" Rose licked her lips, peered towards the door, looking for whoever this Gianna person was.

"Somewhat, but really, Gianna is *your* spy, so to speak, your Familiar." He pulled out a chair and sat all too comfortably across the desk from her. He reached into his tweed jacket, retrieved a silver case. He placed a slim brown cigarette between his lips and lit it.

"I am not a threat to you, Rose. I can assure you of that." Smoke plumed from his nose.

"What do you mean, my Familiar?"

"Your crow is your Familiar," his words puffed white.

Rose stepped back, "*My* crow?" The letter opener slipped from her hand. She backed into the window ledge, her bag behind her feet. Her head swam with recollections of Devil following her, tapping at windows, annoyingly ever-present.

"I can assure you I do not have a crow."

"The moment the book called to you, your heritage came to maturation, and your Familiar was called to your side, Rose."

"My heritage? My what?" Rose could only string two staggard words at a time. *Why was the room spinning?*

"You are a Masciara, my dear, of the House of the Crow."

"I… I am a Carbonelli…" Her voice faded. Mr Borgia seemed distorted. His cigarette smoke coalesced into the shape of a bird… a crow. It flapped around the room, dissipating over her head. The floor was uneven, her feet slipped.

"Yes, you are indeed Carbonelli by name, but Masciara by nature. The common vernacular is Witch."

Rose's knees turned to jelly, she slid to the ground. Her body moved, but she was not in control of it. The room cleared, the wobbling walls eased, and Rose found herself sitting in a chair opposite Mr Borgia. He blew rings of smoke; it smelled sweet, not caustic like other cigarettes did.

"Rose? Can you hear me?"

She nodded, wanting to run, but something… that strange pull she had felt between them, rooted her to the spot.

"I need you to listen very carefully to me, Rose."

Rose stared at him, seemed to see him anew.

"What are you doing to me?"

"Nothing. I'm not in control of who you are."

"I don't understand…"

Mr Borgia sucked deeply on the cigarette and blew the smoke from his nose.

"Surely you suspected something was different about you? You found the book, tried to be rid of it but could not?"

Nothing made sense. She shook her head.

"You see the dead, do you not? Those trapped between this world and the next?"

"No!" Rose snapped.

How could he know?

"I've heard what you see, Rose. I heard your father call to you in the haberdashery, saw the fear in your eyes. That's when I was certain you were a spirit witch like myself."

She was going to vomit, leaned forward, head between her knees. She couldn't catch her breath whilst he sat there calm, collected, divulging things about her no one, not Eric, not even Mama, knew.

"You can't know these things."

"I can, and I do. Your Familiar, Gianna told me exactly so, as did your father, as did Matteo."

Rose shook her head again; her skin felt strange, like it might peel away from her bones.

"I have been looking for another spirit witch for a very long time, one who can see the dead. You see them, don't you?"

"Papa? How do you know of him?" Rose grasped her head, tried to stop the blackness from pressing in. She didn't want to faint, not here, not now, not in front of him.

She tried to concentrate on his words, as outrageous as they sounded.

"You see dead things too?" her voice didn't sound her own… how could it when it spoke out loud of such things?

"I hear them only. I am Masciara, just like you. We both descend from an ancient line of spirit witches that both protect and hunt the dead. Some hear them, some see them, and some both see and hear the dead. Most importantly, together, we are more powerful than alone."

"You hear Papa?"

"I knew him, when he was still in this realm. Now… I only hear him beyond the walls of Rutherford House. The dead tend not to like this place." Another smoke ring haloed his head.

"The dead? Papa? You know he's dead?" Rose's hands balled until her knuckles whitened, "You have his uniform! You killed him!" She tried to stand up, searched for the letter opener again. Her legs wouldn't obey, shock held her in place.

Mr Borgia raised a hand, "I have killed no one, but yes, your Papa was here, he was trying to help me. Unfortunately, our arrangement concluded in unfortunate circumstances."

The room spun out of control. Rose gripped the arms of the chair, her nails biting into the leather. *Tick tock tick tock.* The clock seconds slowed into a syrupy tune. She was falling backwards, the room descended into darkness.

The old woman who forced her to keep the book stood before her… smiling. Her eyes were shiny gold-flecked coal, her movements strange, stuttered, like she was caught in a repetitive loop. Rose found herself in her bedroom at home. The woman was outside her window, tapping a finger upon the pane, whilst Rose felt the weight of the shadows in the corner. Tap, tap, tap. The old woman bent her head forward, both arms circled. Her body blurred; it lifted from the ground, spinning impossibly fast, flecks of black flitted around her, sucked into her. Her body collapsed in on itself, folding like a piece of paper. Black feathers floated upon the air where her body had been. A black crow shook its feathers, stretched its wings, cocked its head and peered through the window at her. Tap, tap, tap, went its beak.

Tap, tap, tap. The sound went on and on, banging in her head. Rose opened her eyes; she was still in the chair, Mr Borgia sat unperturbed in his. *Tap, tap, tap.*

Rose sat up, head pounding. The crow was tapping at the window outside the library.

"Come in Gianna," Mr Borgia said.

The bird stretched its wings and shook its body, the reverse of what she had just dreamt. The crow disappeared, the window rattled slightly and there.... inside the room... was the old woman.

CHAPTER 40

"You!" Rose jumped from the chair; a rush of energy infused her.

Gianna inclined her head, a half-smile upon her lined face. She was short, a little stooped, dressed in a plain black dress, feathers poked through matted grey hair.

Rose looked between Mr Borgia and Gianna and back again.

"You've been..."

"Watching you closely for a while now. Keeping you safe," Gianna said, her voice soft. A gentle smile brought colour to her complexion.

"You had no right... my life, this is *my* life!" Rose pointed hard into her own chest.

"You don't get to come into my life and..."

"Save you from starvation? Show you your true potential?" Mr Borgia stood and took the old woman's hand.

"Gianna sensed your skill and ensured you found the book. She made sure none but the dead with goodwill crossed your path."

Rose backed away, eyes firmly on Mr Borgia and Gianna. She clawed the doorframe, breathing too fast; darkness threatened once more.

"Beloved child... please don't be scared," Gianna reached for Rose, a gentleness in the lines of her smile was something Rose didn't want to acknowledge.

"Get away!" Rose ran. She skidded to a stop. Crows fluttered around the front door, bouncing across the floor, one hung sideways from a

238

smoking thurible. All cawed in deafening unison. They took flight towards her; she felt the beat of their wings.

"No!" Rose turned; couldn't remember how she ascended the stairs so quickly. She pulled on the doors; she thought she'd left them unlocked, but they wouldn't budge. She fumbled for the keys, realised they were in the uniform she'd discarded on the floor maybe an hour ago. She grabbed her head, heard her name being called... deep in her mind.

Rosa. Do not fear us.

The crows burst from the stairwell, circled the landing, feathers fluttered along with the motes in the window light. Rose yanked wildly on the knob, the wild-eyed girl in the mirror was not her... yes, it was. She pulled desperately on the door. "Open, open damn it!" Why wouldn't it obey her like the drawer? Her hands shook until they slipped away, and she fell.

The door clicked open.

Gianna stood inside the doorway.

"Rosa, please, listen?" She reached for Rose; black feathers sprung from her knuckles, her fingernails black claws. Rose screamed, shuffled backwards, somehow pulled herself up, closed her eyes and ran through the crows, back downstairs, and burst from the front doors. She ran until she found herself breathless at the stables.

"Eric? Eric?"

The horses circled in their stalls, snorting as she screamed again. Crows sounded in the distance.

"Eric, where are you?" The crow flew in... Gianna... Devil, sat upon the rafters, pacing, watching with her amber-flecked eyes.

"Leave me alone!"

Rose climbed the loft, missed a rung, slipped and grazed her leg, her shin pounded in pain. She groaned, grit her teeth. Gianna cawed and circled overhead. Rose pushed on, ignored the pulsing in her leg and pulled herself up the ladder. She pushed open a door that led her into a bedroom.

It was musty, Eric's footprints upon the dusty floor. Straw and hay clung to corners and cracks in the walls. His clothes hung upon a wired rack; his beloved peaked cap lay upon a washstand. Sunlight struck through a small window above the cot that was his bed. Rose sat upon it, picked up his pillow, held it to her face, and inhaled the scent of him. She held it tight against her chest. Was he in danger because of her?

A bottle of green liquid sat by his bed, a small glass next to it. She picked it up, sniffed and recoiled. It was alcohol, some kind of strong liquor with an herbed note. She set it back down; he wasn't normally one to imbibe. Rose then recalled seeing Eric heading back to the house earlier; she was sure she had heard him walking up the stairs.

Rose limped back along the driveway; her shin slowed her down, her injured gait crunched too loud along the gravel. She imagined Eric under attack, pecked at by crows, that thing in the walls bearing down on him. Her pain dulled and she ran harder.

The sun dipped behind the clouds; the gentle warmth of the morning was replaced by a frosty bite. She reached the front steps only to find the doors were locked. Rose banged upon them.

"Let me back in!" she screamed.

Rose ran around the back of the house; she couldn't feel anything anymore. Numbness took over. She pushed through sheets flapping on the line, slid across the gravel path of the vegetable garden and came to a shuddering stop when she tumbled into the kitchen.

"What on God's earth?" Martha yelped, "Are you still playing the fool?"

Rose pushed her glasses higher, through heaving breaths, she pointed at Martha.

"You knew! You knew!"

"Knew what?" Martha slapped her knife down, wiped the juices of a butchered bird upon her apron. "I don't know what's got into you, but I was correct as usual. None of you stay. Poor Mrs Rutherford. She can't help herself. None of you have any compassion. You may as well pack your things now!" Martha's voice was shrill, her face pinched in morbid satisfaction.

Rose grimaced, leaned a hand onto the bench, teeth clenched.

Why did her belly have to hurt now?

"It's not Mary, and you know it!"

Martha's expression changed. The crease of her brow relaxed.

"Seems, then, like his Highness has finally found what he needs." She leaned onto the bench and sighed. She looked at Rose, her gaze piercing, "Either help him or get out and run far, far away, Girl."

Rose screamed and ran the corridor, up the service stairs, calling until she was hoarse.

"Eric? Eric, *please*, where are you?"

She ran back to the library. Mr Borgia was gone, the room peppered with black feathers. At the brink of exhaustion, she leaned against the wall, her legs gave way, and she slid to the floor again. Rose tried to calm, to think… to listen to the house.

Voices… not nearby. She checked the corners; there were no shadows here, no ghosts… not like at home. She cocked her head to the side, her eyes rolled towards the ceiling.

"Eric?" His distinct, deep laughter rumbled through the walls. There were cracks in the ceiling, webbing their way across the plaster. A hole in the right corner, an ominous darkness; she could feel its pull, smell the rot of the thing that it hid.

Rose ran back up the stairs, pulling herself around the banister, just in time to see Eric disappearing with Mr Borgia into Mary's rooms. The crows turned their attention to her, cawed deafeningly, then took flight, a black streak down the staircase.

Her body shook, she gasped for breath, banged on the mirrored door. Rose screamed for Eric, but terror stole her voice. She yanked on the mirrored door; it was locked again.

"Let me in!" Rose croaked. She punched the glass, jiggled the knob, staggard back, and leaned forwards on her thighs. Something strange tingled under her skin, an itch needing a scratch, an aching muscle needing to be stretched. Her eyes flicked to the door; teeth clenched.

"Open!"

The handle rotated. Her reflection disappeared as the door creaked open. Rose backed away, the door swung slowly outwards, no one on the other side. She hesitated momentarily, quite ridiculously wondered had she commanded the door open just like the drawer.

Idiot.

It was just another breeze… or was it? Were the crows in her imagination, was Gianna transforming into a bird a figment of her mind gone mad? No… she had seen these things and whatever it all was, it *was* happening to her. She ran onwards, past the dumbwaiter, up the hallway, her reflection a hundred times over followed on. Bursting into Mary's bedroom, she came to a skidding stop, breathless.

"How did you get…" Rose let the question fade.

"Ah, there she is," Mr Borgia said, a smile plastered on his face, his gold tooth caught the light. Eric was close by his side, draining a glass of that green liquor.

"Eric… get away from him!"

Eric's eyes were glassy and red-rimmed, his face flushed.

"Rosie!" Eric held his glass up, smiled groggily. The Frangitelli Mirror captured the drunken wobble of his legs.

"What have you done to him?" Rose noticed a wicker-wrapped bottle of the green liquor on the table with that ornament.

A crow cawed, Rose swivelled around, the room a blur. The doors to the day room were wide open; Mary was on the balcony, oblivious to the goings on. Rose felt compelled to make sure she was ok, took a step towards her, then halted. Gianna, in crow form, leant into Mary's hand, enjoying long slow strokes down her feathered back. Gianna seemed to look Rose's way; she cawed again. Rose turned back to Eric who was florid with drunkenness.

"We have to get out of here, Eric!" Rose lunged for his hand. Eric staggered back, reached for the bottle. Rose picked it up and threw it to the ground; the contents oozed into the edge of a rug and pooled in the crevices on the floorboards.

"What a waste…" Eric slurred, he wobbled backwards. Mr Borgia steadied him; Eric gave him a thumbs up.

"You're drunk!" Rose seethed; her teeth clacked together.

Eric waved a finger at her, "I'm not am!"

"What have you done to him?" She pointed accusingly at Mr Borgia, who was frustratingly calm.

"I have done nothing other than offer him a drink, Rose." He frowned at the dissolving green puddle. "It's most expensive to import."

"What is it?" Rose demanded, "Is it poison?"

Mr Borgia laughed, pressed his hand defensively to his chest.

"Rose! I would never dabble in such mediocre means to accomplish what must be done." He gestured to the stain on the floor, "What you have just wasted is Centerbe, a common Italian liquor, nothing so peasant as poison."

Rose glanced between him, the spill, and Eric, "How much has he had?"

"A shot," Mr Borgia said, pulling a chair out; he pressed Eric's shoulder and sat his unsteady body down.

"He's that inebriated after a single shot?"

He inclined his head, "Let's say it was a mixer, not a straight shot."

"You've drugged him?" Breath punched from Rose.

"Drugged no... never. Relaxed him... yes." Mr Borgia said with cool calm.

Rose lunged to the chair.

"Eric, Eric, come on, we have to get out of here, now! It's not safe here."

Eric was too big, too heavy. She couldn't move him.

"You told me not to come here. You were right," Rose pulled his shoulder; Eric shrugged her off. She slapped her hands to her chest, mouth agape and backed away. Rose eyed the hallway, the doors, the balcony, wondered how she was going to get them out.

"Eric... please..." She begged.

"Rosie..." Eric waved his finger at her again, and slumped deeper into the chair. He hiccupped.

"What I said was... not let my... your..." He belched. "Mmm... magination spoil a..." He hiccupped. "Good... thing." He belched again, wobbled forwards, leaned his hands onto his thighs.

Rose moved in again, grabbed his hand, "Eric, please... I can't carry you out..."

Mr Borgia moved and placed a hand on Eric's shoulder.

"Don't touch him!" Rose yelled.

"Rose, Eric has agreed to stay a while and keep company with Mrs Rutherford whilst you and I attend to some very important matters. I really do need your assistance."

Eric nodded, "Uh... 'sno trouble." His words blurred; his eyes watered.

Rose rushed at them, "Let him …"

Mr Borgia held up a hand, "I'm sorry to do this, but…" He splayed his palm towards the floor, and spoke words she didn't understand.

"Amatiano veru cedata."

Rose's feet stuck to the floor. She wobbled forward.

"What's happening?" She screamed, yanked wildly at her feet. They would not rise from the floor. She circled her arms, trying not to fall forwards. Rose gasped and spluttered, panic well and truly settled in.

"What's happening, Rose, is that I need you to sit down and be quiet, just until I explain our unique circumstances."

Rose screamed, "Help… Martha… Charlie… help me!"

Mr Borgia swiped his hand across his lips and spoke more strange words.

"Alria Garia Ananus."

His accent was deeper, monotone… powerful.

Rose's tongue felt suddenly thick, too big for her mouth, she tried to scream again, but her desperate cries rang only in her head. She couldn't move, couldn't speak. She watched in wide-eyed horror as Mr Borgia placed a hand on Eric's shoulder once more.

"Till we meet again, Eric," Mr Borgia pulled him up and guided a stumbling Eric around the table, past that ornament, towards the Frangitelli Mirror. He positioned Eric until his back reflected upon it. Mr Borgia mumbled something else; it was inaudible… and then he pushed.

Eric fell backwards and kept falling. There was no bang, no breaking glass. Eric splashed into the Frangitelli Mirror, lost in its reflection, swallowed by it, the silver of it lapped like water around the frame.

"Now, Rose, you will listen."

CHAPTER 41

Rose was seated by the round table under the watchful eye of the Frangitelli Mirror and ghastly black vessel. She remained speechless; feet hooked to the floor by some invisible force. In her head, she screamed, even prayed to a God she didn't believe in. Her eyes burned with angry tears, then terrified ones, as she saw Eric's image running through the mirrors. His horrified face bled across the many reflections, his fists banged frantically and silently from within the strange realm.

"He is not in danger; it is, in fact, safer in there than out here," Mr Borgia pulled another chair up and sat across from Rose.

"Gianna?" he called. She flew in, landed on his shoulder. He stroked her inky feathers, "Keep Mrs Rutherford occupied for as long as you can." Gianna bobbed her head, flew back outside.

He looked at Rose, crossed his legs, and rubbed beads of sweat from his top lip.

"Rose, I know this is all very unexpected, perhaps a little frightening, but for your safety, for Eric's, for Mary's, for mine, it is imperative you listen to what I have to say."

Rose shook her head; her skin burned with the effort of trying to find her voice, make her feet bend to her will.

"I was expecting you would take longer to show your potential, settle in before your power presented itself. But nature has a way, and in nature, we trust."

Rose blinked through a fresh flow of tears, shoulders slumped, she ceased a pointless struggle.

"I will remove the spell if you promise to let me speak."

Rose nodded, tried to calm herself, slow her breathing, and drive away the tingling in her lips and fingers.

Mr Borgia clasped his hands and then flicked them towards her.

"Contrarum Alria Garia Ananus at cedata."

Rose's body unlocked; her voice burst from her throat. She ran to the Frangitelli Mirror, clung to its frame, screamed for Eric. He wasn't there. She ran the room, found him banging within a small square mirror near the hearth.

"Eric… Eric!" She screamed. He called back, his voice mute as he punched wildly within the glass. A smokiness surrounded him. His eyes widened, he ran, crossed another mirror. Rose followed, losing him in the murkiness, "Eric!"

Mr Borgia spoke the strange words again.

Rose's feet stuck to the floor; her mouth clamped shut. Arms wrapped around her. Mr Borgia scooped her up, carried her back to the table, sat her on the chair, and pushed her closer to the Frangitelli Mirror. Eric was running circles within it, looking for a way out.

"Very well, we will discuss matters like this then," Mr Borgia sat across from her, smoothed out his pants and jacket.

Rose whimpered through heaving breaths. She was out of her depth, perhaps out of her mind. She blinked her eyes clear of tears and glared at him with as much hatred as she could summon.

"You do not need to like me, Rose, family are funny that way. No matter where you are from, who you are, blood bonds do not always equate to friendship or love. Duty is another thing altogether."

She dug her nails into the chair, sucked in hard breaths.

Family? Friends? They could never be friends.

Mr Borgia cleared his throat, pulled another cigarette from his inside pocket and lit it. The smoke wafted her way, that same herbal sweetness. He blew it towards the Frangitelli Mirror.

"Badesso," he said. The glass reacted when the smoke coated its surface. It wobbled, the silvery glass dissipated until it was an eye of swirling, smoky darkness that lurched towards Eric. He ran, disappearing from sight, reappearing across all the other mirrors, chased by the fog.

"He is safe, as I said before. I just wish you to see something that you shall forego should you refuse to assist me." Mr Borgia's voice was silken as he pointed to the inky Frangitelli Mirror. "Think now, Rose, think of your mother."

Rose did nothing *but* think of Mama and Papa. Heat prickled up her neck; she fought to speak, but her mouth stubbornly refused to open.

"What I mean, Rose, is think of her now, wonder upon what she is doing in this very moment, where she is? Look into the Frangitelli Mirror and think of her right now." He stubbed out the cigarette on his palm; its sweet smoke curled upwards, dissipating into nothingness. He swept his arm towards the mirror, "Think Rose."

Her teeth squeaked, her jaw ached, anger and fear fought for dominance, but neither was helping right now, so she did as he said and stared at the mirror. Rose ran her attention around its ancient frame and noted patches of tarnish deep in the crevasses. The midnight oval of its centre demanded her attention, pulled at her as though they were connected, not unlike that strange feeling she felt the first time she met Mr Borgia. She shifted in her chair, felt ridiculous, looked to Mr Borgia, who reclined with all too much relaxation in his chair. The clocks ticked too loud as she concentrated on the huge mirror. Mary's footsteps clipped on the balcony, the tapping of Gianna's claws on the balustrade… and the rats, the scurrying in the walls, she heard them keenest of all. Now Rose knew that it was much more than vermin living behind the plaster, wood and metal.

Without realising it, her eyes had glazed. Mama came easily to mind, always in the peripheries of her thoughts. Rose's chest clenched. The last memory of Mama was her standing at the front door of their home, distraught, cheeks hollow, her clothes hung from her bones. Shame flushed under Rose's skin. She had been so dismissive to Mama, the secrets she kept about the things that followed her, about why she really fled so far away.

Mama, I'm sorry, the thought rolled through her mind. Over and over, she recalled Mama halving, then quartering her share of their meagre meals, of her secretly sobbing in her bed at night, calling out for Matteo and Papa in her sleep. Tears blurred Rose's vision and settled in hot pools at the base of her glasses. But as her vision cleared, the Frangitelli Mirror seemed to change; she blinked again, sucked in a breath.

The darkness curled into a stormy vortex, the glass undulated in and out as though it was breathing. Something shifted within it, beyond the smoke, behind the dizzying movement. Light pressed in from the edges. Streaks of blue and white became a sky. The smokiness receded to reveal trees, a roof and a front door. Rose sat forward, nostrils flaring. Her house, it was *her* house in the mirror, and someone was walking to the front door, a large sack over their shoulder. The door opened, and there was Mama. Stinging tears flowed harder; Rose blinked impatiently and wriggled in her chair, not understanding what it meant. Was Mama in danger? Rose's breaths accelerated.

Edith clasped her cheeks with surprise, a smile rarely seen blushing her face as the man placed the sack down. He pulled from it bags of flour, candles and matches. There were potatoes, salt and the distinct wrapping of butcher's paper.

The joy on Mama's face melted Rose. The man handed Mama an envelope. He tapped his cap and walked back up the path, disappearing from view. Mama emptied coins into her hand, tears glistened in her eyes. She signed the cross and looked to heaven.

The mirror flashed black, then silver once more. Rose screamed in her mind.

Mama, Mama… I love you.

"That is for just two days of very minimal work. I wish you no harm Rose, that I promise on my very honour." Mr Borgia placed a hand over his heart, "Help me, learn from me, and that delivery will be just the beginning. Both you and I can save your mother… and your father, and liberate yourself as being anything but ordinary."

CHAPTER 42

Rose felt her feet and mouth release, she wiped spittle from her chin.

"What is going on?" her voice was dry, her head still spun. The clocks were still too loud; they struck upon the hour. Midday. How had time passed so quickly?

"What do you mean by save my Papa? He's…"

"Dead, yes, I know this. Yet, he is in need of help, as you well know," Mr Borgia's eyes narrowed on Rose as he lit a new cigarette. His cheeks hollowed as he drew deep on it.

He blew a thick plume of smoke, "I will preface this by admitting that I am quite desperate for your help, Rose. Johnathon Rutherford and I were at one time good friends. But friendships change. Greed, desire, and the need for prestige changed him irrevocably. Some ten years ago, I made an egregious error by allowing Johnathon Rutherford to visit my private residence in Sardinia. In his avarice for ancient artifacts, Johnathon brought into this house something most dangerous, something he had no right to." Smoke billowed from his nostrils.

"As I said earlier, I am a spirit witch, like you, and when a witch enters into a deal, they are bound to it… quite literally. This deal I could not refuse for reasons that will reveal themselves in due course. Until the deal made with Johnathon has been concluded, until a wrong has been righted, I may not leave… I cannot leave. An unforgivable mistake on both his and my part unleashed a great terror in this house, and for ten years I have sought another to help me." He shook his head and licked his lips; the spark in his eyes dulled, "This demon which you have seen, it is stronger than any I've ever encountered. I have tried for a decade to defeat it; I've seen the death and harm it has caused." He sighed, raked his oiled hair. "It is my fault it had the opportunity to make it to these shores, my fault Johnathon's greed brought it here." His eyes reddened, "I have missed my children grow up. I cannot and will not see them again if I am unable to defeat the evil in these walls... and if that is the case, I will die here." Ash fell from the cigarette onto his lap. He brushed it away. His lashes weighed heavy with emotion. This caught Rose off guard, unwound her anger just a little.

"I know this all seems unfathomable, impossible even." Mr Borgia waved his hand, the chair creaked as he stood up.

"It wasn't meant to be you; it was your father who I first sought."

"Papa? What do you mean? He was at war…" Her voice faded, the image of his army uniform in Mr Borgia's rooms slapped sense into her. The words of his unfinished letter bore into her thoughts.

"Papa lied to us…" Rose's lips trembled.

Mr Borgia paced, then rested a hand upon the Frangitelli Mirror.

"Your family on your father's side long ago let their heritage lapse. The witch trials saw to that for so many of us, and who could blame them, really?" He shrugged, "Modern religion has almost been our complete undoing." He shook his head, "Finding kindred these days is difficult, especially so in Australia. This land is so very far away, a different world." Rose felt vulnerable with him towering over her; she stood, edged behind her chair, gripped it for dear life.

"What happened to my Papa?"

Mr Borgia nodded, his expression solemn, lashes still glistening.

"A very good man, the best of men, really. He left his craft in Italy, had not practised in a very long time. Giacomo travelled all the way to Australia to escape it, but still, he came to my aid when I asked, and accepted the bond as I had. He was a good man, a loyal Masciara."

Rose shook her head, squeezed her eyes tight, "He went to war, he did not return, he's… dead." It was a lie and a truth.

"And how do you know he's dead?"

Rose bit her lip, "Because he is."

"But *how* do you know?"

Her lip split between her teeth; warm blood coated the tip of her tongue.

Mr Borgia took a step closer, Rose leaned back.

"How do you *know* he's dead?" Cigarettes and coffee wafted in the air as he neared.

Gianna crowed outside; it made Rose shudder.

"Rose, how..."

"Because I *see* him!" She grabbed her head, "I see the dead. Are you happy?"

She had never admitted that out loud; the words felt strange on her lips.

"What do you want of me? What happened to Papa?"

"Sit."

"No, I'll stand." Rose was angry again, and the anger felt so good, "Just tell me everything, so I can get out of this place!"

Mr Borgia sat back down, Gianna fluttered in, rested upon his shoulder. Then another crow flew in and sat upon his other shoulder. This one seemed to whisper in his ear.

"Very well," Mr Borgia nodded. Seeing Rose's confusion, he then whispered to the second crow, who fluttered to the table with the black vessel.

"You can tell that one is Gianna. If you note, she has a single white spot upon her tail, indicating her advanced age." Gianna cawed at him as though this statement displeased her.

"This fellow is Pero, *my* familiar. We've been paired for a long time. You will get used to Gianna; she is most wise, Pero not so much."

Pero hopped back and pecked at Mr Borgia's hand, "But he is most handsome." Mr Borgia stroked Pero's wings; the crow seemed to forgive the insult and leaned into Mr Borgia's touch.

"I don't want birds... I want an explanation, and I want to leave this place..." Rose stumbled over her words. "After I do whatever it is you need me to do." She couldn't contemplate Mama going hungry ever again... and Eric, she looked to the mirrors... *where is he?*

"Mary is coming in; ring the bell, Rose. We will have Martha sit with her a while."

On cue, Mary wandered in, doll in hand; she stopped, seemed to pause upon Mr Borgia, then looked to Rose.

"I am hungry." Mary wandered away again; a soft lullaby followed her back to the balcony.

"Of course," Rose curtsied awkwardly, side-glanced Mr Borgia.

"I will call Martha." Rose ran down the hall, opened the door to the alcove, and pulled the call bell next to the dumbwaiter. She leaned against the sideboard, took a deep breath, head in hands. *Am I dreaming?*

Something flashed in one of the mirrors.

"Eric?" Rose grabbed a wooden frame, followed the movement to a golden frame and then to a silver.

"Eric?" She pulled the mirror forwards, trying to see him. It slipped from her hands, smacked back against the wall. It cracked. A thin line on the bottom right corner slivered along the edge of its frame. The silver around the crack lost its shine and faded to black. The mirror next to it cracked as well. Rose scrambled back; she hadn't touched that one. Each mirror in the alcove cracked in the same place. The candles flickered, the electric light stuttered as one by one, the mirrors cracked and dulled. The door of the dumbwaiter shuddered, the pulleys within creaked. Something scratched from inside it, something whispered.

"Va Via."

Rose slammed back into the wall just as she heard a key in the door. Martha was about to enter.

Mr Borgia yelled, "Rose! What have you done?"

CHAPTER 43

Mr Borgia burst into the alcove as the door of the dumbwaiter shook ferociously, the vase of lavender and baby's breath smashed to the floor from the vibrations.

"Dio!" He clapped his hand to his head. "You have broken the chain!" He grabbed Rose by her wrists, "Do you realise what you've done?" He glared at her, his mouth opened and closed as though words eluded him, before he let her arms drop.

"Get out of the way!" Mr Borgia kneeled, began circling the doorframe with his fingers. Smoke curled away from the wood, the smell of embers and polish left behind as he burned circles into the doorframe.

"Va Via!"

A gut churning howl erupted from the bowels of Rutherford House. Rose's skin turned to ice. Mr Borgia looked up, he scanned the roof, then the rattling dumbwaiter before he grunted and his movements quickened.

Rose's lips quivered, "What…. What…?" The chandelier spun; its crystal droplets tinkered and clanged louder and louder. Light flickered around the walls, like starlight spinning across the sky. Something shifted in the house like a chord had been struck. The air clawed in and out of her lungs, a new taste of rot upon it.

"Va Via!"

"What's happening?" She raked her face, welts dragged down her cheeks.

"What's happening?" Mr Borgia's shoulders jerked, he seemed to laugh as he completed another circle of the other side of the doorframe, "Resorting to the most rudimentary of repellent spells to protect us from a demon... *that's* what is happening, Rose." He pulled himself up, his face flushed, he dusted ash from his perfectly intact, still smoking fingers.

Mr Borgia took her wrists again; his grip tight, his measured demeanour gone. "A Witch's Mark is weak, it won't last long," he glanced at the charred concentric circles. Sweat ran down his temples, his eyes wide with fear. "The spell of the Frangitelli Mirror is broken. We have little to protect us. We must go on the offensive. Now we must force the Bruxas out!"

He pulled Rose along the hall, his pace brisk, the shake of his hand panicked. She stumbled behind him, trying to understand what was happening. The sweat of his hand let her pull away.

"I don't understand. What have I done?" Rose half yelled as the three cats ran past, their hackles raised. They hid underneath Mary's bed. Their growls only made her blood run colder. Rose backed against Mary's bed; the cats hissed near her feet. Mr Borgia quickly fashioned another Witch's Mark on the doorframe of Mary's room.

"Gianna! Pero!" he called. The birds fluttered in. "The mirror is compromised." Mr Borgia's words were beset with fear. It was then that Rose noticed other mirrors were cracking, one by one, their shiny surfaces dulled, darkness oozed across them... and the house shifted some more.

"Get Mary in front of the Frangitelli Mirror; it can withstand the assault the longest. Stay with her," Mr Borgia ordered.

The birds cawed, then flew out.

"Go with them, Rose, bring Mary inside... now!"

"What about Eric?" Rose followed on, past a wide-eyed Martha, mouth agape, teapot shaking in her hand. Eric was nowhere, the mirrors slick reflections marred one by one as cracks tracked through them.

"He is fine! Just do as I say Rose!" Mr Borgia yelled. Gianna reappeared, flew around Rose and coaxed her outside.

The crows bounced along the balustrade, cawing at Mary. Gianna circled into her human form, Pero upon her shoulder. She spun her hand, a small vortex of white mist seeped from her fingers, a chill wind blew up and tugged at Mary's veil. Mary shivered.

"Come, Lady, come," her old voice coaxed for Mary's attention. Mary paid no heed. "Rose?" Gianna gestured for Rose to go to Mary, she waved her on impatiently, feathers already sprouting along her fingers again.

Rose hesitated as she watched a crack split the balcony tiling, it snaked towards Mary, a hole appeared beside her.

"Va Via." The voice was fainter, but the evil of it set Rose into action.

"Mary?" she called.

Mary turned, "Yes, Dear?" She hugged the chill Gianna had set upon her.

"This cold is not good for Arthur; can't you hear him coughing?" Rose felt sick taking advantage of her malady.

Mary drew the doll closer, leaned an ear towards it.

"Oh my, yes. He is shivering. We must get him inside at once." Mary followed Rose through the dayroom. They hurried into her bedroom, Gianna close behind, returned to crow form.

Mr Borgia had placed a chair in front of the Frangitelli Mirror.

"Dear lady, please, rest yourself," he forced a smile. The glassiness of fear enhanced the amber that ringed his dilated pupils. Rose pulled a blanket from the crib and wrapped it over the doll.

"Thank you, Josephine, you're such a good girl."

"Are you comfortable?" Rose asked, barely able to quell the tremor in her voice. Mary nodded. "Look, Mary, Martha is here with some tea." Each utterance was a struggle for Rose, each word an effort to form.

Martha spilt the tea as she passed a cup to Mary, "There now, Mrs Rutherford."

Mr Borgia circled the dayroom, hand out.

"Chiudere!" The balcony doors slammed shut, their locks clicked with no hand upon them.

He moved to Martha, placed a gentle hand on her shoulder.

"Martha, I would like you to leave early today; take a few days to yourself. I will be attending to this *rat* problem once and for all. Rose will see to Mrs Rutherford's needs. Take the cats with you, let them outside and tell Charlie to have some leave as well," Mr Borgia said.

"Of course," Martha picked up the serving tray, not requiring further convincing. The used tea service rattled in her hands. "Pip, pip!" She called the cats; they needed no coaxing either. They dashed ahead of her, screeching that unnerving wail that only cats did so well. They disappeared down the hall with her. The main doors slammed.

Mr Borgia raised his hand in their direction, repeating the same word, "Chiudere!" The locks clicked into place.

"What's happening?" Rose asked, on the verge of tears.

"Thanks to you, Rose, you're about to find out sooner than I had planned."

"This house is possessed by a demon called a Bruxas. A vile creature that lives upon the souls of newborns." Mr Borgia's hands trembled as he struck a match, held the sizzling flame to another cigarette. He drew deeply and paced around the dayroom, leaving Witch's Marks at every doorway.

"A demon?" Rose searched the mirrors for Eric. "Where is it?"

Eric was still nowhere to be seen. So many mirrors had blacked out, cracked, broken, their reflections a memory.

"It isn't in the mirrors; they are what keep it at bay. They are powered by the Frangitelli Mirror but thanks to you, they all will soon be powerless," Mr Borgia said.

"Thanks to me? You brought me here under false pretences. How can I be at fault? I would never have taken this position, going from one haunted house to another!"

Mr Borgia dragged deep on the cigarette; he blew out from the corner of his mouth, smoke curled above his head. He stubbed the rest of it out on his palm.

"It is not a ghost; I can assure you, that haunts this house. It is the reason you have not seen your father, your brother, or any of the myriad of entities that would assuredly reside here. A Bruxas is that powerful, even the dead fear it."

He must have seen the utter confusion wash over Rose's face.

256

"It lives on souls, Rose. When hungry, it will consume any. No ghost will risk obliteration at the hands of a Bruxas."

As though it was listening, the bones of the house creaked like it was trying to shed its skin. Rose's head snapped up.

Was that an opening in the cornice above Mary's bed?

The house stilled; a silence fell that felt heavier, more ominous.

Rose had so much more to say, more accusations, questions, so many questions, but fear strangled her words. She leaned heavily against a chair, pressed a hand to her mouth.

"Yes… it's better that you listen," Mr Borgia poured the green drink, sculled it as his eyes darted about the room. "You saw the Bruxas last night, didn't you? And it wants you out?"

Rose nodded.

"Believe it or not, that gives me hope. It means it recognises you as a worthy opponent. You have unsettled it."

"I don't understand why any of this is happening." Rose's fingers clawed into the fabric of the chair.

"Why? It is here because of Rutherford's greed, and my selfishness. I am here because of duty to right a wrong, you are here because of your heritage... and the fact that your father was not strong enough against it." Rose's gut dropped.

"It… what happened to Papa?"

"He fought it and lost," Mr Borgia said all too plainly.

"That's why you have his things in your room. You hid his death!" Rose accused; a nail bent painfully back against the chair.

Mr Borgia rounded the room again, his attention now caught upon that hole in the cornice. A crack snaked towards the floor.

"Do you wish to discuss what we cannot change, or save all of our lives?" He held a hand towards the crack and quickly jerked away as though burned, "Because Rose, I can assure you, right now, our lives are in imminent danger."

Rose absently sidled up behind him, feeling it was a safer place to be.

"You owe me *something*. Some form of explanation," she said, eye on that crack as well.

Mr Borgia's shoulders dropped; he ran a hand through his now unkempt hair.

"Johnathon Rutherford was a friend. A lover of antiquities, a collector as you may have gathered." He pointed to the varied ornamentation of the room.

"I may be a witch, but it does not afford one a living in modern times. I was a dealer of antiquities, Johnathon's dealer." He paused to let that sink in.

He lit a new cigarette. The smoke curled around his face. Rose noticed the yellowing that stained his fingers.

"Johnathon had an astute eye, knew a deal, the value of things. But just after the turn of the century, he visited me in Sardinia, as I mentioned and that is where everything went astray." Mr Borgia walked to the table in front of the Frangitelli Mirror. He picked up the ugly black ornament.

"This is a Vasodemonio, a receptacle that entraps dark entities, demons if you will." He flipped the top of it open. It was a vessel. "It should not be here; it should have been destroyed long ago by me."

Rose stared at it, had felt something off about it from the moment she first saw it.

"The first one was commissioned in 1510 by Lucrezia Borgia; you may have heard of her?"

Rose shook her head.

"She was the daughter of Pope Alexander, and a witch hidden within the church… most controversial."

"Her initials are just there, in honour of her devising such a device." He ran a finger across the letters LB inscribed along the base. The house found its voice and groaned again; the sun dipped as the afternoon waned. The glare of the room dulled; even the chandeliers seemed to lose their powerful refraction. Shadows grew, tendrils of darkness crept along the floor, the corners began to take on a thickness that could hide things. Rose shifted with Mr Borgia towards the hearth where the light seemed brightest.

"Lucrezia infamously trapped a most dangerous Bruxas. It had been causing carnage throughout Rome, bringing attention to Masciara and putting our very well-intentioned ancestors in the sights of the church. Once caught, this Bruxas was destroyed by setting the Vasodemonio to flame. The design was then sent to my family estate in Sardinia, hidden away for use when required by Lucrezia and her descendants."

"Your estate?"

"Yes. My family are descended from Lucrezia Borgia."

"Why was this one not destroyed then?"

Mr Borgia nodded slowly; he rubbed a hand over his wearied face, "An obvious and reasonable question." He opened the trunk full of candles, passed some to Rose. He began lighting them, she followed suit, placing them around the room.

"This Bruxas is different."

"How?"

"It is my wife," he said.

"What?" Rose dropped a lit candle, quickly stomped out the flame that caught the edge of the carpet.

"Fifteen years ago, after our third child was born, my wife made a mistake, sought the wrong kind of help when our daughter was ill." He stopped moving. His back to Rose, he held a candle, his head bowed, "Instead of coming to me, she was lured by a dark magik, an evil that promised all that should not be." He rubbed his temple, "Antonietta was asked to pay an unreasonable price, my life for our daughter's. When Antonietta hesitated, she was cursed, turned into a Bruxas."

Rose stopped lighting candles; she bit her lip, "I'm, I'm so sorry."

"Antonietta became trapped between the realms of life and death. She lost her own soul, unable to resist the urge to suck the souls of others. The irony is, she returned and killed the very child she was trying to save… our child." His voice broke then, "I caught her in the act." He pointed to the Vasodemonio. "I had her in it, over a fire pit, but I couldn't do it. I was arrogant, I thought I could find a way to free her, so I left her locked away." He pointed a new cigarette towards the Vasodemonio, the smoke curled protectively around it.

"That's a dreadful story, Mr Borgia." Ice flooded Rose's veins as she stared at the Vasodemonio.

Mr Borgia sighed deeply, "Fate is cruel. Perhaps it was my punishment that Johnathon came across it many years ago when he visited my home. He was not happy when I told him it was not for sale. But he wanted what he could not have. Behind my back, he offered one of my ignorant housekeepers an obscene amount of money.

Unfortunately, in the dead of night, Johnathon took possession of it and fled home... here."

Rose stared at the Vasodemonio, felt the evil of it, unable to comprehend this man's wife was a murderous entity.

"I sent many letters of demand for its return, warned him of the danger. Initially my correspondence went unanswered. Some letters even returned unopened."

He began moving again, "Keep up with the light. We can't run out of light, Rose." He set candles under every electric light to capture as much of what was left of the mirrors as possible. Rose followed suit, feeling the claw of the shadows as she hurriedly set candles in front of the most intact mirrors. The strike of each match, the crackle of each flame was the smallest of reprieves.

"It was not long until I received the first letter from Johnathon. I knew it would happen. He accidentally released the Bruxas. Antonietta attacked his firstborn, then Mary, when she tried to protect Arthur." He picked up the vessel and flicked a small latch on the Vasodemonio. It flipped the top open, "I expect you have seen the results of the attack upon Mary?"

Rose nodded. He slipped from his hand the single glove he wore to reveal gnarled, mangled skin.

"It has attacked many. My wife has no memory of who she was, no ability to resist her nature." He put the glove back and pointed to the open maw of the Vasodemonio.

"Initially, I told Johnathon to leave this open. I sent him Sardinian soil seeded with magik to coax her back in. I couldn't leave my young children to travel half way around the world." He shook his head, pushed the Vasodemonio back to the centre of the table. It loomed larger in the Frangitelli Mirror behind the eerily still silhouette of Mary.

"The Bruxas has decimated this house. Scared off the staff, attacked more than a few in the dead of night. Some were killed." He rubbed that gloved hand, "More letters arrived. Despite the death of the child, Antonietta would not leave. To this day, I don't know why. Bruxas kill and move on. Antonietta didn't." He poured a small glass of Centerbe, offered it to Rose. She shook her head, especially after seeing its effect on Eric. Mr Borgia sculled it.

"After some research within the Masciara community, I sourced the Frangitelli Mirror from the island of Murano." He pointed the empty shot glass at it, "As I mentioned the other day, it was forged by Francesco Frangitelli in the 1700's, a scryer who could enchant anything made of glass. This mirror was created to repel powerful entities, like Bruxas. It was all I could do from a world away, so I shipped it here at great expense. I instructed Johnathon to set it up in the centre of the room, cover the walls in mirrors and leave the rooms lit at all times so the Bruxas would see itself at any point it tried to enter. I hoped that would be enough, that it would tire, retreat… but something keeps it here… its hunger was never sated, despite the fact no other children have entered the home since Arthur Rutherford was murdered."

Mary sobbed, just once. She did not move other than to hold the doll tighter.

"I… I…"

"What is it, Rose?"

"I think I saw what happened to Arthur."

Mary drew a deep breath. "Josephine, Josephine, where are you?" She stood up, looked left and right. "Josephine?"

Gianna snapped back into human form; black feathers fluttered around her. She whispered in Mary's ear, placing a hand on Mary's shoulder. Mary instantly quieted and sat back on the chair. Gianna spun back into crow form, and settled on the back of Mary's chair next to Pero.

"Let's talk out of earshot." Mr Borgia guided Rose deep into the dayroom, had her sit on a chaise longue near the pianoforte.

"Tell me, Rose… what did you see?"

The memory shot through her mind's eye. She took a deep breath and thought what she was about to say couldn't be any more ridiculous than what she was witnessing and hearing.

"I touched the doll."

"And…?" Mr Borgia did not seem angered.

"I think I saw your… the Bruxas… um… when it attacked Arthur. It… she… it looks like a withered old woman… a dead old woman. It had…" Rose hugged the chill from her body. "It had no eyes… just black holes and its mouth…" She gasped, "Oh, I'm so sorry, that was a dreadful thing to say." She slapped her hand to her mouth.

Mr Borgia interrupted, brow furrowed, he paced, "I've come here to kill my wife, Rose. There is no dressing the situation as anything other than the most awful of truths. What you saw is the truth, and that is the bare bones of it." He paced a circle, flipped his pocket watch open and shut, "Perhaps left-over energy from Arthur's soul is attached to the crib?" He rubbed his chin, brow furrowed.

"I need to show you something," Rose said.

Mr Borgia followed her into her bedroom. Rose pointed at the window pane.

"It definitely doesn't want me here."

He leaned over the bed, touched the letters gouged into the glass, jerking quickly back.

"She knows your power even if you do not. When this is done, I will teach you that power. You will come to understand your grimoire, learn to love Gianna and all she can teach you too."

Rose bristled.

"What if I don't want to? What would Mama say? Her faith would… well, it wouldn't approve."

His mouth quirked, "Rose, what is a prayer but a spell to conjure the benefaction of a God? What is church other than a coven that raises a blood and flesh sacrifice of its saviour? Witchcraft is no different. Modern religion practices exactly as we do; they have merely tried to demonise our traditions whilst raising their own. Your mother will have sensed something about your father; she will love you as she always has, once she understands."

"I'm not so sure."

"Well, Rose, unlike religion, we do not force anyone to practice. We do not condemn those who turn away from it. Until you are ready, Gianna will watch over you." He nodded to himself as though the matter was finished, "Now, have you seen anything other than what you saw last night?"

Rose told him about the egg, seeing the Bruxas creep up the wall and disappear into the cornice.

"It is trying to scare you away. It has succeeded with many but it has never needed to resort to showing itself." He made his way to the door, "You are strong and brave, Rose. You *are* the one… most definitely the one I've been searching for. Your Papa would be proud."

Something cracked. Their heads snapped to the mirror at the head of her bed. A thin line spiderwebbed from the bottom to top of the glass, the mirror's reflection dulled and blackened around the edges. Rose looked to the other mirrors, still no sign of Eric. The house groaned; the walls filled with the pitter patter of… something… of it.

"He is safe in there. But *we* are becoming less safe each moment. Every mirror that falters will diminish the Frangitelli Mirror, allowing the Bruxas the opportunity to attack. It thrives in the dark."

Rose's fingers curled; she could almost feel the light being sapped away, felt the touch of things probing from the darkness that lapped at the corner of her eyes. She backed against the bed and swallowed hard.

"I will help you, Mr Borgia, but you will tell me what happened to my father and release Eric as soon as it is done."

"We are in agreement on that. I will need to consult my elders first whilst there is still daylight to protect us. With your ability to see the Bruxas and mine to hear it, I am sure we can divine a new incantation to capture it."

Fatigue washed over Rose, she sat on the edge of her bed, leaned forward, and put her head in her hands.

"While I work out what needs to be done, stay with Pero and Gianna, attend to Mary. If she becomes agitated, give her a sip of the Centerbe. Do not let her leave this wing… not for a moment."

Rose nodded into her hands.

"Okay." Rose felt worse than when she had stayed up all night at home. She wanted to leave, didn't want to acknowledge this new version of herself, but Eric remained somewhere in the depths of the mirrors, in a place she couldn't fathom. She couldn't do anything but what Mr Borgia asked. She had to save Eric… she would do anything to save him. That realisation set something into place within her.

"Do whatever you need to do. I'll do anything as long as you promise to bring Eric back to me."

CHAPTER 44

Sunlight faded to the velvet blue of a starlit night. A half-moon ascended, casting a pale hue across the estate. Rose stared at it through the balcony window. She felt like she was only half of herself too. Yesterday she thought she knew who she was, but now Rose realised she understood only part of herself, the rest a mystery to unravel.

"Rose?"

She turned. Mr Borgia had his grimoire open; its ink-drenched pages held her attention. Something in her wanted to know what those words said, wanted to understand that power. Rose had for so long been searching for strength, to overcome adversity, to defeat fear. She couldn't believe she was looking at the curls and flicks of that strange ink with hope.

"I have what we need to capture the Bruxas together." He pointed for her to sit, "Please…"

She sat on a chair that looked through to Mary's room. Mary remained transfixed in front of the Frangitelli Mirror, the crows on either side.

Mr Borgia sat opposite Rose, he leaned in, and turned the grimoire around. He ran his fingers down a passage of foreign words.

"The calling ideally should be done upon the golden handle of the half-moon. Unfortunately for us, that is in two days' time."

Rose frowned, "What does that mean? We have to stay here for another 2 days?" Her skin prickled.

"To have the ideal force required, yes, but we will do this tonight, at midnight, at the zenith of the moon. There will be no tomorrow for us otherwise." Mr Borgia's eyes were heavy, his skin had lost its golden sheen, a fine black stubble evidence of how very much he was undone.

Rose hugged herself, fingers digging into her arms, "I've no clue how to help. None of this means anything to me."

"You don't need to understand anything, not yet. Your presence, the power running through your veins will be enough. Your ability to see the Bruxas is exactly what will bring it down. When the incantation is struck, you will see it, I will hear it, and then I can point the Vasodemonio in the right direction. Along with the correct incantation, it will have no choice but to relinquish its freedom.

The walls rattled. Another mirror cracked. Mr Borgia narrowed his eyes at the Frangitelli Mirror and rubbed his chin. His fingers dug into the grimoire.

"Are we running out of time?" Rose leaned forward on her chair; her hands ran repetitively along her legs.

"Perhaps… perhaps not. It depends on how strong the power of the mirror is. We need the Frangitelli Mirror intact for as long as possible. How long that will be, I cannot know."

He flipped a page of his book, ran his fingers down the aged paper.

"Hmm." Mr Borgia's finger tapped; he bit his lip in thought whilst peering at The Frangitelli Mirror.

"What is it?" Rose rounded his chair, looked over his shoulder and watched his finger circle a paragraph of strange words.

"We must call the Bruxas three times." He licked his lips, eyes narrowing at the mirror.

"But we also need three people to do so."

"Three people? It's just us."

Something thundered across the roof. They both looked up, wide-eyed.

"We do have three people." Mr Borgia looked to back the Frangitelli Mirror.

"No! You are not using him!"

"What choice do I have?"

"Gianna! She can do it." Rose moved back to stand behind her chair.

Mr Borgia shook his head, "Gianna is old. She can only manifest her human form for minutes at a time. We are already at a disadvantage, thanks to you."

Rose winced at the accusation, felt retaliatory words rise until the overhead lights flickered. Something was being dragged through the ceiling.

"That," Mr Borgia pointed up. "Knows exactly what is going on, and she will do anything to stop us. All we need is a third voice, not a third witch. In this, you have no choice, Rose."

"You will *not* use Eric! He has gone through enough, put his life on the line for a pointless war already."

Mr Borgia closed his grimoire, set it down, "That is why I know he can help. He will fight for others, he is brave."

Rose clenched her teeth; her words slithered through them, "He is ordinary; he isn't… like…us!" *Like us… I'm already accepting it!* Rose wanted to feel shocked, push back at the idea she was one of these… Masciara… but it made some kind of sense to her, was more palatable than losing her mind for the past few years.

"You and I have the power required to recall the Bruxas, but the incantation requires numbers. And numbers it shall have." Mr Borgia lit another cigarette and crossed to the mirror. Mary did not flinch. He blew the smoke towards the Frangitelli Mirror.

"Please, don't, please leave him out of this?" Rose begged behind him.

"You wanted him out; you will receive your wish earlier than expected."

The Frangitelli Mirror warbled, the reflection lapped at its frame. The silver faded into a smokiness.

He spoke quietly.

"Adenum adfonte, Eric Wright."

Mr Borgia sunk his gloved hand into the silvery surface as though it was liquid. He yanked it quickly out, and bunched in his fist was Eric's scruff; his flailing body fell to the ground at Mary's feet. "Eric!" Rose fell by his side, patted him down, checked for injury.

"Oh my God, I'm so sorry," she cried and helped Eric stand. He was so very cold, blubbering incomprehensibly. She guided him to the small dining table, sat him down and wrapped a blanket from Mary's bed around his shoulders. He shivered hard.

"He needs something hot to drink."

Mr Borgia went to pour more Centerbe.

"No more of that poison!" Rose snapped.

Mr Borgia shrugged, picked up a teapot left from Mary's afternoon tea.

"That's no use," Rose said as she squatted and rubbed Eric's legs. She then held his hands, blowing her warm breath onto them.

Mr Borgia placed his hands around the teapot.

"Incanto caldo." Steam began to curl from the spout.

"You have much to learn, Rose." He poured steaming tea into two cups.

"For him." Mr Borgia passed one cup for Eric and took the other cup to Mary, placed it in her hands. Mechanically, she sipped the magical tea.

Rose sniffed the cup he gave her, sipped it. It was strong with tannins but tasted normal and was hot.

"Eric, drink this." She put the cup to his lips, he gulped it down, coughing after the last mouthful.

"I'm sorry Eric, I'm… this is all… I don't want you to be part of this."

"Stop." He put his hands up, "Stop, Rosie."

His hands slipped back to hers, he cupped them and pulled them to his now warm lips.

"I heard it all."

"You could hear us?"

He nodded.

"Eric I…"

Eric held up a hand to stop her.

"Whatever this is… I don't understand. I don't really want to right now." He looked around the room, eyes narrow at Mr Borgia who stood by Mary, watching them.

"All you had to do was ask. You didn't need to drug me. I'd do anything for her."

A lump sat in Rose's throat.

Mr Borgia nodded, "I know, as she would do so for you, that is why you are here, together. Insurance so that I can finally overcome this demon."

"Then why all the deception, tricking her into working here?" Eric pushed himself up, he stood protectively in front of Rose.

Rose rested a hand on his arm, wanting to say stop, but she didn't.

"She is young, raised in ignorance of what she is. She was starving and seeing frightening things. Do you think turning up to her house announcing she is also a witch would have had her come running to my aid?"

"How did you get Papa to agree?"

"Ah, that was altogether different. Your father… what an amazing Muscaria he was."

That word, *was*, made Rose flinch.

"It was a surprise to find him and so close. He had been estranged for a long time, a generous man who was eager to help. Once he knew of the Bruxas, his conscience didn't allow him to refuse."

"Where is Papa?"

Mr Borgia pointed to the ceiling.

"What?" Rose frowned. Both she and Eric looked up.

"It managed to separate us one evening. We had it cornered, but it evaded the incantation we were using. He saw where it went, ran ahead of me. By the time I found him, she was dragging him into the ceiling." Mr Borgia pointed to the hole in the cornice that was now the size of a cricket ball. Something black and oily oozed out of it and slid down the walls.

"He has called to you for two years, Rose, called to you to save him from what is essentially a half death. Defeating the Bruxas not only saves this home but also your father's soul. It has been feeding slowly upon him for all this time.

CHAPTER 45

"He left him there!" Rose cried. Eric followed her around the room, carrying extra pillars as night fell. Rose was still in shock, could only manage to shakily set one candle upon another. They lit them one by one until the rooms were blinding.

"He left Papa trapped here." Tears were gone, Rose sobbed drily. The walls rattled; the ceiling vibrated. She looked up, imagined the horrifying image of her father being feasted upon within the skin and bones of the house. All those visitations, he looked desperate, his mouth gaping, eyes wide with horror. Now she knew why and guilt gnawed her mercilessly.

"Rosie, I'm sorry."

She didn't correct Eric; for some reason, that pet name was now comforting, not annoying.

"It's not your fault; you couldn't have known about your dad."

They passed Mr Borgia, who was reading over the incantations.

"Papa lied to us, Eric. Why does everyone lie? I thought he went to war." Those letters she found in the library now made sense. The war story was just that, a cover story to explain Papa's absence.

Eric shrugged, "I can't imagine it would have been easier for him to say, hey, guess what, I'm a witch, and I'm going on a demon hunting expedition?"

Rose shook her head; tossed her match into the dayroom hearth.

"I guess not." She sat on the piano stool, ran her fingers along the keys.

"I'm sorry I couldn't tell you about the ghosts, Eric, I couldn't tell anyone, and I suppose I can understand why Papa didn't either."

Eric sat next to her; their shoulders touched. Rose felt herself blush, kept talking, hoping Eric didn't notice.

"At first, I thought I was dreaming. It was only at night. Then it started during the day with Papa and Matteo." She looked at Eric, he was studying his hands, thumbs rolling over themselves.

"Then, it was everywhere. In the street, in shops... I couldn't get away from them."

"Your mum didn't see anything?"

"No. Mama just prays day and night. She prays for Papa to come home every day. How could I say I was seeing his ghost, that I knew he was dead? She... both of us were only just hanging on as it was. It would have pushed her too far if I confided in her."

Eric wiped the lonely tear that slid down Rose's cheek, "How long has this been going on?"

"Two years."

"Rosie..." He took one of her hands, "I wish you could have told me."

"You weren't here... not in the beginning."

He nodded, hung his head, his thumb rolled gently over the back of her hand, her fingers curled around his.

"That's true, and ever since then, you've been angry with me."

Rose nodded; another tear ran hot down her face.

"Still angry?"

"I have complicated emotions right now, Eric."

"Yeah, I bet you do."

"What was in the mirror?" Rose asked, sliding further away.

He took a deep breath and let go of her hand.

"Darkness and cold." He raked his hair and sighed, "I thought I was dead for a while."

"I'm so sorry."

"Ahh, I've survived worse." Eric pointed to the scarred nub where his ear used to be and smacked a hand on his bad leg.

"You have, and I'm sorry I didn't appreciate that," Rose edged her hand back towards Eric's.

The pianoforte made a noise. The strike of a key in E flat. A baby wailed.

They looked at each other. Two more keys depressed. They jumped from the stool; the sound of glass cracking echoed from Mary's room.

"Rose!" Mr Borgia yelled.

She ran, Eric in tow. Mr Borgia reached out his hand, shook it impatiently, Rose instinctively slipped her hand into his. It was soft, warm like Papa's.

"It's here!"

CHAPTER 46

The clocks ticked past eight. The moon only halfway to its zenith. The Bruxas thumped within the walls. It was here, there, above, then below.

"I can't see it," Rose said. She held a mirror as a shield, as did Eric. Mr Borgia had the Vasodemonio, he filled it with a handful of enchanted soil and a small square of fabric he had cut from the crib. He then made his way to Mary.

"The fact you cannot see it is good. It means the mirrors are still strong enough." Mr Borgia pulled something from his pocket; a flash of silver glinted as he flicked open a knife.

"Hey!" Eric pushed forwards, "What are you doing?"

"The invocation calls for the blood of the cursed. Technically that would be the child. The Bruxas is seeking something that is not here. Mary as the mother, she is the closest we have. It is just a drop; you need not worry." Mr Borgia picked up one of Mary's hands, pricked a finger through the lace gloves and squeezed blood onto the blade. She did not react. He took the knife back to the Vasodemonio, let it drip inside. A coil of black smoke rose from within it.

"Take the book, practice the words I have underlined… both of you. It does not matter if you mispronounce them; nature understands. When the Bruxas appears, we must be ready and recite the words three times."

Rose picked up the grimoire and opened the page marked with a black ribbon to find the underlined words.

She read them in her head, too scared to utter them out loud.

"Practice Rose. They will not hurt anyone but the Bruxas," Mr Borgia said as he set alight the contents of the Vasodemonio. A flame burst from the vessel, then settled back to a gentle glow.

"C'mon, Rosie, let's do it together." Eric gently nudged her elbow. Rose gulped.

"Actatos Alrax de Braxa," Rose hesitantly spoke the first of the words under her breath. Eric followed suit, mouthing the words awkwardly, then held up his hands.

"Look I'm still here." He smiled at Rose. She felt the tug of a smile, wanted him to smile at her again, but she focused on the book, thoughts of other things neatly tucked away.

"What do they mean?" Rose asked.

"It invokes a demon, forces it to reveal itself and mutes its power against us." Mr Borgia stirred the contents of the Vasodemonio, the glimmer brightened.

"So, it should just go straight into that?" Eric asked, he nodded at the Vasodemonio.

"Yes, but we are not setting the ideal conditions, so… there is a risk it may show up and not do as commanded," Mr Borgia answered.

"Sounds encouraging," Eric muttered. "Better get these words right then."

Eric continued practising the incantation, as did Rose, awaiting the rise of the moon.

The clocks chimed quietly at 10 pm as though they too were wearied. All three stood by Mary, silently reciting the words... preparing.

A brisk wind had picked up, blew in thick clouds that hid the moon's gentle rise.

Mr Borgia peered through the curtains, checking on its progress, when there was a loud knocking at the doors to the wing. They all fell silent. Mr Borgia put a finger to his lips.

There was a louder, more urgent knock. The skittering in the walls rumbled that way.

"Is anyone there?"

"It's Martha!" Rose gasped, "Let her in!"

Mr Borgia set the Vasodemonio down, "Stay there."

He disappeared down the hallway.

Eric pulled Rose into the day room; he craned his head around the doorway.

"What are you doing?"

"Making sure those birds aren't listening… I can't believe I just said that out loud." Eric shook his head. He took Rose's hands in his, his thumbs circling her skin.

"Let's get out of here. This is madness." He whispered urgently.

"We can't." Rose pulled her hands away, immediately longing for their warmth again.

"Why not? I don't know if he's insane or dangerous or both," Eric said.

"There's no way out," Rose replied.

Eric peered quickly about the room and disappeared into the bedroom. She followed him, saw him frantically strip the bedsheets. He dragged them back in, Pero and Gianna watching, but they stayed with Mary.

Eric started knotting the sheets together.

"Rosie, help me. We can slip down the balcony."

Voices carried up from the hallway. The house shuddered; Rose ducked, but this time it was the thunder rolling in. Rain drummed against the windows, drowning the sounds scuttling in the walls. Lightning flashed; the room lit with pale white brilliance.

Rose was immediately drawn back to the crack; it was large enough to fit a head through. She thought of Papa, closed her eyes tight, tried to push away the nightmarish image of him being sucked into the fabric of this house.

Eric tugged her elbow, "C'mon, Rosie, he'll be back any minute."

She pulled away from him.

"Stop… just stop!" Rose held her hands up.

"He's nearly…"

Rose interrupted Eric.

"I can't leave."

Eric stopped knotting the sheets, let his arms drop.

"What...why not? The maniac shoved me into a magic fucking mirror, Rosie. What if that thing really is here? What if it gets to you?" She noticed he didn't refer to the danger to himself.

"It is here, Eric... I saw it, and I've heard it almost since the moment I arrived."

"And you want to stay?"

"Of course not... but I can't leave, not yet." She desperately wanted to leave, but the connection to this house couldn't be severed without helping Papa.

Eric let the sheets fall from his grasp. He pointed through the doorway to where Mary sat, as still as the dead.

"This is *their* problem. It's not here for us. You've been dragged into another person's war." Eric faltered. He looked to the floor, wiped a hand across the light stubble on his chin.

"I see why you were so bloody angry with me," Eric said. "Now I understand."

Footsteps padded slowly up the hallway. Eric collected the sheets, pulled them towards the balcony, and tried to open the doors.

"Shit, they're locked. Is there a key?"

"He locked them."

Eric looked around the room. "I'll find something..."

"I don't want to leave," Rose whispered as loud as she dared.

Eric stopped pulling the drawers of a tallboy.

"What, why?" He made his way back to Rose, "This place isn't safe." He pulled her hands into his, kissed the back of them. Rose's eyes welled; she didn't have the energy to resist and let tears slide down her face.

"Papa, that thing has Papa somewhere in this place. I need to save Papa... or set him free to move on." Rose sobbed. Eric pulled her into his side, she clung to him.

"Rosie..." Eric's words faded.

"He's been calling for help for two years. I've been running from my Papa, my dear Papa who needed me."

Eric rubbed her hair, the urgent panic in his eyes faded.

"Okay, okay." He kissed her hair, his lips lingered, they both quieted, just the sound of their breaths, the pulse of their hearts between them.

Mr Borgia's voice was getting closer.

Eric placed one of Rose's hands on his chest, over his heart. Her breath caught.

"No matter where I've been, the distance between us, it's always been one beat for me, one beat for you, Rosie." He kissed her head again, "And it always will be, Rosie. I'll never leave you again."

"Eric…" Her words were cut off as Eric tipped her face to his, pressed his lips to hers. She felt the tremble in them, the uncertainty. She couldn't blame him. She'd treated him so badly, like he was nothing when in reality, he was everything.

Rose parted her mouth, drew him in. His hesitancy waned, the poison of her anger diminished, and his feather-light touch deepened into an untapped fervour. His tongue swept over her lips, tasted the fear in her, it plunged deep and pressed fear away. Rose groaned, let his strength in, let her anger go. She knew in this moment that if they got through whatever this horror was, she would never let anger or pride come between them again. She didn't want to part, to let go of the heat of his lips, but Mr Borgia's voice was closing in.

Rose pulled away, her hands slid from his back, and ran down to his hands; suddenly shy, she smiled and looked to the floor. Eric squeezed her fingers gently; they broke away when Mr Borgia cleared his throat as he settled a stumbling Martha onto the chaise longue. A flash of something furry ran behind them; it hissed. It was Cathie. She disappeared into Mary's room. Rose worried for the others, but her concern for cats was cut short by the sight of Martha.

"I don't know what happened at all, Sir." Martha was white as a sheet, her lips pasty, her movements staggard.

He gave Martha a shot of Centerbe, she coughed through it but smiled.

"Thank you, I'm so very cold. 'Tis a strange taste, but warming." Martha's voice wavered with a shiver.

"I told you to go home, Martha," Mr Borgia's words were clipped.

"I… I know." Martha frowned, pressed a hand to her chest, looked up at him, confusion glazing her eyes.

"I was picked up as usual at half past five… well, I think I was…" Her words faded; she leaned back, "I think I've had a turn; I can't quite remember."

Rose poured a glass of water, passed it to Martha.

"You're here now; you're safe. We can take you home in the morning," Rose said, not entirely believing in her promise.

Martha looked oddly at Rose as though she didn't recognise her. Her hand shook, Rose helped Martha support the glass up to her mouth, she sipped, and water ran down her chin. Eric pulled a handkerchief from his pocket and passed it to Rose, who dabbed the dribble away.

"Thank you, Dear."

Rose smiled but felt unnerved by Martha's amenable demeanour.

"I'm happy to repay your kindness to me," Rose said, and this was no lie. Although Martha had been ill-tempered with her, she had unquestioningly helped her with her womanly pains.

Martha sipped again, shivered some more. She sighed, leaned back, and looked especially frail. Eric slipped the blanket that had warmed him around Martha's shoulders.

"I helped you?" Martha frowned again.

Rose leaned in and whispered, "Yes, you know, with my women's business." In that moment, Rose realised her pains had completely abated.

Martha still looked confused, smiled unconvincingly, "Of course I did."

Rose helped Martha finish her drink, then put a pillow behind her and left her to rest.

"She seems confused. My grandmother suffered apoplexy, she was a little like this," Eric whispered to Rose.

"I agree. We should keep her warm and call a doctor as soon as we can." Rose nodded.

"I'll find another blanket." Eric made his way back to Mary's bed.

Rose noticed Mr Borgia looking at the knotted sheets Eric had left on the floor.

His brows quirked, but he said nothing, just lit another cigarette.

The silence between them was deafening… the silence, that's when she noticed the walls, the roof, they had gone quiet.

"Where is it?" Rose asked, looking to the ceiling.

"I imagine saving its energy, waiting for the last mirror to crack." Mr Borgia jutted his head towards Mary's room and the Frangitelli Mirror, "It gives us more time to prepare." He parted the drapes, eyed the moon, "Another hour and the moon will be in position."

Martha sighed, her head lolled to one side, her eyes closed.

"She doesn't look well," Rose said as Eric returned, laying another blanket across her legs. Martha didn't notice; her breathing settled into the slow depths of sleep; a light snore fluttered from her lips.

"She is an old woman, a hard-working one at that. Age tends to find us all," Mr Borgia said with a distinct lack of empathy in his voice. "Time is running low, continue practising the invocation."

CHAPTER 47

Mr Borgia roamed the rooms, continuously checking on the mirrors, lighting more candles to capture every possible reflection. The day room and bedroom faded under a sinister, flickering orange.

"I'm not sure about this, Rosie. I've as much magic in me as a horse's arse," Eric laughed nervously. "This is gibberish." He jutted his chin at the grimoire.

"I feel the same," Rose sighed. "But, what choice do we have? I need to save Papa." She pinched the bridge of her nose, resisted the prick of fresh tears, "If this works, if we can catch that thing…" A shiver rippled through her. Eric rubbed her shoulders.

"Sorry, I'm putting doubt in you," he said.

"No, you're right. It does feel ridiculous. Could you imagine telling anyone about this? We'd be locked up for life!"

Eric tapped his head, "This is one tale that stays right here."

Rose smiled, but it wiped from her face when something banged.

All of them looked up, except Martha, who remained in the depths of sleep.

Mr Borgia pressed a finger to his lips, grabbed the Vasodemonio and curled his fingers at them to follow.

Mary had not moved an inch. Her morbid reflection in the Frangitelli Mirror was unsettling.

Mr Borgia pointed at each of them to take up a mirror again. Rose and Eric each lifted a small mirror from the wall, held them against their bodies and followed him to the hallway.

"The very moment you see her, Rose, you tell me which way," Mr Borgia said grimly.

They followed him down the hallway, the silence there broken by the subtle cracking sound of the mirrors continuously fracturing. The light was appreciably lower with so many blacked-out reflections. Rose swallowed hard, took care to step softly, slowly, every sense on edge. Her eyes found the corners, searched the ceiling; the shadows were deeper, the walls split and bulging in multiple places.

Eric edged protectively in front of her, Rose moved in front of him. "Together, we protect each other," she said; he nodded.

A mirror to Rose's left shattered, glass sprayed over them. They ducked, but Rose felt the bite of it.

Mr Borgia spun, faced the Vasodemonio in their direction. "Anul liberatum!"

The floor shuddered, the house groaned, lightning lit the windows. A storm raged both inside and outside. Lightning flashed again; thunder crashed over the top of the house. Mr Borgia's shoulders relaxed; he dropped the hand holding the Vasodemonio back to his side.

"It's just the spell of the mirrors waning; the Bruxas is not here." His eyes were wide, his voice shaky. Rose watched him retreat to the bathroom, recalling that it was his wife he was hunting.

"Rosie, are you okay?" Eric ran his hands over Rose's clothes, flicking glass shards away.

She nodded, "You?"

"I'm fine."

Rose touched Eric's face; her fingers came away bloodied.

"You're hurt, Eric." Fine bloodspots pricked his face, blood trickled to his chin, splashing on his shirt.

He pointed to his scarring, "Felt worse." He touched the left side of Rose's face, and his hand came away bloodied as well.

"I've felt worse too." Rose said.

Another loud bang shuddered up the hall. They halted, Mr Borgia left the bathroom, he opened Rose's bedroom door. They followed him in.

"Just the mirror," Eric said, kicking the frame of a mirror that had fallen glass-first to the floor.

"But how did it fall?" Mr Borgia's question was followed by the slam of the bedroom door and a crash in the ceiling. All three looked up, the scuttling returned with fervour. Rose tried to open the door, but it was jammed.

"Move!" Mr Borgia demanded. He held his palm towards the door.

"Aperi aniamous." The door shook in the frame.

"Aperi aniamous!" He said with more force. The door clicked; it creaked open an inch.

"Out of the way!" Mr Borgia pushed ahead, reached for the handle…

A woman screamed.

"Mary!" Rose exclaimed.

They ran up the hallway, the doors to Mary's rooms slammed shut. The bones of the house cracked, and the remaining mirrors along the hallway exploded one after the other. The sound was ear-splitting. Glass showered them; the sting worse this time. There was nowhere to hide. All three cowered from the razor hail.

"It's now. The time is *now!*" Mr Borgia yelled over the cacophony, raising the Vasodemonio.

"Do you remember…" The whole house shook; they swayed on their feet.

All the lights went out.

Shrouded in darkness, Rose grappled for Eric, their hands found each other quickly. His warm, hers slick and clammy. Mary screamed again; Eric's hand tightened around Rose's.

The storm was between its howling, but the house did not settle. The floor groaned, the walls cracked, underpinning it all was whispering. A coarse voice, running quickly along the still and stagnant air. The hairs on Rose's body stood erect, and her stomach fell.

"Dammelo il bambino."

"Dammelo il bambino."

"Cara Signora."

"Is that?" Eric's voice hitched.

"It's the Bruxas," Rose whispered.

Mary screamed weakly. Lightning struck the house, the hall window imploded, the smell of burning wood tainted the air. Rain and howling wind stormed in, saturating Rose. Eric shielded her with his body.

"Shit, Rosie, what the hell is going on?"

"I don't know!" Her lips trembled uncontrollably.

Mr Borgia thrust the bedroom doors open, the storm curled into Mary's darkened room. Mary screamed again.

"Mary?" Mr Borgia called.

The hearth glimmered insipidly; the darkness swallowed its light. Something growled. The fluttering of bird wings was nearby. Something growled again and the fluttering stopped.

"Mary?" Mr Borgia called again. He stepped cautiously into the room, only the white glow atop the Vasodemonio to guide them. Rose and Eric were close behind.

Rose had not felt such fear since leaving home, since the last time she stayed up all night watching the dead in the corners of her room. This fear, though, it crawled under her skin, slipped through every vein, and coiled tight around her chest. This was not just death, this was a pure, unadulterated evil.

They edged to the hearth. Mr Borgia dipped down, plucked up a fallen candle, and lit it in the gentle flame. An amber halo revealed him from the darkness. A pile of clothing lay at his feet; a dress and shoes. Mr Borgia visibly stiffened and kicked them from his path.

"Take this, hold it in front of your mirror." He passed another to Eric and lit a third for himself.

The whispering recommenced, more softly this time. A baby wailed somewhere in the darkness.

"Dammelo cara Signora, dammelo il bambino," the Bruxas called Mary for the baby.

"She's in here. Can you see her, Rose?" Mr Borgia whispered.

Rose's eyes pained wide, "No."

"Search Rose, she's close," Mr Borgia urged.

"I know," Rose could barely speak for the claws of fear.

"She? It's a she?" Eric whispered in her ear.

"Long story," Rose whispered back.

Mary screamed again, "No! Josephine, help me, help me!" All three spun, candles held high. The faint light caught the reflection of the Frangitelli Mirror. There Mary stood, something in a white shift leaned over her shoulder.

"That's how you got in, Antonietta. Clever girl!" Mr Borgia said.

"Forgive me, beloved, but your time here is done." Mr Borgia's voice was strained now. He sucked in a deep breath and looked over his shoulders, "Rose, Eric, things may get a little uncomfortable, be ready. Do not take your eyes from that, Rose." He pointed at the thing in white.

They edged closer to him in stiff, unwilling movements as he held the Vasodemonio higher.

"Actatos Adra Arata Alal de Bruxas." He pointed towards Mary.

The thing in white screamed and arced back.

"Va Via!"

"It's right in front of us," Mr Borgia whispered. He passed a candle to Eric, "Light as many candles as you can find. Light this place up and do everything I say, okay?"

Eric nodded, even in the dark his face was visibly ashen.

"Rose, repeat after me! Actatos Adra Arata Alal de Bruxas. Eric, you recite the words too whilst you light the candles."

"Yes Sir," Eric was already at the hearth dipping the wick onto dead candles.

Mr Borgia held his mirror higher, the Vasodemonio in his other hand. The room began to glow a little brighter with each candle Eric lit, an eerie orange hue that only added to the dread plucking at Rose.

"Rose, it's time to learn who you really are… now… recite with me."

"Actatos Adra Arata Alal de Bruxas," Mr Borgia commanded, Rose and Eric copied, their words a second behind his. The invocation rolled silkily across Rose's tongue, as easily as English. The thing in white arched back more violently; it screamed; Mary screamed. Light began flooding the room as Eric quickly spread his flame.

"Va Via!" The thing screamed, its spine cracked as it bent almost completely backwards, its head upside down.

"Oh God!" Rose screamed, "Martha!"

Martha's bloodied mouth gawped, her eyes a vacant stare. The collar of her shift was stained red. It was Martha who had hold of Mary.

"Help her!" Rose moved; some stupid unruly part of herself ran to Martha as the room shuddered. She stopped short when she saw Martha's face up close. It was chalk-white, blue veins surged like snakes beneath the skin. Her eyes ink-filled orbs, her wide smile deranged, it bared blood-stained teeth. The fingers of one of her hands were buried deep in Mary's neck. Martha's mouth moved; she hissed in a voice that wasn't hers.

"Va Via!"

"Oh my God!" Rose fell back.

Mr Borgia caught her, his breaths quickened, "It's not Martha anymore."

Wind howled in from the hallway, whipping up linens and dousing the newly lit candles with it.

"Fuck!" Eric yelled. He moved faster, re-lighting as many as he could.

Mr Borgia yelled over the squall, "Say it again, Rose. We have to get the Bruxas out of Martha to catch it."

Rose's lips felt numb, her entire body trembled.

"You can do this Rose; you need to do it… *I* need you to do it." Mr Borgia pulled her hands into his. The wind tugged his hair, snapped it into his glassy eyes. He licked his lips, looked to Martha and back to Rose, "Please, Rose. Help me save Mary, Martha, your Papa, and release Antonietta from this hellscape she endures?" He squeezed her hands. Rose squeezed his back and nodded.

"Okay." Rose breathed deep, set her feet firm against the squalling storm that had taken possession of the house. It buffeted her to and fro, "Let's do this, Mr Borgia."

"Eric?" Mr Borgia yelled.

"Right here." He squeezed in between them and they began.

"Actatos Adra Arata Alal de Bruxas." All three commanded, Rose and Eric more synchronous this time.

Martha howled, her bones snapped; her legs gave way, and the floor cracked underneath her collapse. Her fingers had left bloody holes in

Mary who somehow remained standing in front of the Frangitelli Mirror, doll still in hand.

Martha writhed, blood pooled underneath her.

Rose screamed, "Martha!"

Mr Borgia looked down at Rose, held her hand briefly.

"Martha feels nothing, Rose. She was dead hours ago... I didn't see it until now. That's why she's here. The Bruxas used her to evade the light. Now, let's get it out of her."

"Actatos Adra Arata Alal de Bruxas." All three yelled over and over. Martha curled in a bloody ball, moaning, fitting. The wind shoved them around until Eric fought back the gale to shut the doors and cut it off. Martha's body spun on the floor.

"Va Via, Va Via!"

Mr Borgia closed in on Martha, "See to Mary, Rose," he said and continued the invocation.

Mary was still. Blood oozed thick and viscous from five punctures in her neck; five finger marks. Rose yanked Mary's veil off, and pressed it against her neck to staunch the flow. Blood stained the porcelain of the doll's head.

"Va Via, Va Via!" Martha's body twisted. Her legs and arms snapped fully in half; her body slid across the floor under the power of the invocation.

Rose heard a growl; something touched her ankle. She yelped, looked down to see a cat tail flash from beneath Mary's dress,

"Oh... Cathie! Stupid cat!" Rose half laughed; half cried.

Cathie hissed and stayed hidden beneath Mary's dress.

"Holy mother of fucking God!" Eric dropped the candle. Rose snapped her head back to Martha.

Martha's body started spinning around and around, faster and faster. Rose's mouth fell open, she held onto Mary for support. Mary remained in her own world, silently staring at her own reflection.

"Stay back!" Mr Borgia edged between Martha and the others.

Martha's body stopped suddenly and peeled up from the floor. A sickening sucking sound as an unseen force lifted her into the air, her body suspended. Mr Borgia continued his Masciara attack.

"Speak the words!" He commanded. Rose and Eric joined in as Martha's mouth widened unnaturally. The jaw cracked, fell limp. A soul-crushing scream pierced the room. The doors slammed open, and once more, the storm raged within Rutherford House.

All three recommenced the invocation. Martha's body lifted higher; the scream more intense. Rose wanted to cover her ears but was still staunching the blood on Mary's neck.

Something snaked out across Martha's tongue. Something clawed from within her mouth. A crooked finger, then another.

"Oh..." Rose vomited. More fingers squeezed from Martha's mouth, ripped at her cheeks until a bony arm slithered out through her split lips. Her flesh tore, and Rose retched again at the smell of old, clotted blood.

Eric slid back behind Rose, wrapped his arms around her. They watched in horror, whispering the invocation as another arm peeled out of Martha and split her whole face in two. Body fluids splashed to the floor.

Mr Borgia chanted louder. His shirt wet down the back, his voice tiring.

"Hold this and don't stop repeating the spell." Rose pressed Eric's hand on Mary's neck and forced herself, willed herself with every bone in her body, to join Mr Borgia.

Rose helped exorcise the demon from Martha.

CHAPTER 48

Mr Borgia's breaths were stuttered as he muttered his spell for the doors to close.

"Aperi aniamous." Open doors slammed shut, locks clicked into place. The storm cut off again, yet a very different storm still raged inside as the Bruxas defiled Martha.

Mr Borgia held the Vasodemonio up, edged a little closer to Martha. Rose could smell the salt of his fear. She reached a hand to his back; she felt his body tremble.

"Are you okay?" she panted; exhaustion had an iron grip on her as well.

"She is… this thing is much stronger than I thought," he gasped.

There was a sickening stretching sound. Rose gripped Mr Borgia's shirt. Martha's face fell away into two halves, held onto her body only by the skin

"Ugh… oh my God," Rose cried, hand pressed against her mouth. The Bruxas' arms squeezed out of Martha's neck cavity; blood pumped like a fountain for a few moments. Slick and red, a corpse-like head birthed from Martha's body. A head, shoulders, and an emaciated grey body writhed out of the old woman. When its hips were exposed, it glared down, black-eyed, at the three of them. Cathie howled and spat.

"Va Via, e mia!" A bony finger pointed towards Mary. The Bruxas' voice oozed like liquid hate; an oily substance dribbled down its chin.

"We will not leave. Nothing here belongs to you!" Mr Borgia seethed, and stared at the hovering remains of Martha.

"You see her?" Mr Borgia asked.

"Yes… and I'm glad you can't see her. She's right in front of us. She's… uh… coming out of Martha." Acid burned Rose's throat again.

Mr Borgia sucked in a breath, he sobbed just a moment then yelled the invocation louder, held his mirror at just the right angle towards Martha's body, ensuring the reflections flashed brightly at the Bruxas. It screeched, shimmied and flicked Martha's body away. She slumped broken to the floor; discarded like rubbish. The Bruxas leapt to the ceiling, scuttled like a bug, howling its way to the hole in the cornice. Just like the other night, the Bruxas compacted itself down and slid like a snake back within the fabric of the house.

Mr Borgia slumped to the ground. Beaded with exhaustion, he rested his head in his hands, and the Vasodemonio glowed silently by his side.

No one spoke for a while. Eric was a new shade of pale with his hand still pressed against Mary's neck, his attention now upon the scarring across her face.

"I'll do this, you sit a moment, Eric." Rose took over. Eric slumped on the bed.

The Bruxas thundered through the roof and clawed through the walls. The house rumbled; light slowly succumbed to darkness as the candles died out one by one. Only a few stubs kept burning, and they were moved in to the centre of Mary's room, to keep the Frangitelli Mirror alight.

Eric slid from the bed, "What's that?" He bent down, peering under the dressing table. He reached in, his hands pulled back, heavy with Pero and Gianna. The crows stirred from unconsciousness. Both were wet and dishevelled. Eric wrapped them in a towel and set them by the hearth. Gianna rolled to her feet first, shook her feathers out. She hopped over to Eric, cocked her eyes up. She cawed, shook again and transformed into her elderly human self.

Eric stumbled back to the bed.

"See him to a chair and drink, Rose. I will tend to this," Gianna said, her words stretched, the sound of the crow in them. She took over tending Mary's wounds, "Go. Sit." She waved Rose away with bony, claw-like hands.

Rose reached for Eric, his hand slid into hers; Mary's blood coated his palm, glued their skin together. She sat him in a chair on the opposite side of the room.

Eric squeezed Rose's hand harder. Colour hadn't returned to his face; his eyes were glazed and wide, and she knew they were hooked on the bloodied remains of Martha.

"It's just like…" he stumbled; his lips trembled, his voice only a thread.

"You're not on the front anymore. I'm here." Rose kissed his forehead. He pulled her closer. "The enemy…" he gripped so tight her hand began to tingle. Rose peeled his fingers away, the blood between pulled at her skin as their hands separated. Bile rose in her throat; Martha's putrid remains were impossible to ignore.

Rose swallowed back nausea, looked to Mary and caught Gianna's attention.

"Come now Rose, learn." Gianna beckoned to Rose with a long black fingernail. Eric squeezed Rose's fingers blue again.

"It's okay, Eric, Gianna's a… friend." Rose was surprised at how easily that word came to her. It felt intrinsic for some reason, as though Gianna had always been there. Rose made her way to Gianna.

"Thank you, Gianna," Mr Borgia said, reaching out as Pero finally made his way to him. The bird hopped onto his arm, sidled up to his shoulder and settled at the crook of his neck. It made a noise… somewhat like the purr of a cat. "Thank you, Eric, for helping our Familiars."

Eric looked at him, through him, his eyes still seeing something more than what was happening in the present. He pulled his knees up, hugged them to his chest.

Gianna picked up Mary's bloodied veil from the floor, and pressed a thumb into the fabric.

Mary shivered, her scarred face still staring, wide-eyed and dazed into the Frangitelli Mirror. The blood-stained doll remained pressed firmly against her chest.

"Be still, dear lady," Gianna said, "Take this." She dropped the veil into Rose's hands.

"You will do as I do." Gianna pressed her thumb, impregnated with blood against Mary's forehead.

"Agla aglala," Gianna said the words quickly like the calls of a crow, not the sing-song of Mr Borgia's incantations.

Mary shuddered.

"What are you doing?" Rose asked.

"Less talk, more action. Do as I have done." Gianna jutted her chin at the veil, "Hurry, my time runs short." Gianna shivered; feathers sprouted in her wiry grey hair. Her eyes blacked around the edges; her mouth looked a little peaked.

"Hurry, Rose, Gianna cannot stay human for long. Do as she says… learn." Mr Borgia said.

Rose pressed her thumb into the sticky fabric. Gianna, impatient, grabbed Rose's hand and pressed her thumb against Mary's forehead.

"Say the words, Agla, aglala. Imagine stemming the tide of a river."

Rose hesitantly said the words.

"Agalalala." She felt stupid.

"No," Gianna coughed; it came out as a caw. The gnarled veins on the back of her hands now covered in black down, her lips elongated a little more. "Hurry, child."

Rose repeated the words.

"Rose, you must speak a healing summons correctly."

Rose looked at Mary, the chalkiness of her skin was frightening, even the redness of the scarring had drained. Her neck still bled profusely; her skin was deathly cold.

Rose took a breath, closed her eyes, imagined a river being dammed.

"Agla aglala." Her tongue felt a little numb, her thumb prickled, and something twanged in her belly. Her eyes snapped open.

Mary's neck, though smeared crimson, no longer pulsed. Rose reached for the wounds, they were crusted over, she yanked her hand away. She caught Eric watching her but couldn't decipher the emotion that clouded his face.

"I did that?" Rose asked Gianna. She turned her bloody hand over, stared at it, wondering where, how, and why this had worked.

Gianna opened her mouth to answer, but it was the call of the crow that erupted. She shook, shivered, spun like a spinning top and snapped back into her bird form. Gianna flapped around Rose, came to settle on her shoulder, and leaned her head into Rose's neck.

Gianna's voice rang in Rose's thoughts.

You are indeed a Masciara in the making.

CHAPTER 49

"We need the power back on," Mr Borgia said, pulling himself up, eyes to the ceiling where the Bruxas raged and thumped within the house.

"It will make another attack soon, and we have no new candles to light." He made it to the window, still puffing hard as though he'd run a mile.

"It is only just midnight. I need to gather my strength back so we can try again. Until then, we need as much light as possible to repel the Bruxas. We need to check the fuse box."

"Can't you just magic them on?" Rose waved her hands in the air.

For the first time since she arrived at Rutherford House, Mr Borgia laughed.

"Whilst that would be convenient right now. Unfortunately, I do not have dominion over all things. We are spirit witches, Rose, our strength is dealing with them, not parlour tricks."

"But you locked and unlocked all the doors?"

He nodded. "That is easy. It's merely the movement of air. Electricity is a very different element."

"Where is the fuse box?" Eric said, his voice a shadow of itself.

"Under the main stairwell, near the service stairs," Mr Borgia answered. "There are spare fuses there as well."

"I'll go," Eric pulled himself up, trying and failing to avoid looking at the remnants of Martha. Rose quickly pulled one of the knotted sheets apart and threw it over her body.

"I'll go with you," Rose said.

"No, you stay here." Eric put his hand against Rose.

"She will go with you. She can see the Bruxas, she now has the skill to repel it. Even if she can't, Rose will hear it coming, and you can run from it. If you go alone, Eric, it will do to you what it did to Martha. It can possess a human, not a witch. Gianna will be with you as well."

Gianna cawed loudly in Rose's ear.

"Okay, I can hear you." Rose pressed her ear; Gianna nuzzled into Rose's hair apologetically.

Rose didn't relish the idea of going downstairs, back into the dark, sinking into the shadows where nothing but evil lurked. Still, she wasn't about to let Eric go alone. She picked up a candelabra of three half-gone candles and passed it to Eric, carrying a single candlestick herself. The warmth of their glow added colour to Eric's skin; he didn't look quite so pasty, so very petrified.

"Go!" Mr Borgia waved them off, "I will need only a short time to recuperate, then we call the Bruxas in for good."

Every mirror in the hallway was damaged, many were completely blacked out, some no longer had glass at all. The candlelight distorted in the fractured surfaces; the ambience more sinister by the moment. Gianna took flight, disappeared into the shadows and circled back again.

We must hurry. It will soon know where you are and what you are doing. Gianna spoke in Rose's mind again before settling back on her shoulder.

Darkness pressed in on them, and they hugged together to stay within the orb of candlelight.

Rose unlocked the main doors, her hand hovering over the handle.

"What is it?" Eric asked, immediately looking behind himself.

"Can you hear that?" Rose gasped, mouth agape, she leaned towards the dumbwaiter.

"I can't hear anything." Eric pressed closer, his hand slipping back into Rose's.

In there. Gianna pointed her beak forwards. Her claws dug into Rose's shoulders, the bird's feathers brushed her neck, but it was somehow reassuring, comforting, when every sense told Rose to run.

"There, in there!" Rose leaned over the sideboard, as close to the nailed-shut dumbwaiter as she could. She gasped. "Crying, I hear something crying."

"It's probably the wind," Eric responded, not a shred of conviction in his words.

Rose's fingers gouged into the sideboard, "Oh, my God. It's a baby!" Rose gasped.

The dumbwaiter shuddered. She fell back, Gianna fluttered from her shoulders, attacked the dumbwaiter, swooped over and over, smashing her beak into it.

Go now. I will keep it here as long as I can, Gianna cried.

The wooden door rattled; the screeching of its pully system groaned within the wall.

Eric pulled Rose away, had them out the main doors, and running down the stairs.

The candlelight trailed behind, their feet plunged into the thick night, almost falling down each step. When they hit the lower floor, Rose pulled Eric around the balustrade, they thumped their backs against a wall, gasping. Only two candles remained alight.

"Fuck, what the fuck?" Eric sucked for air, his candle quivered, Rose could feel the fear rattling through him, "Sorry, Rose, my language."

"For goodness' sake, you think I care about fucking profanity?"

Eric's face fell. So did Rose's.

"That was fucking rude of me." Rose broke the silence.

They burst into a nervous, hushed laughter. Eric pulled her into his chest, holding his candle above her head.

"Oh, Rosie..."

"I'm clearly no lady."

"You're the best kind of lady, Rosie."

His warmth flooded her. She nestled into his body. They stayed still, quiet, sought a singular moment of comfort.

"I'm sorry, Eric," Rose whispered into his chest.

"Shh." He pulled her closer until all she heard was that heart that beat for her.

"I've treated you so badly." Her tears wet his shirt.

"No, you've just tried to survive." He kissed the top of her head, she clung to him, never wanting to move, but upstairs thundered, the vibration rattled the wall behind them. They lurched apart.

"Let's survive this and make up for wasted time later." Rose trailed her candle along the underside of the staircase until she found a door set into it.

"Here, this must be it." She pulled a circular latch, held her candle inside.

It was a small, dark space curtained with webs.

"Ugh!" Rose jerked away, quickly slapping musty webs from her arm.

"Here, let me. I'd rather spiders than that thing." Eric held his candelabra inside, swept it around, the webs melted away.

"There, better."

"Check the fuse box. I want to get out of here." Rose hugged her body with her free hand.

Eric fumbled inside the cupboard; Rose stood guard. The hallway stretched out in front of her, the servants' stairs to her left – inky nothingness to disappear into. She shivered, waved her candle around, searched where it's light spilled.

By the doorway that led to the kitchen, a basket and a hat lay strewn on the floor. Rose knelt and flipped the basket over. It was Martha's. Rose jerked her hand from it, a new chill clung to her. She swept her light left to right, up and down.

A faint sound drew her left, between the servant stairs and the fuse cupboard.

"Did you hear that?"

"No, what is it?" Eric's voice was muffled inside the cupboard.

"The baby, you can't hear the crying?"

"No."

The baby cried again; another sound underpinned it. Rose leaned forwards and searched the black wall of nothingness in front of her.

Bambin… Bambin… A muted voice repeated over and over. She pressed her ear to the wall.

Bambin... o...Bambin... ooooo.

"Papa?" Rose slapped her hand on the papered wall. She thumped it. "Papa, Papa?"

"Rosie?"

"Papa, I can hear him. He's in there!" She flushed hot, and her words bled together, "Papa... Papa... Papaaa!" Her hands splayed over the wall.

"Rosie, shh. You'll make that thing find us. Come here." Eric pulled her hands from the wall, kissed her softly on her head. "You need to look at this."

Rose sobbed as she bent into the cupboard, blinked her eyes, and followed the trail of Eric's hand to the fuse box. "Look." He gulped hard, "I think we're stuffed."

The fuse box was ripped to pieces, the wires snapped, fuses hung dead. The box tipped sideways off its brackets; its wood casing gouged. Rose's candlelight flooded the walls, they were all marred with deep claw marks.

"This is not good," Eric said. The walls quivered. The baby screamed. Rose squeezed her eyes tight, shook her head as her father whispered loud in her mind.

Bambin...o. She pressed her ear to the wall again. "Papa. Where are you?"

The whispers faded, "Papa, please?" Rose sobbed.

Eric pulled her back into his arms, "We better get back and..."

Something disturbed the air. Gianna flew in, fluttered around them. *Upstairs now.* She tugged on Rose's sleeve with her beak.

They pounded up the stairs as the entire house seemed to shift. The floors vibrated underfoot; the stairs felt like they might sink away. Rose made it to the landing first, turned around for Eric as the staircase exploded in front of him, sending him flying backwards.

'Eric!"

He was swallowed by the darkness. Gianna squawked, flew circles around Rose, drove her away from the carnage. Rose coughed, the air thick with dust, the taste of wood and rot upon it.

"Eric!" she screamed when she saw a hand claw out of the hole in the staircase. She stumbled up the last few stairs.

The baby wailed, the storm thundered, Papa bellowed in her mind again. Rose was rigid as she watched the Bruxas pull itself from within the belly of the house.

Her flame shook so hard it threatened to douse. She backed up towards the mirrored door, Gianna flew back and forth between her and the Bruxas.

It slithered its body out until it stood tall. It cracked its neck to the right and stretched its long limbs, the sinews snapping. Something fetid eked from it. The air buzzed with an uncomfortable tactile feeling, like running your hand the wrong way along velvet. It ascended. Rose tripped on her dress, slithered back along the floor until she backed into the mirrored door.

"Get away!" Rose yelled. The Bruxas jutted forwards. Rose scrambled to her feet and held the candle to the reflection. The Bruxas stopped dead, a bony hand to its eyes; it screeched so loud Rose's ears rung.

It reared back. Gianna flew at it over and over until it smacked her down. Her little body thumped somewhere in the darkness.

"Va Via." The Bruxas drawled, cocked its head, seemed to look downstairs. Eric was groaning somewhere below.

"No, Antonietta, you stop!" Rose turned around, took the base of her candlestick and smashed the mirror.

"You'll not have him! You'll have me!"

Darkness fell upon her; Rose pulled the door open and ran.

CHAPTER 50

Rose burst into Mary's room, "It's coming!"

"The lights?"

"It's destroyed the wiring!" Rose yelled, hearing the Bruxas thunder up the hallway.

Mr Borgia grabbed the last pillars, put them in front of the Frangitelli Mirror. The effect haloed the ghastly pallor of Mary. She barely looked alive. She still clung to the doll.

Mr Borgia thrust another mirror into Rose's hands.

Rose's mirror cracked, then another did. The room became a symphony of fracturing glass.

"Oh God!" Rose screamed.

Mr Borgia stood at the back of Mary, "Get on the other side of her. We do this now, or we die… all of us."

Eric flashed into Rose's mind… *was he already dead?* Her heart thundered too hard, the room a blur.

"Which way Rose?"

She pointed towards the doors and Mr Borgia held the Vasodemonio towards to Bruxas and began reciting the invocation. Rose's mind was cluttered, she couldn't remember the words, she opened her mouth as the Bruxas smashed into the bedroom.

Mary screamed. A long, loud wail. The Bruxas hissed, backed away from the small glimmer of light and the power of the Frangitelli Mirror.

Rose guided Mr Borgia so that the Vasodemonio followed the Bruxas' movements. It crawled like a spider up the wall and hung in a corner. It rattled and chittered like a cockroach.

Mr Borgia continued his words, Mary screamed and screamed until she collapsed.

The doll fell with her; it hit the floor at Rose's feet, the porcelain head cracked open. The wail of the baby's cries intensified. Rose knelt to Mary and felt the pulse on her neck. It was there but faint and rapid. She was so very cold.

"Do you hear the baby? Tell me, you hear that?" Rose's whole body shook.

Mr Borgia finished a round of the invocation, "It is inconsequential. You must invocate with me!"

"But we need three...and Eric..."

"At this point, Rose... anything is better than what she has in store for us when the mirror finally succumbs to darkness." He seemed to collapse in on himself, "I should've been stronger. I should have burned her the day I caught her. She isn't my wife anymore. We have to bring her down, and now."

"Ok... ok... just let me help Mary." Rose let her hand slide from Mary's throat. She pulled Mary's arm, which had landed awkwardly underneath her back. As she did so, her foot knocked the doll, and its head lolled, revealing a wide gap where it had cracked open.

"Oh my God!" Rose jerked away.

"What is it?"

"It can't be..." Rose's breaths hastened.

Mr Borgia dared not look down as he held the Vasodmonio ready.

"It's..." Rose reached her trembling fingers to the doll and poked the cool porcelain. It seemed solid, filled with something.

"Oh no... no." She poked it again; a wedge of porcelain fell away.

Rose stood up, "I know why the Bruxas is still here, why it never went away."

Mr Borgia glanced briefly down; confusion screwed up his face.

The Bruxas scattered behind the drapes of the ceiling. Its shape bulged against the fabric.

"Dammelo il bambino!" Its claws scraped along the roof, ripped through the fabric lining.

Rose pointed to the broken doll.

"The baby…. Arthur… he's inside the doll."

Mr Borgia picked up the doll. Peeled the porcelain from the face revealing the mummified remnants of a newborn.

"Dio Mio," sadness stained his voice, he cradled it as Mary had. "I can hear its cries."

Rose pressed a hand to her mouth, "I think that's what Papa has been trying to say. He's been trying to say bambino, and I never understood. I was too frightened to really hear him." Everything dawned on her all at once. She wasn't being haunted; she was being guided. Papa was trying to lead her to him, to tell her the secret of Rutherford House.

Guilt and relief washed through her.

"I know what you meant now, Papa," she called out, hoping that wherever he was, that he heard her.

The candles burned low, a mere inch or so left. The Bruxas' movements intensified, the clawing louder, the demands more insistent.

"Dammelo il bambino!"

"Dammelo il bambino!"

The sound it made could have been a million crawling things… but it was one demon, an impossible-to-kill thing of evil.

"Mia Bambino!" Delight lifted its voice into a reverberating vibrato.

"It's not your baby!" Rose hissed at it and lifted her candle close to the mirror, retrieved the smaller fractured one and angled it towards it to reflect upon the roof. The Bruxas screamed and scuttled away; its chittering was still too close.

"We're running out of light," Mr Borgia gasped, all arrogance gone as he looked solemnly at Rose. "I'm not sure how to overcome it." His eyes misted, "I'm sorry."

Rose looked between him and the remains of Arthur, then to the Frangitelli Mirror.

Hesitantly, she reached for Arthur and let her finger graze a piece of porcelain still stuck across the scalp. She peered down at Mary, newly appreciating what she had done, what she had endured to save the soul of her child.

"She hid him," Rose said.

"She hid him so the Bruxas couldn't take all of him. That's why I can… why we both hear his cries. Part of his soul must still be in there."

Mr Borgia's eyes cleared; the sharpness returned, "That's why it never left; it hadn't finished what it started." He looked down at the infant corpse, brows drawn, lips tight, "I never imagined this was the reason. I didn't know the strength of Mary."

Rose looked again at the Frangitelli Mirror, "We need to hide Arthur, get him out of the house, to somewhere the Bruxas can't ever touch him or Mary."

Deep creases formed between Mr Borgia's brows, then he followed Rose's attention to the Frangitelli Mirror.

"What you did to Eric? Can you do that to Arthur?"

Mr Borgia nodded, he chuckled, "Clever witch."

He peeled the rest of the porcelain from Arthur, revealing the shrivelled little body.

He held the infant, almost lovingly against his chest with one hand, kneeled and rested his other against Mary's forehead, "Rest easy dear lady, you are a mother above all others."

"Find an intact mirror, Rose, and hurry."

Rose took her candle stub and ran through the rooms; Pero flew beside her. She worried on Gianna, couldn't think long of Eric or she would collapse. They had to defeat this thing; she had no chance of helping Eric until then.

Everything was destroyed, every single mirror. Her breaths became more desperate, her pulse pounded in her head. Rose stopped and tried to think.

"How big does it have to be?"

"It doesn't matter," Mr Borgia responded.

Rose ran to Mary's dressing table, flipped over her hand mirror. It was unbroken. She snatched it up.

"Put Arthur in the mirror, then follow me with that thing. I think I know exactly what to do." She pointed to the Vasodemonio.

Mr Borgia nodded, held Arthur's remains closer, and stepped towards the Frangitelli Mirror. The last two candles flickered, only minutes of light left in them. The Bruxas stirred, its scratching more intense than before.

"Nascondemerato." Mr Borgia took another step and plunged Arthur into the Frangitelli Mirror.

The Bruxas screamed.

Rose saw Arthur's remains appear in the hand mirror, she shoved it deep into her pocket.

"Run, Rose, run!"

CHAPTER 51

The house groaned. Rose sprinted down the hall. Pero flapped behind her. Mr Borgia yelled invocations frantically in the distance. She kicked the door to the stairs, it hung from one hinge. The Bruxas exploded from the dumbwaiter, raked its nails down her back.

"Argh!" Rose screamed, arched away as pain seared down her spine. She fell, crawled on hand and knee for the stairs, felt wetness seep around her torso, her whole body trembled. She spun around and crawled backwards, eye on the colourless image of the Bruxas being attacked by Pero. It screamed, slashed at Pero. Its head snapped to the right as Mr Borgia's spells sounded closer. Rose pulled herself from the floor whilst it was distracted and ran, swallowed into the darkness of the house.

Rose couldn't feel her body. There was no pain anymore. There was nothing. She moved like a mindless automaton; instinct pushed her forwards. It was so very dark; a bluish Luna hue barely touched the top of the stairs.

Rose slipped down the first few steps, her dress caught around her feet. She bunched the hem, found a better footing, jumped over the gaping hole left by the Bruxas, and tumbled to the first landing. Breathless, she frantically felt for the mirror; its glass was smooth, it was intact.

She took the next step but her foot caught on something; she grappled for balance on the balustrade, half slid on her backside down the rest. Her feet hit the ground floor, and she lurched into the velvet blackness towards the thin strip of moonlight on either side of the front doors.

Rose wrestled with the handle; the door rattled on its hinges. She fumbled for the lock; her fingers didn't do what she wanted. The entire house rumbled, the very core of it seemed to tremble. Pain resurged and called for her attention, she gasped, felt the call of unconsciousness.

"No, no, no!" She gulped for air, shook her head to clear it, grit her teeth against the agony, imagined it was her courses, she dealt with that, she could deal with this. Sweat slicked her fingers as they slipped around the door, searching.

At last, she found the latch, twisted it and yanked the door open. The storm hit her cold and hard. Sheet lightning lit the gardens, she ran to the left, rounded the house, and past the vegetable gardens. She ran full pelt into something.

Rose fell, stones ground into her elbows.

"Rosie!" Eric stood above her, a blazing torch in his grip.

"Eric?" she gasped as he pulled her up, hugged her tight. "Oh my God, you're okay." The storm buffeted them closer.

"What's ..." His hand came away wet from her back, "Oh God, Rosie..." He turned her around and he gasped again, gently prodding at her back. "Rosie, we gotta get out of here!" Eric carefully turned her back, held her chin with a single finger. Rain sizzled through his flame, and the storm sucked at it, threatening to douse its life-saving light.

"I'm ok," she said. "I'm ok."

"Sure?" He frowned, glanced at her blood that soaked his hand. Rose nodded and quickly felt his face, his warmth, and the soft gleam of love in his eyes.

"You're you?" Her fingers curled gently against his skin.

"I was coming back for you but needed something to defend you." He waved the flame; it sizzled and snapped.

"We're not going back there, but we can't leave yet either." Rose grabbed Eric's hand, pulled him into a run.

She felt for the mirror. It was still intact.

"Where are we going?"

"Cemetery," she gasped as they ran. Eric didn't ask questions as they ran on, down the back path, past the skeletal lines of the orchard.

Something grazed past Rose's ear; she yelped and ducked.

It is coming after you. Gianna flew ahead. Something deep in Rose flipped with relief that Gianna was okay, then froze with terror that the Bruxas was headed for them.

Rose cut through a silvery frost blanketing the grass. Eric's torch light sliced through the night, burnt away the thickness of the fog, revealing the path ahead.

Rain pelted, drenched them both, slicked the ground, and ate at the flame.

A guttural scream breached the roar of the storm. Rose looked back over her shoulder, saw movement flash through the shadows behind them.

"Faster," she screamed as the Bruxas' hellish cries rolled along the breath of the storm. They hit the path by the lake, their boots slipped in the mud, the thickness of it slowing their pace. Rose peered over her shoulder again, blinked rain from her eyes. She swallowed a scream.

The Bruxas flashed through the gaps of the trees; its wet rot penetrating her next breath.

They hit the lake bridge. Rose felt emptiness behind her; darkness enveloped the way ahead. She skidded to a stop when she realised Eric had let go of her hand.

"Eric?"

"I'll keep it away, do what you need to do!"

"Eric, no!"

"Rosie… I love you… just go!"

The Bruxas screamed; she could feel its wrath, smell the death of it meld to the wind.

"Eric…" Her lips trembled, she gulped for air, hands dug into the balustrade.

"I love you too."

"Go, Rosie, go now!" Eric yelled.

Rose forced herself to the other side of the bridge, sobbing the entire way. Every cruel word she had said to Eric, each time she had turned her back on him, punched the breath from her. In this moment, she realised how pointlessly cruel she had been, how fear and pride had ruled her every move. If they survived this…

The darkness was vacuous, the moon sucked away by smothering clouds. Rose couldn't see the way forward. She recalled when Mary brought her here, just two short days ago. She ran blindly up the rise of the island to her right, her feet sodden, she slipped every other step. A flash of lightning lit up the hedge; Rose forced her legs to move, rounded it and found herself at the cemetery. The gravestones were deep in shadow, they looked like rotten teeth dotted across the earth.

She fell at a grave. There was no light to read the words. How could she tell which was which? Rose ran her fingers over the wet stone, tried to feel the shape of the engraved names. Her fingers were numb, the stone slippery.

"Damn it!" She pressed her fingers into the indentations again but couldn't visualise what she was feeling.

She ran from grave to grave, praying the moon would find its way through the clouds. She could barely see her own hand in front of her face. The Bruxas howled; she could almost feel its breath.

Her fingers were numb, everything bathed in the night; she panicked. *Where was Arthur's grave? Near the mausoleum, or was it off to the side?*

"Help me!" She screamed to no one in particular in fits of tears. The storm answered with a harder downpour, lightning snaked overhead and lit the graveyard momentarily. Rose saw the small grave near the front of the mausoleum, the one with the tiny metal fence. The gravestone with barely a word inscribed on it.

"Arthur!" Rose whispered.

She was exhausted, couldn't stand, pulled herself through the mud on her hands and knees.

Eric screamed her name. Rose couldn't move any faster, could feel death clawing for her, could taste it with every gasp.

Rosa? Rosa? Someone called in her mind.

Something glimmered behind the grave she was only a few feet from. She blinked wildly, hope soaring, thinking it was Eric.

Knees screaming in pain, nails ripped and stinging, Rose clawed forward, shook the water from her glasses, set them back and blinked. Her chin trembled.

"Papa?"

He hovered next to the tiny grave in his overalls and work boots, something in his hand.

Rosa?

"Papa?"

A shovel tumbled from his grasp; he looked beyond Rose as the Bruxas' screams were impossibly near.

He moved towards Rose, leaned down, placed his hand on her cheek, his touch cold, the echo of it infused warmth into her heart. Papa then walked straight through her.

"Papa!" Rose cried; her body shuddered but strength returned.

He turned around and smiled at her, "Ti amo, Bella."

The hedge rustled; branches snapped. The Bruxas burst through, its grotesque form stretched high above her father. It lunged for him, and he fought back.

That's when Rose realised he was helping her. He had always been trying to help her. He was sacrificing the last of himself for her.

Rose lunged for the shovel and dug into Arthur's grave, sobbing profusely, crying his name.

"Papa, Papa!" She slammed the shovel down over and over, her vision blurred under the driving rain.

The one mercy of the storm, the ground was soft, and the shovel sunk in easily, but it was a grave, the digging felt never-ending.

Rose heard Papa yell the words Mr Borgia had, magik words, words of a witch; she heard his cries, felt the pain of each blow when the Bruxas made contact with his soul.

Rose dug harder; cried for Papa, for Mama, Matteo and for Eric.

The shovel suddenly pulled from her hands.

"I've got this!" Eric dug deep into the grave. The metal rang out with each strike.

"Do your witchy stuff."

"I…I don't know…"

Rose looked over her shoulder and saw the faint image of Papa. Rain seared through his spirit; the sweep of Bruxas' claws visible through his torso. Papa fought with his words, tried to give Rose as much time as possible, but the Bruxas was forcing him back, pushing him down. Papa's light was fading.

Eric dug faster, mud flicked in Rose's face, torrential rain almost blinded her. Papa's glow dimmed to a bare flicker. The Bruxas looked up at Rose, its depthless sockets met hers, and it smiled as it plunged Papa into the ground.

Rose screamed from the very centre of herself.

Gone... he was truly gone. She couldn't hear him, feel him, couldn't smell the rot of his death, the call of his voice.

"Papa?" She sobbed from her very soul, and something shifted inside. Rose ground her teeth and wobbled as she pulled herself up. Anger seared hot under her frigid skin. The Bruxas made its way towards her, a slow cockiness in its movements. It smiled, knowing it had won.

Rose could see the grimoire in her mind; she flicked through the pages Mr Borgia had shown her. One incantation seemed to leap from her memory, the words coated her tongue.

Rose bit her lip hard until blood drizzled down her chin. She dabbed a finger in her mouth, one by one, wrote the letters on her skin. The rain did not touch the bloodied words, it seemed to bend around her whole body.

"Buona Jacumora," she said slowly, deliberately. The Bruxas halted, seemed to freeze, unsure. Rose dipped a finger in her mouth again, backed up and stilled Eric's digging.

"Rosie?" He stared as she dabbed the same words upon his chest.

"Now dig as fast as you can!"

"Buona Jacumora," Rose called with more gusto, feeling the words drive up from within her. They slipped so easily from her mouth, the power of them drowned out the noise of fear.

The Bruxas screeched, coiled back, clawed at its head.

She repeated the spell to repel the demon's power. Over and over, Rosie held a hand up to the demon and yelled with more ferocity each time, "Buona Jacumora."

"I've found a coffin!" Eric yelped.

"Open it, quickly," Rose said, not disrupting her incantation as the Bruxas writhed in front of her.

Eric gasped and grunted as he struggled with the coffin deep in the grave, but Rose couldn't help him.

A light bounced through the darkness beyond the Bruxas.

Mr Borgia, bloodied and limping, burst through the hedge behind the Bruxas.

"It's in front of you!" Rose yelled. He raised the Vasodemonio, arced along the graveyard towards Rose, head cocked, listening to its movements.

The Bruxas howled and cursed, curled up in a ball. It could neither attack them nor flee. It was too driven for the soul of Arthur, but also too bound by their magik to attack.

Rose and Mr Borgia held their ground. She guided him, pointed out each movement the Bruxas made.

With each word spoken, Rose felt a powerful surge, felt a shift within herself.

"It's open!" Eric shouted.

Rose spun around to see Eric climbing out of the grave. A little coffin lay open on its side. She pulled the mirror from her pocket.

"What are you doing?" Eric asked, looking at the mirror.

"Arthur's in the mirror. I'm giving him the burial he deserved." Rose kissed the mirror. "Goodbye little one." She set the mirror into the empty casket and pushed the lid back down.

Mr Borgia stood at the gravestone as they slid the coffin back into the earth and began pushing slushy mud back over the casket. It thudded onto the old wood.

The Bruxas screamed wildly, as Mr Borgia kept his words and the Vasodemonio pointed towards its objections.

"Non! non!"

"Rose, help me!" Mr Borgia called; exhaustion thinned his voice. Lightning cracked overhead, the Vasodemonio hung heavily in his hands.

The Bruxas spun around, thinned into a long strip along the ground. It snapped back into a stooped, rotting old woman.

"Mia Bambino!" she hissed at them both.

Mr Borgia stuttered, "I… I can see you, Antonietta." He blinked rapidly, seemingly frozen as the Bruxas inched forward.

The Bruxas showed no reaction to hearing her human name. Her mouth elongated; razor sharp teeth protruded from it. She hissed like a snake.

Rose backed up. "Mr Borgia?"

Mr Borgia licked his lips, cocked his head to one side, then breathed out slowly. He held up the Vasodemonio, "You are my wife no more, and no more shall you cause terror."

Rose eased back to his side.

She helped him as he pointed the Vasodemonio at the Bruxas, and they spoke the invocation together.

"Actatos Adibaga Sabaoth Adonay."

"Actatos Adibaga Sabaoth Adonay."

"Actatos Adibaga Sabaoth Adonay."

The Vasodemonio glowed. The Bruxas recoiled, screamed, hid its face, then stretched out and peered at the Vasodemonio as though it were a drug it could not resist. It retracted, reached a bony hand to it, pulled away again.

"Actatos Adibaga Sabaoth Adonay."

"Actatos Adibaga Sabaoth Adonay."

The Bruxas was both drawn to it and repelled at the same time, but the more they called to it, the weaker it became. The Bruxas shrivelled with every word spoken. Its body shimmered then dulled, became as see through as a sheet of glass.

"Actatos Adibaga Sabaoth Adonay."

"Actatos Adibaga Sabaoth Adonay."

The Bruxas groaned, its body folded in two. As though an invisible hand plucked it up, it sailed through the air, twisted into a tight coil and plunged into the Vasodemonio.

Mr Borgia slammed the lid shut. He gasped for breath, eyes blinking, wide and disbelieving. He stood for a while, the rain coming in sheets, buffeting his body as he stared at the vessel that held what had once been the love of his life. Rose let him be, but stood in solidarity with him in the storm.

"Eric? The torch, do you still have it?" Mr Borgia broke his silence when the rain eased and the wind stilled.

"Yes, it's nearly out." He passed the branch to Mr Borgia, the wood a glowing ember with no flame.

"Thank you," Mr Borgia said and touched it to the Vasodemonio. It took a moment, but the heat caught, a small flame licked up the length of the vessel. He set it down as the fire took hold. The three of them watched it burn, heard the morose howl of the soul within fade until there was nothing but soggy ash and silence left.

CHAPTER 52

It had seemed like a nightmare when Rose woke up in the stables, snuggled against Eric. Charlie had roused them, shocked to find them nestled in the hay stacks, the cats purring amongst their feet. Pero and Gianna roosted in the rafters.

Sun shone with a spring warmth, the air light, pungent with eucalypt and wattle. When they left the stables, any semblance that the previous night was a mere dream was dashed with one glance at the remains of Rutherford House.

A shattered façade, scorched along the western side where lightning had struck, and fire had taken hold. The house would have been ash were it not for the ferocious storm dousing the flames. But there it stood, bathed in warmth, windows blown out, roof shingles peppered the front lawn. The front door banged on one hinge, tugged by a light tepid breeze.

Rose groaned as she pulled the girth around one of the Rutherford horses. She leaned into the warmth of the horse and could have slept standing. The reality of the night was biting painfully into her back, across her entire body.

Eric rested his hand over hers, "Let me do that."

Rose smiled and relented. Eric buckled the saddle, pulled the reigns over the horse's head and led it out to where Charlie had pulled up the carriage. Mary was already inside. Veiled, still, silent. Charlie opened the door, "Pip, pip!" The cats dashed from the stables and leapt in with Mary. The door clicked shut.

Charlie had asked no questions, just faded a few shades of pale when he saw the house, the blood-stained clothes and found them all hiding in the stables.

Rose clung to Eric. They were battered inside and out, weighed down by what they had witnessed, but they were alive.

Mr Borgia secured a large case to the back of the carriage, slipped a thick envelope into Charlie's pocket. He shook the old man's hand and patted him on the shoulder. Charlie nodded, climbed aboard the carriage and clicked his tongue. The carriage lurched forward. They all stood in wearied silence, watching the carriage and Mary disappear around the drive.

"Where is she going?" Rose asked.

"For now, St Agatha's convent. It's a few hours away. She will convalesce there. I need to attend to matters here and make sense of what is left. When she is strong enough, I will take Mary abroad to Sardinia. She can take the sea air and sun, make a new life."

He struck a match to a cigarette; Rose couldn't ignore the nervous shake of his hand. Mr Borgia looked older, a strike of grey through his hair that wasn't there yesterday.

"What about Martha?" Rose's voice hitched.

"I will bury her here after you have gone. She had no family; no one will ask questions."

This made Rose so very sad. To have no one to mourn you, no one to realise you are gone.

"I will visit her… in the future," she said.

Mr Borgia nodded. He pulled another envelope from inside his ripped Tweed coat. The crispness of his white shirt was no more; the deep brown of old blood smeared it from collar to belt.

"This is for you."

Rose took the envelope, opened the documents within it. Her name was newly etched atop the deed of ownership of Rutherford House. Rose gasped.

"What? I don't understand?" The papers quivered in her hands.

"When I was bound to this house, the agreement was that I would receive full ownership of it. I have been here for too long and I miss what's left of my family too much. I have less need of it than you."

He seemed to see the reluctance in Rose's gaze.

"Sell it. Use that money to take care of your mother, make a future for you all."

Rose stared open-mouthed at the deed.

"I will return to Italy in a week's time. Should you need me in the future, you need only send word."

"Will I see you again?" Rose asked. She felt strangely empty with the thought of him leaving. Despite everything, he was part of who she was, part of a heritage she was yet to know, and a connection to Papa.

"In time, I will return, but until then, you have her and all her attitude to guide you." Mr Borgia smiled and rolled his eyes towards Gianna, who circled overhead and cawed in a most annoyed tone.

There are twenty pounds in the envelope as well. Ride on to Brighton Hill. I have called ahead and booked you a comfortable room at the Ploughers Arms Hotel. Rest tonight. Continue on home tomorrow morning."

"Thank you," Rose said. Eric reached forwards and offered his hand. They shook in silence.

CHAPTER 53

When they turned into Banksia Lane late the next afternoon, Rose let out a breath. A weight lifted from her as she stared down the tree-lined lane. The shadows held a different feeling. The depth and smell of them were no longer an assault on her senses, no longer something to fear.

Rose reached for Eric's hand as they walked alongside their horses.

"I'm sorry," Rose said.

"We've been over this."

"No, I mean, I'm sorry for the future, for who I am, for what I am," Rose said.

"Rosie, if you can accept me, I can love you no matter who you are, even if it's riding a broomstick." He winked at her.

She elbowed him, and they both laughed.

As they walked up to her house, Rose noticed something by the front door shining in a wedge of sunlight.

Her mouth dropped open. The front gate squeaked as Rose ran up the garden path. Her reflection grew larger the closer she came to the Frangitelli Mirror. It was intact, an envelope wedged in its frame.

Rose opened it.

In case you need it someday.
Most sincerely yours,
Mr Christiano Dino Borgia.

Thank you for reading the Frangitelli Mirror.
If you enjoyed this story, please take a moment to leave a review
on your favourite review site. This story will forever be grateful.

For more information on any of my books,
please scan below to visit my website.
Thank you.

www.grthomasbooks.com

This book was over two years in the making. From the first inkling of an idea inspired by the cover art that I found on a cover design website, The Frangitelli mirror has evolved into a story that has captured elements of myself and my own ancestors from the early 20th century.

As always, my ever-patient husband and children have endured many conversations about the development of the plot, the characters, the depth of spookiness I should delve into. I thank them so very much for listening, perhaps under duress, and providing me a solid and enduring support network.

To my wonderful formatter, Becky, of Platform House Publishing. Without fail, you make my words look so much prettier than the scrappy word documents I send you. I could never replace you. Thank you so very much.

To Kay of Full Proof Editing, your patience with me being horrendously late with the deadline to send in my manuscript will not be forgotten. Thank you once again for polishing the story and making it shine.

To Marisa Noelle, a dear friend and extraordinarily talented author. Thank you for your generous critique of this story, you really shone a light upon what was important. Thank you so much for the time you put into the feedback you gave me.

To my readers, this book has seen the most support, pre-publication, all thanks to your enthusiasm to have it ready to go. I have been overwhelmed by the encouragement you have given me. I hope you enjoy the end result.

Please follow me on my socials for all updates on this and other works.
    Instagram: @grthomas2014
    TikTok: @grthomasindieauthor